RIVER OF DEATH
NIGHT WITHOUT END

ALISTAIR MACLEAN

River of Death

Night Without End

BOOK CLUB ASSOCIATES LONDON

River of Death
First published 1981

© Alistair MacLean 1981

Night Without End
First published 1960

© Gilach A.G., 1959

This combined edition published 1982 by
Book Club Associates
by arrangement with William Collins Sons & Co Ltd

Printed in Great Britain by
Richard Clay (The Chaucer Press) Ltd
Bungay, Suffolk

ALISTAIR MACLEAN

River of Death

To Gisela

PROLOGUE

Darkness was falling over the ancient Grecian monastery and the
first of the evening stars were beginning to twinkle in the cloudless
Aegean sky. The sea was calm, the air was still and did indeed, as
is so often claimed for it, smell of wine and roses. A yellow moon,
almost full, had just cleared the horizon and bathed in its soft and
benign light the softly rolling landscape and lent a magical
quality to the otherwise rather harsh and forbidding outlines of
the dark and brooding monastery which, any evidence to the
contrary, slumbered on peacefully as it had done for countless
centuries gone by.

At that moment, unfortunately, conditions inside the monastery
could hardly be said to reflect the dream-like outer world. Magic
had taken wings, no-one slumbered, peace was markedly absent,
darkness had given way to a score of smoking oil torches and
there was little enough around in the way of wine and roses.
Eight uniformed members of the Nazi S.S. were carrying oaken
chests across the flagged hallway. The brass-bound boxes were
small but so heavy that it required four men to carry one of them:
a sergeant supervised their operations.

Watching them were four men. Two of those were high-ranking
S.S. officers: of those, one, Wolfgang Von Manteuffel, a tall, thin
man with cold blue eyes, was a major-general, no more than thirty-
five years old: the second, Heinrich Spaatz, a thick-set, swarthy
man who had apparently elected to choose a scowl as his permanent expression in life, was a colonel of about the same age.
The other two watchers were monks in cowled brown habits, old
proud men but now with mingled fear and pride in their eyes,
eyes that never left the oaken chests. Von Manteuffel touched the
sergeant with the tip of his gold-handled malacca cane which
could hardly have been regulation issue to S.S. officers.

'A spot-check, I think, Sergeant.'

The sergeant gave orders to the nearest group who, not without

7

difficulty, lowered their chest to the floor. The sergeant knelt, knocked away the retaining pins in the iron hasps and lifted the hinged lid, the screeching of the ancient metal being testimony enough to the fact that many years must have passed since this had last been done. Even in the wavering light of the malodorous oil torches the revealed contents glittered as if they were alive. The chest contained literally thousands of golden coins, so fresh and gleaming they could have been minted that same day. Von Manteuffel contemplatively stirred the coins with the tip of his cane, looked with satisfaction at the resulting iridescence, then turned to Spaatz.

'Genuine, you would say, Heinrich?'

'I am shocked,' Spaatz said. He didn't look it. 'Shocked beyond words. The holy fathers traffic in dross?'

Von Manteuffel shook his head sadly. 'You can't trust anyone these days,'

With what appeared to be as much a physical effort as an exercise of will, one of the monks averted his fascinated gaze from the glittering chest and looked at Von Manteuffel. He was a very thin man, very stooped, very old—he must have been nearer ninety than eighty. His face was carefully expressionless, but there wasn't much he could do about his stricken eyes.

'These treasures are God's,' he said, 'and we have guarded them for generations. Now we have broken our trust.'

'You can't take all the credit for that,' Von Manteuffel said. 'We helped. Don't worry, we'll look after them for you.'

'Yes, indeed,' Spaatz said. 'Be of good cheer, father. We shall prove worthy of our stewardship.'

They stood in silence until the last of the treasure chests was removed, then Von Manteuffel gestured towards a heavy oaken door.

'Join your comrades. I'm sure you will be released as soon as our planes are heard to leave.'

The two old men, clearly as broken in spirit as they were in body, did as ordered, Von Manteuffel closing the door behind them and sliding home the two heavy bolts. The troopers entered, carrying a fifty-litre drum of petrol which they laid on its side close to and facing the oaken door. It was clear that they had been well briefed in advance. One trooper unscrewed the cap of the petrol drum while the other laid a trail of gunpowder to the outside doorway. More than half of the petrol gushed out on to the

8

flags, some of it seeping under the oaken door: the trooper seemed content that the rest of the petrol should remain inside the drum. Following the departing troopers, Von Manteuffel and Spaatz walked away and halted at the outside doorway. Von Manteuffel struck a match and dropped it on the gunpowder fuse: for all the expression that his face registered he could have been sitting in a church.

The airfield was only two minutes' walk away and by the time the S.S. officers arrived there the troopers had finished loading and securing the chests aboard the two Junkers 88s, engines already running, parked side by side on the tarmac. At a word from Von Manteuffel, the troopers ran forward and scrambled aboard the farther plane: Von Manteuffel and Spaatz, doubtless to emphasize the superiority of the officer class, sauntered leisurely to the nearer one. Three minutes later both planes were airborne. In robbery, looting and plundering, as in all else, Teutonic efficiency shone through.

At the rear of the lead plane, beyond rows of boxes secured to painstakingly prepared racks on the floor, Von Manteuffel and Spaatz sat with glasses in their hands. They appeared calm and unworried and had about them the air of men secure in the knowledge that behind them lay a job well done. Spaatz glanced casually out of a window. He had no trouble at all in locating what he knew he was bound to locate. A thousand, maybe fifteen hundred feet below the gently banking wing, a large building burnt ferociously, illuminating the landscape, shore and sea for almost half a mile around. Spaatz touched Von Manteuffel on the arm and pointed. Von Manteuffel glanced through the window and almost immediately looked indifferently away.

'War is hell,' he said. He sipped his cognac, looted, of course, from France and touched the nearest chest with his cane. 'Nothing but the best for our fat friend. What value would you put on our latest contribution to his coffers?'

'I'm no expert, Wolfgang.' Spaatz considered. 'A hundred million deutschmarks?.'

'A conservative estimate, my dear Heinrich, very conservative. And to think he already has a thousand million overseas.'

'I've heard it was more. In any event, we will not dispute the fact that the Fieldmarshal is a man of gargantuan appetites. You only have to look at him. Do you think *he* will some day look at *this*?' Von Manteuffel smiled and took another sip of his cognac.

'How long will it take to fix things, Wolfgang?'

'How long will the Third Reich last? Weeks?'

'Not if our beloved Fuehrer remains as commander-in-chief.'

Spaatz looked gloomy. 'And I, alas, am about to join him in Berlin where I shall remain to the bitter end.'

'The *very* end, Heinrich?'

Spaatz grimaced. 'A hasty amendment. Almost the bitter end.'

'And I shall be in Wilhelmshaven.'

'Naturally. A code word?'

Von Manteuffel pondered briefly, then said: 'We fight to the death.'

Spaatz sipped his cognac and smiled sadly. 'Cynicism, Wolfgang, never did become you.'

At the best of times the docks at Wilhelmshaven would have no difficulty in turning away the tourist trade. And that present moment was not the best of times. It was cold and raining and very dark. The darkness was quite understandable for the port was bracing itself for the by now inevitable attack by the R.A.F.'s Lancasters on the North Sea submarine base or what, by this time, was left of it. There was one small area of illumination and subdued illumination at that for it came from low-powered lamps in hooded shades. Faint though this area of light was, it still contrasted sufficiently with the total blackness around to offer marauding bombers a pin-point identification marker for the bombardiers crouched in the noses of the planes of the surely approaching squadrons. No-one in Wilhelmshaven was feeling terribly happy about those lights, but then no-one was anxious to question the orders of the S.S. general responsible for their being switched on, especially when that general was carrying with him the personal seal of Fieldmarshal Goering.

General Von Manteuffel stood on the bridge of one of the latest of the German Navy's longest range U-boats. Beside him stood a very apprehensive U-boat captain who clearly didn't relish the prospect of being caught moored alongside a quay when the R.A.F. appeared as he was certain they would. He had about him the air of a man who would have loved nothing better than to pace up and down in an agony of frustration, only there isn't much room for pacing on the conning-tower of a submarine. He cleared his throat in the loud and unmistakable fashion of one who is not about to speak lightly.

'General Von Manteuffel. I must insist that we leave now. Immediately. We are in mortal danger.'

'My dear Captain Reinhardt, I don't fancy mortal danger any more than you do.' Von Manteuffel didn't give the impression of caring about any danger, mortal or otherwise. 'But the Reichsmarshal has a very short way of dealing with subordinates who disobey his orders.'

'I'll take a chance on that.' Captain Reinhardt didn't just sound desperate, he was desperate. 'I'm sure Admiral Doenitz——'

'I wasn't thinking about you and Admiral Doenitz. I was thinking about the Reichsmarshal and myself.'

'Those Lancasters carry ten-ton bombs,' Captain Reinhardt said unhappily. 'Ten tons! It took only two to finish off the *Tirpitz*. The *Tirpitz*, the most powerful battleship in the world. Can you imagine——'

'I can imagine all too well. I can also imagine the wrath of the Reichsmarshal. The second truck, God knows why, has been delayed. We stay.'

He turned and looked along the quay where groups of men were hurriedly unloading boxes from a military truck and staggering with them across the quay and up the gangway to an opened hatchway for'ard of the bridge. Small boxes but inordinately heavy: they were, unmistakably, the oaken chests that had been looted from the Greek monastery. No-one had to exhort those men to greater effort: they, too, knew all about the Lancasters and were as conscious as any of the imminent danger, the threat to their lives.

A bell rang on the bridge. Captain Reinhardt lifted a phone, listened then turned to Von Manteuffel.

'A top priority call from Berlin, General. You can take it from here or privately below.'

'Here will do,' Von Manteuffel said. He took the phone from Reinhardt. 'Ah! Colonel Spaatz.'

'We fight to the death,' Spaatz said. 'The Russians are at the gates of Berlin.'

'My God! So soon?' Von Manteuffel appeared to be genuinely upset at the news as, indeed in the circumstances, he had every right to be. 'My blessings on you, Colonel Spaatz. I know you will do your duty by the Fatherland.'

'As will every true German.' Spaatz's tone, as clearly overheard by Captain Reinhardt, was a splendid amalgam of resolution and resignation. 'We fall where we stand. The last plane out leaves in five minutes.'

'My hopes and prayers are with you, my dear Heinrich. Heil Hitler!'

Von Manteuffel handed back the phone, looked out towards the quay, stiffened then turned urgently towards the captain.

'Look there! The second truck has just arrived. Every man you can spare for the job!'

'Every man I can spare for the job is already on the job.' Captain Reinhardt seemed oddly resigned. 'They all want to live just as much as you and I do.'

High above the North Sea the air thundered and reverberated to the throbbing roar of scores of aero engines. On the Lancaster flight deck of the point plane of the squadrons, the captain turned to his navigator.

'Our E.T.A. over target area?'

'Twenty-two minutes,' the navigator said. 'Heaven help those poor sods in Wilhelmshaven tonight.'

'Never mind about the poor sods in Wilhelmshaven,' the captain said. 'Spare a thought for us poor sods up here. We must be on their screens by now.'

At that precise instant another aircraft, a Junkers 88, was approaching Wilhelmshaven from the east. There were only two people aboard, which seemed a poor turn-out for what was supposed to be the last plane out of Berlin. Colonel Spaatz, seated beside the pilot, looked uncommonly nervous and unhappy, a state of mind that was not induced by the fact that their Junkers was being almost continuously bracketed by exploding anti-aircraft shells—practically the entire length of their flight lay over what was now Allied-occupied territory. Colonel Spaatz had other things on his mind. He glanced anxiously at his watch and turned impatiently to the pilot.

'Faster, man! Faster!'

'Impossible, Colonel.'

Both troopers and seamen were working in a frenzy of activity to transfer the remaining treasure chests from the second military truck to the submarine. Suddenly, the air raid warning sirens began their ululating banshee wailing. As if by command, and in spite of the fact that they had known this was inevitable, the workers stopped and looked fearfully into the night sky. Then, once more, again as if by command, they resumed their frantic efforts. It would have appeared impossible that they could have improved upon their previous work-rate but this they unquestionably did. It is one thing to be almost certain that the enemy may appear at any time: it is quite another to have the last lingering vestiges of hope vanish and know that the Lancasters are upon you.

Five minutes later the first bomb fell.

Fifteen minutes later the Wilhelmshaven naval base appeared to be on fire. Clearly, this was no run-of-the-mill raid. By this time Von Manteuffel could have ordered the most powerful arc-lamps, searchlights if necessary, to be switched on and it wouldn't have made the slightest difference. The entire dock area was an inferno of dense and evil-smelling smoke shot through with great columns of flame, through which shadowy Dante-esque figures moved as in some nameless nightmare, seemingly as oblivious of their surroundings as they were of the screaming aero engines, the ear-numbing explosion of bombs, the sharp whip-like cracks of heavy anti-aircraft fire, the ceaseless stuttering of machine-guns, although what the machine-guns hoped to achieve was difficult to imagine. Through all this the S.S. men and the seamen, reduced now, despite all their will to the contrary, to almost zombie slow motion by the increasingly heavy burden of the chests, continued their by now fatalistic loading of the submarine.

On the conning-tower of the submarine both Von Manteuffel and Captain Reinhardt were coughing harshly as the dense and evil-smelling smoke from the burning oil tanks enveloped them. Tears streamed down the cheeks of both men.

Captain Reinhardt said: 'God's sake, that last one was a ten-tonner. And straight on top of the U-boat pens. Concrete ten feet thick, twenty, what does it matter? There can't be a man left alive there now, the concussion would have killed them all. In heaven's name, General let's go. We've had the devil's own luck till now. We can come back when it's all over.'

'Look, my dear Captain, the air raid is at its height now. Try moving out of the harbour now, a slow business as you know, and you have as good a chance of being blown out of the water as you have alongside the quay here.'

'Maybe so, Herr General, maybe so. But at least we'd be *doing* something.' Reinhardt paused, then went on: 'If I may say so without offence, sir, surely you must know that a captain is in command of his own vessel.'

'Even as a soldier I know that, Captain. I also know that you're not in command until you have cast off and are under way. We complete loading.'

'I could be court-martialled for saying this, but you are in-human, General. The devil rides your back.'

Von Manteuffel nodded. 'He does, he does.'

At the Wilhelmshaven airfield a dimly seen plane, later identifiable as a Junkers 88, made so violently bumpy a touch-down that its undercarriage could well have collapsed under the impact. The bumpiness was understandable, the drifting smoke being so intense that the pilot could make only a blind guess as to his height above the runway. Under normal conditions he would never have dreamed of attempting so hazardous a landing but the conditions were far from normal. Colonel Spaatz was a man of a highly persuasive cast of mind. Even before the plane had rolled to rest he had the door open, peering anxiously for his waiting transport. When he finally saw it—an open Mercedes staff car—he was aboard it within twenty seconds, urging the driver to make all possible haste.

The smoke surrounding the submarine was, if anything, even denser and more acrid than it had been minutes before although a sudden gusting wind, no doubt the result of the firestorm, gave promise of an early amelioration of the conditions. But choking and half-blinding through the smoke still was it didn't prevent Von Manteuffel from seeing what, despite his coolly relaxed calm, he had so desperately wanted to see.

'That's it, then, Captain Reinhardt, that's it. The last chest aboard. And now your men aboard, Captain, and let the devil ride on *your* back.'

Captain Reinhardt was hardly in the frame of mind to require any second bidding. Shouting hoarsely to make himself heard above the still thunderous din, he ordered his men aboard, ropes to be cast off and engines slow ahead. The last of his men were still frantically climbing up the sliding gangway as the submarine inched away from the quayside. It hadn't moved more than a few feet when the sound of a motor car screeching and skidding

14

to a halt made Von Manteuffel turn sharply and look at the quay.

Spaatz had leapt from the Mercedes while it was still moving. He stumbled, recovered himself, and stared at the still very slowly moving submarine, his face contorted in desperate anxiety.

'Wolfgang!' Spaatz's voice wasn't a shout, it was a scream. 'Wolfgang! God's sake, wait!' Then the anxiety on his face yielded abruptly to an expression of utter incredulity: Von Manteuffel had a pistol lined up on him. For some seconds Spaatz remained quite still, shocked into a frozen and uncomprehending immobility, then comprehension came with the crack of Von Manteuffel's pistol and he hurled himself to the ground as a bullet struck only a foot away. Spaatz dragged his Luger from its holster and emptied it after the slowly moving submarine which, apart from giving vent to his feelings, was an otherwise futile gesture as the conning-tower was apparently empty, Von Manteuffel and Captain Reinhardt having obviously and prudently ducked beneath the shelter of the steel walls off which Spaatz's bullets ricocheted harmlessly. And then, abruptly, the submarine was lost in the swirling banks of smoke.

Spaatz pushed himself to his hands and knees and then stood upright and stared in bitter fury in the direction of the vanished submarine.

'May your soul rot in hell, Major-General Von Manteuffel,' Spaatz said softly. 'The Nazi Party's funds. The S.S. funds. Part of Hitler's and Goering's private fortunes. And now the treasures from Greece. My dear and trusted friend.'

He smiled almost reminiscently.

'But it's a small world, Wolfie, my friend, a small world and I'll find you. Besides, the Third Reich is gone. A man must have something to live for.'

Unhurriedly, he reloaded his Luger, brushed the mud and moisture from his clothes and walked steadily towards the Mercedes staff car.

The pilot was in his seat, poring over a chart, when Spaatz clambered aboard the Junkers 88 and took his seat beside him. The pilot looked at him in mild astonishment.

Spaatz said: 'Your tanks?'

'Full. I—I didn't expect you, Colonel. I was about to leave for Berlin.'

'Madrid.'

'Madrid?' This time the astonishment was more than mild. 'But my orders——'

'Here are your new orders,' Spaatz said. He produced his Luger.

1

The cabin of the thirty-seater aircraft was battered, scruffy, unclean and more than a little noisome, which pretty accurately reflected the general appearance of the passengers who would never have made it to the ranks of the international jet-set. Two of them could have been classified as exceptions or at least as being different from the others although neither of them would have made the jet-set division either, lacking, as they did, the pseudo-aristocratic veneer of your true wealthy and idle layabout. One, who called himself Edward Hiller—in this remote area of southern Brazil it was considered poor form to go by your own given name—was around thirty-five, thick-set, fair-haired, hard-faced, obviously European or American and dressed in tan bush-drills. He seemed to spend most of his time in moodily examining the scenery, which, in truth, was hardly worth the examining, inasmuch as it duplicated tens of thousands of square miles in that virtually unknown part of the world: all that was to be seen was an Amazonian tributary meandering its way through the endless green of the rain forest of the Planalto de Mato Grosso. The second exception—again because he seemed not unacquainted with the basic principles of hygiene—claimed to be called Serrano, was dressed in a reasonably off-white suit, was about the same age as Hiller, slender, black haired, black moustached, swarthy and could have been Mexican. He wasn't examining the scenery: he was examining Hiller, and closely at that.

'We are about to land at Romono.' The loud-speaker was scratchy, tinny and the words almost indistinguishable.

'Please fasten seat-belts.'

The plane banked, lost altitude rapidly and made its approach directly above and along the line of the river. Several hundred feet below the flight-path a small, open out-board motor-boat was making its slow way up-stream.

This craft—on closer inspection a very dilapidated craft

indeed—had three occupants. The largest of the three, one John Hamilton, was tall, broad-shouldered, powerfully built and about forty years of age. He had keen brown eyes, but that was about the only identifiable feature of his face as he was uncommonly dirty, dishevelled and unshaven, giving the impression that he had recently endured some harrowing ordeal, an impression heightened by the fact that his filthy clothes were torn and his face, neck and shoulders were liberally blood-stained. Comparatively, his two companions were presentable. They were lean, wiry and at least ten years younger than Hamilton. Clearly of Latin stock, their olive-tinged faces were lively, humorous and intelligent and they looked so much alike that they could have been identical twins, which they were. For reasons best known to themselves they liked to be known as Ramon and Navarro. They considered Hamilton —whose given name was, oddly enough, Hamilton—with critical and speculative eyes.

Ramon said: 'You look bad.'

Navarro nodded his agreement. 'Anyone can see he's been through a lot. But do you think he looks bad enough?'

'Perhaps not,' Ramon said judicially. 'A soupçon, perhaps. A little touch here, a little touch there. He leaned forward and proceeded to widen some of the already existing rents in Hamilton's clothing. Navarro stooped, touched some small animal lying on the floorboards, brought up a bloodied hand and added a few more artistically decorative crimson touches to Hamilton's face, neck and chest then leaned back to examine his handiwork critically. He appeared more than satisfied with the result of his creative handiwork.

'My God!' He shook his head in sorrowful admiration. 'You really have had it rough, Mr Hamilton.'

The faded, peeling sign on the airport building—hardly more than a shack—read: 'Welcome to Romono International Airport' which was, in its own way, a tribute to the blind optimism of the person who had authorized it or the courage of the man who had painted it as no 'international' plane had ever landed or ever would land there, not only because no-one in his right senses would ever voluntarily come from abroad to visit Romono in the first place but primarily because the single grass runway was so short that no aircraft designed later than the forty-year-old DC3 could possibly hope to land there.

The aircraft that had been making the down-river approach landed and managed, not without some difficulty, to stop just short of the ramshackle terminal. The passengers disembarked and made for the waiting airport bus that was to take them into town.

Serrano kept a prudent ten passengers behind Hiller but was less fortunate when they boarded the bus. He found himself four seats ahead of Hiller and therefore was in no position to observe him any more. Hiller was now observing Serrano, very thoughtfully.

Hamilton's boat was now closing in on the river bank. Hamilton said: 'However humble, there's no place like home.'

Using the word 'humble' Hamilton was guilty of a grave understatement. Romono was, quite simply, a jungle slum and an outstandingly malodorous example of the genre. On the left bank of the aptly named Rio da Morte, it stood partly on a filled-in, miasmic swamp, partly in a clearing that had been painfully hacked out from a forest and jungle that pressed in menacingly on every side, anxious to reclaim its own. The town looked as if it might contain perhaps three thousand inhabitants: probably there were double that number as three or four persons to a room represented the accommodation norm of Romono. A typically sleazy end-of-the-line—only there was no line—frontier town, it was squalid, decaying and singularly unprepossessing, a maze of narrow, haphazardly criss-crossing alleys—by no stretch of the imagination could they have been called streets—with the buildings ranging from dilapidated wooden shacks through wine-shops, gambling dens and bordellos to a large and largely false-fronted hotel rejoicing according to a garish blue neon sign, in the name of the   OTEL DE   ARIS, some misfortune having clearly overtaken the missing capitals H and P.

The waterfront was splendidly in keeping with the town. It was difficult to say where the river bank began for almost all of it was lined with house-boats—there had to be some name for those floating monstrosities—relying for their construction almost entirely on tar paper. Between the house-boats were piles of driftwood, oil cans, bottles, garbage, sewage and great swarms of flies. The stench was overwhelming. Hygiene, had it ever come to Romono, had gratefully abandoned it a long time ago.

The three men reached the bank, disembarked and tied up the boat. Hamilton said: 'When you're ready, take off for Brasilia. I'll join you in the Imperial.'

19

Navarro said: 'Draw your marble bath, my lord? Lay out your best tuxedo?'

'Something like that. Three suites, the best. After all, we're not paying for it.'

'Who is?'

'Mr Smith. He doesn't know it yet, of course, but he'll pay.'

Ramon said curiously: 'You know this Mr Smith? Met him, I mean?'

'No.'

'Then might it not be wise to wait for the invitation first?'

'No reason to wait. Invitation's guaranteed. Our friend must be nearly out of his mind by now.'

'You're being downright cruel to that poor Mr Hiller,' Navarro said reproachfully. 'He must have gone out of his mind during the three days we stayed with your Muscia Indian friends.'

'Not him. He's sure he *knows* he knows. When you get to the Imperial keep close to a phone and away from your usual dives.'

Ramon looked hurt. 'There *are* no dives in our fair capital, Mr Hamilton.'

'You'll soon put that right.' Hamilton left them and made his way in the gathering dusk through winding, ill-lit alleyways until he had passed clear through the town and emerged on its western perimeter. Here, on the outskirts of the town and on the very edge of the forest and jungle, stood what had once passed for a log cabin but was now no more than a hut and even at that, one would have thought, a hut scarcely fit for animal far less human habitation: the grass and weed covered walls leaned in at crazy angles, the door was badly warped and the single window had hardly an unbroken pane of glass left in it. Hamilton, not without some difficulty, managed to wrench open the creaking door and passed inside.

He located and lit a guttering oil lamp which gave off light and smoke in about equal proportions. From what little could be seen from the fitful yellow illumination, the interior of the hut was a faithful complement of the exterior. The hut was very sparsely furnished with the bare essentials for existence—a dilapidated bed, a couple of bentwood chairs in no better condition than the bed, a warped deal table with two drawers, some shelving and a cooker with some traces of the original black enamel showing under the almost total covering of brown rust. On the face of it, Hamilton didn't care too much for the sybaritic life.

20

He sat wearily on the bed which, predictably, sagged and creaked in an alarmingly disconcerting fashion. He reached under the bed, came up with a bottle of some undetermined liquid, drank deeply from the neck and set the bottle down somewhat unsteadily on the table.

Hamilton was not unobserved. A figure had appeared just outside the window and was peering inside from a prudent distance, a probably unnecessary precaution. It is more difficult to see from a lighted area to a darkened one than the other way round and the windows were so filthy that it was difficult to see through them anyway. The watcher's face was indistinct, but the identity of the man not hard to guess: Serrano was probably the only man in Romono who wore a suit, far less an off white one. Serrano was smiling, a smile composed of an odd mixture of amusement, satisfaction and contempt.

Hamilton extracted two leather pouches from the torn remains of his buttoned pockets and poured the contents of one of them into the palm of his hand, staring in rapt admiration at the handful of rough cut diamonds which he let trickle on to the table. With an unsteady hand he fortified himself with another drink then opened the other pouch and emptied the contents on the table. They were coins, glittering golden coins; all told there must have been at least fifty of them.

Gold, it is said, has attracted men from the beginning of recorded time. It unquestionably attracted Serrano. Seemingly oblivious of the possibility of discovery he had moved closer to the window, so close indeed, that a keen eyed and observant person inside the hut might well have seen the pale blur of his face. But Hamilton was being neither keen eyed nor observant: he just stared in apparent fascination at the treasure before him. So did Serrano. The amusement and contempt had disappeared from his face, the unblinking eyes seemed huge in his face and his tongue licked his lips almost continuously.

Hamilton took a camera from his rucksack, removed a cassette of exposed film, examined it closely for a moment, and, in doing so, dislodged two diamonds which fell and rolled under the table, apparently unobserved. He put the cassette on a shelf beside some other cassettes and cheap camera equipment then turned his attention to the coins again. He picked one up and examined it carefully, almost as if seeing it for the first time.

The coin, indisputably gold, did not appear to be of any South

American origin—the likeness of the engraved head was unmistakably of classical Greek or Latin origin. He looked at the obverse side: the characters, clear and unblemished, were unmistakably Greek. Hamilton sighed, lowered some more of the rapidly diminishing contents of the bottle, returned the coins to the pouch, paused as if in thought, shook some coins into his hand, put them in a trouser pocket, put the pouch into one of his buttoned shirt pockets, returned the diamonds to their pouch and his other buttoned pocket, had a last drink, turned out the oil lamp and left. He made no attempt to lock the door for the sufficient reason that, even with the door as fully closed as it would go, there was still a two inch gap between the key bolt and door jamb. Although it was by now almost dark he did not appear to require any light to see where he was going: within a minute he vanished into the shanty town maze of corrugated iron and tar paper shacks which formed the salubrious suburbs of Romono.

Serrano waited a prudent five minutes, then entered, a small flashlight in his hand. He lit the oil lamp placing it on a shelf where it could not be seen directly from the outside then, using his flashlight, located the fallen diamonds under the table and placed them on the table top. He crossed to the shelves, took the cassette which Hamilton had placed there, replaced it with another from the pile of cassettes and had just put the cassette on the table beside the diamonds when he became suddenly and uncomfortably conscious of the fact that he was not alone. He whirled around and found himself staring into the muzzle of a rifle expertly and unwaveringly held in Hiller's hand.

'Well, well,' Hiller said genially. 'A collector, I see. Your name?'

'Serrano.' Serrano didn't look any too happy. 'Why are you pointing that gun at me?'

'Calling cards you can't get in Romono, so I use this instead. Are you carrying a gun, Serrano?'

'No.'

'If you are and I find it I'm going to kill you.' Hiller was still geniality itself. 'Are you carrying a gun, Serrano?'

Serrano reached slowly for an inside pocket. Hiller said: 'The classic way, of course, my friend. Finger and thumb on the gun barrel then gently on the table.'

Serrano carefully, as directed, produced a small snub-nosed automatic and laid it on the table. Hiller advanced and pocketed it, along with the diamonds and the cassette.

'You've been following me all day,' Hiller said consideringly. 'For hours before we boarded that plane. And I saw you the previous day and the day before that. In fact, I've seen you quite a few times in the past weeks. You really should get yourself another suit, Serrano, a shadower in a white suit is no shadower at all.' His tone changed in a fashion that Serrano clearly didn't care much for. '*Why* are you following me, Serrano?'

'It's not you I'm after,' Serrano said. 'We're both interested in the same man.'

Hiller lifted his gun a perceptible inch. If he'd lifted it only one millimetre it would have carried sufficient significance for Serrano who was in an increasingly apprehensive state of mind. 'I'm not sure,' Hiller said, 'that I like being followed around.'

'Jesus!' Serrano's apprehension had become very marked indeed. 'You'd kill a man for a thing like that?'

'What are vermin to me?' Hiller said carelessly. 'But you can stop knocking your knees together. I've no intention of killing you—at least, not yet. I wouldn't kill a man just for following me around. But I wouldn't draw the line at shattering a knee-cap so that you couldn't totter around after me for a few months to come.'

'I won't talk to anyone,' Serrano said fervently. 'I swear to God I won't.'

'Aha! That's interesting. If you were going to talk who would you talk to, Serrano?'

'Nobody. Nobody. Who would I talk to? That was just a manner of speaking.'

'Was it now? But if you *were* to talk, what would you tell them?'

'What could I tell them? All I know—well, I don't know, but I'm pretty sure—is that Hamilton is into something big. Gold, diamonds, something like that—he's found a cache somewhere. I know that you're on his track, Mr Hiller. That's why I am following you.'

'You know my name. How come?'

'You're a pretty important man around these parts, Mr Hiller.' Serrano was trying to be ingratiating but he wasn't very good at it. A sudden thought appeared to occur to him for he brightened and said: 'Seeing we're both after the same man, Mr Hiller, we could be partners.'

'Partners!'

'I can help you, Mr Hiller.' Serrano was eagerness itself but

23

whether from the prospect of partnership or the understandable desire not to be crippled by Hiller it was difficult to say. 'I *can* help you. I swear I can.'

'A terrified rat will swear to anything.'

'I can prove what I say.' Serrano seemed to have regained a measure of confidence. 'I can take you to within five miles of the Lost City.'

Hiller's initial reaction was one of astonishment and suspicion.

'What do you know about it?' He paused and recovered himself. 'Well, I suppose everybody's heard about the Lost City. Hamilton's always shooting off his mouth about it.'

'Mebbe so. Mebbe so.' Serrano, sensing the change in the atmosphere, was almost relaxed now. 'But how many have followed him four times to within a few miles of it?' If Serrano had been at the gambling table he'd have leaned back in his chair, his trump card played.

Hiller had become very interested indeed, even to the extent of lowering, then pocketing, his own gun.

'You have a rough idea where it is?'

'Rough?' Immediate danger past, Serrano invested himself with an air very close to benign superiority. 'Close is more like it. Very close.'

'Then if you've come all that close why don't you go looking for it yourself?'

'Look for it myself!' Serrano looked almost shocked. 'Mr Hiller, you must be out of your mind. You don't understand what you're talking about. Have you *any* idea what the Indian tribes in the area are like?'

'Pacified, according to the Indian Protection Service.'

'Pacified?' Serrano gave a contemptuous laugh. 'Pacified? There isn't enough money in the country to make those desk-bound pansies leave those lovely air-conditioned offices in Brasilia and go see for themselves. They're terrified, just plain terrified. Even their field-agents—and there are some pretty tough cookies among them—are terrified and won't go near the area. Well, four of them did go there once some years back, but none of them ever returned. And if they're terrified, Mr Hiller, I'm terrified too.'

'That creates quite a problem.' Not surprisingly, Hiller had become quite thoughtful. 'An approach problem. What's so special about those bloodthirsty people? There are many tribes who don't care all that much for people from the outside, what you and I would regard as other civilized people.' Apparently Hiller saw nothing incongruous in categorizing himself and Serrano as 'civilized'.

'Special? I'll tell you what's special about them. They're the most savage tribes in the Mato Grosso. Correction. They're the most savage tribes in the whole of South America. Not one of them have moved out of the Stone Age so far. In fact, they must be a damned sight worse than the Stone Age people. If the Stone Age people had been like them they'd have wiped each other out— when those tribes up there have nothing better to do, they just go around massacring each other—to keep their hand in, I suppose —and there would have been no human left on this planet today.

'There are three tribes up there, Mr Hiller. First, there are the Chapates. God knows they're bad enough, but all they do is use their blowpipes, pump a few curare-tipped poison darts into you and leave you lying there. Almost civilized, you might say. The Horenas are a bit different. They use darts that only knock you unconscious; then you're dragged back to their village and tortured to death—this, I understand, can take a day or two—then they cut off your head and shrink it. But when it comes to sheer savagery, the Muscias are the pick of the bunch—I don't think any white man has ever seen them. But one or two of the outside Indians who have met them and survived say that they're cannibals and if they see what they regard as being a particularly appetizing meal they dump him alive into boiling water. Something like lobsters, you know. Go looking for a lost city surrounded by all those monsters? Why don't *you* go looking? I can point you in the right direction. Me, I only like cooking pots from the outside.'

'Well, maybe I'll have to do a little more thinking on that one.' Absently, almost, he handed Serrano back his gun. Hiller was no mean psychologist when it came to gauging the extent of a man's cupidity. Hiller said: 'Where do you live?'

'A room in the Hotel de Paris.'

'If you saw me in the bar there?'

'I've never seen you before in my life.'

An unbiased guide-book to the better taverns of South America would have had some difficulty in finding the space to list the bar of the Hotel de Paris, Romono, in its pages. The bar was not a thing of beauty. The indeterminately coloured paint, what little

25

there was of it, was peeling and blistered, the splintered wooden floor was blackened and filthy and the rough-cut softwood bar bore the imprint of the passage of time. A thousand spilt drinks, a thousand stubbed-out cigars. It was not a place for the fastidious.

The clientele, fortunately, were not of an overly fastidious nature. Exclusively male and dressed for the most part in scarecrow's clothing, they were rough, uncouth, ill-favoured and hard-drinking. Especially hard-drinking. As many customers as possible—and there were many—pushed up to the bar and consumed huge quantities of what could only be described as rot-gut whisky. There were a scattering of bentwood chairs and rickety tables, largely unoccupied. The citizens of Romono were mostly vertical drinkers. Among the currently vertical were both Hiller and Serrano, separated from each other by a prudent distance.

In such surroundings, then, the entrance of Hamilton did not provoke the horror stricken reaction that it would have in the plusher caravanserais of Brasilia or Rio. Even so, his appearance was sufficient to cause a marked drop in the conversational level. With his tangled hair, a week's growth of matted and bloodied beard, and ripped and blood-stained shirt he looked as if he had just returned from the scene of a successfully if messily executed triple murder. His expression—as was indeed customary with him —lacked anything in the way of encouragement towards social chit chat. He ignored the stares and although the crowd before the bar was at least four deep a path opened magically before him. In Romono, such a path always opened for John Hamilton, a man very obviously held, and for a variety of good reasons, in considerable respect by his fellow citizens.

A large, very fat barman, the boss of the four men serving non-stop behind the bar, hurried forward towards Hamilton. His egg-bald pate gleamed in the light: inevitably, he was known as Curly.

'Mr Hamilton!'

'Whisky.'

'God's name, Mr Hamilton. What happened?'

'You deaf?'

'Right away, Mr Hamilton.'

Curly reached under the bar, produced a special bottle and poured a generous measure. That Hamilton should be thus privileged apparently aroused no resentment among the onlookers, not so much because of their innate courtesy, of which they had

26

none, but because Hamilton had demonstrated in the past his reaction to those who interfered in what he regarded as his own private business: he'd only had to do it once, but once had been enough.

Curly's plump, genial face was alive with curiosity as were those of the bystanders. But Hamilton was not a man to share confidences as everyone was well aware. He tossed two Greek coins on to the bar. Hiller, who was standing close by, observed this and his face grew very still indeed. His face was not the only one to assume sudden immobility.

'Bank's shut,' Hamilton said. 'Those do?'

Curly picked up the two shining coins and examined them with an air of unfeigned reverence.

'Will those do? *Will those do!* Yes, Mr Hamilton, I think those will do. Gold! Pure gold! This is going to buy you an awful lot of Scotch, Mr Hamilton, an awful lot. One of those I'm going to keep for myself. Yes, sir. The other I'll take and have valued in the bank tomorrow.'

'Up to you,' Hamilton said indifferently.

Curly examined the coins more closely and said: 'Greek, aren't they?'

'Looks like,' Hamilton said with the same indifference. He drank some of his Scotch and looked at Curly with a speculative eye. 'You wouldn't, of course, be dreaming of asking me if I went all the way to Greece to get those?'

'Certainly not,' Curly said hastily. 'Certainly not. Will I—will I get the doctor, Mr Hamilton?'

'Thanks. But it's not my blood.'

'How many of them? Who did this to you—I mean, who did you do it to?'

'Just two. Horenas. Same again.'

Although most people at the bar were still looking at Hamilton or the coins, the hubbub of conversation was slowly resuming. Hiller, glass in hand, elbowed his purposeful way towards Hamilton who regarded Hiller's approach with his customary lack of enthusiasm.

Hiller said: 'I hope you'll excuse me. I don't want to intrude, Hamilton. I understand that after tangling with head hunters a man would like some peace and quiet. But what I'd like to say to you is important. Believe me. Could I have a word?'

'About what?' Hamilton's tone was less than encouraging

27

'And I don't like discussing business—I assume it is business—with a dozen pairs of ears hanging on to every word we say.'

Hiller looked around. Inevitably, their conversation was attracting attention. Hamilton paused for a moment, as if in thought, then picked up his bottle, jerked his head and led the way to the corner table most remote from the bar. Hamilton, as always, looked aggressive and forbidding and his tone matched his expression.

'Out with it,' he said, 'and no shilly-shallying.'

Hiller took no offence. 'Suits me. That's the way I like it, the only way to do business. I'll lay it on the line. It's my belief you've found this Lost City of yours. I know a man who'd pay you a six figure fee to take him there. That straight enough for you?'

'If you throw away that rot gut rubbish you have there I'll give you some decent Scotch.' Hiller did as requested and Hamilton topped up both glasses. Hiller was clearly aware that Hamilton was less interested in dispensing hospitality than in having time to think and from the just perceptibly slurred note in Hamilton's voice it could well have been that he could be taking just slightly longer than normal to think quickly and clearly.

'Well, I'll say this,' Hamilton said, 'you don't beat about the bush. Who says I've found the Lost City?'

'Nobody. How could they? No one knows where you go when you leave Romono—except maybe those two young side-kicks of yours.' Hiller smiled thinly. 'They don't look like the type that would talk too much.'

'Side-kicks?'

'Oh, come off it, Hamilton. The twins. Everybody in Romono knows them. But it would be my guess that *you* would be the only person to know the exact location. So, okay, I'm only going on a hunch—and a couple of brand new golden coins that may be a thousand years old, two thousand. Just supposing.'

'Supposing what?'

'Supposing you'd found it, of course.'

'Cruzeiros?'

Hiller kept his face impassive, a rather remarkable feat in view of the wave of elation that had just swept through him. When a man talks money it means that he is prepared to dicker, to make a deal, and Hamilton had the means to bargain. Hamilton had his *quid pro quo* and that could mean only one thing—he knew where

28

the Lost City was. He had his fish hooked, Hiller thought exultantly: now all he had to do was gaff and land him. That might well take time, Hiller knew, but he had every confidence in himself: he rather fancied his prowess as a fisherman.

'U.S. dollars,' Hiller said.

Hamilton thought this over for a few moments then said: 'An attractive proposition. Very attractive. But I don't accept propositions from strangers. You see, Hiller, I don't know you, what you are, what you do, and how come you are empowered to make this proposition.'

'A con man, possibly?'

'Possibly.'

'Oh, come. We've had a drink a dozen times in the past months. Strangers? Hadly. We all know why you've been searching those damned forests for the past four months and other huge stretches of the Amazon and Paraná basins for the past four years. For the fabled Lost City of the Mato Grosso—if that is indeed where it is—for the golden people who lived there—who may still live there—most of all for the fabled man who found it. Huston. Dr Hannibal Huston. The famous explorer who vanished into the forests all those many years ago and was never seen again.'

'You talk in clichés,' Hamilton said.

Hiller smiled. 'What newspaperman doesn't?'

'Newspaperman?'

'Yes.'

'Odd. I'd have put you down for something else.'

Hiller laughed. 'A con? A convict on the lam? Nothing so romantic, I'm afraid.' He leaned forward, suddenly serious. 'Listen. As I said, we all know why you're out here—no offence, Hamilton, but goodness knows you've told everyone often enough—although why I don't know—I'd have thought you'd have kept it secret from everybody.'

'Three good reasons, my friend. In the first place, there has to be some reason to account for my presence here. Secondly, anybody will tell you that I know the Mato Grosso better than any white man and no one would dream of following me where I go. Finally, the more people who know what I'm after the greater the likelihood that some person, some time and in some place will drop a hint or a clue that could be invaluable to me.'

'I was under the impression that you didn't require hints or clues any longer.'

'That's just as maybe. Just you go ahead and form any impressions you like.'

'Well, all right. So. Ninety nine per cent of the people laugh at your wild notions, as they call them—though God knows there's not a man in Romono would dare say it to your face. But I belong to the one per cent. I believe you. I further believe that your search is over and that the dream has come true. I'd like to share in a dream, I'd like to help a man, my employer, make his dream come true.'

'I'm deeply moved,' Hamilton said sardonically. 'I'm sorry—well, no, I'm not really—but something gives here that I just can't figure. And besides, Hiller, you are an unknown quantity.'

'Is the McCormick-Mackenzie International?'

'Is it what?'

'Unknown.'

'Of course not. One of the biggest multinational companies in the Americas. Probably the usual bunch of crooks using the usual screen of a battery of similarly crooked international lawyers to bend the laws any which way that suits them.'

Hiller took a deep breath, manfully restraining himself. 'Because I'm in the position of asking a favour of you, Hamilton, I won't take exception to that. In point of fact the record of McCormick-Mackenzie is impeccable. They have never been investigated, far less impeached on any count.'

'Smart lawyers. Like I said.'

'You can be glad that Joshua Smith is not here to hear you say that.'

Hamilton was unimpressed. 'He the owner?'

'Yes. And the Chairman and Managing Director.'

'The multi-millionaire industrialist? If we're talking about the same man?'

'We are.'

'*And* the owner of the largest newspaper and magazine chain in the Americas. Well, well, well.' He broke off and stared at Hiller. 'So that's why you——'

'Exactly.'

'So. He's your boss, a newspaper magnate. And you're one of his newspapermen, and a pretty senior one at that, I would guess—I mean, he wouldn't send out a cub reporter on a story like this. Very well. Your connections, your credentials established. But I still don't see——'

30

'What don't you see?'

'This man. Joshua Smith. A multi-millionaire. A bulti-million-aire. Anyway, as rich as Croesus. What's left on earth for him that he doesn't already have? What more can a man like that want?' Hamilton took a long pull at his whisky. 'In short, what's in it for him?'

'You are a suspicious bastard, aren't you, Hamilton? Money? Of course not. Are you in it for the money? Of course not. A man like you could make money anywhere. No, and again no. Like you—and, if I may say, a little bit like myself—he's a man with a dream, a dream that's become an obsession. I don't know which fascinates him the more, the Huston case or the Lost City, although I don't suppose you can really separate the two. I mean, you can't have the one without the other.' He paused and smiled, almost dreamily. 'And what a story for his publishing empire.'

'And that, I take it, is your part of the dream?'

'What else?'

Hamilton considered, using some more Scotch to help him with his consideration. 'Mustn't rush things, mustn't rush things. A man needs time to think about these things.'

'Of course. How much time?'

'Two hours?'

'Sure. My place. The Negresco.' Hiller looked around him and gave a mock shudder which could almost have been real. 'It's almost as good as it is here.'

Hamilton drained his glass, rose, picked up his bottle, nodded and left. No one could have accused him of being under the weather but his gait didn't appear to be quite as steady as it might have been. Hiller looked around until he located Serrano who had been looking straight at him. Hiller glanced after the departing Hamilton, looked back at Serrano and nodded almost imperceptibly. Serrano did the same in return and disappeared after Hamilton.

Romono had not yet got around to, and was unlikely ever to get around to, street lighting with the result that the alleyways, in the occasional absence of saloons and bordellos fronting on them, tended to be very poorly lit. Hamilton, all trace of his unsteady gait vanished, strode briskly along, clearly unbothered by the fitful or non-existent lighting. He rounded a corner, carried on a few yards, stopped suddenly and turned into a narrow and almost totally dark alleyway. He didn't go far into the alley—

not more than two feet. He poked his head cautiously out from his narrow niche and peered back along the way he had just come.

He saw no more than he had expected to see. Serrano had just come into view. Serrano, it was clear, wasn't out for any leisurely evening stroll. He was walking so quickly that he was almost running. Hamilton shrank back into the shadows. He no longer had to depend on his hearing. Serrano was wearing steel-tipped shoes which no doubt he found indispensable for the subtler intricacies of unarmed combat. On a still night Serrano could have been heard a hundred yards away.

Hamilton, no more than another shadow in his shadowy place of concealment, listened to the rapidly approaching footsteps. Serrano, almost running now, looked neither to right nor to left but just peered anxiously ahead in quest of his suddenly and mysteriously vanished quarry. He was still peering anxiously ahead when he passed the alleyway entrance. Hamilton, a shadow detaching itself from the deeper shadow behind, stepped out swiftly and in silence brought his locked hands down on the base of Serrano's neck. He caught the already unconscious man before he could strike the ground and dragged him into the dark concealment. From Serrano's breast pocket he removed a well filled wallet, extracted a gratifying wad of cruzeiro notes, pocketed them, dropped the empty wallet on top of Serrano's prone form and continued on his way, this time without a backward glance. He had no doubt that Serrano had been on his own.

Back in his tumbledown hut, the guttering oil lamp lit, Hamilton sat on his coat and pondered the reason for his being shadowed. That Serrano had acted under Hiller's instructions he did not for a moment doubt. He did not think that Serrano had intended to waylay or attack him for he could not doubt that Hiller was almost desperately anxious to have his services and an injured Hamilton would be the last thing he would want on his hands. Nor could robbery have been a motive—although they may well have seen the bulges of the two pouches in his shirt pockets—and Hamilton had been well aware that Serrano had been watching him through the hut window—comparatively petty theft would not have interested Hiller; what he was after was the pot of gold at the foot of the rainbow and only he, Hamilton, knew where that rainbow ended.

That Hiller and his boss Smith had dreams Hamilton did not

for a moment doubt: what he did doubt, and profoundly, was Hiller's version of those dreams.

Hiller had wanted to find out if he had been going to contact his two young assistants or other unknown parties. Perhaps he thought that Hamilton might lead him to a larger and worthwhile cache of gold and diamonds. Perhaps he thought Hamilton had gone to make some mysterious phone call. Perhaps anything. On balance, Hamilton thought, it was just because Hiller was of a highly suspicious nature and just wanted to know what, if anything Hamilton was up to. There could be no other explanation and it seemed pointless to waste further time and thought on it.

Hamilton poured himself a small drink—the nondescript bottle did in fact contain an excellent Highland malt which his friend Curly had obtained for him—and topped it up with some mineral water: the Romono water supply was an excellent specific for those who wanted to be laid low with dysentery, cholera, and a variety of other unpleasant tropical diseases.

Hamilton smiled to himself. When Serrano came to and reported his woes to his master, neither he nor Hiller would be in any doubt as to the identity of the assailant responsible for the sore and stiff neck from which Serrano would assuredly be suffering. If nothing else, Hamilton mused, it would teach them to be rather more circumspect and respectful in their future dealings with him. Hamilton had no doubts whatsoever that he would be meeting Serrano—officially—in the very near future and would thereafter be seeing quite a deal of him.

Hamilton took a sip of his drink, dropped to his knees, ran his hand over the floor under the table, found nothing and smiled in satisfaction. He crossed to the shelving, picked up a solitary cassette, examined it carefully and smiled in even wider satisfaction. He drained his glass, turned out the light and headed back into town.

In his room in the Hotel Negresco—the famous hotel in Nice would have cringed at the thought that such a hovel should bear the same name—Hiller was making—or trying to make—a telephone call, his face bearing the unmistakable expression of long suffering impatience that characterized any person so foolhardy as to try to phone out of Romono. But at long last his patience was rewarded and his face lit up.

'Aha!' he said. His voice, understandably, had a note almost of triumph in it. 'At last, at last! Mr Smith, if you please.'

2

The drawing-room of Joshua Smith's villa—the Villa Haydn in Brasilia—demonstrated beyond all question the vast gulf that lay between a bulti-millionaire and the merely rich. The furnishings, mainly Louis XIV and not the shadow of an imitation in sight, the drapes, from Belgium and Malta, the carpets, ancient Persian to the last one, and the pictures, ranging all the way from Dutch Old Masters to the Impressionists, all spoke not only of immense wealth but also a hedonistic determination to use it to its maximum. But for all that vast opulence there was nonetheless displayed an exquisite good taste in that everything matched and blended in something very, very close to perfection. Clearly, no modern interior decorator had been allowed within a mile of the place.

The owner matched up magnificently to all this magnificence. He was a large, well-built and dinner-suited man of late middle age who looked absolutely at home in one of the huge armchairs that he occupied close to a sparkling pine log fire.

Joshua Smith, still dark in both hair and moustache, the one brushed straight back, the other neatly trimmed, was a smooth and urbane man, but not too smooth, not too urbane, much given to smiling and invariably kind and courteous to his inferiors which, in his case, meant just about everybody in sight. With the passage of time, the carefully and painstakingly acquired geniality and urbanity had become second nature to him (although some of the original ruthlessness had had to remain to account for his untold millions). Only a specialist could have detected the extensive plastic surgery that had transformed Smith's face from what it once had been.

There was another man in his drawing room, and a young woman. Jack Tracy was a young-middle-aged man, blond, with a pock-marked face and a general air of capable toughness about him. The toughness and capability were undoubtedly there—

34

they had to be for any man to be the general manager of Smith's vast chain of newspapers and magazines.

Maria Schneider, with her slightly dusky skin and brown eyes, could have been South American, Southern Mediterranean or Middle Eastern. Her hair was the colour of a raven. Whatever her nationality she was indisputably beautiful with a rather inscrutable face but invariably watchful penetrating eyes. She didn't look kind or sensitive but was both. She looked intelligent and had to be: when not doubling—as rumour had it—as Smith's mistress she was his private and confidential secretary and it was no rumour that she was remarkably skilled in her official capacity.

The phone rang. Maria answered, told the caller to hold and brought the phone on its extension cord across to Smith's armchair. He took the phone and listened briefly.

'Ah, Hiller!' Smith, unusually for him, leant forward in his armchair. There was anticipation in both his voice and posture. 'You have, I trust, some encouraging news for me. You have? Good, good, good. Proceed.'

Smith listened in silence to what Hiller had to say, the expression on his face gradually changing from pleasure to the near beatific. It was a measure of the man's self-control that, although apparently in a near transport of excitement, he refrained from either exclamations, questions or interruptions and heard Hiller through in silence to the end.

'Excellent!' Smith was positively jubilant. 'Truly excellent. Frederik, you have just made me the happiest man in Brazil.' Although Hiller claimed to be called Edward, his true given name would have appeared to be otherwise. 'Nor, I assure you, will you have cause to regret this day. My car will await you and your friends at the airport at eleven a.m.' He replaced the receiver. 'I said I could wait forever. Forever is today.'

Moments passed while he gazed sightlessly into the flames. Tracy and Maria looked at each other without expression. Smith sighed, gradually bestirred himself, leaned back into his armchair, reached into his pocket, brought out a gold coin, and examined it intently.

'My talisman,' he said. He still didn't appear to be quite with them. 'Thirty long years I've had it and I've looked at it every day in those thirty years. Hiller has seen this very coin. He says the ones this man Hamilton has are identical in every way. Hiller is

35

not a man to make mistakes so this can mean only one thing. Hamilton has found what can only be the foot of the rainbow.'

Tracy said: 'And at the far end of the rainbow lies a pot of gold?'

Smith looked at him without really seeing him. 'Who cares about the gold?'

There was a long and, for Tracy and Maria, rather uncomfortable silence. Smith sighed again and replaced the coin in his pocket.

'Another thing,' Smith went on. 'Hamilton appears to have stumbled across some sort of an El Dorado.'

'It seems less and less likely that Hamilton is the kind of man to stumble across anything,' Maria said. 'He's a hunter, a seeker— but never a stumbler. He has sources of information denied other so-called civilized people, especially among the tribes not yet classified as pacified. He starts off with some sort of clue that points him in the right direction then starts quartering the ground, narrowing the area of search until he finally pin-points what he's after. The element of chance doesn't enter into that man's calculations.'

'You might be right, my dear,' Smith said. 'In fact you're almost certainly right. Anyway, what matters is that Hiller says that Hamilton seems to have located some diamond hoard.'

Maria said: 'Part of the war loot?'

'Overseas investments, my dear, overseas investments. Never war loot. In this case, however, no. They are uncut—rough cut, rather—Brazilian diamonds. And Hiller is an expert on diamonds —God knows he's stolen enough in his lifetime. Anyway, it appears that Hamilton has fallen for Hiller's story, hook, line and sinker—in Hiller's rather uninspired phrase. Two birds with one stone—he's found both the European gold and the Brazilian diamonds. Looks as if this is going to be even easier than we thought.'

Tracy looked vaguely troubled. 'He hasn't the reputation for being an easy man.'

'Among the tribes of the Mato Grosso, agreed,' Smith said. He smiled as if anticipating some future pleasure. 'But he's going to find himself in a different kind of jungle here.'

'Maybe you overlook one thing,' Maria said soberly. 'Maybe you're overlooking the fact that you've got to go back into that jungle with him.'

*

Hiller, in his room in the Hotel Negresco, was studying a gold coin which he held in his hand when he was disturbed by an erratic knock on the door. He pulled out a gun, held it behind his back, crossed to the door and opened it.

Hiller put his gun away: the precaution had been unnecessary. Serrano, both hands clutching the back of his neck, swayed dizzily and practically fell into the room.

'Brandy!' Serrano's voice was a strangled croak.

'What the hell's happened to you?'

'Brandy!'

'Brandy coming up,' Hiller said resignedly. He gave a generous double to Serrano who downed it in a single gulp. He had just finished his third brandy and was pouring out his tale of woe when another sharp rat-tat-tat came on the door, this knocking far from erratic. Again Hiller took his precautionary measures and again they proved unnecessary. The Hamilton who stood in the doorway was scarcely recognizable as the Hamilton of two hours previously. Two hours in the Hotel de Paris's grandiloquently named Presidential suite—no president had ever or would ever stay there, but it had the only bath in the hotel not corroded with rust—had transformed him. He had bathed and was clean-shaven. He wore a fresh set of khaki drills, a fresh khaki shirt without a rent in sight and even a pair of gleaming new shoes.

Hiller glanced at his watch. 'Two hours precisely. You are very punctual.'

'The politeness of princes.' Hamilton entered the room and caught sight of Serrano who was busy pouring himself another large brandy. By this time it was difficult to judge whether he was suffering the more from the effects of the blow or the brandy. Holding the glass in one rather unsteady hand and massaging the back of his neck with the other, he continued the restorative process without seeming to notice Hamilton.

Hamilton said: 'Who's this character?'

'Serrano,' Hiller said. 'An old friend.' It would have been impossible to guess from Hiller's casual off-handedness that he'd met Serrano for the first time only that evening. 'Don't worry. He can be trusted.'

'Delighted to hear it,' Hamilton said. He couldn't remember the month or the year when he last trusted anybody. 'Makes a welcome change in this day and age.' He peered at Serrano with the air of a concerned and kindly healer. 'Looks to me as if he's coming down with something.'

'He's been down,' Hiller said. 'Mugged.' He was observing Hamilton closely but could well have spared himself the trouble.

'Mugged?' Hamilton looked mildly astonished. 'He was walking the streets this time of night?'

'Yes.'

'And alone?'

'Yes,' Hiller said and added in what he probably regarded as a rather pointed fashion: '*You* walk alone at night.'

'I know Romono,' Hamilton said. 'Much more importantly, Romono knows me.' He looked pityingly at Serrano. 'I'll bet you weren't even walking in the middle of the road—and I'll bet you're that much lighter by the weight of your wallet.'

Serrano nodded, scowled, said nothing and got back to his self-medication.

'Life's a great teacher,' Hamilton said absently. 'But it beats me how a citizen of Romono could be so damned stupid. Okay, Hiller, when do we leave?'

Hiller had already turned towards a glass fronted wall cupboard. 'Scotch?' he said. 'No fire water. Guaranteed.' He showed Hamilton a famous proprietary brand of Scotch with the seal unbroken.

'Thanks.'

Hiller's gesture had not been motivated by an undiluted spirit of hospitality. He had turned his back on Hamilton to conceal what he knew must have been a momentary flash of triumph in his face; moreover, this was definitely a moment for celebration. Back in the bar of the Hotel de Paris he had been sure that he had his fish hooked: now he had it gaffed and landed.

'Cheers,' he said. 'We leave at first light tomorrow.'

'How do we go?'

'Bush plane to Cuiabá.' He paused then added apologetically: 'Rickety old bus of cardboard and wire but it's never come down yet. After that, Smith's private jet. That's something else again. It will be waiting for us at Cuiabá.'

'How do you know?'

Hiller nodded towards the phone. 'Carrier pigeon.'

'Pretty sure of yourself, weren't you?'

'Not really. We like to arrange things in advance. I just go on probabilities.' Hiller shrugged. 'One call to fix things, then another

38

call to cancel. Then from Cuiabá to Smith's private airfield in Brasilia.' He nodded towards Serrano. 'He's coming with us.'

'Why?'

'Why ever not?' Hiller even managed to look puzzled. 'My friend. Smith's employee. Good jungle man.'

'Always wanted to meet one of those.' Hamilton looked consideringly at Serrano. 'One can only hope that he's a little bit more alert in the depths of the Mato Grosso than he is in the alleys of Romono.'

Serrano had nothing to say to this but he was, clearly, thinking: prudently he refrained from voicing his thoughts.

Smith, it would seem, was both a considerate man and one who thought of everything. Not only had he stocked his Lear with a splendid variety of liquor, liqueurs, wines and beers, he'd even provided an exceptionally attractive stewardess to serve them up. All three men—Hamilton, Hiller and Serrano—had long, cold drinks in their hands. Hamilton gazed happily at the green immensity of the Amazonian rain forest passing by beneath them.

'This fairly beats hacking your way through that lot down there,' he said. He looked round the cabin of the luxuriously appointed jet. 'But this is for the carriage trade. What transport is Smith thinking of using when we make our trip into the Mato Grosso?'

'No idea,' Hiller said. 'Matters like that, Smith doesn't consult me. He's got his own advisers for that. You'll be seeing him in a couple of hours. I suppose he'll tell you then.'

'I don't think you quite understand,' Hamilton said in an almost gently explanatory tone. 'I only asked what transport he was *thinking* of using. Any decisions he and his experts have made are not really very relevant.'

Hiller looked at him in slow disbelief. '*You* are going to tell *him* what we're to use?'

Hamilton beckoned the stewardess, smiled and handed over his glass for a refill. 'Nothing like savouring the good life—while it lasts.' He turned to Hiller. 'Yes, that's the idea.'

'I can see,' Hiller said heavily, 'that you and Smith are going to get along just fine.'

'Oh, I hope so, I hope so. You said we'd be seeing him in two hours. Could you make it three?' He looked disparagingly at his wrinkled khaki drills. 'These look well enough in Romono, but I have to see a tailor before I go calling on multi-millionaires.

You say we're being met when we arrive. You think you can drop me off at the Grand?'

'Jesus!' Hiller was clearly taken aback. 'The Grand—*and* a tailor. That's expensive. How come? Last night in the bar you said you had no money.'

'I came into some later on.'

Hiller and Serrano exchanged very peculiar looks. Hamilton continued to gaze placidly out of the window.

As promised a car met them at the private airport in Brasilia. 'Car' was really too mundane a word to describe it. It was an enormous maroon Rolls-Royce, big enough, one would have thought, to accommodate a football team. In the back it had television, a bar and even an ice-maker. Up front—very far up front —were two uniformed men in dark green livery. One drove the car: the other's main function in life appeared to be opening doors when the back seat—seats—passengers entered or left. The engine, predictably, was soundless. If it were part of Smith's pattern to awe visitors he most certainly succeeded in the case of Serrano. Hamilton appeared quite unimpressed, possibly because he was too busy inspecting the bar; Smith had somehow overlooked providing a stewardess for the rear of the Rolls.

They drove through the wide avenues of that futuristic city and pulled up outside the Grand Hotel. Hamilton dismounted—the door having magically been opened for him, of course—and passed swiftly through the revolving door. Once inside, he looked out through the glassed-in porch. The Rolls, already more than a hundred yards away, was turning a corner to the left. Hamilton waited until it had disappeared from sight, left by the revolving door by which he had entered and started to walk briskly back in the direction from which they had come. He gave the impression of one who knew the city, and he did: he knew Brasilia very well indeed.

Five minutes after dropping Hamilton the Rolls pulled up outside a photographer's shop. Hiller went inside, approached a smiling and affable assistant and handed over the film that had been taken from Hamilton.

'Have this developed and sent to Mr Joshua Smith, Haydn Villa.' There was no need for Hiller to add the word 'immediately'. Smith's name guaranteed immediacy. Hiller went on: 'No copy is to be made of this film and neither the person who develops it nor any other member of your staff is ever to discuss it. I hope that is clearly understood.'

'Yes, sir. Of course, sir.' The smile and the affability had vanished to be replaced by total obsequiousness. 'Speed and secrecy. Those are guaranteed, sir.'

'And a perfect print?'

'If the negative is perfect so will the print be.'

Hiller couldn't think of how else he could threaten the now thoroughly apprehensive assistant so he nodded and left.

Another ten minutes later and Hiller and Serrano were in the drawing-room of the Villa Haydn. Serrano was seated, as were Tracy, Maria and a fourth and as yet unidentified man. Smith talked somewhat apart with Hiller—'somewhat apart' in that huge drawing-room meant a considerable distance—glancing occasionally in Serrano's direction.

Hiller said: 'Of course, I can't vouch for him. But he knows an awful lot that we don't and I can always see to it that he'll make no trouble. Come to that, so would Hamilton. Hamilton has a rough way of dealing with people who step out of line.' Hiller went on to tell the sad tale of Serrano's mugging.

'Well, if you say so, Hiller.' Smith sounded doubtful and if there was one thing Smith didn't like it was being doubtful about anything. 'You certainly haven't let me down so far.' He paused. 'But your friend Serrano seems to have no history, no past.'

'Neither have most men in the Mato Grosso. Usually for the simple reason that they have *too* much of a past. But he knows his jungle—and he knows more Indian dialects than any man except maybe Hamilton. Certainly more than any man in the Indian Protection Service.'

'All right.' Smith had made up his mind and seemed relieved for that. 'And he's been close to the Lost City. Could be a useful back-up man.'

Hiller nodded towards the unidentified person, a tall, very heavily built, darkly handsome man in his mid-thirties.

'Who's that, Mr Smith?'

'Heffner. My chief staff photographer.'

Hiller said: 'Mr Smith!'

'Hamilton would think it extremely strange if I didn't take a staff photographer along on this historic trip,' Smith said reason-

41

ably. He smiled slightly. 'I will confess, though, that he can use one or two instruments other than his cameras.'

'I'll bet he can.' Hiller looked at Heffner with even closer interest. 'Another with or without a past?'

Smith smiled again but made no answer. A phone rang. Tracy, who was nearest to it, picked it up, listened briefly and replaced the receiver.

'Well, well. Surprise, surprise. The Grand Hotel has no one registered there under the name of Hamilton. Not only that, no member of the staff can recall ever seeing a man answering to the description.'

Hamilton, at that moment, was in a lavishly furnished suite in the Hotel Imperial.

Ramon and Navarro, seated on a couch, were admiring Hamilton, who was admiring himself in front of a full-length mirror.

'Always did fancy myself in a fawn seersucker,' Hamilton said complacently. 'Don't you agree? This should knock Smith for six.'

'I don't know about Smith,' Ramon said, 'but in that outfit you'd terrify even the Muscias. So no trouble with getting the invitation?'

'None. When he saw me flashing those gold coins in public he must have panicked in case someone else would step in fast. Now, I'm pleased to say, he's convinced he's got me hooked.'

'You still think that gold hoard exists?' Navarro said.

'I'm convinced it *did* exist. Not that it *does*.'

'Then why did you want those coins?'

'When this is over they will be returned and the money reimbursed—all except the two that are now in the possession of Curly, the head barman at the Hotel de Paris. But those were necessary: the shark, as we know, took the bait.'

'So, no hoard, huh?' Ramon said. 'Disappointing.'

'There is a hoard and a huge one. But not of those coins. Perhaps melted down, although that's unlikely. What is likely is that it's been split up into private collectors' hands. If you want to dispose of an art treasure, be it a stolen Tintoretto or a Penny Black, then Brazil is *the* place in the world. The number of Brazilian millionaires who spend hours in their air-conditioned, humidity-controlled, burglar-proof deep underground cellars gloating over

42

stolen Old Masters boggles the imagination. Ramon, there's a wet bar right behind you, and I'm developing a sore and thirsty throat from lecturing callow youngsters on the facts of criminal life.'

Ramon grinned, rose and brought a large whisky and soda to Hamilton and a soda each for himself and his brother—the twins never drank anything stronger.

Having eased his throat, Hamilton said: 'What did you get on Smith?'

'Nothing more than you expected,' Ramon said. 'The number of companies he controls is beyond counting. He's a financial genius, charming and courteous, totally ruthless in his business dealings and must by any reckoning be the richest man in the Southern hemisphere. A sort of Howard Hughes in reverse. About Hughes's early days everything was known in detail but the latter part of his life was so wrapped in mystery that many people who should have been in a position to know could scarcely believe that he died on that flight from Mexico to the States, having been firmly convinced that he had died many years previously. Smith? Dead opposite. His past is a closed book and he never talks about it: neither do any of his colleagues, friends or supposed intimates —no-one really knows whether he *has* any intimates—for the good reason that none of them was around in his early days. Today, his life is an open book. He conceals nothing and operates in a totally straightforward fashion. Any one of the shareholders in his forty-odd companies can inspect the firm's books whenever they wish. He appears to have absolutely nothing to hide and I would suppose when you are as brilliant as he unquestionably is there's just no point in being dishonest. After all, what's the point in it if you can make more money being honest? Today he knows everybody's business and lets anyone who wishes know all about his businesses.'

'He's got something to hide,' Hamilton said. 'I know he has.'

Navarro said: 'What?'

'That's what we're going to find out, isn't it?' Hamilton said.

'I wish you wouldn't play your cards so close to your chest,' Navarro said.

'What cards?'

'We look forward to watching you at work, Mr Hamilton,' Ramon said. His tone was neutral to the point of being ambiguous. 'It should be worth watching. By every account, the man is totally

43

above suspicion. He goes everywhere, sees everyone, knows everyone. And everyone knows that he and the President are blood brothers.'

The President's blood brother was leaning forward in a chair in his splendid drawing-room, oblivious of the company around him, staring in fascination at the silver screen. The room had been so efficiently darkened by the heavy drapes that he would have had difficulty in seeing those around him: had it been broad daylight, he still wouldn't have seen them. His absorption was total.

The transparencies were of superb quality, taken with a superb camera by an expert photographer who knew precisely what he was about. The colour was true, the clarity and the resolution impeccable. And the projector the best that Smith's money could buy.

The first group showed a ruined and ancient city, impossibly clinging to the top of a narrow plateau with, at the far end, a breathtakingly well-preserved ziggurat, as imposing as the best surviving works of the Aztecs or the Maya.

A second group showed one side of the city perched on the edge of a cliff that dropped vertically to a river and the rain forest beyond. The third group showed the other side of the city overlooking a similar gorge with a river sliding swiftly past in the distant depths. A fourth group, clearly taken from the top of the hills, showed a reverse view of the ancient city, with a brief glimpse of scrub-land beyond—once obviously terraced for cultivation—and with the two cliff-sides meeting in the middle distance. A fifth group, obviously taken 180° from the same position, showed a flat, grassy plateau, the sides curving to meet like the bows of a boat. Nearly incredible as those pictures were, the next few groups were staggering.

They were taken from the air and as transparency succeeded transparency, it became evident that they, like a number of the previous ones, could only have been taken from a helicopter.

The first of those helicopter shots showed the entire ruined city from above. The second, from perhaps five hundred feet higher up, showed that the city was perched on top of a vertically-sided, boat-shaped pinnacle of rock splitting a river which swept by on either side of it. Both arms of the river were rock-strewn, foaming white and clearly unnavigable. The third and fourth groups, from an even higher altitude, were a shock: taken hori-

44

zontally they showed pictures of a densely crowded rain-forest, reaching out, it seemed, almost to touch the camera and extending, unbroken, to the distant horizon. The fifth set, vertically downwards, made it clear that the great outer cliff-walls of the twin gorges were at least several hundred feet higher than the top of the cliff-walls that formed the island on which the Lost City was built. The sixth group, taken at a still higher elevation, showed just a narrow gap between two great stretches of forest reaching towards each other, with the Lost City just vaguely visible in the gloomy depths below. The seventh and last group, taken anywhere between five hundred and a thousand feet higher up again, revealed nothing but the continuous majestic sweep of the Amazonian rain-forest, unbroken from pictorial horizon to pictorial horizon.

It was small wonder, then, that the planes on the Brazilian ordnance survey services, whose pilots claimed, probably rightly, to have criss-crossed every square mile of the Mato Grosso, had never discovered the site of the Lost City. It just could not be seen from the air. But the ancients had stumbled across it, discovered the most invisible, the most inaccessible, the most impregnable fortress ever created by nature or devised by man.

The viewers in the Villa Haydn drawing-room had sat throughout in silence. They knew they had seen something that no white man with the exception of Hamilton and his helicopter pilot, had ever seen before, something, perhaps, that no-one had ever seen for generations, maybe even for centuries. They were hard people, tough people, cynical people, people who counted value only in the terms of cost, people conditioned to disbelieve, almost automatically, the evidence of their own eyes: but there is yet to be born a man or woman the atavistic depths of whose soul cannot be touched by that one questing finger that will not be denied, that primitive ancestral awe inseparable from watching the veil of unsuspected history being swept aside.

The slowly comprehending silence stretched out for at least a minute. Then, almost inaudibly, Smith exhaled his breath in a long sigh.

'Son-of-a-gun,' he whispered. 'Son-of-a-gun. He found it.'

'If your intention was to impress us,' Maria said, 'you've succeeded. What on earth was that? And *where* is it?'

'The Lost City.' Smith spoke absently. 'Brazil. In the Mato Grosso.'

'The *Brazilians* built pyramids?'

'Not that I know of. May have been some other race. Anyway, they're not pyramids, they're—Tracy, this is more in your field.'

'Well. Not really my field either. One of our magazines had an article on those so-called pyramids and I spent a couple of days with the writer and photographer on the job. Curiosity only, and wasted curiosity—I didn't learn much. Pyramid-shaped, sure, but those stepped-sided and flat-topped structures are called ziggurats. No-one knows where they originated although it is known that the Assyrians and Babylonians had them. Oddly enough, this style bypassed the virtually neighbouring country of Egypt, which went in for the smooth-sided and conically-topped version, but turned up again in ancient Mexico where some are still to be seen. Archaeologists and such-like use this as a powerful argument of prehistoric contact between east and west but the only sure fact is that their origins are lost in the mists of those same prehistoric times. My word, Mr Smith, this is going to drive those poor archaeologists up the wall. A ziggurat in the Mato Grosso.'

'Ricardo?' Hamilton said. 'I shall be leaving our friend's place in about two hours' time. I'll be driving—moment.' He broke off and turned to Ramon lounging in the couch in the Imperial suite. 'Ramon, what shall I be driving?'

'Black Cadillac.'

'A black Cadillac,' Hamilton said into the phone. 'I do not wish to be followed. Thank you.'

46

3

There were six people in Smith's drawing-room that sunny afternoon—Smith himself, Tracy, Maria, Hiller, Serrano and Hamilton. All had glasses in their hands.

'Another?' said Smith. His hand reached out to touch the button that would summon the butler.

Hamilton said: 'I'd rather talk.'

Smith raised an eyebrow in slight if genuine astonishment. Not only had he heard from Hiller of Hamilton's reputation as a hard drinker, but his slightest suggestion was usually treated as a royal command. He withdrew his hand from the buzzer.

'As you wish. So we are agreed on the purpose of our visit. I tell you, Hamilton, I have done many things in the past that have given me a great deal of pleasure, but I've never been so excited——'

Hamilton interrupted him, something no-one ever did to Smith. 'Let's get down to details.'

'By God, you *are* in a hurry. I'd have thought that after four years——'

'It's a lot longer than that. But even after only four years a man starts to become a little impatient.' He pointed towards Maria and Tracy. People never pointed in Smith's drawing-room. 'Who are they?'

'We all know your rough diamond reputation, Hamilton.' When Smith chose to use a cold tone he could do so most effectively. 'But there's no need to be rude.'

Hamilton shook his head. 'Not rude. Just a man, as you observed, in a hurry. I just like to check on the company I'm keeping. As you do.'

'As I do?' Again the eyebrow. 'My dear fellow, if you would kindly explain——'

'And that's another thing,' Hamilton said. That made it twice in thirty seconds that Smith had been interrupted, which must have constituted some sort of a record. 'I don't like being condescended to. I am not your dear fellow. I am not, as you may come to learn, anybody's dear fellow. As you do, I said. Check up. Or perhaps you don't know the identity of the person who rang the Grand Hotel to see if I was actually staying there?'

It was a guess, but in the circumstances a safe one, and the flickered glance between Smith and Tracy was all the confirmation Hamilton required. He nodded towards Tracy.

'See what I mean,' Hamilton said. 'That's the nosey bastard. Who is he?'

'You would insult my guests, Hamilton?' Smith's tone was now positively arctic.

'I don't much care who I insult—or should I say "whom"? He's still a nosey bastard. Another thing, when I ask questions about people I do it honestly and in the open, not behind their backs. Who is he?'

'Tracy,' Smith said stiffly, 'is the managing director of McCormick-Mackenzie International Publications Division.' Hamilton looked unimpressed. 'Maria is my confidential secretary and, I might add, a close personal friend.'

Hamilton looked away from Tracy and Maria almost as if he had already dismissed them from his mind as being of no importance. 'I'm not interested in your relationships. My fee.'

Smith was obviously taken aback. Gentlemen did not discuss business negotiations in this crude and abrupt fashion. Momentarily, his expression hovered between astonishment and anger. Many years had passed since any man had dared talk to him in such a way. He required considerable will-power to repress his anger.

'Hiller mentioned it, I think,' Smith said. 'A six-figure sum. One hundred thousand dollars—U.S. dollars—friend.'

'I'm not your friend. A quarter million.'

'Ludicrous.'

'I could say "Thanks for the drink" and walk out. I'm not childish. I hope you're not either.'

Smith had not become the man he was without the ability to make his mind up very rapidly indeed. Without in any way appearing to capitulate he capitulated immediately.

'A man would want an awful lot of service for money like that.'

'Let's get our terms clear. You get co-operation, not service.

I'll return to this point later. I regard my fee as being far from excessive in view of the fact that I'm damned certain you're in this not just to get a few nice photographs and a human interest story. Who ever heard of Joshua Smith engaging upon any enterprise where money was not the prime and motivating factor?'

'As far as the past is concerned I would agree with you.' Smith's voice was quiet. 'In this particular instance money is not the principal factor.'

Hamilton nodded in acknowledgment. 'That could well be. In this particular instance I could well believe you.' Smith looked taken aback at Hamilton's concession, then his expression changed to one of speculation. Hamilton smiled. 'You're doubtless trying to figure out what I've figured out as the other motivation. You need not concern yourself for that in no way concerns me. Now, transportation?'

'What? What was that?' Smith had been caught off-balance by the sudden switch in topic which he should not have been as it was a favourite tactic of his own. 'Ah! Transportation.'

'Yes. What kind of transportation—air and water, we can forget land—do your companies have available?'

'A great deal, as you can imagine. What we don't have we can hire although I should think the need would be unlikely. Tracy has all the details. Tracy, by the way, is both a qualified pilot and helicopter pilot.'

'Helps. Where are the details?'

'Tracy has the details.' Smith said this in such a way as to convey the impression that he was not the man to be concerned with details, which was probably quite an accurate impression for he was famous for his gift in picking top-flight lieutenants and delegating the bulk of the executive work to them. Tracy, who had been following the conversation closely, rose, crossed to where they were standing and handed Hamilton a folder. The expression on Tracy's face bespoke a marked lack of affection: managing directors do not take kindly to being called nosey bastards. Hamilton appeared to notice nothing amiss.

He took the folder, read rapidly through the loose-leaf contents, pausing briefly now and again as something in particular caught his attention, then closed the folder. One could have been forgiven for assuming that Hamilton had already absorbed the contents: he probably had. For once, Hamilton seemed fairly impressed.

'Quite an air/sea fleet, haven't you? Everything from a Boeing 727 to a Piper Comanche. Double rotor freight helicopter—this is a Sikorsky Skycrane?'

'Yes.'

'And a hovercraft. Can the helicopter lift the hovercraft?'

'Naturally. That's why it was bought.'

'Where's the hovercraft? Corrientes?'

Smith said: 'How the devil do you know?'

'Logic. Wouldn't be much good to you here or in Rio, would it? I'll take this folder. See you this evening.'

'This evening?' Smith looked unhappy. 'Damn it, man, we have to draw up our plans and——'

'I'll draw up the plans. I'll explain them when I return with my assistants this evening.'

'Damn it all, Hamilton, *I* am putting up all the money. The man who pays the piper calls the tune.'

'This time out, you're second fiddle.'

Hamilton left, leaving behind him a brief but profound silence. Tracy said: 'Well. Of all the arrogant, hard-nosed, intransigent bastards——'

'Agreed, agreed,' Smith said. 'But he holds the cards, all of them.' He looked thoughtful. 'Enigma. Rough, tough, but dresses well, speaks well, obviously at home in any territory. Nuances, clever nuances. At ease in my drawing-room. Not many strangers are. Come to that, nobody is.'

Tracy said: 'And he's come to the conclusion that this Lost City is so dangerously inaccessible that he's not prepared to try the same route again. So—a helicopter. Or hovercraft.'

'I wonder.' Smith was still looking thoughtful. 'Why else would a man like that throw in his lot with us?'

'Because he's convinced he can eat us alive,' Maria said. She paused. 'Maybe he will at that.'

Smith looked at her without expression then crossed to the dining-room window. Hamilton was just moving away in his black Cadillac. A chauffeur stopped polishing a nondescript Ford, glanced towards Smith's window, nodded, climbed into his car and followed the Cadillac.

Hamilton was driving down one of Brasilia's broad boulevards. He consulted his rear mirror. The Ford was about two hundred yards behind. Hamilton increased his speed. So did the Ford. Both cars were now travelling well above the speed limit. A

police car appeared behind the Ford, switched on the siren, overtook and flagged the Ford to a stop.

The Ministry of Justice was a rather splendid building and the large airy office in which Hamilton sat opposite across a polished leather table from Colonel Ricardo Diaz was suitably sumptuous. Diaz, in an immaculately cut uniform, was large, tanned and looked competent to a degree, which indeed he was. Diaz took a sip of some indeterminate liquid and sighed.

'About Smith, Mr Hamilton, you know as much as we do—everything and nothing. His past is a mystery, his present an open book that anyone is welcome to read. The dividing line between the present and the past can't be precisely delineated but it is known that he appeared—or, rather, emerged or surfaced in Santa Catherina, a province with a traditionally heavy Germanic settlement, in the late forties. Whether he is of similar origin is not known: his English is as immaculate as his Portuguese but, as far as is known, he has never been heard to speak German.

'His first business venture was to produce a newspaper aimed primarily at the native German speakers in the province but printed in Portuguese: it was conservative and strongly pro-establishment and marked the beginning of a long and close association with the government of the time, an association that has persisted, despite changes of government, until this day.

'He then branched out into the fields of early plastics and early ball-point pens. Smith was never an innovator—he was and remains a take-over specialist and a share manipulator of genius. Both the publishing and the industrial sides of his business expanded at a remarkable speed and within ten years he was, by any standards, a very wealthy man.'

Hamilton said: 'He couldn't have been without the odd cruzeiro to begin with.'

'Agreed. Expansion on a scale such as Smith's must have called for a great deal of capital.'

'And the source of capital is unknown?'

'Totally. But that's nothing to hold against any man. In this country—as in many others—we don't care to enquire too closely into those things.

'Now we come to Tracy. He is indeed the general manager of Smith's publication division. Very tough, very able, nothing known about him in the criminal line, which could mean that he's either

51

honest or very clever. The best you can say of him is that he's a soldier of fortune. The police are certain that the bulk of his activities are illegal—diamonds have an odd habit of disappearing when he's in the neighbourhood—but he's never been arrested far less convicted. Serrano is a small-time crook, not too bright and a fearful coward.'

'He can't be all that cowardly if he ventures alone into the rain-forests of the Mato Grosso. Not many white people would.'

'That thought, I admit, has also occurred to me. I'm merely passing on reported reputation, accuracy not guaranteed. Now, Heffner. Heffner's the joker. Wouldn't recognize a camera if he tripped over one. Well known to the New York police. Associated with crimes of violence and alleged gangland killings, but he's always beaten the rap. Not too surprisingly really—no police in any country are going to come over all zealous and excited when one hoodlum dispatches another. Curious fellow. Usually well spoken and civilized enough—look at those pillars of society, the Mafia bosses—but the veneer vanishes when he gets next to a bottle of bourbon. And he has a weakness for bourbon.'

'And all this leaves Smith unaffected?'

'Nothing known against him, as I said, but you can't associate with characters like Hiller, Heffner and Tracy without some tar rubbing off. Could well be the other way round, of course.' He looked up as a knock came at the door. 'Come in, come in.'

Ramon and Navarro entered. The twins were clad in khaki suits and smiling cheerfully. Diaz looked at them and winced.

'The famous Detective-Sergeant Herera and the famous Detective-Sergeant Herera. Or infamous. You are far from home, gentlemen.'

'Senor Hamilton's fault, sir.' Ramon spread his hands apologetically. 'He's always leading us astray.'

'Mary's little lambs. Ah. Major.'

A young officer entered and unrolled on the table a map of Southern Brazil. It was marked with legends of varying kinds. Differently coloured flags in circles and squares indicated different tribes, races and languages. Other symbols indicated the state of hostility or friendliness of the tribes.

The major said: 'This is the most up-to-date picture the Indian Protection Service can give you. There are some places, you understand, where even the Service do not care to investigate too closely. Most of the tribes are friendly—pacified, if you like. Some are

52

hostile. Nearly always the white man's fault. A very few cannibal tribes. Those are known.'

'And to be avoided, of course. The Chapate, Horenas and Muscias especially.'

Hamilton pointed at a town on the map and looked at Diaz. 'Corrientes. Smith has a hovercraft there—for obvious reasons. It's at the junction of the Paraná and Paraguay rivers and he must be pretty sure the Lost City lies near the head-waters of one of those. I'm going up the Paraguay. I don't know it well, there may be bad rapids for all I know, but the helicopter can help if there are.'

Diaz said: 'Your friend has a helicopter?'

'My friend, as you call him, has got everything. This is a giant—a Sikorsky Skycrane. Well enough named—it can just about lift any damn thing. We'll base the helicopter at Asunción. The hovercraft can go up in three stages—to either Puerto Casado or Puerto Sastre in Paraguay, then into Brazil to Corumbá then finally to Cuiabá. From there the helicopter can airlift it to Rio da Morte.'

'And you would like to have some units of the Federal army exercising near Cuiabá, is that it?'

'If it can be arranged.'

'That has already been done.'

'I am in your debt, Colonel Diaz.'

'It would be more accurate to say that we are in your debt. If, that is to say——'

'*If* I come back?'

'Precisely.'

Hamilton gestured towards the two young men. 'With the heavenly two to watch my back, what harm can befall me?'

Diaz looked at him briefly and doubtfully then pressed a button. An aide came in carrying a brown leather case, extracted what looked to be a large movie camera and handed it to Hamilton, who pressed a button on the base. There came the faint whirring noise typical of an electric-powered camera.

Diaz said: 'You won't believe this, but it will even take pictures if you wish.'

Hamilton smiled but without humour. 'I don't think I'll be indulging in any photography this time out. What's the radio transmitting range?'

'Five hundred kilometres.'

'Enough. Waterproof?'

'Naturally. You leave tomorrow?'

'No. We have to get provisions and jungle gear and fly them to Cuiabá. We must get the hovercraft on the move. More important, though, I must go ahead and check on our friend Mr Jones.'

'Back to the Colony?'

'Back to the Colony.'

Diaz said slowly: 'You are an extraordinarily persistent man, Mr Hamilton. God knows you've every right to be.' He shook his head. 'I greatly fear for the health of your travelling companions in your forthcoming expedition.'

Hamilton had rejoined his travelling companions-to-be. Outside the uncurtained windows of the Villa Haydn's drawing-room the sky was dark: the room itself was brightly but not harshly lit by the light from the three crystal chandeliers. There were nine people in the room, most of them standing, most of them with aperitif glasses in their hands. Present were Hamilton, the twin Sergeants Herera, Smith and his entourage. Heffner, to whom Hamilton had just been introduced, was slightly flushed of face, slightly loud of voice and was sitting on an arm of the chair Maria was occupying. Tracy was regarding him with disfavour.

Smith said to Hamilton: 'I must say your heavenly twins, as you call them, have an air of competence about them.'

'They're not much at home in drawing-rooms. But in the jungle, yes. They're good. Squirrel-hunter's eyes.'

'Meaning?'

'Either of them, with his rifle, can hit a playing-card at a hundred yards. Most people can't even see a card at that distance.'

'That meant to sound intimidating, threatening?'

'Neither. Reassuring. Very useful accomplishment when wild boars or alligators or head-hunters or cannibals come at you. Let's not confuse this coming trip with a Sunday school picnic.'

'I'm aware of that.' Smith was trying to sound patient. 'Well, your plan sounds reasonable. We leave in a couple of days?'

'More like a week. I repeat, no picnic: you don't go dashing off into the Amazonian rain-forest at a couple of hours' notice, especially when you are going to be passing through hostile territory—and, believe me, we will be. We have to allow several days for the hovercraft to get up to Cuiabá—we don't know what difficulties it might encounter. Then we have to get all our provisions and equipment and fly them over to Cuiabá. At least, you will. I have some business to attend to first.'

Smith raised an eyebrow. He was very good at raising eyebrows. 'What business?'

'Sorry.' Hamilton didn't sound sorry. 'Where can one hire a helicopter in this city?'

Smith took a deep breath then clearly made up his mind to ignore the outright rebuff. 'Well, you know I have this freight Sikorsky——'

'That lumbering giant? No thank you.'

'I have a smaller one. And a pilot.'

'Again, no thanks. Tracy's not the only one who can fly a helicopter.'

Smith looked at him in silence. His face was without expression but it was not difficult to guess what he was thinking: it would have been perfectly in keeping with Hamilton's secretive nature, his policy of never letting his left hand know what his right was doing, to have flown his own helicopter over the Lost City, so that no other person could share his knowledge. At last Smith said: 'Gracious, aren't you? You don't see a little friction arising when we set off on this search?'

Hamilton shrugged indifferently. 'It isn't a search. I know where I'm going. And if you think some friction is going to arise, then why don't you leave behind those liable to give rise to friction? It's a matter of indifference to me who comes along.'

'I'll decide that, Hamilton.'

'Will you, now?' Again the same indifferent, infuriating shrug. 'I don't think you've quite got the picture yet.'

It was significant of Smith's perturbation that he actually went to the bar and poured another drink for himself. Normally, indeed invariably, he would have summoned his butler to perform such menial tasks. He returned to Hamilton and said: 'Another point. You got your own way about making the plans—but we haven't yet decided who's going to be in charge of our little expedition, have we?'

'I have. I am.'

Smith's impassive air deserted him. He looked every inch the bulti-millionaire he was reputed to be.

'I repeat, Hamilton, I'm the paymaster.'

'The ship-owner pays his captain. Who's in charge at sea?

Even more importantly, who's in charge in the jungle? You wouldn't last a day without me.'

There was a sudden silence in the room. The tension between the two men was all too obvious. Heffner rose from the arm of the chair, lurched once and then crossed to where the two men were standing. The light of battle was in his truculent and bloodshot eyes.

'But, boss! You don't seem to understand.' Heffner didn't speak the words, he sneered them. 'This is the intrepid explorer himself. The one and only Hamilton. Haven't you heard? Hamilton is always in charge.'

Hamilton glanced briefly at Heffner then at Smith. 'This is the kind of irritant I mean. Born to give trouble, bound to give rise to friction. What function does he perform?'

'My chief staff photographer.'

'Looks the artistic type. He coming along?'

'Of course he is.' Smith's tone was glacial. 'Why on earth do you think Mr Tracy and I brought him down here?'

'I thought maybe he had to leave some place in a hurry.'

Heffner took a step closer. 'What does that mean, Hamilton?'

'Nothing, really. I just thought that maybe your friends in the New York police department were beginning to take too close an interest in you.'

Heffner was momentarily taken aback, then he took another menacing step forward. 'I don't know what the hell you mean. You wouldn't think of stopping me, would you, Hamilton?'

'Stopping you from coming along, dear me, no.'

Ramon looked at Navarro. Both men winced.

'Amazing,' Heffner said. 'All you require is twenty pounds over a man to make him see it your way.'

'Provided, of course, that you're half-way sober by that time.'

Heffner gazed at him in alcoholic disbelief then swung a round-house right at Hamilton's head. Hamilton moved inside it and brought up his own right in a wicked jab as Heffner's fist swept harmlessly by his head. Grey-faced and doubled over, Heffner sank to his knees, his hands clutching his midriff.

Ramon said thoughtfully: 'I do believe, Senor Hamilton, that he's half-way sober already.'

'A short way with mutineers, eh?' Smith was unmoved by the plight of his trusty chief photographer, and his irritation had given way to curiosity. 'You seem to know something about Heffner?'

'I read the occasional New York paper,' Hamilton said. 'Bit late when I get them, mind you, but that hardly matters as Heffner's activities cover a fair period. What the Americans call a scoff-law. Suspected involvement in various crimes of violence, even gangland killings. He's cleverer than he looks, which I don't believe, or he has a clever lawyer. Anyway, he's always beaten the rap so far. It is impossible, Mr Smith, that you had no inkling of this.'

'I confess that there have been stories, rumours. I discount them. Two things. He knows his job and a man is innocent until proved guilty.' Smith paused and went on: 'You know anything to my detriment?'

'Nothing. Everybody knows your life is an open book. A man in your position can't afford to have it otherwise.'

'Me?' said Tracy.

'I don't want to hurt your feelings but I never heard of you until today.'

Smith glanced down casually at a still prostrate Heffner, as if seeing him for the first time, and rang a bell. The butler entered. His face remained expressionless at the sight of the man on the floor: it was not difficult to imagine that he had seen such things before.

'Mr Heffner is unwell,' Smith said. 'Have him taken to his quarters. Dinner is ready?'

'Yes, sir.'

As they left the drawing-room Maria took Hamilton's arm. In a quiet voice she said: 'I wish you hadn't done that.'

'Don't tell me I've unwittingly clobbered your fiancé?'

'My fiancé! I can't stand him. But he has a long memory—and a bad reputation.'

Hamilton patted her hand. 'Next time I'll turn the other cheek.'

She snatched her hand away and walked quickly ahead of him.

Dinner over, Hamilton and the twins left in the black Cadillac. Navarro said admiringly: 'So now Heffner is labelled in their minds as your bad apple in the barrel while Smith, Tracy, Hiller and for all I know Serrano think that they are the driven snow. You really are a fearful liar, Senor Hamilton.'

'One really has to be modest about such things. As in all else practice makes perfect.'

4

As dusk approached, a helicopter, equipped with both floats and skids, set down on a sandy stretch on the left bank of the River Paraná. Both up-river and down, on the same bank, as far as the eye could see in the gloom, stretched the dense and virtually impenetrable rain forest of the region. The far side of the river, the right or western bank, was invisible in the gathering gloom: at this point, close to where the River Iquelmi flowed into the Paraná, the parent river was more than five miles wide.

The helicopter cabin was dimly lit even although the precaution had been taken of pulling black drapes across the windows. Hamilton, Navarro and Ramon were having their evening meal of cold meat, bread, beer and soda—the beer for Hamilton, soda for the twins.

Ramon shivered theatrically. 'I don't think I much care for this place.'

'Not many people do,' Hamilton said. 'But it suits Brown—alias Mr Jones—and his friends well enough. Defensively speaking, it's probably the most impregnable place in South America. Years ago I traced Brown and his fellow-refugees to a place called San Carlos de Bariloche near Lake Ranco on the Argentine–Chilean border. God knows that was fortress enough, but he didn't feel secure even there so he moved to a hide-out in the Chilean Andes, then came here.'

Navarro said: 'He knew you were after him?'

'Yes. For years. Our wealthy friend in Brasilia has been after him for much, much longer. There may well be others.'

'And now he no longer feels secure even here?'

'I'm almost certain he doesn't. I know he was in the Lost City this year, and several times in the past few years. But he likes his comforts and there are none in that ruin. He may have taken a chance and returned. It's highly unlikely, but I have to check. Otherwise there's no point in going to the Lost City.'

'You have to have this confrontation between Brown and his friend.'

'Yes. I have no proof. This—ah—meeting will give me all the proof I ever require.'

'Remind me to take care of myself. I want to be alive to see it.' Navarro turned and gazed at the curtain facing down-stream. 'It will not be easy to get into this place?'

'It will not be easy. Brown's estate here—it's known as Kolonie Waldner 555—is better guarded than the Presidential Palace. The estate is hotching with trained killers as guards—and when I say that I mean they're trained and proven killers. There's dense jungle to the north and south—Paraguay lies to the south and Brown is a close friend of the President there—there's this river to the east and a large number of German settlements, populated almost exclusively by ex-members of the S.S. lie astride the roads to Asunción and Bella Vista. You won't even find a single river pilot here who is Brazilian born, they're all Germans from the River Elbe.'

Ramon said: 'In view of the fact of what you've just told us, a thought occurs to me. How *do* we get in?'

'I'll admit I've given the matter some thought myself. Not much option really. There's a road used by supply trucks, but it's too long, too dangerous and has to pass through an armed gatehouse with electrified fences stretching away on both sides. There's also a landing stage about ten miles downriver from here—about fifteen miles north of the Paraguayan border. The road up to the compound is about a mile long and usually heavily patrolled. But it's the only other way. At least there are no electrified fences along the right bank of the Paraná—or there weren't the last time I was there. We'll wait two hours and move on in.'

'Would it be in order,' Navarro said, 'if we gave you what is known as a couple of old-fashioned looks?'

'Help yourself,' Hamilton said agreeably. He opened a ruck-sack, brought out three silenced Lugers, three spare magazines and three sheathed hunting knives and distributed those. 'Sleep if you can. I'll watch.'

The helicopter, not under power, drifted with the current down the right bank of the Paraná, keeping as close inshore as possible to avoid the bright light of a brilliant half moon riding high in a cloudless sky. A door in the fuselage opened, a figure appeared, stepped down on to one of the pontoons and lowered an anchor quietly to the bed of the river. A second figure appeared with a bulky package under his arm: there came a subdued hiss and within thirty seconds a rubberized dinghy was fully inflated. A third man emerged from the fuselage carrying a small outboard motor and a medium-sized battery. The first two men stepped gingerly into the dinghy and took those items from him: the engine was clamped on to the transom aft, the battery lowered to the duckboard floor and coupled up to the engine.

The engine, once started, was almost soundless and the south-east wind, the prevailing one in that area, carried what little noise there was upstream. The painter was unhitched from the heli-copter and the dinghy moved downstream. The three occupants were crouched forward, listening intently and peering, not without some apprehension, into the gloom beneath the overhanging branches of the rain-forest trees.

A hundred yards ahead the river curved to the right. Hamilton switched off the electric motor, the twins dipped paddles into the water and very soon, a paddle occasionally touching the bank, they rounded the bend.

The landing stage, less than two hundred yards ahead, pro-jected out into the river for a distance of twenty feet. Behind it, on land, there was a guard-house which threw enough light to illuminate the cracked and splintered timber of the stage and two men, rifles shoulder-slung, maintaining a comfortable and relaxed guard on a couple of bentwood chairs. Both were smoking and they were sharing a bottle. They stood up as two other men came out from the guard-house. They talked briefly, then the two relieving guards took over their chairs—and the bottle—while the previous guards went inside the guard-house.

The dinghy grounded silently on the muddy bank of the river and was secured by its painter to the low-hanging branch of a tree. The three men disembarked and disappeared into the undergrowth.

After they had gone about ten yards Hamilton said to Navarro in a barely audible whisper: 'What did I tell you? No electrified fences.'

'Watch out for the bear-traps.'

There were four men inside the guard-house, all dressed in uni-forms of the field-grey colour used by the Wehrmacht in the Second World War. Fully clad, they were lying on camp beds: three were asleep or appeared to be. The fourth was reading a magazine. Some instinct—there was certainly no sound—made him glance upwards and towards the doorway.

Ramon and Navarro were smiling benevolently at him. There was nothing particularly benevolent, however, about the discouragingly steady silenced Lugers held in their hands.

On the landing stage the two new guards were gazing out over the Paraná when someone cleared his throat, almost apologetically, behind them. They immediately swung around. Hamilton wasn't even bothering to smile.

Inside the guard-house all six guards were securely bound beyond any hope of escape and were more than adequately gagged. Ramon looked at the two telephones then questioningly at Hamilton, who nodded and said: 'No chances.'

Ramon sliced through the wires while Navarro started to collect the prisoners' rifles. He said to Hamilton: 'Still no chances?'

Hamilton nodded. The three men left, threw the rifles into the Paraná, then began to move up the road connecting the landing stage with Kolonie 555. The twins pressed in closely to the forest on the left-hand side of the road while Hamilton kept to the right. They moved slowly, with the stealth and silence of Indians: they had long moved at will through the disaffected tribes of the Mato Grosso.

When they were only yards from the compound Hamilton waved his two companions to a halt. The compound of the Kolonie was well lit by the moon. It was built in the basic form of a barrack square and was perhaps fifty yards across. Eight huts faced on to this central square. Most of those were extremely ramshackle, but one at the far left of the square was a solidly built bungalow. Close by that was an arched metal shed and, beyond that, a short runway. At the entrance to the compound, diagonally across the square from the bungalow, was a thatched hut which could well have been a guard-house, a probability reinforced by the fact that a solitary figure leaned against the entrance wall. Like his colleagues on the landing stage he was in para-military uniform and carried a slung rifle.

Hamilton gestured to Ramon, who waved back. The three men vanished into the undergrowth.

The sentry, still leaning against the wall, had his head tilted back, a bottle to his lips. There came the sound of a muffled blow,

61

the sentry's eyes turned up in his head and three disembodied hands appeared from apparently nowhere. One took the bottle from the already powerless hand while the other two took him under the armpits as he began to sag.

In what was indeed the guard-house six more men lay trussed and gagged. Hamilton, alone in the middle of the room and engaged in rendering rifles and pistols inoperable, looked up as Ramon and Navarro, each with torch in hand, re-entered the room, shaking their heads. The three men left and began to move around the other huts. As they passed by each one, on each occasion Hamilton and Ramon remained outside while Navarro entered. Each time Navarro emerged, shaking his head. Finally, they arrived at the last building, the solidly constructed bungalow. All three entered. Hamilton, in the lead, found a switch and flooded the room with light.

It was a combination office and living quarters and furnished in considerable comfort. Drawers and filing cabinets were searched but they had nothing that interested Hamilton. They moved on to another apartment, a bedroom and again a very comfortable place of accommodation. Pride of place on the walls were given to three framed and inscribed photographs—those of Hitler, Goebbels and Stroessner, a former Paraguayan president. The contents of the wardrobes were very sparse, indicating that the owner had removed the bulk of the contents. In one cupboard stood a pair of brown riding boots. The Nazis had always insisted on black riding boots, despising brown ones as being decadent: Stroessner, on the other hand, had favoured brown.

From there the three moved into what was Brown's communication centre, containing two large multicalibrated transceivers of the latest design. They located a tool-box and while Hamilton and Ramon used chisels and screwdrivers to remove the faceplates and destroy the inner mechanisms, Navarro located all the spares and reduced them too to scrap metal and shattered glass.

Navarro said: 'He's also got a very nice radio and transmitting set here.'

'You know what to do, don't you?'

Navarro knew what to do. From there they moved on to the arched metal shed. It was rather a remarkable place inasmuch as there ran down the middle of it what must have been the Kolonie's pride and joy, a genuine full-length American bowling alley. They paid no attention to this. What did attract their attention was a Piper Cub in a bay alongside the bowling alley. It took the men less than ten minutes to ensure that that particular Piper Cub would never fly again.

On their way back to the Paraná, this time walking openly in the middle of the road, Ramon said: 'So your friend *has* gone.'

'In that inelegant phrase, the bird has flown the coop, taking most of his hard cases with him—Nazis, renegade Poles, renegade Ukrainians. As fine a collection of war criminals as you'll ever meet. This bunch here belong strictly to the second division.'

'Where do you think they've gone?'

'We'll ask, shall we?'

The three men entered the landing-stage guard-house. Wordlessly, they sliced the ankle-bonds of one of the prisoners, removed his gag, dragged him to his feet and led him outside down to the river edge of the landing stage.

Hamilton said: 'Brown had three Piper Cubs. Where have the other two gone?'

The guard spat in contempt. At a signal from Hamilton, Navarro cut the back of the guard's hand. The blood flowed freely. The guard was then led forward until he was teetering on the very edge of the landing-stage.

'Piranha,' Hamilton said, 'can smell blood at a quarter of a mile. Ninety seconds and you'll be white bones. If a crocodile doesn't get you first. Either way, being eaten to death is unpleasant.'

The guard looked in horror at his bleeding hand. He was trembling. 'North,' he said. 'North to Campo Grande.'

'And after that?'

'I swear to God——'

'Throw him in.'

'Planalto de Mato Grosso. That's all I know. I swear to you——'

Hamilton said wearily: 'Stop your damned swearing. I believe you. Brown would never entrust his secrets to vermin.'

Ramon said: 'What do we do with the prisoners?'

'Nothing.'

'But——'

'But nothing. I daresay someone will happen by and free them. Take this character inside and hobble and gag him.'

Navarro looked doubtful. 'It's a pretty deep cut. He could bleed to death.'

'Dear oh dear.'

5

Hamilton, Ramon and Navarro were in a taxi driving along one of Brasilia's broad boulevards. Ramon said: 'This woman, Maria, she comes?'

Hamilton looked at him and smiled. 'She comes.'

'There will be danger.'

'The more, the better. It will at least help to keep those clowns under control.'

Navarro was thoughtfully silent for a moment then he said: 'My brother and I hate all they stand for. But you, Senor Hamilton, hate so much more.'

'I have the reason. But I don't hate them.'

Ramon and Navarro looked at each other in lost comprehension then nodded as if in understanding.

A Rolls-Royce and a Cadillac had been backed out of Smith's six-car garage to make storage room for what Smith regarded as being more important, however temporarily, than the two cars. Hamilton, in the company of the eight people who were going to accompany him, surveyed, with an apparently uncritical eye, the extremely comprehensive layout of the most modern and expensive equipment necessary for survival in the Amazonian rain-forests. He took his time about it, so much so in fact that one or two of the watchers were beginning to look, if not apprehensive, then at least uncomfortable. Smith was not one of those. There was a slight tightening of the lips presumably indicative of a growing impatience. It was almost a law of nature that tycoons do not care to be kept waiting. Smith immediately proved that his patience was on a very short fuse indeed.

'Well, Hamilton? Well?'

'So. How the multi——or is it bulti-?——millionaire travels into the boondocks. But good, really excellent.'

Smith visibly relaxed.

'But there's one exception, though.'

'Indeed?' One has to be very wealthy before one can—or is permitted to—raise one's eyebrows in the proper fashion. 'And what might that be?'

'Nothing missing, I assure you. Just some items surplus to requirements. Who are those guns and pistols for?'

'Us.'

'No deal. Ramon, Navarro and I carry weapons. You don't. None of you do.'

'We do.'

'Deal's off.'

'Why?'

'You are children in the rain-forests. No pop-guns for kids.'

'But Hiller and Serrano——'

'I admit they know more than you do. That doesn't mean very much. In the Mato Grosso they might even rate as adolescents. Forget what they've ever told you.'

Smith lifted his shoulders, looked at the rather splendid armoury of weapons he had assembled, then back at Hamilton. 'Self-protection——'

'We'll protect you. I don't much fancy the prospect of you lot going around shooting harmless animals and innocent Indians. Even less do I fancy the prospect of being shot in the back when I've finally shown you where the Lost City is.'

Heffner stepped forward. He obviously had no doubt that the reference had been to himself. His fingers were actually clutching and unclutching, his face dusky with anger. 'Look here, Hamilton——'

'I'd rather not.'

'Stop it.' Smith's voice was cold and incisive but when he spoke again the tone had changed to one of bitterness and left no doubt that he was addressing Hamilton. 'If I may say so, you have a splendid capacity for making friends.'

'Oddly enough, I do. I have quite a few in this city alone. But before I make a man my friend I have to make sure he's not my enemy or potential enemy. Very sensitive about those things, I am. But so's my back—sensitive, I mean, sensitive to having a knife stuck in it. I should know, I've had it done twice to me. I suppose I should have you all searched for flick-knives or some such toys but in your case I really don't think I'll bother. The harmless animals and innocent Indians are safe from any ill

65

intentions you may develop, for, quite frankly, I can't see any of you lot taking on an armed Indian or a jaguar with what is, after all, little more than a pen-knife.' He made a small gesture with his right hand, as contemptuous as it was dismissive, and from the sudden tightening and whitening of Smith's lips, it occurred to Hamilton, not for the first time, that Smith might well and easily be the most dangerous man of them all.

Hamilton gestured again, this time towards the very considerable pile of equipment lying on the garage floor. 'How did those arrive—the packaging, I mean?'

'Crates. We crate them up again?'

'No. Too damned awkward to handle aboard a helicopter or hovercraft. I think——'

'Waterproof canvas bags.' He smiled at the slight surprise on Hamilton's face. 'We thought you might require something like that.' He pointed towards two large cardboard boxes. 'We bought them at the same time as we got the equipment. We're not mentally retarded, you know.'

'Fine. Your plane, a DC6, I understand—what's its state of readiness?'

'Superfluous question.'

'I suppose. Where are the hovercraft and helicopter?'

'Almost at Cuiabá.'

'Shall we join them?'

The DC6 parked at the end of the runway of Smith's private airfield may not have been in the first flush of youth but if the gleaming fuselage were anything to go by its condition would have ranked anywhere as immaculate. Hamilton, Ramon and Navarro, aided by an unexpectedly helpful Serrano, were supervising the loading of the cargo. It was a thorough, rigorous, painstaking supervision. Each canvas bag in turn was opened, its contents removed, examined, returned and the bag then sealed to make it waterproof. It was a necessarily lengthy and time-consuming process and Smith's patience was eroding rapidly.

He said sourly: 'Don't take many chances, do you?'

Hamilton glanced at him briefly. 'How did you make your millions?'

Smith turned and clambered aboard the aircraft.

*

After half-an-hour's flying time out from Brasilia the passengers, with the exception of Hamilton, were all asleep or trying to sleep. No-one, it seemed, felt philosophical enough or relaxed enough to read: the clamour from the ancient engines was so great as to make conversation virtually impossible. Hamilton, as if prompted by some instinct, looked around and his gaze focused.

Heffner, sprawled in his seat, appeared, from his partly opened mouth and slow deep breathing, to be asleep, a probability lent credence by the fact that his white drill jacket, inadvertently unbuttoned, lay so as to reveal under his left armpit a white felt container which had obviously been designed to accommodate the aluminium flask inside. This did not give concern to Hamilton: it was perfectly in character with the man. What did concern him was that on the other side of his chest could just be seen a small pearl-handled gun in a white felt under-arm holster.

Hamilton rose and made his way aft to the rear end of the compartment where the equipment, provisions and personal luggage were stored. It made for a very considerable pile, but Hamilton didn't have to rummage around to find what he was looking for—when loading he had made a mental note of where every item had been stored. He retrieved his rucksack, opened it, looked casually around to see that he was unobserved, removed a pistol and thrust it into an inside pocket of his bush jacket. He replaced the rucksack and resumed his seat up front.

The flight to Cuiabá airport had been uneventful and so now was the landing. The passengers disembarked and gazed around them in something like wonder, which was more than understandable as the contrast between Cuiabá and Brasilia was rather more than marked.

Maria was gazing around her in apparent disbelief. She said: 'So *this* is the jungle. Quite, quite fascinating.'

'This is civilization,' Hamilton said. He pointed to the east. 'The jungle lies over there. That's where we'll be very soon and once we get there perhaps you'd sell your soul to be back here.' He turned and said sharply to Heffner: 'Where do you think you're going?'

Heffner had been walking in the direction of the airport building. Now he stopped, turned and looked at Hamilton with a languid, insolent air.

'Talking to me?'

'I'm looking at you and I don't squint. Where are you going?'

'Look, I can't see it's any of your business, but I'm going to a bar. I'm thirsty. Any objections?'

'Every objection. We're all thirsty. But there's work to be done. I want all the equipment, food and luggage transferred to that DC3 there, and I want it done now. Two hours on and it will be too hot to work.'

Heffner glared at him, then looked at Smith, who shook his head. Sullenly, Heffner retraced his steps and approached Hamilton, his face heavy with anger. 'Next time I'll be ready, so don't be fooled by last time.'

Hamilton turned to Smith and said, almost wearily: 'He's your employee. Any more trouble or threats of trouble and he's on the DC6 back to Brasilia. If you disagree, I'm on the plane back there. Simple choice.'

Hamilton brushed contemptuously by Heffner who stared after him with clenched fists. Smith took Heffner by the arm and led him to one side, clearly having trouble keeping his anger in check. He said, low-voiced: 'Damned if I don't agree with Hamilton. Want to ruin everything? There's a time and a place to get tough and this is neither the time nor the place. Bear in mind that we're entirely dependent upon Hamilton. You understand?'

'Sorry, boss. It's just that the bastard is so damned arrogant. Pride cometh before a fall. My turn will come and the fall is going to be a mighty big one.'

Smith was almost kind. 'I don't think you quite understand. Hamilton regards you as a potential troublemaker—which, I have to say, you are—and he's the sort of man who will eliminate any potential source of trouble. God, man, can't you see? He's trying to provoke you so that he can have a reason, or at least an excuse, for disposing of you.'

'And how would he do that?'

'Having you sent back to Brasilia.'

'And failing that?'

'Don't even let us talk about such things.'

'I can take care of myself, Mr Smith.'

'Taking care of yourself is one thing. Taking care of Hamilton is another kettle of fish altogether.'

They watched, some of them with evident apprehension, as a giant twin-rotored helicopter, cables attached to four lifting bolts, clawed its way into the air, raising a small hovercraft with it. The hovercraft's rate of climb was barely perceptible. At five hundred feet, it slowly began to move due east.

Smith said uneasily: 'Those hills look mighty high to me. Sure they'll make it?'

'You'd better hope so. After all, they're your machines.' Hamilton shook his head. 'Do you think the pilot would have taken off unless he knew it was on the cards? Only three thousand feet. No trouble.'

'How far?'

'The head-waters of the Rio da Morte is only a hundred miles away. To reach the landing-strip? Perhaps eighty. In half-an-hour's time we'll leave in the DC3. We'll still be there before them.'

Hamilton moved off and sat by the side of the river, idly lobbing stones into the dark waters. Some minutes later Maria appeared and stood uncertainly beside him. Hamilton looked up, smiled briefly, then glanced indifferently away.

She said: 'Is it safe to sit here?'

'Boy-friend let you off the leash?'

'He's not my boy-friend.' She spoke with such vehemence that Hamilton looked at her quizzically.

'You could have fooled me. Misinterpretations, so easily come by. You have come, no doubt, or been sent to ask a few craftily probing questions?'

She said quietly: 'Do you have to insult everybody? Wound everybody? Antagonize everybody? Provoke everybody? Back in Brasilia you said you had friends. It is difficult to understand how you came by them.'

Hamilton looked at her in some perplexity then smiled. 'Now look who's doing the insulting.'

'Between gratuitous insults and the plain truth there's a big difference. I'm sorry to have disturbed you.' She turned to walk away.

'Oh, come and sit down. Childish, childish. Maybe I can ask a few probing questions while you congratulate yourself on having found a chink in Hamilton's armour. I suppose that could be misinterpreted as an insult, too. Just sit down.'

She looked at him doubtfully. 'I asked if it's safe to sit here.'

'A damn sight safer than trying to cross a street in Brasilia.'

She sat down gingerly, a prudent two feet away from him. 'Things can creep up on you.'

'You've read the wrong books or talked to the wrong people. Who or what is going to creep up on us? Indians? There's not a hostile Indian within two hundred miles of here. Alligators, jaguars, snakes—they're a damned sight more anxious to avoid you than you are to avoid them. There are only two dangerous things in the forest—the *quiexada*, the wild boar, and the *carangageiros*. They attack on sight.'

'The caran what?'

'Giant spiders. Great hairy creatures the size of soup plates. They come at you one yard at a time. Jumping, I mean. One yard and that's it.'

'How horrible!'

'No problem. None in those parts. Besides, you didn't have to come.'

'Here we go again.' Maria shook her head. 'You really don't care much for us, do you?'

'A man has to be alone at times.'

'Evasion, evasion.' She shook her head again. 'You're always alone. Married?'

'No.'

'But you were.' It wasn't a question, it was a statement.

Hamilton looked at her, at the remarkable brown eyes which reminded him painfully of the only pair he'd ever seen like them. 'You can tell?'

'I can tell.'

'Well, yes.'

'Divorced?'

'No.'

'No? You mean——'

'Yes.'

'Oh! Oh, I am sorry. How—how did she die?'

'Come on. Plane to catch.'

'Please. What happened?'

'She was murdered.' Hamilton stared out across the river, wondering what had caused him to make this admission to a total stranger. Ramon and Navarro knew, but they were the only two in the world he'd told. Perhaps a minute passed before he became conscious of the light touch of finger-tips on his forearm. Hamilton turned to look at her and knew at once that she wasn't seeing him: the big brown eyes were masked in tears. Hamilton's first reaction was one of an almost bemused incom-

70

prehension: this was totally out of character with the image she—ably abetted by Smith—projected of herself as a worldly-wise, street-wise cosmopolitan.

Hamilton gently touched the back of her hand and at first she didn't appear to notice. Perhaps half a minute passed before she wiped her eyes with the back of her free hand, disengaged her other hand, smiled apologetically and said: 'I'm sorry. What must you think of me?'

'I think I may have misjudged you. I also think that in some way, some time, you may have suffered a lot.'

She had nothing to say to this, just wiped her eyes again, rose and turned away.

'Battered' is the adjective invariably and usually inevitably used to describe vintage and superannuated DC3s and this one was no exception: if anything it was an epitome, a prime example. The gleaming fuselage of yesteryear was but a fond and distant memory, the metal skin was pitted and scarred and appeared to be held together chiefly by large areas of rust: the engines, when started up, were a splendid complement to the rest of the plane, coughing, spluttering and vibrating to such an extent that it seemed improbable that they would not be shaken free from the airframe. But the plane lived up to its reputation of being one of the toughest and most durable ever built. With what seemed a Herculean effort—it couldn't have been, it was under-loaded—it clambered off the runway and headed east into the late afternoon sky.

There were eleven people in the plane, Hamilton's party, the pilot and co-pilot. Heffner, as was customary, was taking counsel with a bottle of Scotch: the aluminium flask, presumably, was being held as an emergency reserve. Seated across the aisle from Hamilton, he turned to him and spoke or, rather, shouted, for the rackety clamour from the ancient engines was almost deafening.

'Wouldn't kill you to tell us your plans, would it, Hamilton?'

'No, it wouldn't kill me. But what does that matter? How's that going to help you?'

'Curiosity.'

'No secret. We land at Romono airstrip about the same time as the helicopter and hovercraft. Helicopter refuels—even those big birds have only a limited range—takes the hovercraft down-stream, leaves it, returns and takes us down to join it in the morning.'

71

Smith, sitting in the seat next to Hamilton and listening, put a cupped hand to Hamilton's ear and said: 'How far downstream and why?'

'I'd say about sixty miles. There are falls about fifty miles from Romono. Not even a hovercraft could negotiate them so this is the only way we can get it past there.'

Heffner said: 'Do you have a map?'

'As it happens, I have. Not that I require it. Why do you ask?'

'If anything happens to you it would be nice to know where we are.'

'You better pray nothing happens to me. Without me, you're finished.'

Smith said into Hamilton's ear: 'You have to antagonize him? You have to be so arrogant? You have to provoke him?'

Hamilton looked at him, his face cold. 'I don't have to. But it's a pleasure.'

Romono airstrip, like Romono itself, looked, as it always did, a miasmic horror. The DC3 and the helicopter-cum-hovercraft arrived on the strip within minutes of each other. The helicopter's rotor had hardly stopped when a small fuel tanker moved out towards it.

The passengers disembarked from the DC3 and looked around them. Their expressions ranged from the incredulous to the appalled.

Smith contented himself with saying merely: 'Good God!'

'I don't believe it,' Heffner said. 'What a stinking, nauseating dump. Jesus, Hamilton, is this the best you could do for us?'

'What are you complaining about?' Hamilton pointed to the tin shed which constituted both the arrival and departure terminals. 'Look at that sign there. Romono International Airport. What is more reassuring than that? This time tomorrow, gentlemen, you may well be thinking of this as home sweet home. Enjoy it. Think of it as the last outpost of civilization. Look, as the poet says, your last on all things lovely every hour. Take what you need for the night. We have a splendid hotel here—the Hotel de Paris. Those who don't fancy it—well, I'm sure Hiller will put you up.' He paused. 'On second thoughts, I think I could have a better use for Hiller.'

Smith said: 'What kind of use?'

'With your permission, of course. You know that this hover-craft is the lynch-pin to everything?'

'I'm not a fool.'

'The hovercraft will be anchored tonight in very dicey waters indeed. By which I mean that the natives on either side of the Rio da Morte range from the unreliable to the downright hostile. So, it must be guarded. I suggest that this is not a task for one man, Kellner, the pilot, to do. In fact, I'm not suggesting, I'm telling you. Even if a man could keep awake all night, it would still be extremely difficult. So, another guard. I suggest Hiller.' He turned to Hiller. 'How are you with automatic weapons?'

'Can find my way around, I guess.'

'Fine.' He turned back to Smith. 'You'll find a bus waiting outside the terminal.' He reboarded the plane and emerged two minutes later bearing two automatic weapons and some drums of ammunition. By this time Hiller was alone. 'Let's go to the hover-craft.'

Kellner, the hovercraft pilot, was standing by his craft. He was thirtyish, sun-tanned, tough.

Hamilton said: 'When you anchor tonight don't forget to do so in mid-stream.'

'There'll be a reason for that?' Kellner, clearly, was an Irish-man.

'Because if you tie up to either bank the chances are good that you'll wake up with your throat cut. Only, of course, you don't wake up.'

'I don't think I'd like that.' Kellner didn't seem unduly per-turbed. 'Mid-stream for me.'

'Even there you won't necessarily be safe. That's why Hiller is coming with you—needs two men to guard against an attack from both sides. And that's why we have those two nasty little Israeli sub-machines along.'

'I see.' Kellner paused. 'I'm not much sure that I care for killing helpless Indians.'

'When those same helpless Indians puncture your hide with a few dozen darts and arrowheads, all suitably or perhaps even lethally poisoned, you might change your mind.'

'I've already changed it.'

'Know anything about guns?'

'I was in the S.A.S. If that means anything to you.'

'It means a great deal to me.' The S.A.S. was Britain's elite

73

commando regiment. 'Well, that saves me explaining those little toys to you, I suppose.'

'I know them.'

'One of my luckier days,' Hamilton said. 'Well, see you both tomorrow.'

The saloon of the Hotel de Paris, after closing hours, had six occupants. Heffner, glass in hand, was slumped in a chair, but his eyes were open: Hamilton, Ramon, Navarro, Serrano and Tracy were asleep or apparently so, stretched out on benches or on the floor. Bedrooms were, that night, at a premium in the Hotel de Paris. As they were all equally dreadful and bug-ridden, Hamilton had explained, this was not a matter for excessive regret.

Heffner stirred, stooped, removed his boots, rose and padded his noiseless way across to the bar, deposited his glass on the counter, then crossed silently to the nearest rucksack. It was, inevitably, Hamilton's. Heffner opened it, searched briefly, removed a map, and studied it intently for some minutes before returning it to the rucksack. He returned to the bar, poured himself a generous measure of the Hotel de Paris's Scotch. Wherever the birthplace of that particular brand was it hadn't been among the highlands and islands of Scotland. He returned to his seat, replaced his shoes, leaned back in his chair to enjoy his night-cap, spluttered and emptied half the contents on the floor.

Hamilton, Ramon and Navarro, heads propped on hands, were regarding him with a quietly speculative air.

Hamilton said: 'Well, did you find what you were looking for?'

Heffner didn't say whether he had or not.

'One of the three of us is going to keep an eye on you for the remainder of the night. You try to stir from that chair and I will take the greatest pleasure in clobbering you. I don't much care for people who meddle in my private belongings.'

Hamilton and the twins slept soundly throughout the night. Heffner did not once leave his chair.

6

Just after dawn, the helicopter pilot, John Silver—generally known as Long John—was at the controls. The party of nine embarked and stowed their overnight luggage with the food and equipment that had been transferred from the DC3. Hamilton took the co-pilot's seat. So cavernous was the interior of the giant helicopter that it seemed virtually empty. It rose effortlessly and flew more or less east, paralleling the course of the Rio da Morte. All the passengers had their heads craned, peering through what few windows there were: they were seeing for the first time the true Amazonian rain-forest.

Hamilton turned in his seat and pointed forward. 'That's an interesting sight.' His voice was a shout.

On a wide mud flat, perhaps almost a mile long, and on the left bank, scores of alligators lay motionless as if asleep.

'Good God!' It was Smith. 'Good God! Are there so many 'gators in the world?' He shouted to Silver: 'Take her down, man, take her down!' Then to Heffner: 'Your camera! Quick!' He paused, as if in sudden thought, then turned to Hamilton. 'Or should I have asked the expedition commander's permission?'

Hamilton shrugged. 'What's five minutes?'

The helicopter came down over the river in great sweeping, controlled circles. Long John was clearly a first-rate pilot.

The alligators, hemmed in the narrow strip between forest and river, seemed to stretch as far as the eye could see. It was, depending upon one's point of view, a fascinating, horrifying or terrifying spectacle.

Tracy said, almost in awe: 'My word, I wouldn't care to crash-land amongst that lot.'

Hamilton looked at him. 'Believe me, that's the least of the dangers down there.'

'The least?'

'This is the heart of the Chapate territory.'

75

'That meant to mean something to me?'

'You have a short memory. I've mentioned them before. It would mean something to you if you ended up in one of their cooking-pots.'

Smith looked at him doubtfully, clearly not knowing whether to believe him or not, then turned to the pilot.

'That's low enough, Silver.' He twisted in his seat and shouted at the top of his voice: 'God's sake, man, hurry!'

'Moment, moment,' Heffner bawled back. 'There's such a damned jumble of equipment here.'

There was, in fact, no jumble whatsoever. Heffner had already found his own camera, which lay at his feet. In Hamilton's rucksack he had found something that he had missed the previous night for the good enough reason that he hadn't been looking for it. He held a leather-bound case in his hand, the one Colonel Diaz had given to Hamilton. He extracted the camera from the case, looked at it in some puzzlement, then pressed a switch in the side. A flap fell down, noiselessly, on oiled hinges. His face registered at first bafflement, then understanding. The interior of the camera consisted of a beautifully made transistorized radio transceiver. Even more importantly it bore some embossed words in Portuguese. Heffner could read Portuguese. He read the words and his understanding deepened. The radio was the property of the Brazilian Defence Ministry which made Hamilton a government agent. He clicked the flap in position.

'Heffner!' Smith had twisted again in his seat. 'Heffner, if you—Heffner!'

Heffner, radio case in one hand and his pearl-handled pistol in the other, approached. His face was a smiling mask of vindictive triumph. He called out: 'Hamilton!'

Hamilton swung around, saw the wickedly smiling face, his own camera held high and the pearl-handled pistol and at once threw himself to the floor of the aisle, his gun coming clear of his bush jacket. Even so, despite the swiftness of Hamilton's movement, Heffner should have had no trouble in disposing of Hamilton, for he had the clear drop on him and his temporarily defenceless target was feet away. But Heffner had spent a long night of agony in the Hotel de Paris. As a consequence, his hand was less than steady, his reactions were impaired, his co-ordination considerably worse.

Heffner, his face contorted, fired twice. With the first came a

76

cry of pain from the flight-deck. With the second the helicopter gave a sudden lurch. Then Hamilton fired, just once, and a red rose bloomed in the centre of Heffner's forehead.

Hamilton took three quick steps up the aisle and had reached Heffner before anyone else had begun to move. He stooped over the dead man, retrieved the camera-radio case, checked that it was closed, then straightened. Smith appeared beside him, a badly shaken man, and stared down in horror at Heffner.

'Between the eyes, between the eyes.' Smith shook his head in total disbelief. 'Between the eyes. Christ, man, did you have to do that?'

'Three things,' Hamilton said. If he was upset, he had his distress well under control. 'I tried to wing him, and I'm a good shot, especially at four paces, but the helicopter lurched. He twice tried to kill me before I pulled the trigger. Third place. I gave orders that no-one was to carry guns. As far as I'm concerned, he's dead by his own hand. God's sake, why did he pull a gun on me? Was he mad?'

Smith, perhaps fortunately, was given no time to lend consideration to either of those things, even had he then been of a mind to, which he almost certainly was not. The helicopter had given another and even more violent lurch, and although it still carried a good deal of forward momentum, seemed to be fluttering and falling from the sky like a wounded bird. It was a singularly unpleasant sensation

Hamilton ran forward, clutching at whatever he could to maintain his balance. Silver, blood streaming from a cheek wound, was fighting to regain control of the uncontrollable helicopter.

Hamilton said: 'Quick! Can I help?'

'Help? No. I can't even help myself.'

'What's happened?'

'First shot burnt my face. Nothing. Superficial. Second shot must have gone through one or more hydraulic lines. Can't see exactly but it can't have been anything else. What happened back there?'

'Heffner. Had to shoot him. He tried to shoot me, but he got you and your controls instead.'

'No loss.' Considering the circumstances, Silver was remarkably phlegmatic. 'Heffner, I mean. This machine is a different matter altogether.'

Hamilton took a quick look backwards. The scene, understandably, was one of confusion and consternation although there were no signs of panic. Maria, Serrano and Tracy, all three with almost comically dazed expressions, were sitting or sprawling in the central aisle. The others clung desperately to their seats as the helicopter gyrated through the sky. Luggage, provisions and equipment were strewn everywhere.

Hamilton turned again and pressed his face close to the windscreen. The now pendulum-like motion of the craft was making the land below swing to and fro in a crazy fashion. The river was still directly beneath: the one plus factor appeared to be that they had now left behind them the mud-flats where the alligators had lain in so lifeless a manner. Hamilton became suddenly aware that an island, perhaps two hundred yards long by half as wide, lay ahead of them in the precise middle of the river, at a distance of about half a mile: it was wooded but not heavily so. Hamilton turned to Silver.

'This thing float?'

'Like a stone.'

'See that island ahead?'

They were now less than two hundred feet above the broad brown waters of the river: the island was about a quarter of a mile ahead.

'I can see it,' Silver said. 'I can also see all those trees. Look, Hamilton, control is close to zero. I'll never get it down in one piece.'

Hamilton looked at him coldly. 'Never mind the damned chopper. Can you get *us* down in one piece?'

Silver glanced briefly at Hamilton, shrugged and said nothing.

The island was now two hundred yards distant. As a landing ground it looked increasingly discouraging. Apart from scattered trees it was, but for one tiny clearing, thickly covered with dense undergrowth. Even for a helicopter in perfect health it would have made an almost impossible landing site.

Even in that moment of emergency some instinct made Hamilton glance to the left. Directly opposite the island, at about fifty yards' distance and on the bank of the river, was a large native village. From the expression—or lack of it—on Hamilton's face it was clear that he didn't care for large native villages, or, at least, this particular one.

Silver's face, streaked with rivulets of sweat and blood, reflected a mixture of determination and desperation, with the

78

former predominating. The passengers, tense, immobile, gripped fiercely at any available support and stared mutely ahead. They, too, could see what was about to happen.

The helicopter, swinging and side-slipping, weaved its unpredictable way towards the island. Silver was unable to bring the helicopter to the hover. As they approached this one much too small clearing, the helicopter was still going too fast. Its ground-level clearance was by then no more than ten feet. The trees and undergrowth rushed at them with accelerating speed.

Silver said: 'No fire?'

'No fire.'

'No ignition.' Silver switched off.

One second later the helicopter dipped sharply, crashed into the undergrowth, slid about twenty feet and came to a jarring stop against the bole of a large tree.

For a few moments the silence was complete. The engine roar had vanished. It was a silence compounded of the dazed shock caused by the violence of their landing and the relief of finding themselves still alive. No-one appeared to have sustained any injury.

Hamilton reached out and touched Silver's arm. 'I'll bet you couldn't do that again.'

Silver dabbed at his wounded cheek. 'I wouldn't ever care to try.' If he was in any way proud of his magnificent airmanship it didn't show.

'Out! All out!' Smith's voice was a stentorian shout, he seemed unaware that normal conversational tones were again in order. 'We can go up any moment.'

'Don't be so silly.' Hamilton sounded weary. 'Ignition's off. Stay put.'

'If I want to go out——'

'Then that's your business. Nobody's going to stop you. Later on, we'll bury your boots.'

'What the hell is that meant to mean?'

'A civilized interment of the remains. Maybe even those won't be left.'

'If you'd be——'

'Look out of your window.'

Smith looked at Hamilton then turned to the window, standing so as to achieve a ground view. His eyes widened, his lips parted and his complexion changed for the worse. Two very large alligators were only feet from the helicopter, fearsome jaws agape, their huge tails swinging ominously from side to side. Wordlessly, Smith sat down.

Hamilton said: 'I warned you before you left, the Mato Grosso is no place for mindless little children. Our two friends out there are just waiting for such children. And not only those two. There'll be more around, lots of them. Also snakes, tarantulas and suchlike. Not to mention——' He broke off and pointed to the port windscreen. 'I'd rather you didn't have to but take a look anyway.'

They did as he asked. Among the trees on the left bank could be seen a number of huts, perhaps twenty in all with an especially large circular one in the centre. Several columns of smoke shimmered up into the morning air. Canoes, and what looked like a pinnace, fronted the village. A large number of natives, nearly naked, stood on the bank, talking and gesticulating.

'But this is luck,' Smith said.

'You should have stayed in Brasilia.' Hamilton sounded unwontedly sour. 'Sure it's luck—the most fiendishly bad luck. I see the chiefs are getting ready.'

There was a fairly long silence then Maria said almost in a whisper: 'The Chapate?'

'None else. Complete, as you can now see, with olive branches and calling cards.'

Every native ashore was now armed or was in the process of getting armed. They carried spears, bows and arrows, blowpipes and machetes. The angry expressions on their faces went well with the menacing gesticulations in the direction of the island.

'They'll be calling soon,' Hamilton said, 'and not for tea. Maria, would you give Mr Silver a hand to fix up his face?'

Tracy said: 'But we're safe here, surely? We have guns, plenty. They're carrying nothing that could penetrate our screens, far less the fuselage.'

'True. Ramon, Navarro, get your rifles and come with me.'

Smith said: 'What are you going to do?'

'Discourage them. From crossing. Shame, really. They may not even know what a gun is.'

'Tracy made sense,' Smith said. 'We're safe here. You *have* to be a hero?'

Hamilton stared at him until Smith looked uncomfortable. Hamilton said: 'Heroism doesn't enter into it, just survival. I

wonder whether *you* would be half-way brave enough to fight
for your own survival. I suggest you leave this to someone who
knows how the Chapate wage war. Or do you want to be ready
for immediate consumption when they get you?'

'What's that supposed to mean?' Smith tried to sound blustery
but his heart wasn't in it, his ego had been too severely dented.

'Just this. If they get as much as a foothold on this island the
first thing they'll do is to set fire to the undergrowth and roast
you alive in this metal coffin.'

There was a silence that lasted until Hamilton, Ramon and
Navarro had left the helicopter.

Ramon, the first to touch the ground, had his rifle on the nearest alligator immediately but the precaution proved needless:
both alligators immediately turned and scuttled away into the
undergrowth.

Hamilton said: 'Just keep an eye on our backs, Ramon.'
Ramon nodded. Hamilton and Navarro moved towards the rear,
took shelter behind the tail of the helicopter and looked cautiously
ashore.

A squat, powerfully built Indian dressed in a pink feather
head-dress, teeth necklace, a series of arm bracelets and little
else—definitely the chief—was ordering warriors into half-a-
dozen canoes. He himself was standing on the bank.

Navarro looked at Hamilton, his reluctance plain. He said:
'No choice?'

With equal regret Hamilton agreed, shaking his head. Navarro
lifted his rifle, aimed and fired in one swift motion. The report of
the rifle momentarily paralysed all activity on the bank. Only the
chief moved: he cried out in pain and clutched his upper right
arm. A second later, while the warriors were still immobilized
in shock, another report was heard and another warrior struck in
precisely the same place. Navarro was clearly a marksman of the
most extraordinary accuracy.

Navarro said: 'Not nice, Senor Hamilton.'

'Not nice. As the old saying goes, it's people like us who have
made people like them what they are. But this is hardly the time
and place to explain that to them.'

Ashore the warriors rapidly abandoned their canoes and ran
for the shelter of their huts and the forest, taking the two wounded
men with them. From those shelters they could be seen almost
immediately drawing bows and lifting blowpipes to their mouths.

Hamilton and Navarro prudently dropped behind cover as arrows and darts rattled and rebounded harmlessly off the fuselage. Navarro shook his head in sorrow and wonderment. 'I'll bet they've never even *heard* a rifle report before. It is something less than a fair contest, Senor Hamilton.'

Hamilton nodded, but made no comment for comment would have been superfluous. He said: 'That's all for now. I don't think they'll try anything again before dark. But I'll keep watch—or arrange for others to do it. Meantime, you and Ramon get rid of our four-legged friends and the creepy-crawlies. Try to chase them away, shoo them away. If you have to shoot, for goodness sake don't do it by the water's edge or in the water. Bath-time tonight and I don't want to attract every piranha for miles around.'

Hamilton reboarded the helicopter. Tracy said: 'That was quite a hailstorm out there. Arrows and darts, I assume?'

'Didn't you see?'

'I wasn't too keen on looking. I'm sure those windows are made of toughened glass but I wasn't going to be the one to put them to the test. Poisoned?'

'Certainly. But, almost equally certainly, no curare, nothing lethal. They have a less final but equally effective poison that merely stuns. Too much curare affects the flavour of the stew.'

Smith said sourly: 'You certainly have a summary way of dealing with the opposition.'

'I should have parleyed with them? The brightly coloured beads approach? Why don't you go and try it?' Smith said nothing. 'If you have any futile suggestions to offer, I suggest you either translate them into action or shut up. There's a limit to the number of niggling remarks a man can take.'

Silver, his face bandaged, intervened pacifically. 'And now?'

'A lovely long siesta until dusk. For me, that is. I shall have to ask you to take turns in keeping watch. Not only the village, but as far upstream and downstream as you can see—the Chapate might contemplate launching a canoe attack at some distance from their village although I consider it highly unlikely. If anything happens, let me know. Ramon and Navarro should be back in twenty minutes; don't bother letting me know.'

Tracy said: 'You place a great deal of faith in your lieutenants.'
'Total.'

Smith said: 'So we keep awake while you sleep. Why?'

'Recharging my batteries for the night ahead.'

'And then?'

Hamilton sighed. 'This helicopter, obviously, will never be airborne again so we have to find some other means of rejoining the hovercraft, which I reckon must be about thirty miles downstream. We can't go by land. It would take us days to hack our way down there and, anyway, the Chapate would get us before we covered a mile. We need a boat. So we'll borrow one from the Chapate. There's a nice, big and very ancient motor launch moored to the bank there. Not their property for a certainty: the original owners were probably eaten long ago. And the engine will be a solid block of rust and quite useless. But we don't need power to go downstream.'

Tracy said: 'And how do you propose we—ah—obtain this boat, Mr Hamilton?'

'I'll get it. After sunset.' He smiled faintly. 'That's why I intend recharging my batteries in advance.'

Smith said: 'You really do have to be a hero, Hamilton, don't you?'

'And you'll really never learn, will you? No, I don't have to be a hero. I don't want to be a hero. You can go instead. You be the hero. Go on. Volunteer. Impress your girl-friend.'

Smith slowly unclenched his fists and turned away. Hamilton sat and appeared to compose himself for slumber, oblivious of the dead Heffner laid now across the aisle from him. The others looked at one another in silence.

It was many hours later, at dusk, when Hamilton said: 'Everything packed? Guns, ammunition, last night's overnight bags, food, water, medicines. And Silver, the chopper's two compasses might come in handy.'

Silver indicated a box by his feet. 'They're already in there.'

'Excellent.' Hamilton looked around him. 'Well, that seems to be all. Heigh-ho, I think.'

'What do you mean, that seems to be all?' Smith said. He nodded towards the dead Heffner. 'How about him?'

'Well, how about him?'

'You going to leave him here?'

'That's up to you.' Hamilton spoke with an almost massive indifference. He did not have to spell out his meaning. Smith turned and stumbled down the helicopter steps.

At the downstream end of the island, only Navarro, of all the party, was absent. In the gathering darkness Hamilton again checked all the various packs. He seemed satisfied.

'There will be a moon,' he said, 'but it will be too late to save us. Moonrise is in about two and a half hours. When they attack—there's no "if" about it—it must be inside those two and a half hours, which means it could be any time now although I should guess that they'll wait a bit until it is as dark as possible. Ramon, join Navarro now. If they attack before you get my signal, hold them off as best you can for as long as you can. If my signal comes first, get back here at once. Tracy?'

Tracy said: 'I can tell you, I haven't been too happy here for the past hour. No, no alligators. No sign. Not a ripple. No gun?'

'Guns make noises. Guns get wet.'

Maria shivered and pointed to his big sheath knife. 'And that does neither?'

'Sometimes the first blow doesn't kill. Then there can be a lot of noise. But no heroics. I don't expect to have to use it. If I do, it means I've botched my job.'

Hamilton looked out across the river. The darkness had now so deepened that the shoreline was no more than a dimly seen blur. He checked that the coil of rope, the waterproof torch and the sheath knife were securely attached to his waist, walked noiselessly into the river and then slowly, silently, began to swim.

The water was warm, the current was gentle and around him he could see nothing but the calm dark water. Suddenly, he stopped swimming, trod water and stared ahead. He could see what he imagined to be a tiny ripple in the black smoothness without being able to see what caused it. His right hand came clear of the water, clenched round the haft of his sheath knife. The tiny ripple was still there but even as he strained to watch it, it disappeared. Hamilton replaced the knife in its sheath. He wasn't the first person to have mistaken a drifting log for a crocodile, a considerably healthier position than the other way round. He resumed his silent swimming.

A minute later he drifted in towards the bank and caught hold of a convenient tree root. He straightened, paused, looked carefully around, listened intently then emerged swiftly and silently from the river and disappeared into the forest.

A hundred yards brought him to the perimeter of the village. There were at least a score of native huts, haphazardly arranged, none of them showing any sign of life. In their approximate centre was the much larger circular hut: light could be seen through the numerous chinks in its walls. Ghostlike, Hamilton moved off to his right and moved round the perimeter of the village until he was directly to the rear of the large hut. Here he waited until he was sure—or as sure as he could possibly be—that he was alone then moved forward to the rear of the hut. He selected a small, lighted chink in the wall and peered through it.

The communal hut was illuminated by some scores of tallow tapers. It was completely unfurnished. Dozens of natives were standing several deep round a cleared space in the middle where an elderly man was using a stick to make a diagram on the sand-covered floor while at the same time explaining something in an unintelligible tongue. The diagram was the outline of the island. Also shown was the left bank of the river on which the village stood. The speaker had drawn lines from the village, from above the village and from below the village, all towards the island. A multi-pronged attack was to be launched on the helicopter and its passengers. The lecturer lifted his stick from time to time and pointed it at various natives: it was apparent that he was allocating canoe crews for their lines of attack.

Hamilton moved away in the direction of the upper river bank, still circling the village perimeter. As he passed the last hut, he stopped. At least twenty canoes, some quite large, were tethered to the bank. Almost at the end of the row, up-river, was the dilapidated, paint-flaked motor launch, a little over twenty feet in length. It was deep in the water but floating so to that extent might be deemed riverworthy.

Two Indian warriors, talking quietly, stood guard at the downstream end of the row of canoes. As Hamilton watched, one of them gestured towards the village and walked away. Hamilton moved around to one side of the hut and crouched there: the Indian walked by on the other side.

Another problem had arisen, one that Hamilton could well have done without. Even fifteen minutes ago he could have remained where he had been and the remaining Indian could have come within a few feet without seeing him. Not any more. The sun was gone, moonrise was still some time away, but, unfortunately, the evening clouds which, earlier, had so obligingly offered concealment, had passed away and the southern skies were alive with stars—and in the tropics stars always seem so much bigger

85

and brighter than they do in temperate climes. Visibility had become disconcertingly good.

Hamilton knew that the last thing he could afford to do was to wait. He straightened and advanced soundlessly, knife held in the throwing position. The Indian was gazing out towards the island, now quite visible. A shadow appeared behind him and there came the sound of a sharp but solid blow as the haft of Hamilton's knife caught him on the base of the neck. Hamilton caught him as he was about to topple into the water and lowered him none too gently to the bank.

Hamilton ran upstream. He came to the motor launch, pulled out his signal torch, hooded the beam with his hand and shone it inside.

The launch was filthy and had at least four inches of water in the bottom. The torch beam lit on the centrally positioned engine which, as Hamilton had expected, was now no more than a solid block of rust. Floating incongruously in its vicinity were three cooking pans, obviously intended as bailers, at a guess the property of some optimistic but now departed missionaries. The beam played swiftly around the entire interior of the boat. There was no means of propulsion whatsoever: no mast, no sail, no oars, not even a solitary paddle.

Hamilton straightened and moved quickly to examine some of the nearest canoes. Within a minute he had collected at least a dozen paddles. He deposited those in the launch, hurried away, selected two large canoes and pulled them close to the launch. He unwound the rope around his waist, cut off two sections and used those to tie the canoes in tandem to the launch. He sliced through the manila painter, pushed the launch into deeper water, scrambled in, seized a paddle and began to move silently away from the bank.

Paddling the launch—and its attendant canoes—diagonally downstream, Hamilton was soon making heavy weather of it. The launch was naturally cumbersome and made more so by the amount of water in it and Hamilton, able to use only one paddle, had to switch continuously from side to side to keep it on course. Briefly, he paused, located what he could discern to be the upstream end of the island, now almost directly opposite him, pulled out his torch and pressed the button three times. He then pointed his torch diagonally downstream and flashed again three times. He replaced his torch and resumed paddling.

86

Ashore, an Indian warrior emerged from the communal hut, and walked casually towards the upper river-bank. Suddenly, he hurried forward and stooped over an Indian lying face-down on the bank. A trickle of blood was coming from what was the beginning of a massive bruise on the base of his neck. His fellow tribesman straightened and began to shout, repeatedly and urgently.

Hamilton momentarily ceased paddling and glanced involuntarily over his shoulder. Then he bent himself again to his task but with even more energy this time.

Ramon and Navarro, as by pre-arrangement, had already begun to move to the other end of the island. Now they stopped abruptly when they heard the cry ashore, a cry now taken up by the shouting of many more angry voices.

Ramon said: 'I think Senor Hamilton must have been up to something. I also think we'd better wait a little.'

The two men crouched on the island shore, rifles at the ready, and peered out across the channel. The bulky outline of Hamilton's launch and the two canoes he was towing were now visible not thirty yards from where they were. Not as visible, but still distinct enough to be unmistakable, were the shadowy forms of canoes putting out from the village in pursuit.

Ramon shouted: 'As close to the island as you can. We'll cover you.'

Hamilton glanced over his shoulder. The nearest of half a dozen canoes was already less than thirty yards away. Two men stood in the bows, one with a blowpipe to his mouth, the other pulling back the string of his bow.

Hamilton crouched as low as possible in the boat, glancing almost desperately to his right. He could now see both Ramon and Navarro and he could see that they had their rifles levelled. The two shots came simultaneously. The warrior with the blowpipe toppled backwards in the canoe: the one with the drawn bow pitched into the water, his arrow hissing harmlessly into the river.

'Quickly,' Hamilton called. 'Join the others.'

Ramon and Navarro loosed off a few more shots, more for the sake of discouragement than with the intent of hitting anything, then began to run. Thirty seconds later they rejoined the remainder of the party at the downstream end of the island, all looking anxiously up-river. Hamilton was struggling, unsuccessfully, to

87

bring his unwieldy trio of boats ashore: it looked as if he would miss the tip of the island by feet only.

Ramon and Navarro handed over their rifles, plunged into the river, seized the bows of the motor-launch and turned it into the shore. There were no orders given, no shouts for haste: such were needless. Within seconds all the equipment and passengers were aboard the motor-launch, the boat pushed off and paddles distributed. They cast frequent and apprehensive glances astern but there was no cause for concern. The canoes, unmistakably, were dropping behind. There was going to be no pursuit.

Smith said, not even grudgingly: 'That was rather well managed, Hamilton. And now?'

'First we bail out. There should be three cooking pans floating around somewhere. Then we move out into the middle of the river—just in case they've sent some sharp-shooters down the left bank. There's going to be a full moon shortly, the skies are cloudless so we might as well carry on. Kellner and Hiller must be distinctly worried about us by this time.'

Tracy said: 'Why the two empty canoes?'

'I told you yesterday evening that there were falls about fifty miles below the town. That's why we had to airlift the hovercraft beyond them. The falls are about twenty miles farther on now. We'll have to make a portage there and it would be impossible to make it with this elephant. When we get there and have emptied her we'll give her a shove over the edge. Maybe she'll survive, the falls are only fifteen feet.'

Some little time later the now bailed-out motor-launch glided gently down the centre of the river, six men at the paddles but not exerting themselves; the current bore them along. The newly risen moon gleamed softly on the brown water. It was a peaceful scene.

Five hours later, as Hamilton guided the launch into the left bank, the passengers could distinctly hear the sound of the falls ahead, no Niagara roar, but unmistakably falls. They made the bank and tied up to a tree. The portage was not more than a hundred yards. First all the equipment, food and personal luggage were carried down, then the two canoes, and just in case the motor-launch should survive its fall, the three cooking utensils for bailing as well.

Hamilton and Navarro climbed into a canoe and reached a spot where the white water ended about a hundred feet below the foot of the falls and paddled gently to maintain position. Both men were looking up-river towards the falls beyond which, they knew, Ramon was at work.

For half a minute there was only the brown-white smoothness of the Rio da Morte sliding vertically downwards. Then the bows of the motor-launch came in sight, appeared to hesitate, until suddenly the entire boat was over and plunging down. There was a loud smack and a considerable cloud of spray as the launch first entered the water then disappeared entirely. All of ten seconds elapsed before it reappeared. But reappear it did, remarkably, right side up.

The launch, so full of water that there were only about four inches of freeboard left, drifted sluggishly downstream until Hamilton got a line aboard. With no little difficulty he and Navarro towed it to the left bank and tied up. Bailing operations commenced.

The brightly illuminated hovercraft lay anchored in mid-river. Navigation, deck and cabin lights were on. Kellner and Hiller were already close to despair because the expected arrivals were already fifteen hours late and it hardly seemed likely that if they hadn't arrived by that time that they would be arriving at all. They had no cause for worry as far as they themselves were concerned. They had only to continue down-river till they came to the junction with the Araguaia and some form of civilization. Both men were prepared to wait indefinitely and both for the same unexplained reason: they had faith in Hamilton's powers of survival. And so Kellner had his hovercraft lit up like a Christmas tree. He was taking no chances that the helicopter would bypass him in the darkness.

He and Hiller, both men with their machine-pistols immediately and constantly ready to hand, stood on the brief after-deck between the fans, ears always straining for the first faint intimation of the rackety clamour of the Sikorsky. But it was his eyes that gave Kellner the answer he was waiting for, not his ears. He peered up-river, peered more closely, then switched on and trained the hovercraft's powerful searchlight.

A powerless but impassively manned motor-launch and two canoes had just appeared in line ahead round a bend in the Rio da Morte.

7

The hovercraft's cabin was luxuriously furnished although on a necessarily small scale. The bar was splendidly if selectively equipped and, at the moment, well patronized. Most of the passengers from the wrecked helicopter gave the impression of having escaped from the jaws of death. The atmosphere was relaxed, almost convivial, and the spirit of the departed Heffner did not appear to hover over the company.

Hamilton said to Kellner: 'Any trouble during the night?'

'Not really. A couple of canoe-loads of Indians approached us just after midnight. We turned the searchlight on them and they turned and headed back for shore.'

'No shooting?'

'None.'

'Good. Now, the big question tomorrow is the rapids that the Indians call the Hoehna.'

'Rapids?' Kellner said. 'There are no rapids shown on the chart.'

'I daresay. Nevertheless, they're there. Never been through them myself although I've seen them from the air. Don't look anything special from up there, but then nothing ever does. Much experience with rapids?'

'A fair bit,' Kellner said. 'Nothing that a boat hasn't navigated though.'

'I'm told boats have made it throught the Hoehna.'

'So where's the problem? A hovercraft can navigate rapids that no boat made by man could ever hope to.'

Serrano said: 'Knowing you, Senor Hamilton, I thought you would have had us on our way by this time. A clear night. Bright moon. A beautiful night for sailing. Or is it "flying" in one of those machines?'

'We need a good night's rest, all of us. It's going to be a hard day tomorrow. The Hoehna rapids are less than a hundred miles away. How long to get there, Kellner?'

'Three hours. Less if you want.'

'One does not navigate rapids by night. And only a madman goes there in the hours of darkness. Because of the Horena, you see.'

Tracy said: 'The Horena? Another Indian tribe?'

'Yes.'

'Like the Chapate?'

'They're not at all like the Chapate. The Horena are the Roman lions, the Chapate the Christians. The Horena put the fear of living death into the Chapate.'

'But you said the Muscias——'

'Ah! The Muscias are to the Horena what the Horena are to the Chapate. Or so they say. Goodnight!'

'Rapids!' Ramon called out. 'Rapids ahead!'

In the two and a half hours since the hovercraft's dawn departure the Rio da Morte, though flowing at a rate of about fifteen knots, had been almost glassily calm and, although visibility had been poor because of fairly heavy rain, no problems had been encountered. But now conditions had dramatically altered. At first indistinctly through the now sheeting rain, but then suddenly, frighteningly, and all too vividly rocks could be seen, some jagged, some curved, thrusting up from the river bed. For as far as the eye could see hundreds of them spanned the entire width of the river with white-veined, seething water coursing down between them. The hovercraft, throttled back to a point where directional control could just be maintained, was almost at once into this white and seething cauldron.

When Kellner had said that he had some little experience of navigating rapids he had been doing himself less than justice. As far as the untrained observer could see, he was masterly. He was positively dancing a jig at the controls. He no longer had the throttle pulled back but kept altering it between half and full ahead which, considering their speed, might have seemed foolhardy, but wasn't. By doing this and by ignoring the air ducts and maintaining the cushion pressure as high as possible he could all the more easily avoid making violent course alterations which would have slewed the hovercraft broadside and into disaster. Instead, he was deliberately aiming for and riding his hovercraft over the less fearsome rocks in his path. Even here he had to be selective, searching out the more rounded rocks and avoiding the jagged ones which, at that speed, would have ripped even the abnormally tough apron skirts, leading to the collapse of the cushion and turning the hovercraft into a boat which would then have foundered in short order. One moment he was jerking the pitch control back, putting power on the left fan, then if this proved insufficient, applying right rudder to give him directional stability while only seconds later he had to reverse the procedure. His task was made harder by the fact that even the high-speed windscreen wipers were capable only intermittently of clearing the spray and rain.

Kellner said to Hamilton who was seated beside him: 'Tell me again about all those boats that were supposed to navigate the Hoehna.'

'I guess I must have been misinformed.'

Further back in the hovercraft no-one spoke because all their energies were concentrated on hanging on to their seats. The general effect of the motion was that of a roller-coaster—except that this roller-coaster, unlike the fairground type, also shook violently from side to side.

Up front, Kellner said: 'Do you see what I see?'

Some fifty yards ahead the river appeared to come to an abrupt end. They were obviously approaching a waterfall of sorts.

'Unfortunately. What are you going to do about it?'

'Funny.'

The hovercraft was being swept helplessly along to what was indeed a waterfull. The drop in the river level must have been at least ten feet. Kellner was doing the only thing he could do—trying to keep the hovercraft on a perfectly straight course.

The hovercraft swept over the fall, dipped sharply and plunged downwards at an angle of forty-five degrees. With an explosion of sound and spray, the hovercraft momentarily disappeared save for the stern. Not only the bows but part of the front of the cabin had gone completely under and in that way and at that angle the hovercraft remained for several seconds before it slowly struggled to the surface again, water cascading off its decks. It settled deeper in the water, the effect of partially losing its air cushion when the stern had come completely clear of the water.

The interior of the craft was a scene of appalling confusion. The angle of fall and the stunning impact had catapulted everyone to the deck. Equipment which had been stored but not lashed aft was now scattered throughout the cabin. To make matters worse, a window had been smashed and hundreds of gallons of water were sloshing about the interior of the cabin. One by one the passengers struggled upright. They were bruised, dazed and slightly concussed, but there seemed to be no broken bones.

As the air cushion began to fill again and the water gurgled away through the self-draining ports, they could feel the hovercraft rise slowly to its normal position.

Three times in the next few minutes the hovercraft went through a similar experience, although none of the overfalls were as high as the first time. At last the hovercraft passed into an area of smooth, rock-free water, but it was then another danger manifested itself. The forested banks gave way to what was at first low rock, which quickly became higher and higher until they were passing through what was virtually a cliff-sided canyon. At the same time the river swiftly narrowed to about a third of its original width and the speed of the river and hence that of the hovercraft rapidly more than doubled.

Hamilton and Kellner stared through the windscreens, glanced at each other, then looked forward again. Ahead, the steep-sided river walls fell sharply away, but this promised no surcease. A quarter of a mile ahead a jumble of huge black rocks blocked the river from side to side.

'Bloody charts!' Kellner said.

'Indeed.'

'Pity, really. These machines are very expensive.'

'Make for the left.'

'Any particular reason?'

'The Horena live on the right bank.'

'Left, as the man says.'

The rocks were about three hundred yards away. They appeared to form an impenetrable barrier, no two sufficiently far apart to afford passage to the hovercraft.

Hamilton and Kellner looked at each other. Simultaneously they shrugged. Hamilton turned and faced the rear.

'Hang on tight,' he said. 'We're about to stop very suddenly.' He had no sooner spoken than he realized that his warning had been unnecessary. They had seen what was coming up. They were already hanging on for dear life.

The rocks were now no more than a hundred yards distant. Kellner was guiding the craft towards the biggest gap between any two of them, the first and second from the left bank.

For one brief moment it seemed that the hovercraft might just have one chance of making the passage as Kellner arrowed straight for the centre of the gap. The craft's bows passed through but that was all: the passage was at least eighteen inches narrower than the midships beam of the hovercraft. With a grinding, screeching tearing of metal, the hovercraft came to an abrupt halt, immovably jammed.

Kellner went into reverse and applied maximum power. Nothing happened. Kellner eased off the fans but kept the engine running to maintain the cushion. He straightened up, muttering to himself, 'Now with an ocean-going tug . . .'

Ten minutes later there was a pile of rucksacks, canvas bags and other improvised luggage containers on deck and Hamilton was securing a rope around his waist. He said: 'It's only twenty feet to that bank but the water's mighty fast so kindly don't let go of the end of that rope.'

It was a danger, but not the only one. Even as he finished speaking there came a sudden grunt and Kellner collapsed to the deck. A dart protruded from the back of his neck. Hamilton swung round.

On the far right bank, less than fifty yards away, stood a group of Indians, ten or twelve in all. Every man had a blowpipe to his mouth.

'Horena!' Hamilton shouted. 'Down! Take cover behind the cabin, inside the cabin. Ramon! Navarro!'

Almost immediately, Ramon and Navarro, all humanitarian principles forgotten at the sight of Kellner, were on the cabin roof, stretched out on their elbows, rifles in hand. More darts struck the metal sheathing but none found a target. In three seconds the twins fired six shots. At five hundred yards either man was accurate. At fifty yards they were deadly. One after another, in those few seconds, three Horena toppled into the river, three others crumpled and died where they stood amd the others melted away.

Hamilton gazed down in bitterness at the lifeless Kellner. Not for the Horena the use of timbo, the poisonous bark of a forest vine which merely stunned: the dart which took Kellner had been tipped with curare.

Hamilton said: 'If it weren't for Kellner we'd all be dead. And now Kellner is dead.' Without another word he jumped into the river. The only danger here was the speed of the water: neither alligators nor piranha ever inhabit rapids.

94

boars which had redoubled their efforts. Both men started firing and within seconds a dozen *quiexada* lay dead.

Navarro said: 'Next time I go boar hunting—if there is a next time—I shall bring a sub-machine-gun with me. My magazine is empty.'

'Mine too.'

The sight of their dead companions seemed only to increase the blood lust of the boars. They tore at the roots with savage frenzy —and, already, several of the roots had been severed.

Navarro said: 'Senor Hamilton, either I'm shaking or this tree is becoming rather—what is the word for it?'

'Wobbly?'

'Wobbly.'

'I don't think. I know.'

A rifle shot rang out and a boar dropped dead. Hamilton and Navarro swung round to look back the way they had come. Ramon, who seemed to be carrying a pack of some sort on his back, was less than forty yards away and was prudently standing by a low-branched tree. He fired steadily and with deadly accuracy. Suddenly an empty click was heard. Hamilton and Navarro looked at each other thoughtfully, but Ramon remained unperturbed. He reached into his pocket, extracted another magazine clip, fitted it and resumed firing. Three more shots and it finally dawned on the *quiexada* that they were on to a hiding to nothing. Those that remained turned and ran off into the forest.

The three men walked back towards the camp, dragging a *quiexada* behind them. Ramon said: 'I heard the shooting so I came. Of course, I brought plenty of spare ammunition with me.' Deadpan, he patted a bulging pocket, then shrugged apologetically. 'All my fault. I should never have let you go alone. One has to be a man of the forest——'

'Oh, shut up,' Hamilton said. 'Thoughtful of you to bring my rucksack along with you.'

Ramon said pontifically: 'One should not expose the weak-minded to temptation.'

'Do be quiet,' Navarro said. He turned to Hamilton. 'God only knows he was insufferable enough before. But now, after this——'

The cooking fire burned in the near darkness and boar steaks sizzled in a glowing bed of coals.

Smith said: 'I appreciate the necessity for all the shots. But if the Horena are around—well, that must have attracted the attention of everyone within miles.'

'No worry,' Hamilton said. 'No Horena will ever attack at night. If he dies at night his soul will wander for ever in the hereafter. His gods must see him die.' He prodded a steak with his sheath knife. 'I would say those are just about ready.' Ready or not, the steaks were dispatched with every sign of gusto and when they were finished Hamilton said: 'Better if it had hung a week, but tasty, tasty. Bed. We leave at dawn. I'll keep the first watch.'

They prepared for sleep, some lying on waterproof sheets, others in lightweight hammocks slung between trees at the edge of the clearing. Hamilton flung some fuel on the fire and kept on flinging it until it flared up so brightly that the flames were almost ten feet high. Machete in hand, Hamilton departed to obtain some more fuel and returned with an armful of branches most of which he cast on the already blazing fire.

Smith said: 'Well, granted, granted, you know how to make bonfires. But what's it all in aid of?'

'Safety measures. Keeps the creepy-crawlies at bay. Wild animals fear fire.' He was to be proved half right, half wrong.

He was on his third fuel-hunting trip and was returning to camp when he heard the piercing scream of fear. He dropped the fuel and ran into the brightly lit clearing. He knew the high-pitched scream would only have come from Maria and as he closed on her hammock the reason for her terror was obvious: a giant anaconda, at least thirty feet in length and with its tail still anchored to one of the trees that supported Maria's hammock, had one of its deadly coils wrapped round the base of her hammock. She was in no way pinned down, just too paralysed with fear to move. The anaconda's vast jaws were agape.

It was not Hamilton's first anaconda and he had a nodding respect for them but no more. A full-grown specimen can swallow a 150-pound prey in its entirety. But while they could be endlessly patient, even cunning, in waiting for their next meal to come along, they were extremely slow-witted in action. While Maria continued to scream in the same mindless terror, he approached within feet of the fearsome head. No more than any other creature on earth could an anaconda withstand three Luger bullets in the head: it died immediately, but even in its death the coil slipped over the girl's ankles and continued to contract. Hamilton struggled to pull the slimy coil free but was brushed aside by Ramon who carefully placed two rifle bullets into the upper centre of the coil, severing the main spinal nerve. The anaconda at once went limp.

Hamilton carried her across to his groundsheet close by the fire. She was in a state of mild shock. Keep a shocked patient warm, Hamilton had often heard, and the thought had no sooner occurred to him than Ramon knelt alongside, a sleeping-bag in his hands. Together they eased the girl inside, zipped up the bag and sat to wait. Navarro came to join them and jerked a thumb in the direction of an apparently sleeping Smith.

'Observe our gallant hero,' he said. 'Asleep? He's wide awake. Has been all the time. I watched him.'

Ramon said complainingly: 'You might have come and watched us.'

'When you and Senor Hamilton can't take care of a simple-minded reptile like that it's time for us all to retire. I saw his face and he was terrified, seemed quite unable to move: not, I am sure, that he wanted to move or had any intention of moving. Has the girl been hurt?'

'Not physically,' Hamilton said. 'I'm afraid this is basically my fault. I had a big fire going to frighten off wild animals. Well, anacondas are also wild creatures and as frightened of fire as any other. This one just wanted out: it was the devil's bad luck that it was roosting in the tree that helped support Maria's hammock. I'm pretty sure she would have come to no harm. The reptile was simply easing its way down the tree. Apart from the fact that its belly is swollen and obviously would not be requiring another meal for a fortnight, it probably had a much greater matter on its mind, such as getting the hell out of here. All very unfortunate but no harm done.'

'Perhaps,' Ramon said. 'I hope.'

'You hope?' Hamilton said.

'Trauma,' Ramon said. 'How deep does a trauma lie? This has been a traumatic experience. But I think that's only a side issue. I have the feeling that her whole life has been a traumatic experience.'

'You plunging into the deep waters of psychology, psychiatry or what-have-you, Ramon?' Hamilton didn't smile as he spoke.

'I agree with Ramon,' Navarro said. 'Twins, you know,' he added apologetically. 'Something is wrong or not what it appears

101

to be. Her actions, her behaviour, the way she talks and smiles—
I find it hard to believe that this is a bad person, a common whore.
Smith, we know, *is* a bad person. She doesn't care for him, any
fool can see that. So what goes on?'

'Well,' Hamilton said judicially, 'he's got a lot to offer——'

'Ignore Senor Hamilton,' Ramon said. 'He's just trying to
provoke us.'

Navarro nodded in agreement then said: 'I think she is a prisoner
in some way or another.'

'Possibly,' Hamilton said. 'Possibly. Has it occurred to either
of you that *he* might be in some way *her* prisoner, without ever
knowing it?'

Navarro looked at Ramon, then accusingly at Hamilton.
'There you go again, Senor Hamilton. You know something that
we don't know and you're not telling us.'

'I know nothing that you don't know and far be it from me to
suggest that I look more closely and, perhaps, think a little more
deeply. But, then, you are young.'

'Young?' Navarro was indignant. 'Neither of us, Senor Hamilton, will ever see thirty again.'

'That's what I meant.' He put his fingers to his lips. Beside
him, Maria was stirring. She opened her eyes, still huge with fear
and horror. Hamilton touched her gently on the shoulder.

'It's all right now,' he said gently. 'It's all over.'

'That horrible, ghastly head.' Her voice was no more than a
husky whisper and she was shaking. Ramon rose and walked
away. 'That awful snake——'

'The snake is dead,' Hamilton said. 'And you are unharmed.
We promise you, no harm will come to you.'

She lay there breathing shallowly, her eyes closed. She opened
them again when Ramon returned and knelt by her side. He had
an aluminium cup in one hand, a bottle in the other.

Hamilton said: 'And what do we have here?'

'The finest cognac,' Ramon replied. 'As is only to be expected.
Smith's private supplies.'

'I don't like brandy,' she said.

'Ramon is right. You'd better like it. You need it.'

Ramon poured a generous measure. She tasted it, coughed,
screwed her eyes shut and emptied the cup in two gulps.

'Good girl,' Hamilton said.

'Awful,' she said. She looked at Ramon. 'But thank you. I feel

At first he was swept downstream and had to be hauled back. On the second attempt he succeeded in reaching the bank. He stood there some time, regaining his breath—the buffeting had been severe—then undid the rope around his waist and secured it to the bole of a tree. Another rope was thrown across to him. This he passed round a branch and threw back to the hovercraft where, in turn, it was passed round a fan bracket and thrown back to Hamilton, forming, in effect, an endless pulley.

The first item of equipment—Hamilton's own rucksack—was ferried across, well clear of the water, as was all the rest of the equipment. The members of the party had to make it the wet way.

8

Sweat-soaked and stumbling, mostly from near exhaustion, the heavily laden party of nine made their painfully slow way through the afternoon gloom of the rain-forest. Even at high noon there was never more than half-light in its depths. The crowns of the great liana-festooned trees stretched out and intertwined a hundred feet or more above the ground, effectively blocking out the sunlight.

Progress was not slow because they had to hack their way with machetes through the dense undergrowth, because of dense under-growth there was none. For plants to grow at ground-level, sunshine is essential. Jungle, in the true African sense of the term, did not exist. The progress was slow primarily because there was as much swampland as there was firm ground and quicksands were an ever-present peril. A man could step confidently on to what appeared to be an inviting stretch of greensward and on his second step find himself shoulder deep in a swamp. For safe locomotion in the forest, a probe, in the form of a hacked-off and trimmed branch, was essential. For every mile covered as the crow flew, it was not uncommon to have to traverse five miles. That, and the time it took to locate patches of firm ground, made for time-consuming, frustrating and exhausting travel.

Smith, in particular, was making heavy weather of it. His clothes were so saturated with sweat that he might well have just been dragged from the river. His legs had gone rubbery and he was gasping for breath.

Smith said: 'What the hell are you trying to prove, Hamilton? How tough you are and how out of condition we city dwellers are? God's sake, man, a break. An hour wouldn't kill us, would it?'

'No. But the Horena might.'

'But you said their territory was on the right bank.'

'That's what I believe. But don't forget: we killed six of their men. Great lads for revenge, the Horena. I wouldn't put it past them to have crossed the river and be following us. There could be a hundred of them within a hundred yards of here, just waiting to get within blowpipe range, and we wouldn't know a thing about it until too late.'

Smith, it appeared, was possessed of reserves of strength and endurance of which he had been unaware. He hurried on.

Towards evening, they reached a small and largely swampy clearing. Most of the party were now shambling, not walking.

'Enough,' Hamilton said. 'We'll make camp.'

With the approach of dusk the forest appeared to come alive. All around them was sound. Mainly, it came from birds—parrots, macaws, parakeets. But there was animal life too. Monkeys screeched, bull-frogs barked and now and again the deeply muffled roar of a jaguar came at them from the depths of the forest.

Everywhere there were creepers, vines, parasitic orchids and there, in the clearing, exotic flowers of almost every conceivable colour. The air was damp and fetid, a miasmic smell all-prevalent, the heat over-powering and leaden and enervating, the floor underfoot almost an unbroken expanse of thick, clinging, evil-smelling mud.

Everyone, even Hamilton, sank gratefully to what few patches of dry ground they could find. Over the river, not much higher than the tree-tops, several birds, with huge wing-spreads, seemed suspended against the sky, for their wings were motionless. They looked evil, sinister.

Maria said: 'What are those horrible-looking creatures?'

'Urubus,' Hamilton said. 'Amazonian vultures. They seem to be looking for something.'

Maria shuddered. Everybody gazed unhappily at the vultures.

'A poor choice, I suppose,' Hamilton said. 'The cooking-pots, head-hunters or the vultures. And speaking of cooking-pots, some fresh meat might help. Curassow—a kind of wild turkey—armadillo, wild boar, all very tasty. Navarro?'

Ramon said: 'I'll come too.'

'You stay, Ramon. A little more thoughtfulness, please. Someone has to look after these poor souls.'

Tracy said: 'To keep an eye on us, you mean.'

'I don't see what mischief you can get up to here.'

'Your haversack.'

'I don't understand.'

Tracy said deliberately: 'Heffner appeared to find something there just before you murdered him.'

Ramon said: 'Before Mr Heffner met his unfortunate end is what Mr Tracy means.'

Hamilton eyed Tracy thoughtfully then turned away into the forest, Navarro following. Less than two hundred yards from the camp Hamilton put a restraining hand on Navarro's arm and pointed ahead. Not forty yards away was a *quiexada*, that most savage of all the world's wild boars. They are so devoid of fear that they have been known to invade towns in herds, driving the citizens into their houses.

'Supper,' Hamilton said.

Navarro nodded and raised his rifle. One single shot was all that Navarro would ever need. They began to make their way towards the dead animal then halted abruptly. A herd of perhaps three dozen *quiexada* had suddenly appeared from the forest. They halted, pawed the ground, then came on again. There was no mistaking their intention.

Only on the riversides do Amazonian trees have branches, for only there can they get sunlight. Hamilton and Navarro reached the lowermost branches of the nearest tree a short distance ahead of the boars, which proceeded to encircle the tree and then as if in response to some unseen signal, began to use their vicious tusks to savage the roots of the tree. The roots of the Amazonian trees, like those of the giant sequoia of California, are extremely long—and extremely shallow.

'I would say they have done this sort of thing before,' Navarro said. 'How long is this going to take, do you think?'

'Not long at all.'

Hamilton sighted his pistol and shot a *quiexada* that seemed to be more industrious than its companions. The dead animal toppled into the river. Within seconds, the smooth surface of the river was disturbed by a myriad ripples and there came the high-pitched, spinechilling buzzing whine as the needle teeth of the voracious piranha proceeded to strip the *quiexada* to the bone

Navarro cleared his throat and said: 'Perhaps you should have shot one not quite so close to the river.'

Hamilton said: '*Quiexada* to one side, piranha to the other. You don't by any chance see a constrictor lurking in the branches above?'

Involuntarily, Navarro glanced upwards, then down at the

98

Tracy stared at him, still in wonderment, and shook his head.

Suddenly people, scores of them, began to emerge from the communal hut. That they were not Amazonian Indians was obvious from the fact that there were as many woman as men among them: normally, in the Amazonian basin, women are banned from the meeting places of elders and warriors. All were of the same copper colour, all possessed of a proud, almost regal bearing. They began to disperse towards their huts.

Smith touched Hamilton on the arm and said in a low voice: 'Who are those people?'

'The Muscias.' Smith turned pale.

'Goddamned Muscias!' he said in a vicious whisper. 'What the hell are you playing at? Head-hunters, you said. Head-shrinkers! Cannibals! I'm off!'

'Off where, you clown? You've got no place left to run to. Stay here. *Don't, don't, don't* show yourselves.'

The advice was probably superfluous. No-one, clearly, had the slightest intention of showing himself.

Hamilton rose and walked confidently into the clearing. He had gone at least ten paces before he was noticed. There was a sudden silence, the babble of voices ceased, then the chatter redoubled in volume. An exceptionally tall Indian, old and with his forearms almost covered in what were unquestionably gold bracelets, gazed for some seconds then ran forward. He and Hamilton embraced each other.

The old man, who was surely the chief, and Hamilton engaged in an animated, if incomprehensible, coversation. The chief, with an expression of incredulity on his face, repeatedly shook his head. Just as firmly Hamilton nodded his. Suddenly, Hamilton extended his right arm and made a semi-circular motion, bringing his arm to a sudden halt. The chief looked long at him, seized him by the arms, smiled and nodded his head. He turned and spoke rapidly to his people.

Tracy said: 'I'd say those two people have met somewhere before.'

The chief finished addressing his people, all of whom had now gathered in the clearing, and spoke again to Hamilton, who nodded and turned.

Hamilton shouted to his waiting companions: 'You can come now. Keep your hands well away from any weapon.'

Not quite dazedly, but not understanding what was happening, the other members of the party entered the clearing.

Hamilton said: 'This is Chief Corumba.' He introduced each of the eight in turn. The chief gravely acknowledged each introduction, shaking each in turn by hand.

Hiller said: 'But Indians don't shake hands.'

'This Indian does.'

Maria touched Hamilton on the arm. 'But those savage headhunters——'

'These are the kindliest, most gentle, most peaceable people on earth. In their language they do not have a word for war because they do not know what war is. They are a lost children from a lost age and the people who built the Lost City.'

Serrano said: 'And I thought I knew more about the tribes of the Mato Grosso than any man alive.'

'And so you may, Serrano, so you may. If, that is to say, I can take the word of Colonel Diaz.'

'Colonel Diaz?' Smith said. He was clearly floundering in deep water. 'Who's Colonel Diaz?'

'A friend of mine.'

Tracy said: 'But their ferocious reputation——'

'A fiction invented by Dr Hannibal Huston, the man who found these lost people. He thought that such a reputation might ensure them—what shall we say?—a little privacy.'

'Huston?' Hiller said. 'Huston? You—you found Huston?'

'Years ago.'

'But you've only been in the Mato Grosso for four months.'

'I have known it for many years. Remember in the Hotel de Paris in Romono you mentioned my search for the golden people? I forgot to mention that I also met them years ago. Here they are. The Children of the Sun.'

Maria said: 'And Dr Huston is still in the Lost City?'

'He's still there. Come, I believe these good people want to offer us some hospitality. First, however, I owe you a small explanation about them.'

'High time, too,' Smith said. 'Why all the dramatic, stealthy approach to them?'

'Because if we had approached as a group they would have run away. They have every good reason to fear those from the outside world. We, ironically known as the *civilizados*—in practically everything that matters they're a damned sight more civilized than we are—bring them so-called progress, which harms them, so-called change, which harms them, so-called civilization, which harms them even more, and disease, which kills them. These people have no natural resistance to measles or influenza. Either of those are to them what bubonic plague was to Europeans and Asiatics in the Middle Ages. Half a tribe can be wiped out in a fortnight. The same thing happened to the people of Tierra del Fuego. Well-meaning missionaries gave them simple clothes, primarily so that the women could cover their nakedness. The blankets came from a hospital where there had been a measles epidemic. Most of the people were wiped out.'

Tracy said: 'But our presence here. Surely that endangers them?'

'No. Almost half the Muscias were destroyed by measles or influenza or a combination of both. These people here are the survivors, having acquired natural immunity the hard way. As I said, it was Dr Huston who found them. Although mainly famous as an explorer, his real life's work lay elsewhere. He was one of the original *sertanistas*—men wise in jungle ways—and a founder member of the FUNAI, the National Foundation for the Indian, people who dedicate their lives to protecting the Indians and rendering them harmless to *civilizados*. "Pacification" is the term generally used but in truth what they mainly required was protection *against* the *civilizados*. Sure, many of the tribes were genuinely savage—well, not so many, there are less than two hundred thousand pure-blood Indians left—but their savagery sprang from fear and very understandably so. Even in modern times, those civilized gentlemen from the outer world, and by no means all Brazilians, either, have machine-gunned them, dynamited them from the air and given them poisoned food.'

'This is all news to me,' Smith said, 'and I've lived in this country for many years. Frankly, I find it very hard to believe.'

'Serrano will confirm it.'

'I confirm it. I take it that you, too, are a *sertanista*.'

'Yes. Not always a very happy job. We have our failures. The Chapate and the Horena, as you've seen, are not too keen on the idea of co-operation with the outside world. And, inevitably, we bring disease as we did here. Come along, Chief Corumba is summoning us to eat. It may taste a little odd, but I can assure you that no harm will come to any of you.'

*

One hour later the visitors were still seated around a rough wooden table outside the communal hut. Before them lay the remains of an excellent if rather exotic meal—game, fish, fruit and other unknown delicacies concerning the nature of which it had been thought more prudent not to ask: all had been washed down with *cachassa*, a rather potent brew. At the end, Hamilton thanked Chief Corumba on behalf of all of them and turned to the others.

'I think it's time we were on our way.'

Tracy said: 'One thing intrigues me. I've never seen so many gold ornaments in my life.'

'I thought that might intrigue you.'

'Where do these people come from?'

'They don't know themselves. A lost people who have lost everything and that includes their history. It was Dr Huston's theory that they are the descendants of the Quimbaya, an ancient tribe from the Cauca or Magdalena valleys in the western Andes of Colombia.'

Smith stared at him. 'So what in God's name are they doing here?'

'Nobody knows. Huston thinks they left their homeland all those hundreds of years ago. He thinks they may have fled to the east, found the head-waters of the Amazon, come all the way down until they reached the Rio Tocantis, turned up that until they came to the Araguaia, then up the Rio da Morte. Again, who knows? Stranger migrations have happened. It could have taken them generations: they were weighed down with many possessions. I believe it. Wait till you see the Lost City and you'll understand why I do believe it.'

Smith said: 'How far away is this damned city?'

'Five hours. Six.'

'Five hours!'

'And easy going. Uphill, but no swamps, no quicksands.' He turned to Chief Corumba, who smiled and again warmly embraced Hamilton.

'Wishing us good luck?' Smith said.

'Among quite a few other things. I'll have a longer chat with him tomorrow.'

'Tomorrow!'

'Why ever not?'

Smith, Tracy and Hiller exchanged flickering glances. None of the three said anything.

Just before they walked away Hamilton spoke quietly to Maria. 'Stay behind with these people. They will look after you, I promise. Where we're going is no place for a lady.'

'I'm coming.'

'Suit yourself. There's an excellent chance you'll be dead by nightfall.'

'You don't much care for me, do you?'

'Enough to ask you to stay behind.'

In the late afternoon Hamilton and his party were still making their way towards the Lost City. The going underfoot was excellent, dry, leafy and springy.

Unfortunately for people like Smith, the incline was fairly severe and the heat was, of course, as always oppressive.

Hamilton said: 'I think we'll have a half-hour break here. We're ahead of time—we can't move in until it's dark. Besides, some of you may think you've earned a rest.'

'Too bloody right, we have,' Smith said. 'How much longer do you intend to crucify us?'

He sank wearily to the ground and mopped his streaming face with a bandana. He was not the only one to do so. With the exception of Hamilton and the twins, everyone seemed to be suffering from a shortage of breath and leaden, aching legs. Hamilton had, indeed, been setting a brisk pace.

'You've done very well, all of you,' Hamilton said. 'Mind you, you might have done even better if you hadn't guzzled and drunk like pigs down in the village. We've climbed almost two thousand feet since leaving there.'

Smith said: 'How—much—longer?'

'From here to the top? Another half hour. No more. I'm afraid we'll have to do a bit more climbing after that—downhill, mind you, but a pretty steep downhill.'

'Half an hour,' Smith said. 'Nothing.'

'Wait until you start going down.'

'The last lap,' Hamilton said. 'We are ten yards from the brink of a ravine. Anyone who hasn't a head for heights had better say so now.'

If anyone didn't have a head for heights he or she wasn't saying so. Hamilton began to crawl forward. The rest followed. Hamilton stopped and motioned to the others to join him.

Hamilton said: 'You see what I see?'

Smith said: 'Jesus!'

Maria said: 'The Lost City!'

Tracy said: 'Shangri-la!'

'El Dorado,' Hamilton said.

'What?' Smith said. 'What was that?'

'Nothing, really. There never was an El Dorado. It means the golden man. New Inca rulers were covered in gold dust and dipped—only temporarily, of course—in a lake. You see that peculiar stepped pyramid with the flat top at the far end?'

The question was really unnecessary It was the dominant feature of the Lost City.

'That's one of the reasons—there are two others—why Huston thought that the Children of the Sun came from Colombia. It's what you call a ziggurat. Originally it was a temple—tower in Babylonia or Assyria. No traces of those remain in the Old World—the Egyptians built a quite different form of pyramid.'

Tracy said, as if not knowing: 'This is the only one?'

'By no means. You'll find well-preserved examples in Mexico, Guatemala, Bolivia and Peru. But only in Central America and the north-west of South America. But nowhere else in the world—except here.'

Serrano said: 'So they're Andean. You couldn't ask for better proof.'

'You couldn't. But I have it.'

'Complete proof? Total?'

'I'll show you later.' He pointed with outstretched arm. 'You see those steps?'

Stretching from the river to the top of the plateau and hewn from the vertical rock-face, the stone stairway, terrifying to look at even from a distance, angled upwards at 45°.

'Two hundred and forty-eight steps,' Hamilton said, 'each thirty inches wide. Worn, smooth and slippery—and no hand rail.'

Tracy said: 'Who counted them?'

'I did.'

'You mean——'

'Yes. Wouldn't do it again, though. There had been a hand rail once and I'd brought along equipment to rig a rope rail. It's still on the hovercraft—for obvious reasons.'

'Mr Hamilton!' Silver spoke in an urgent whisper. 'Mr Hamilton!'

'What's the excitement about?'

'I saw someone moving in the ruins down there. I swear to it.'

'The pilot's eagle-eye, eh? No need to swear to anything. There are quite a number of people down there. Why do you think I didn't fly in by helicopter?'

Serrano said: 'They are not friends, no?'

'No.' He turned to Smith. 'Speaking of helicopters, I don't have to explain the lay-out of this place to you. You know it already.'

'I don't understand.'

'That film cassette you had Hiller steal for you.'

'I don't know what——'

'I took them a year ago. I left Hiller no option but to steal them. Taken from a helicopter. Not bad for an amateur, were they?'

Smith didn't say whether they were or not. He, Hiller and Tracy had again, momentarily, assumed very odd expressions, mainly of deep unease.

Hamilton said: 'Look to your left there. Just where the river forks to go round the island.'

At a distance of about half a mile and about three hundred feet below their present elevation a spidery, sagging, and apparently twisted series of ropes spanned the gorge between the top of the plateau and a point about half-way up the top of the cliff on which they were lying. Immediately below the cliff anchorage a small waterfall raced out into the river.

'A rope bridge,' Hamilton said. 'Well, a liana bridge. Or a straw bridge. Those normally renewed once a year. This one can't have been renewed for at least five years. Must be in a pretty rotten state by this time.'

'So?' Smith said. The apprehension in his voice was unmistakable.

'So that's the way we go in.'

The silence that followed was long and profound.

At last Serrano said: 'Another proof of Andean ancestry, no? I mean, there *are* no rope bridges in the Mato Grosso—well, there's not one now—nor, as far as I know, anywhere in Brazil. The Indians never learnt how to make them. Why should they have done—they never needed them. But the Incas and their descendants knew how to make them—living in the Andes, they had to know.'

111

'I've seen one,' Hamilton said. 'On the Apurimac river, high up in Peru—about twelve thousand feet. They use six heavy braided straw cables for the main supports—four for the footpaths, two for the hand rails. Smaller ropes for closing in the sides and a bed of twigs spread over the footpath so that only a three-year-old could possibly fall through. Can support scores of people when new. I'm afraid this one is not new.'

A narrow cleft ran down the cliff at an angle of close on 60°. A small stream, probably fed from some spring above, fell, rather than flowed down this cleft, leaping whitely from spur to spur. On one side of this cleft a series of rough steps had been cut, obviously a very long time ago.

Hamilton and the others started to descend. It was a fairly arduous descent but not really either difficult or dangerous as Hamilton had taken the precaution of binding together a series of tough lianas, anchoring one end to a tree and letting the rest fall down the cleft.

At the foot of the cleft, just above where the waterfall arced out above the river, a platform, about eight feet by eight, had been quarried out of the cliff-face. Hamilton was already standing there. One by one he was joined by the others.

Hamilton moved to examine a stone bollard and an iron post that had been hammered into the platform. Three now threadbare lianas were attached to both. Hamilton produced his sheath knife and scraped at the iron post. Thick brown flakes were shaved away.

'Keep your voices down,' Hamilton said. 'Rusty, isn't it?' He turned away to look over the gorge. The others did the same. The straw bridge was very flimsy and clearly venerable. Both the hand supports and the footpath were severely frayed. Several of the straw ropes appeared to have rotted and fallen away.

Hamilton said: 'Not in the best condition, wouldn't you say?'

Smith, his eyes wide, was obviously appalled. 'Good God in heaven. That's suicide. Only a madman would go on it. Do you expect me to risk my life on that?'

'Of course not. Why on earth would you? You're only here for the story, for the pictures. You'd be crazy to risk your life just for that. Tell you what. Give me your camera and I'll take the pictures for you. And don't forget—the people over there may not be welcoming trespassers.'

Smith was silent for some time, then said: 'I'm a man who sees things through to the end.'

'Maybe the end is closer than you think. It's dark enough now. I'm going first.'

Navarro said: 'Senor Hamilton. I am much lighter——'

'Thank you. But that's just the point. I'm a heavy man and I'm carrying a heavy pack. If it takes my weight—well, you should all be okay.'

Ramon said: 'A thought occurs to me.'

'And to me.' He moved towards the straw bridge.

'What was that meant to mean?' Maria said.

'He thinks, perhaps, that they will have a welcome mat out over there.'

'Oh. A guard.'

Hamilton moved steadily across the straw bridge. That is, he made steady progress. The bridge itself was shockingly unsteady, swaying from side to side. Hamilton was now more than half-way across. The bridge sagged so badly in the middle that he had to haul himself up a fairly steep incline. But he was experiencing no great difficulty. He arrived safely on a platform similar to the one he had left on the other side of the gorge. He crouched low, for the platform was only a few feet lower than the plateau. Cautiously, he lifted his head.

There was, indeed, a guard, but he was not taking his duties too seriously. He was smoking a cigarette and, of all things, relaxing in a deck chair. Hamilton's bent arm was raised to shoulder level. His handkerchief-wrapped hand held the blade of his heavy sheath knife. The guard drew deeply on his cigarette, clearly illuminating his face. He made no sound as the haft of the knife struck him between the eyes, just tipped to one side and fell out of his chair.

Hamilton turned and flashed his torch three times. Within minutes he was joined one by one by eight people who had not enjoyed their passage across the rope bridge.

Hamilton said: 'Let's go and see the boss man.' He could find his way blindfolded and led them silently through the ancient ruins. Shortly he stopped and pointed.

There was a large and fairly new wooden hall with lights showing. The sound of voices carried.

'Barracks,' Hamilton said. 'Mess hall and sleeping accommodation. Guards.'

Tracy said: 'Guards? Why?'

'Guilty conscience somewhere.'

'What's that noise?' Smith said.

'Generator.'

'Where do we go from here?'

'There.' Hamilton pointed again. At the foot of the giant ziggurat was another but much smaller wooden building. Lights also shone from that building.

'That's where the guilty conscience lives.' Hamilton was silent for a few moments. 'The man who every night feels dead feet trampling over his grave.'

Silver said: 'Mr Hamilton——'

'Nothing, nothing. Ramon, Navarro. I wonder if you see what I see?'

'Yes, indeed,' Ramon said. 'There are two men standing in the shadow of that porch.'

Hamilton seemed to ponder for a few moments. 'I wonder what they could be doing there?'

'We'll go and ask them.'

Ramon and Navarro melted into the shadows.

Smith said: 'Who are these two? Your assistants, I mean. They are not Brazilian.'

'No.'

'European?'

'Yes.'

Ramon and Navarro returned as silently and unobtrusively as they had left.

'Well,' Hamilton said. 'What did they say?'

'Not a great deal,' Navarro said. 'I think they may tell us when they wake up.'

9

Inside the smaller wooden house was a large dining-cum-living-room. The walls were much behung with flags, banners, portraits, swords, rapiers, guns and pictures, all German. Behind a table a large, rather red-faced, heavily jowled man was eating a solitary meal to be washed down by beer from a pewter litre mug beside him. He looked up in amazement as the door crashed open.

Hamilton, pistol in hand, entered. He was followed by Smith, then the others.

'*Guten abend*,' Hamilton said. 'I've brought an old friend along to see you.' He nodded towards Smith. 'I think old friends should smile and shake hands and say "hallo", don't you? You don't?'

Hamilton's pistol fired, gouging a hole in the seated man's desk.

'Nervous hands,' Hamilton said. 'Ramon?'

Ramon went behind the desk and removed a gun from an already half-opened drawer.

'Try the other drawer,' Hamilton said. Ramon did so and came up with a second gun.

'Can't really blame you,' Hamilton said. 'There are thieves and robbers everywhere these days. Well. Embarrassing silences bother me. Let me introduce you to each other. Behind the desk, Major-General Wolfgang Von Manteuffel of the S.S., variously known as Brown or Jones. Beside me, Colonel Heinrich Spaatz, also known as Smith, also of the S.S., Inspector General and Assistant Inspector General of the north and central Polish concentration and extermination camps, thieves on a colossal scale, murderers of old men in Holy orders and despoilers of monasteries. Remember, that's where you last met—in that Grecian monastery where you cremated the monks. But, then, you were specialists in cremation, weren't you?'

They weren't saying whether they were or not. The stillness in the room was total. All eyes were on Hamilton with the exception

115

of those of Von Manteuffel and Spaatz: they had eyes only for each other.

'Sad,' Hamilton said. 'Very sad. Spaatz came all this long way to see you, Von Manteuffel. Admittedly, he came to kill you, but he did come. Something, I believe, to do with a rainy night in the Wilhemshaven docks.'

There came the sharp crack of a small-bore automatic. Hamilton looked at Tracy who, gun loose in an already nerveless hand, was sinking to the floor and from the state of his head it was clear he would never rise again. Maria had a gun in her hand and was very pale.

Hamilton said: 'My gun is on you.'

She put her automatic back in her bush jacket pocket. 'He was going to kill you.'

'He was,' Ramon said.

Hamilton looked at her in bafflement. '*He* was going to kill *me*, so *you* killed *him*?'

'I was waiting for it.'

Navarro said thoughtfully, 'I do believe the young lady is not all that we thought she was.'

'So it would seem.' Hamilton was equally thoughtful. He said to her: 'Whose side *are* you on?'

'Yours.'

Spaatz at last looked away from Von Manteuffel and stared at her in total incredulity. She went on quietly: 'It is sometimes quite difficult to tell a Jewish girl from other girls.'

Hamilton said: 'Israeli?'

'Yes.'

'Intelligence?'

'Yes.'

'Ah! Would you like to shoot Spaatz too?'

'They want him back in Tel Aviv.'

'Failing that?'

'Yes.'

'My apologies, and without any reservations. You're becoming quite unpopular, Spaatz. But not yet in Von Manteuffel's class. The Israelis want him for obvious reasons. The Greeks'—he nodded to Ramon and Navarro in turn—'those two gentlemen are Greek army intelligence officers—want you for equally obvious reasons.' He looked at Hiller. 'They supplied me with those gold coins, by the way.' He turned back to Von Manteuffel.

116

'The Brazilian government want you for dispossessing the Muscia tribe and for the killing of many of them and *I* want you for the murder of Dr Hannibal Huston and his daughter, Lucy.'

Von Manteuffel smiled and spoke for the first time. 'I'm afraid you all want a great deal. And I'm afraid you're not going to get it.'

There came a loud crashing of glass and simultaneously the barrels of three sub-machine-guns protruded through three smashed windows.

Von Manteuffel smiled contentedly. 'Any person found with a gun on him will be shot out of hand. Do I have to tell you what to do next?'

He didn't. All guns were dropped on the floor, including two that Hamilton had not known that Spaatz and Hiller were carrying.

'So.' Von Manteuffel nodded in satisfaction. 'So much better than a blood bath, don't you think? Simpletons! How do you think I have survived for so long? By taking endless precautions. Such as this little press button my right foot rests on.'

He broke off as four armed men entered and watched them in silence as they searched the captives for further weapons. Predictably, they found none.

'And the rucksacks,' Von Manteuffel said.

Again the search failed to turn up any weapon.

Von Manteuffel said: 'I would have a word with my old friend Heinrich, who would appear to have come a very long way for nothing. Ah, and this man.' He indicated Hiller. 'I gather he's an accomplice of my dear ex-comrade in arms. The rest—take them and their pestilential luggage across to the old grain store. Perhaps I shall be subjecting them to some intensive and, I fear, very painful questioning. On the other hand, perhaps not. I shall decide after I've had my chat with Heinrich.'

10

The old grain store was built entirely of beautifully cut and fitted stone without any mortar whatsoever. It was about twenty feet by twelve, and had three storage bins on either side. The sides and the partitions of the bins were made of heavy adze-cut wood. A single weak and naked electric lamp, suspended from the ceiling, burned in the centre of the store. There were no windows and only one door-opening without a door, which the presence outside of a man with a cocked machine carbine made superfluous anyway. There were no furnishings of any description. Hamilton and his fellow captives had nothing to do but to look at each other or at the sentry, who faced them, his elderly but no doubt still lethal Schmeisser levelled directly at them: he had about him the look of a man who was yearning for an excuse to use it.

Navarro finally broke the silence. 'I fear for the health of our Mr Smith. Hiller, too, come to that.'

'Never mind about *their* damned health,' Hamilton said. 'Start fearing for your own. When he's finished with those two who do you think is next on his list, whether or not he indulges in a little torture beforehand?' He sighed. 'Trust old trusty secret agent Hamilton to tell all. Von Manteuffel knows who I am, who Maria is, and who you two so-called Greek intelligence officers are. He can't let us live and I'm afraid he can't let Silver or Serrano live either—obviously.'

'Speaking of Serrano,' Ramon said, 'could I have a word with you?'

'Go ahead.'

'In private, if you please.'

'If that's what you want.' The two men moved to a corner of the room where Ramon spoke in a low rapid tone. Hamilton lifted his eyebrows and his face registered surprise, an emotion he had practically never betrayed. Then he shrugged his shoulders, nodded twice, turned thoughtfully away and looked at the sentry.

'Big man,' Hamilton said. 'My size. Black from head to toe—beret, jacket, trousers, shoes. I want those clothes. More importantly, I want that gun. Even more importantly still, I want them both fast.'

'Easy,' Ramon said. 'Just ask him.'

Hamilton didn't reply. Savagely, almost, and to the accompaniment of the indrawn hiss of Maria's breath, he bit the ball of his left thumb. At once the blood began to flow. He squeezed the torn flesh until the blood flowed even more freely, then smeared it over Ramon's uncomprehending face.

'All in the interest of art,' Hamilton told him. 'Brother, what a fight this is going to be.'

The 'fight' started in the corner of the store, just out of the sentry's line of sight. The sentry would have been less than human not to locate the source of the sound of the heavy blows, the shouting and swearing. He moved forward into the doorway.

Hamilton and Ramon were belabouring each other mightily, fighting in apparently vicious fury, kicking and punching and obviously intent on inflicting grievous and mutual bodily harm. The sentry was clearly startled, but not suspicious. He had a heavily brutalized face behind which there lurked no great intelligence.

'Stop that!' he shouted. 'You madmen! Stop it or——'

He broke off as one of the combatants received a seemingly murderous blow and came staggering to fall flat on his back, half in and half out of the doorway, eyes turned up in his head, the face masked with blood. The sentry stepped by him, ready to quell any further signs of trouble. Ramon's hands closed round his ankles.

Four men prepared to carry three blanket-covered, stretchered forms from Von Manteuffel's room. Von Manteuffel said: 'It can be fatal to allow an enemy to live longer than is necessary.' He paused, briefly, for thought. 'Over the side with them. Think of all those poor starving piranha. As for our other friends in the grain store, I don't think they can supply me with any more useful information. You know what to do.'

'Yes, Herr General,' one of the men said. 'We know what to do.' His face was wolfish in anticipation.

Von Manteuffel glanced at his watch. 'I will expect you back

119

in exactly five minutes. After you've given the piranha their second course.'

A figure, dressed all in black, faced the grain store with a levelled Schmeisser in his hands. He heard the sound of footsteps some way off and glanced quickly over his shoulder. Four men—the four who had disposed of Spaatz and Hiller—were about thirty yards away: their machine carbines were shoulder slung. The dark figure continued to gaze at the door of the grain store, waited until his ears told him that the approaching group were no more than five yards away, then swung round with his Schmeisser blazing.

Maria said in a subdued tone: 'You play for keeps, don't you? You didn't *have* to kill them.'

'True. True. But, then, I didn't want them to kill me. You don't play footsy with cornered rats. Those are desperate men and you can bet that each one is a trained, efficient and practised killer. I don't much feel like apologizing.'

'And no need,' said Ramon who, like his brother, had remained unmoved by the proceedings. 'The only good Nazi is one who has stopped breathing. So. Five guns. What do we do?'

'We stay here because here we're safe. Von Manteuffel may have thirty, forty men, maybe even more. Out in the open we'd be massacred.' He glanced down at the stirring figure of the sentry. 'Ah! Junior is coming to. I think we'll send him for a little walk so that he can apprise his boss that there's been a slight change in the *status quo*. Remove his uniform—should give Von Manteuffel quite a turn.'

Von Manteuffel was making some notes at his desk when the knock came on the door. He glanced at his watch and smiled in satisfaction. Exactly five minutes had elapsed since his four men had departed, just over two minutes since he had heard the burst of machine-gun fire which could only have signalled the end of the six captives. He called out permission to enter, made a final note, said: 'You are very punctual,' and looked up. His expression of surprise vanished and his eyes opened almost impossibly widely. The stumbling figure before him was clad only in his underclothes.

The store was deep in shadow. The single lamp had been switched off and what little light there was came from a newly risen moon.

'Fifteen minutes and nothing,' Navarro said. 'Is that good?'

'It's inevitable, I suppose,' Hamilton said. 'We're in darkness. Von Manteuffel's men are exposed, or would be if they showed themselves and they don't dare show themselves. What can they do? Smoke us out if the wind is right? But no wind, so no smoke.'

Ramon said: 'Starve us out?'

'We should live that long.'

The time crawled by. Apart from Navarro, who stood by the doorway, everyone was lying down. They may or may not have been trying to sleep for some had their eyes shut but were unquestionably wide awake. Navarro said: 'Two hours. That's two hours gone now. Still nothing.'

'Would you mind, watchman? I'm trying to sleep.' Hamilton sat up. 'Don't think I will sleep. They *may* be up to something. I've no cigarettes. Anybody? No?' Serrano offered a packet. 'I thought you were asleep. Thanks. You know, I wasn't quite sure whether or not to believe what you told me, but I believe you now if for no other reason than the fact that it has to be as you say. So I guess I owe you an apology.' He paused reflectively: 'Apologizing seems to have become a habit with me.'

Ramon said curiously: 'May we know what the present apology is about?'

'Of course. Serrano is government. On the need-to-know principle, I suppose, Colonel Diaz kind of forgot to tell me.'

'Government?'

'Ministry of Culture. Fine Arts.'

'God help us all,' Ramon said. 'I would have thought there were enough genuine vultures in those godforsaken parts without adding culture vultures to the list. What on earth are you doing here, Serrano?'

'That's what I hope to find out.'

'Forthcoming, aren't we? Senor Hamilton?'

'I told you, I only learnt of this a couple of hours ago.'

Ramon looked at him reproachfully. 'Senor Hamilton, you're at it again.'

'At what?'

'Being enigmatic and evasive.'

Hamilton shrugged and said nothing. Serrano said: 'An honest doubt doesn't require an apology.'

'There's a little more to it than that,' Hamilton said. 'I thought

121

you were Hiller's man. Back in Romono, that is, when I first met you. I'm afraid I'm the person who clobbered you. I'll give you back the money I took from your wallet. There's not much I can do about your stiff neck. Forgive me.'

'Forgive, forgive,' Maria said. 'I don't suppose anyone is going to forgive me.'

There was a brief silence, then Hamilton said, mildly enough: 'I have apologized.'

'Apologies and forgiveness are not the same thing and you're clearly of the opinion that my association—that's the nicest way I can put it—was unforgivable. It all depends upon who is doing the judging and casting the first stones. All four of my grandparents died in Auschwitz and the chances are high that it was Von Manteuffel or Spaatz who sent them there. Or both. I suppose the world is tired of hearing about it, but six million Jews did die in the concentration camps. Was I so wrong? I knew if I stayed with Smith long enough he'd lead me to Von Manteuffel and he was the one we really wanted. I knew of only one way of staying with him. So I—we—found Von Manteuffel. Was I so wrong?'

'Tel Aviv?' Hamilton made no attempt to conceal his distaste. 'Another of those barbaric Eichmann show trials?'

'Yes.'

'Von Manteuffel will never leave the Lost City.'

'This Dr Huston,' Serrano said carefully. 'He meant so much? And his daughter?'

'Yes.'

'You were here at the time they—ah—died?'

'Murdered. No. I was in Vienna. But a friend of mine—Jim Clinton—was here. He buried them. He even gave them a tombstone and inscription—burnt on wood with a red-hot poker. Von Manteuffel killed him also—some time later.'

'Vienna?' Maria said. 'Wiesenthal? The Institute?'

Serrano said: 'What's this, young lady?'

'You should watch those slips of the tongue, Mr Serrano, such as calling me a young lady. The Institute is a Jewish central organization for hunting down war criminals. Based in Austria, not Israel. Mr Hamilton, why can they never let the left hand know what the right is doing?'

'Same old need-to-know principle, I suppose. All that I really know is that I'd a double reason for hunting Von Manteuffel down. I got close to him twice in the Argentine, twice in Chile,

122

once in Bolivia, twice in the Kolonie 555. An elusive character, always on the run, always surrounded by his Nazi thugs. But I've caught up with him.'

'Or the other way around,' Serrano said.

Hamilton remained silent.

'Your friends are buried here?'

'Yes.'

'I'm hungry and I'm thirsty,' Navarro said plaintively. It was half an hour before dawn.

'I am deeply moved by your sufferings,' Hamilton said. 'What's a damned sight more important is that you're alive. I didn't want to depress anyone any more than we already were by saying what was in my mind, but I didn't really think we'd see the night out.'

Ramon said: 'And how could that have been?'

'Quite simple, really. Lots of ways. With a small cannon, a rocket launcher, any kind of anti-aircraft gun or a mortar. They could have directed two or three very nasty pounds of high explosive straight through this open doorway. Maybe the shrapnel would not have got us all, but the concussion in this confined space would have finished us off. Or they could have crawled over the grain store roof from the back and lobbed in a few grenades or a stick or so of blasting powder. The effect would have been the same. Maybe they didn't have any of those materials to hand, which I don't for a moment believe—Von Manteuffel lugs around with him enough weaponry and artillery for an armoured battalion. Maybe the idea just didn't occur to them, which I don't believe either. I think that Von Manteuffel believes, as he has reason to, that we are dangerous in the dark and is waiting for daylight before moving in for the kill.'

Serrano said unhappily: 'It will be daylight quite soon.'

'It will, won't it?' In the first faint glimmering of light Maria, Serrano and Silver stared at Hamilton without comprehension as he extracted the camera from his haversack, opened it, released the flap to display the transceiver, extended an aerial and spoke into the microphone.

'Night-watch,' Hamilton said. 'Night-watch.'

The speaker crackled and the reply was immediate.

'We have you, Night-watch.'

'Now.'

'Now it is. How many vultures?'

'Thirty. Forty. A guess.'

'Repeat after me: Stay under cover. Napalm.'

'Stay under cover. Napalm.' Hamilton switched off. 'Useful, no? Very thoughtful is Colonel Diaz.'

'Napalm!' Ramon said.

'You heard the man.'

'But napalm!'

'Very tough, those airborne commandos. But, no, they don't use it directly. They've no intention of dropping the stuff on us. They ring the area. Not a new technique but very intimidating.'

Hamilton made another switch on the camera and a faint bleeping sound could be heard.

'Homing signal,' Ramon explained to no-one in particular. 'How else do you think they'd ever locate this place?'

'You've got everything organized, haven't you?' Maria sounded slightly bitter. 'Never thought to tell us, did you?'

'Why should I?' Hamilton said indifferently. 'Nobody ever tells me anything.'

'How long will they take to get here?'

'Twenty minutes. No more.'

'And dawn is in about the same time?'

'About.'

'It's starting to get light already. They could still attack before your friends get here.'

'Most unlikely. In the first place, it'll take Von Manteuffel and his minions some time to get organized and if we can't hold them off for a few minutes after that then we've no right to be here in the first place. Secondly, as soon as they hear the sound of the helicopter engines they're going to forget all about us.'

It was becoming quite light now but still the courtyard remained deserted. If Von Manteuffel and his men were preparing to launch an attack they were being extremely discreet about it.

By and by Ramon said: 'Engines. I can hear them now. They're coming in from the south.'

'I don't hear them myself, but if you say they're coming in, then they're coming in. Do you see what I see, Ramon?'

'Yes, indeed. I see a man on the roof of their mess hall with a pair of binoculars to his eyes. He must have good hearing, too. The legs?'

'If you would.'

In his typical one-sweep movement Ramon lifted his rifle

and squeezed the trigger. The man with the binoculars collapsed to the roof then, after some seconds, scuttled crab-wise away on two hands and a knee, dragging a useless leg behind him.

Hamilton said: 'Our friend, General Von Manteuffel, must, as they say, be losing his cool or he wouldn't have taken a stupid liberty like that. I don't think we'll be seeing any more sky-watchers.' He paused. 'I can hear them now.'

The sound of the aero-engines was now unmistakable and increased rapidly in strength as the craft approached: finally, the rackety clamour of the engines reached an almost intolerable pitch as three large gunships began to descend between the reverberating walls of the cliff-sides.

Hamilton said: 'Inside, I think.'

Maria paused in the doorway. 'Okay to look?'

Hamilton pushed her roughly inside and behind a wooden partition where he joined her.

'Napalm, you ninny. Some of that stuff could fly loose.'

'Rockets? Bombs?'

'Jesus! This is an historic monument.'

Moments later, almost having to shout to make herself heard over the clamour, she said: 'That awful smell.'

'Napalm.'

'Shouldn't we—shouldn't we go out and help them?'

'Help them? We'd only be in their way. Believe me, those lads don't require help of any kind. And has it occurred to you that they'd probably mow us down before we got three paces beyond that doorway? They don't know who we are and airborne commandos have the odd habit of shooting you first and asking who you are afterwards. A little discretion and patience until peace and calm reign again.'

The peace and calm came within two minutes. The sound of the helicopter engines died away. A klaxon sounded, presumably to indicate an all-clear. Not one shot had been fired.

Hamilton said: 'I think the intrepid Captain Hamilton and his gallant crew may now safely risk a peek outside.' They filed out through the open doorway.

Three gunships stood in the courtyard before the ziggurat. The ruins of the ancient city were ringed with smoke from the still burning napalm. At least fifty commandos, looking very tough and very competent and certainly armed to the teeth, had their guns trained on about three dozen of Von Manteuffel's followers, while four commandos, one of them carrying a carton of handcuffs which had been brought along for the purpose, moved along them securing their wrists behind their backs. In the forefront of the captives was Von Manteuffel himself, already handcuffed.

As Hamilton and the others reached the centre of the courtyard an Army officer advanced to meet them.

'Mr Hamilton?' he said. 'Major Ramirez. At your service.'

'You have already been of more than enough service.' They shook hands. 'We are most grateful. That really was efficient.'

'My men are disappointed,' Ramirez said. 'We had expected a rather more—ah—challenging training exercise. You wish to leave now?'

'An hour, if we may.' Hamilton pointed to Von Manteuffel. 'I'd like to speak to that man.'

Von Manteuffel was brought forward between two soldiers. His face was grey and without expression.

Hamilton said: 'Major, this is Major-General Wolfgang Von Manteuffel of the S.S.'

'The last of the infamous Nazi war-time criminals, no? I do not have to shake hands?'

'No.' Hamilton looked consideringly at Von Manteuffel. 'You have, of course, murdered Colonel Spaatz. And Hiller. Along, of course, with Dr Huston, his daughter, scores of Muscias and God knows how many others. To every road there is an end. With your permission, Major, there are a couple of things I would like to show Von Manteuffel.'

Accompanied by a group of soldiers armed with shovels, powerful electric torches and two large battery-powered flood-lamps, they made their way towards the base of the ziggurat.

'This ziggurat is unique,' Hamilton said. 'Every other known one is solid throughout. This one has been hollowed out and honeycombed like the great Egyptian ones. Please follow me.'

He led them along a winding, crumbling passageway until they came to a low, vaulted cavern, smooth-walled, with no further passage-way leading from it. The floor was deeply covered with broken fragments of rock and a great deal of gravel to a depth of between one and two feet. Hamilton spoke to Ramirez and indicated a particular area: eight soldiers with shovels immediately began to excavate this area. In a short time an area of about six feet by six had been cleared to reveal a square slab of stone with

126

an inset iron ring at either end. Crowbars were inserted into the rings and the slab, not without some considerable difficulty, lifted clear.

A shallow flight of stairs led down from the opening in the cavern floor. They moved down these, along a rough-hewn passage and halted before a heavy wooden door

Hamilton said: 'Well, Serrano, this is where you come into your own. As for you, Von Manteuffel, let your last reflections on earth be the most ironic you've ever had. You'd have given your heart and your soul—if you ever had one—for what lies beyond that door but you sat atop it all those years and never dreamed it was there.'

He paused, as if deep in thought, then said: 'It's a mite dark in there. There are no windows or lights. If you would be so kind, Major, as to have your men switch on all torches and floodlamps. I'm afraid the air will also be a bit musty, but it won't kill you. Ramon, Navarro, give me a hand with this door.'

The door proved to be reluctant to yield, but with a sepulchral creaking sound, yield it eventually did. Hamilton took one of the floodlights and passed through, the others crowding close behind.

The large square cavern was hewn from the solid rock. All four sides had stepped rock shelves cut into them to a depth of fifteen inches. The spectacle was astonishing, far beyond any belief: the entire cavern gleamed and glittered with thousands upon thousands of artifacts in solid gold.

There were bowls, crocks, crockery, all in solid gold. There were helmets, shields, plaques, necklets, busts and figurines, all in solid gold. There were bells, flutes, ocarinos, rope-chains, vases, breast-plates, open-work head-dresses, filigree masks and knives, all in solid gold. There were monkeys, alligators, snakes, eagles and condors, pelicans and vultures and innumerable jaguars, all in solid gold. And for good measure there were half a dozen open boxes, sparkling and glittering with an untold fortune in precious stones, more than half of them emeralds. It was a treasure house inconceivably far beyond the dreams of avarice.

It seemed as if the awed silence would last for ever. Serrano, at last, was the first to speak.

'The lost treasure of the Indies. The El Dorado of a million dreams. The Spanish always believed that some vanished tribe had taken with them a huge treasure trove such as this: mankind has believed in the myth ever since and thousands have lost their lives in the search for the El Dorado. But it was no myth, no myth.'

Serrano, it was clear, was scarcely capable of believing the evidence of his eyes.

'It was a myth, all right,' Hamilton said. 'But the golden treasure was there all right but everybody looked for it in the wrong place—up in the Guianas. And they all looked for the wrong thing—they thought it was royal Inca gold. But it wasn't. The people who made those were the Quimbaya of the Cauca valley, the greatest masters of the goldsmith's art in history. For them gold had no commercial value, it was solely a thing of beauty.'

'And the Spaniards would have melted the lot and sent it back to Spain in ingot form. Mr Hamilton, you have done the world of art an immeasurable service. And you were the only non-Indian alive who knew of this. You could have been the richest man alive.'

Hamilton shrugged. 'Once a Quimbaya, always a Quimbaya.'

Ramirez said: 'What will become of this?'

'It is to be a national museum. The rightful owners, the Muscias, will return and become the custodians. Few people, I'm afraid, will ever see this—just accredited scholars from all over the world and but a few of those at a time. The Brazilian government—who don't even know the location of this place yet—is determined that the Muscias, what's left of them, will not be destroyed by civilization.'

Hamilton looked at Von Manteuffel who was gazing, trance-like, at the immense fortune that had lain beneath his feet. He was stunned. But then so, too, was everyone else.

Hamilton said: 'Von Manteuffel.' Von Manteuffel turned his head slowly and looked at him like a sightless man.

'Come. I have one last thing to show you.'

Hamilton led the way into another, much smaller cavern. Side by side at the far end lay two stone sarcophagi. Above each was a plain pine board with poker-burnt inscriptions.

Hamilton said: 'A friend of mine did those, Von Manteuffel. Jim Clinton. Remember Jim Clinton? You should. After all, you murdered him shortly afterwards. Read them. Read them aloud.'

Still in the same odd sightless fashion Von Manteuffel looked slowly around, looked at Hamilton, and read: 'Dr Hannibal Huston. R.I.P.'

'And the other?' Hamilton said.

'Lucy Huston Hamilton. Beloved wife of John Hamilton. R.I.P.'

Everyone stared at Hamilton. Shocked comprehension came slowly but it came.

Von Manteuffel said: 'I am a dead man.'

Hamilton, with Ramon and Navarro, Von Manteuffel and the others trudging along closely behind, made their way to a helicopter which was parked at the edge of the courtyard only yards from the rim of the plateau. Suddenly Von Manteuffel, wrists still handcuffed behind his back, ran towards the edge of the cliff. Ramon started after him, but Hamilton caught him by the arm.

'Let him be. You heard what he said. He's a dead man.'

ALISTAIR MACLEAN

Night Without End

To Bunty

CONTENTS

CHAPTER ONE

MONDAY MIDNIGHT

It was Jackstraw who heard it first—it was always Jackstraw, whose hearing was an even match for his phenomenal eyesight, who heard things first. Tired of having my exposed hands alternately frozen, I had dropped my book, zipped my sleeping-bag up to the chin and was drowsily watching him carving figurines from a length of inferior narwhal tusk when his hands suddenly fell still and he sat quite motionless. Then, unhurriedly as always, he dropped the piece of bone into the coffee-pan that simmered gently by the side of our oil-burner stove—curio collectors paid fancy prices for what they imagined to be the dark ivory of fossilized elephant tusks—rose and put his ear to the ventilation shaft, his eyes remote in the unseeing gaze of a man lost in listening. A couple of seconds were enough.

'Aeroplane,' he announced casually.

'Aeroplane!' I propped myself up on an elbow and stared at him. 'Jackstraw, you've been hitting the methylated spirits again.'

'Indeed, no, Dr Mason.' The blue eyes, so incongruously at variance with the swarthy face and the broad Eskimo cheekbones, crinkled into a smile: coffee was Jackstraw's strongest tipple and we both knew it. 'I can hear it plainly now. You must come and listen.'

'No thanks.' It had taken me fifteen minutes to thaw out the frozen condensation in my sleeping-bag, and I was just beginning to feel warm for the first time. Heaven only knew that the presence of a plane in the heart of that desolate ice plateau was singular enough—in the four months since our I.G.Y. station had been set up this was the first time we had had any contact, however indirectly, with the world and the civilization that lay so unimaginably beyond our horizons—but it wasn't going to help either the plane or myself if I got my feet frozen again. I lay back and stared up through our two plate glass skylights: but as always they were completely opaque, covered with a thick coating

135

of rime and dusting of snow. I looked away from the skylights across to where Joss, our young Cockney radioman, was stirring uneasily in his sleep, then back to Jackstraw.

'Still hear it?'

'Getting louder all the time, Dr Mason. Louder and closer.'

I wondered vaguely—vaguely and a trifle irritably, for this was our world, a tightly-knit, compact little world, and visitors weren't welcome—what plane it could be. A met. plane from Thule possibly. Possibly, but unlikely: Thule was all of six hundred miles away, and our own weather reports went there three times a day. Or perhaps a Strategic Air Command bomber testing out the DEW-line—the American's distant early warning radar system—or even some civilian proving flight on a new trans-polar route. Or maybe some base plane from down by God-thaab——

'Dr Mason!' Jackstraw's voice was quick, urgent. 'It's in trouble, I think. It's circling us—lower and closer all the time. A big plane, I'm sure: many motors.'

'Damn!' I said feelingly. I reached out for the silk gloves that always hung at night above my head, pulled them on, unzipped my sleeping-bag, swore under my breath as the freezing air struck at my shivering skin, and grabbed for my clothes. Half an hour only since I had put them off, but already they were stiff, awkward to handle and abominably cold—it was a rare day indeed when the temperature inside the cabin rose above freezing point. But I had them on—long underwear, woollen shirt, breeches, silk-lined woollen parka, two pairs of socks and my felt cabin shoes—in thirty seconds flat. In latitude 72.40 north, 8,000 feet up on the Greenland ice-cap, self-preservation makes for a remarkable turn of speed. I crossed the cabin to where no more than a nose showed through a tiny gap in a sleeping-bag.

'Wake up, Joss.' I shook him until he reached out a hand and pushed the hood off his dark tousled head. 'Wake up, boy. It looks as if we might need you.'

'What—what's the trouble?' He rubbed the sleep from his eyes and stared up at the chronometer above his head. 'Midnight! I've been asleep only half an hour.'

'I know. Sorry. But get a move on.' I recrossed the cabin, passed by the big R.C.A. transmitter and stove, and halted in front of the instrument table. The register showed the wind ENE., velocity 15 knots—near enough 17 miles per hour, but on a night like this, with the ice-crystals and drift lifting off the ice-cap, clogging and slowing up the anemometer cups, the true speed was probably half as much again. And the pen of the alcohol thermograph was running evenly along the red circle of 40 degrees below zero—72 degrees of frost. I thought of the evil combination of these two factors of wind and cold and felt my skin crawl.

Already Jackstraw was silently climbing into his furs. I did the same—caribou trousers and parka with reindeer fur trimmed hood, all beautifully tailored by Jackstraw's wife—sealskin boots, woollen mittens and reindeer gloves. I could hear the plane quite clearly now, and so too, I could see, did Joss. The deep even throb of its motors was plain even above the frantic rattling of the anemometer cups.

'It's—it's an aeroplane!' You could see that he was still trying to convince himself.

'What did you think it was—one of your precious London double-deckers?' I slipped snow-mask and goggles round my neck and picked up a torch from the shelf beside the stove: it was kept there to keep the dry batteries from freezing. 'Been circling for the past two or three minutes. Jackstraw thinks it's in trouble, and I agree.'

Joss listened.

'Engines sound O.K. to me.'

'And to me. But engine failure is only one of a dozen possible reasons.'

'But why circle here?'

'How the devil should I know? Probably because he can see our lights—the only lights, at a guess, in 50,000 square miles. And if he has to put down, which God forbid, he stands his only chance of survival if he puts down near some human habitation.'

'Heaven help them,' Joss said soberly. He added something else, but I didn't wait to hear. I wanted to get up top as quickly as possible.

To leave our cabin, we had to use a trap-door, not an ordinary door. Our cabin, a prefabricated, sectioned structure that had been hauled up from the coast on tractor sleds during the month of July, was deep-sunk in a great oblong hole that had been gouged out from the surface of the ice-cap, so that only the top few inches of its flat roof projected above ground level. The trap-door, hinged at both ends so that it could open either upwards or downwards, was reached by a short steep flight of steps.

137

I climbed the first two of these, took down the wooden mallet that hung there permanently by the wall and pounded round the already bruised and splintered edges of the trap to loosen the ice that held it locked fast. This was an almost invariable routine: whenever the trap had previously been opened for any length of time at all, the layer of warm air that always lay under the roof seeped slowly out, melting the surrounding snow—which promptly turned to ice when the trap was closed again.

Tonight the ice cracked easily. I got my shoulder under the trap, levered upwards against the accumulated drift of snow above, and scrambled out.

I was prepared for what awaited me up top—the gasping, panic-stricken feeling of suffocation as the warm air was sucked from my lungs by that deadly, numbing cold—but even so I wasn't sufficiently prepared. The wind speed was far higher than I had feared. Bent double and coughing violently, breathing shallowly to avoid frosting my lungs, I turned my back to the wind, breathed into my reindeer gloves, slipped on my snow mask and goggles and straightened. Jackstraw was already standing by my side.

The wind on the ice-cap never howled or shrieked. It moaned, instead, a low-pitched, unutterably eerie ululation: a requiem for the damned, if ever there was one, the agony of some soul lost in torment. The same moan had driven men mad before now: less than two months previously I had had to send our tractor mechanic, a completely broken youngster who had lost all contact with the last shadow of reality, back to our Uplavnik base. The wind had done that to him.

Tonight its desolate threnody boomed and faded, boomed and faded in the lower registers of sound with an intensity which I had seldom heard, while its fingers plucked at the tightly strung guy ropes of the radio antenna and instrument shelters to provide its own whistling obbligato of unearthly music. But I was in no mood then to listen to its music, and, indeed, that sepulchral wailing was not the dominant sound on the ice-cap that night.

The throbbing roar of big aero engines, surging and receding as the wind gusted and fell away, like surf on some distant shore, was very close now. The sound lay to windward of us at that moment, and we turned to face it, but we were blind. Although the sky was overcast, there was no snow that night—at any time, heavy snowfalls, strangely enough, are all but unknown on the

138

Greenland ice-cap—but the air was full of millions of driving, needle-pointed ice spicules that swept towards us out of the impenetrable darkness to the east, clogging up our goggles in a matter of seconds and stinging the narrow exposed area of my face between mask and goggles like a thousand infuriated hornets. A sharp, exquisite pain, a pain that vanished almost in the moment of arrival as the countless sub-zero spicules dug deep with their anaesthetizing needles and drove all sensation from the skin. But I knew this ominous absence of feeling all too well. Once again I turned my back to the wind, kneaded the deadened flesh with mittened hands till the blood came throbbing back, then pulled my snow-mask higher still.

The plane was flying in an anti-clockwise direction, following, it seemed, the path of an irregular oval, for the sound of its motors faded slightly as it curved round to north and west. But within thirty seconds it was approaching again, in a swelling thunder of sound, to the south-west—to the leeward of us, that was—and I could tell from Jackstraw's explosive ejaculation of sound, muffled behind his mask, that he had seen it at the same moment as myself.

It was less than half a mile distant, no more than five hundred feet above the ice-cap, and during the five seconds it remained inside my line of vision I felt my mouth go dry and my heart begin to thud heavily in my chest. No S.A.C. bomber this, nor a Thule met. plane, both with crews highly trained in the grim craft of Arctic survival. That long row of brightly illuminated cabin windows could belong to only one thing—a trans-Atlantic or trans-Polar airliner.

'You saw it, Dr Mason?' Jackstraw's snow-mask was close to my ear.

'I saw it.' It was all I could think to say. But what I was seeing then was not the plane, now again vanished into the flying ice and drift, but the inside of the plane, with the passengers—God, how many passengers, fifty, seventy?—sitting in the cosy security of their pressurized cabin with an air-conditioned temperature of 70° F., then the crash, the tearing, jagged screeching that set the teeth on edge as the thin metal shell ripped along its length and the tidal wave of that dreadful cold, 110 degrees below cabin temperature, swept in and engulfed the survivors, the dazed, the injured, the unconscious and the dying as they sat or lay crumpled in the wreckage of the seats, clad only in thin suits and dresses. . . .

The plane had completed a full circuit and was coming round again. If anything, it was even closer this time, at least a hundred feet lower, and it seemed to have lost some speed. It might have been doing 120, perhaps 130 miles an hour, I was no expert in these things, but for that size of plane, so close to the ground, it seemed a dangerously low speed. I wondered just how effective the pilot's windscreen wipers would be against these flying ice spicules.

And then I forgot all about that, forgot all about everything except the desperate, urgent need for speed. Just before the plane had turned round to the east again and so out of the line of our blinded vision, it had seemed to dip and at the same instant two powerful lights stabbed out into the darkness, the one lancing straight ahead, a narrow powerful beam glittering and gleaming with millions of sparkling diamond points of flame as the ice-crystals in the air flashed across its path, the other, a broader fan of light, pointing downwards and only slightly ahead, its oval outline flitting across the frozen snow like some flickering will o' the wisp. I grabbed Jackstraw's arm and put my head close to his.

'He's going to land! He's looking for a place to put down. Get the dogs, harness them up.' We had a tractor, but heaven only knew how long it would have taken to start it on a night like this. 'I'll give you a hand as soon as I can.'

He nodded, turned and was lost to sight in a moment. I turned too, cursed as my face collided with the slatted sides of the instrument shelter, then jumped for the hatch, sliding down to the floor of the cabin on back and arms without bothering to use the steps. Joss already completely clad in his furs but with the hood of his parka hanging over his shoulders, was just emerging from the food and fuel tunnel which led off from the other end of the cabin, his arms loaded with equipment.

'Grab all the warm clothing you can find, Joss,' I told him quickly. I was trying to think as quickly and coherently as I was talking, to figure out everything that we might require, but it wasn't easy, that intense cold numbed the mind almost as much as it did the body. 'Sleeping-bags, blankets, spare coats, shirts, it doesn't matter what they are. Shove them into a couple of gunny sacks.'

'You think they're going to land, sir?' Curiosity, anticipation, horror—each struggled for supremacy in the thin, dark intelligent face. 'You really think so?'

'I think they're going to try. What have you got there?'

'Fire bombs, a couple of Pyrenes.' He dumped them by the stove. 'Hope they're not solid.'

'Good boy. And a couple of the tractor extinguishers—the Nu-Swifts, G-1000, I think.' A great help these little things are going to be, I thought, if several thousand gallons of petrol decides to go up in flames. 'Fireaxes, crowbars, canes, the homing spool—for heaven's sake don't forget the homing spool—and the searchlight battery. Be sure to wrap that up well.'

'Bandages?'

'No need. Seventy degrees of frost will freeze blood and seal a wound quicker than any bandage. But bring the morphia kit. Any water in these two buckets?'

'Full. But more ice than water.'

'Put them on the stove—and don't forget to turn out the stove and both the lights before you leave.' Incongruously enough, we who could survive in the Arctic only by virtue of fire, feared it above all else. 'Pile the rest of the stuff up by the instrument shelter.'

I found Jackstraw, working only by the feeble light of his torch, outside the lean-to drift-walled shelter that we had built for the dogs from empty packing cases and an old tractor tarpaulin. He appeared to be fighting a losing battle in the centre of a milling pack of snarling, yelping dogs, but the appearance was illusion only: already he had four of the dogs off the tethering cable and the sledge tracelines snapped into their harness.

'How's it coming?' I shouted.

'Easy.' I could almost see the crinkling grin behind the snow mask. 'I caught most of them asleep, and Balto is a great help—he's in a very bad temper at being woken up.'

Balto was Jackstraw's lead dog—a huge, 90-pound, half-wolf, half-Siberian, direct descendant of, and named for the famous dog that had trekked with Amundsen, and who later, in the terrible winter of '25, his sledge-driver blind behind him, had led his team through driving blizzards and far sub-zero cold to bring the life-giving anti-toxin into the diphtheria-stricken town of Nome, Alaska. Jackstraw's Balto was another such: powerful, intelligent, fiercely loyal to his master—although not above baring his wolf's fangs as he made a token pass at him from time to time —and, above all, like all good lead dogs, a ruthless disciplinarian with his team-mates. He was exercising that disciplinary authority now—snarling, pushing and none-too-gently nipping the recalcitrant and the slow-coaches, quelling insubordination in its earliest infancy.

'I'll leave you to it, then. I'll get the searchlight.' I made off towards the mound of snow that loomed high to the westward of the cabin, broke step and listened. There was no sound to be heard, nothing but the low-pitched moan of the wind on the ice-cap, the eternal rattling of the anemometer cups. I turned back to Jackstraw, my face bent against the knifing wind.

'The plane—have you heard the plane, Jackstraw. I can't hear a thing.'

Jackstraw straightened, pulled off his parka hood and stood still, hands cupped to his ears. Then he shook his head briefly and replaced the hood.

'My God!' I looked at him. 'Maybe they've crashed already.'

Again the shake of the head.

'Why not?' I demanded. 'On a night like this you wouldn't hear a thing if they crashed half a mile downwind.'

'I'd have felt it, Dr Mason.'

I nodded slowly, said nothing. He was right, of course. The frozen surface of this frozen land transmitted vibration like a tuning-fork. Last July, seventy miles inland, we had distinctly felt the vibration of the ice-cap as an iceberg had broken off from a glacier in a hanging valley and toppled into the fjord below. Maybe the pilot had lost his bearings, maybe he was flying in ever-widening circles trying to pick up our lights again, but at least there was hope yet.

I hurried across to where the tractor, sheeted in tarpaulin, lay close in to the high snow wall that had been cut down the middle of a drift. It took me a couple of minutes to clear away the accumulated snow at one end and wriggle in under the tarpaulin. There was no question of trying to lift it—its impregnated oils had frozen solid and it would have cracked and torn under any pressure.

The searchlight, fixed to a couple of bolts on the tractor bonnet, was held down by two quick release butterfly nuts. In these latitudes, quick-release was a misnomer: the nuts invariably froze after even the briefest exposure. The accepted practice was to remove one's gloves and close mittened hands round the nuts until body heat warmed and expanded them enough to permit unscrewing. But there was no time for that tonight: I tapped the bolts with a spanner from the tool box and the steel pins, made brittle by the intense cold, sheared as if made from the cheapest cast iron.

I crawled out at the foot of the tarpaulin, searchlight clutched under one arm, and as soon as I straightened I heard it again—the roar of aero engines, closing rapidly. They sounded very near, very low, but I wasted no time trying to locate the plane. Head lowered against the wind and the needle-sharp lances of the flying ice, I felt rather than saw my way back to the cabin hatch and was brought up short by Jackstraw's steadying hand. He and Joss were busy loading equipment aboard the sledge and lashing it down, and as I stooped to help them something above my head fizzled and spluttered into a blinding white glare that threw everything into a harsh black and white relief of frozen snow and impenetrable shadow. Joss, remembering what I had completely forgotten—that dousing our cabin lights would have robbed the pilot of his beacon—had ignited a magnesium flare in the slats of the instrument shelter.

We all turned as the plane came into our vision again, to the south, and it was at once apparent why we had lost all sight and sound of it. The pilot must have made a figure of eight turn out in the darkness, had reversed his approach circle, and was flying from east to west: less than two hundred feet up, undercarriage still retracted, it passed within a couple of hundred yards of us like some monstrous bird. Both headlights were now dipped, the twin beams a glitter of kaleidoscopic light in the ice-filled darkness of the sky, the twin oval pools of light, interlocking now and very bright, racing neck and neck across the snow. And then these pools, increasing as rapidly in size as they diminished in strength, slipped away to the left as the plane banked sharply to the right and came curving round clockwise to the north. I knew now what the pilot was intending and my hands clenched helplessly inside mittens and gloves. But there was nothing I could do about this.

'The antenna!' I shouted. 'Follow out the line of the antenna.' I stooped and gave the sledge its initial shove as Jackstraw shouted at Balto. Joss was by my side, head close to mine.

'What's happening? Why are we——'

'He's coming down this time. I'm sure of it. To the north.'

'The north?' Not even the snow-mask could hide the horror in his voice. 'He'll kill himself. He'll kill all of them. The hummocks——'

143

'I know.' The land to the north-east was broken and uneven, the ice raised up by some quirk of nature into a series of tiny hillocks, ten, twenty feet high, tiny but the only ones within a hundred miles. 'But he's going to do it, all the same. A belly-landing with the wheels up. That's why he reversed his circle. He wants to land upwind to give himself the minimum stalling ground speed.'

'He could land to the south, into the wind.' Joss sounded almost desperate. 'It's a billiard-table there.'

'He could, but he won't.' I had to shout the words to make myself heard above the wind. 'He's nobody's fool. He knows if he lands to windward of us, even a hundred yards to windward, the chances of finding our lights, our cabin, in this weather just don't exist. He's got to land upwind. He's just *got* to.'

There was a long silence as we staggered forward, head and shoulders bent almost to waist level against the wind and ice-filled drift, then Joss moved close again.

'Maybe he'll see the hummocks in time. Maybe he can——'

'He'll never see them,' I said flatly. 'Flying into this stuff he can't possibly see a hundred yards in front of him.'

The radio antenna, rime-coated now to almost fifty times its normal size, sagging deeply and swaying pendulum-like in the wind between each pair of fourteen-foot poles that supported it, stretched away almost 250 feet to the north. We were following the line of this, groping our way blindly from pole to pole and almost at the end of the line, when the roar of the aircraft engines, for the last few seconds no more than a subdued murmur in the night as the wind carried the sound from us, suddenly swelled and increased to a deafening crescendo as I shouted a warning to the others and flung myself flat on the ground: the huge dark shape of the airliner swept directly over us even as I fell. I would have sworn, at the time, that I could have reached out and touched it with my hand, but it must have cleared us by at least ten feet—the antenna poles, we later discovered, were undamaged.

Like a fool, I immediately leapt to my feet to try to get a bearing on the vanishing plane and was literally blown head over heels by the tremendous slipstream from the four great propellers, slid helplessly across the frozen crust of the snow and fetched up on my back almost twenty feet from where I had been standing. Cursing, bruised and not a little dazed, I got to my feet again, started off in the direction where I could hear the dogs barking and howling in a paroxysm of fear and excitement, then stopped abruptly and stood quite still. The engines had died, all four of them had died in an instant, and that could mean only one thing: the airliner was about to touch down.

Even with the realization a jarring vibration, of a power and intensity far beyond anything I had expected, reached my feet through the frozen crust of the ice-cap. No ordinary touchdown that, I knew, not even for a belly-landing: the pilot must have overestimated his height and set his ship down with force enough to crumple the fuselage, to wreck the plane on the spot.

But he hadn't. I was prone on the frozen snow again, ear pressed hard against it, and I could half hear, half feel, a kind of hissing tremor which could only have come from the fuselage, no doubt already splintered and ripped, sliding over the ice, gouging a furrowed path through it. How long this sound continued, I couldn't be sure—six seconds, perhaps eight. And then, all at once, came another earth tremor, severer by far than the first, and I heard clearly, even above the gale, the sudden sharp sound of the crash, the grinding tearing scream of metal being twisted and tortured out of shape. And then, abruptly, silence—a silence deep and still and ominous, and the sound of the wind in the darkness was no sound at all.

Shakily, I rose to my feet. It was then I realized for the first time that I had lost my snow-mask—it must have been ripped off as I had rolled along the ground. I brought out my torch from under my parka—it was always kept there as even a dry battery could freeze and give no light at all if the temperature fell low enough—and probed around in the darkness. But there was no sign of it, the wind could have carried it a hundred yards away by this time. A bad business, indeed, but there was no help for it. I didn't like to think what my face would be like by the time I arrived back at the cabin.

Joss and Jackstraw were still trying to quieten the dogs when I rejoined them.

'You all right, sir?' Joss asked. He took a step closer. 'Good lord you've lost your mask!'

'I know. It doesn't matter.' It did matter, for already I could feel the burning sensation in my throat and lungs every time I breathed. 'Did you get a bearing on that plane?'

'Roughly. Due east, I should say.'

'Jackstraw?'

'A little north of east, I think.' He stretched out his hand, pointing straight into the eye of the wind.

'We'll go east.' Somebody had to make the decision, somebody had to be wrong, and it might as well be me. 'We'll go east—Joss, how long is that spool?'

'Four hundred yards. More or less.'

'So. Four hundred yards, then due north. That plane is bound to have left tracks in the snow: with luck, we'll cut across them. Let's hope to heaven it did touch down less than four hundred yards from here.'

I took the end of the line from the spool, went to the nearest antenna pole, broke off the four-foot-long flag-like frost feathers —weird growths of the crystal aggregates of rime that streamed out almost horizontally to leeward—and made fast the end of the line round the pole. I really made it fast—our lives depended on that line, and without it we could never find our way back to the antenna, and so eventually to the cabin, through the pitch-dark confusion of that gale-ridden arctic night. There was no possibility of retracing steps through the snow: in that intense cold, the rime crusted snow was compacted into a frozen *névé* that was but one degree removed from ice, of an iron-hard consistency that would show nothing less than the crimp marks of a five-ton tractor.

We started off at once, with the wind almost in our faces, but slightly to the left. I was in the lead, Jackstraw came behind with the dogs and Joss brought up the rear, unreeling the line from the homing spool against the pressure of the return winding spring.

Without my mask, that blinding suffocating drift was a nightmare, a cruel refinement of contrasting torture where the burning in my throat contrasted with the pain of my freezing face for dominance in my mind. I was coughing constantly in the superchilled air, no matter how I tried to cover mouth and nose with a gloved hand, no matter how shallowly I breathed to avoid frosting my lungs.

The devil of it was, shallow breathing was impossible. We were running now, running as fast as the ice-glazed slipperiness of the surface and our bulky furs would allow, for to unprotected people exposed to these temperatures, to that murderous drift-filled gale, life or death was simply a factor of speed, of the duration of exposure. Maybe the plane had ripped open or broken in

146

half, catapulting the survivors out on to the ice-cap—if there were any suvivors: for them, either immediate death as the heart failed in the near impossible task of adjusting the body to an instantaneous change of over 100° F., or death by exposure within five minutes. Or maybe they were all trapped inside, slowly freezing. How to get at them? How to transport them all back to the cabin? But only the first few to be taken could have any hope. And even if we did get them all back, how to feed them—for our own supplies were already dangerously low? And where, in heaven's name, were we going to put them all?

Jackstraw's shout checked me so suddenly that I stumbled and all but fell. I turned back, and Joss came running up.

'The end of the line?' I asked.

He nodded, flashed a torch in my face. 'Your nose and cheek— both gone. They look bad.'

Gloves off, I kneaded my face vigorously with my mittened hands until I felt the blood pounding painfully back, then took the old jersey which Jackstraw dug out from a gunny sack and wrapped it round my face. It wasn't much, but it was better than nothing.

We struck off to the north, with the wind on our right cheeks —I had no option but to gamble on the hope that the wind had neither backed nor veered—our torches probing the ground in front of us, stopping every fifteen or twenty feet to drive a pointed bamboo marker into the frozen ground. We had covered fifty yards without sighting anything, and I was just beginning to become convinced that we must still be well to the west of the plane's touchdown point and wondering what in the world we should do next when we almost literally stumbled into an eighteen inch deep, ten foot wide depression in the snow-crust of the ice-cap.

This was it, no question about that. By a one in a hundred chance we had hit on the very spot where the plane had touched down—or crashed down, if the size of the depression in that frozen snow were anything to go by. To the left, the west, the ground was virginal, unmarked—ten feet to that side and we should have missed it altogether. To the east, the deep depression shelved rapidly upwards, its smooth convexity now marred by two large gouge marks, one in the centre and one to the right of the track, as if a pair of gigantic ploughs had furrowed through the ground: part of the under fuselage must have been ripped

147

open by the impact—it would have been a wonder had it not been. Some way farther to the east, and well to the right of the main track, two other grooves, parallel and of a shallow bowl shape, had been torn in the snow. The gouge marks, plainly, of the still-racing propellers: the plane must have tilted over on its right wing just after the moment of landing.

To see all this took no longer than to sweep a torch through a swift semi-circle. I shouted to Joss to take another bundle of canes and prop up the homing spool line that led back to the antenna—if this weren't done it would drift over and be lost to sight in ten minutes—and then rejoin us: then I turned and ran after Jackstraw who had already urged his team forwards and eastwards along the track of the crashed plane.

The wind was worse than ever, the drift an almost solid wall that reduced our speed to a lurching stumble and forced us to lean far into it to maintain our balance. Two hundred yards, three hundred, and then, almost a quarter of a mile from where it had touched down we found the airliner simply by walking straight into it. It had slewed almost 90 degrees as it had come to a halt, and was lying square across its own path, still resting on even keel.

In the feeble light of my torch the airliner, even although its fuselage rested on the ground, seemed immensely high and to stretch away for a vast distance on either side, but for all its great size there was something peculiarly pathetic and forlorn about it. But this, of course, was purely subjective, the knowledge in my own mind that this crippled giant would never leave here again.

I could hear no movement, see no movement. High above my head a faint blue light seemed to glow behind some of the cabin windows but apart from that there was no sign of life at all.

CHAPTER TWO

MONDAY 1 A.M.–2 A.M.

My greatest fear had already proved groundless—there was no sign of fire anywhere, no flickering red to see, no hidden crackling to hear. It was still possible that some small tongue of flame was creeping along inside the fuselage or wings looking for the petrol or oil that would help it blaze into destructive life—and with that wind to fan the flames, destruction would have been complete—but it hardly seemed worth worrying about: and it was unlikely that any pilot cool-headed enough to turn off the ignition would have forgotten to shut down the petrol lines.

Already Jackstraw had plugged our searchlight into the dry battery and handed me the lamp. I pressed the switch, and it worked: a narrow but powerful beam good for six hundred yards in normal conditions. I swung the beam to my right, then brought it slowly forward.

Whatever colours the plane may have had originally, it was impossible to distinguish any of them now. The entire fuselage was already shrouded in a sheet of thin rimed ice, dazzling to the eye, reflecting the light with the intensity, almost, of a chromed mirror. The tail unit was intact. So, too, was the fuselage for half its length, then crumpled and torn underneath, directly opposite the spot where we stood. The left wing was tilted upwards at an angle of about five degrees above the normal—the plane wasn't on such an even keel as I had first thought. From where I stood this wing blocked off my view of the front, but just above and beyond it I saw something that made me temporarily forget the urgency of my concern for those inside and stand there, stockstill, the beam trained unwaveringly on that spot.

Even under the coating of ice the big bold lettering M.Y.T.H. was clearly visible. M.Y.T.H.! What on earth was a M.Y.T.H. airliner doing in this part of the world? The S.A.S. and K.L.M., I knew, operated trans-arctic flights from Copenhagen and Amsterdam to Winnipeg, Los Angeles and Vancouver via Sondre

Strömfjord, about an hour and a half's flying time away to the south-west on the west coast of Greenland, just on the Arctic Circle, and I was pretty sure that Pan American and Trans World operated reciprocal services on the same route. It was just barely possible that freak weather conditions had forced one of these planes far enough off course to account for its presence here, but if I was right about the M.Y.T.H., it just wasn't possible——

'I've found the door, Dr Mason.' Jackstraw had taken my arm, jerking me out of my reverie, and was pointing to a big oval door with its lowest point just at our eye-level. 'We will try these, perhaps?'

I heard the metallic clang as he lifted a couple of crowbars off the sledge, and nodded. We could only try. I set the searchlight on the snow, adjusted it on its gimbals so as to illuminate the door, took one of the crowbars and thrust it beneath the foot of the oval, the flattened end sliding easily between door and fuselage. Jackstraw did the same. We heaved together, but nothing happened. Again we heaved, and again, our feet coming clear of the ground, but the door remained immovable. To localize pressure, we concentrated on one bar, and this time we felt something giving: but it was the lever, not the door. With a pistol-shot crack, the cold-weakened crowbar snapped six inches from the end and we both landed on our backs.

Even the urgency of the moment, my almost complete lack of knowledge about planes, was no excuse. I cursed my stupidity in wasting valuable time trying to force open a massive door locked on the inside by heavy clips designed to withstand an internal pressure of many thousands of pounds, grabbed searchlight and battery, ducked round under the towering tail assembly into the full force of the wind and flying drift and moved forward till I came to the right wing.

Its tip was buried deep under the frozen snow, the airscrew blades bent back at right angles to their normal line. I thought perhaps I might try to scramble up the wing towards the fuselage and smash in one of the cabin windows, but after a couple of seconds wild slithering on the ice-sheeted wing in that gusting gale wind I gave up the idea. To maintain a foothold was quite impossible: besides, it was doubtful whether I could have smashed in a window anyway. Like the door, the windows were designed to withstand great pressures.

Stumbling, slipping, we ran round the buried tip of the wing, and clear in sight now was the ice hummock that had brought the big airliner to its sudden halt. About fifteen feet high and twenty wide at the base, it lay in the right angle formed by the front of the fuselage and the leading edge of the wing. But it wasn't the root of the wing that had absorbed the initial impact, a glance at the nose of the aircraft was enough to show that. The plane must have crashed into the ice-mound just to right of centre of the control cabin: the windscreens were smashed, the fuselage ripped open and crushed back for six or seven feet. What had happened to the pilot sitting on that side at the moment of the telescopic impact just didn't bear thinking about: but at least we had found our way in.

I set the searchlight so that its beam illuminated the wrecked control cabin, gauged the distance to the lower sill of the windscreen—it must have been fully nine feet—and jumped. My gloved hands hooked on firmly but slipped almost at once on the ice-rimed surface. I grabbed for a purchase grip on one of the windscreen pillars, felt my fingers striking against solid glass on both sides—the winscreen hadn't been as completely shattered as I had imagined—and was on the point of losing my hold altogether when Jackstraw moved forward swiftly and took my weight.

With my knees on his shoulders and a fireaxe in my hand it took me no more than two minutes to smash away the glass that clung to the pillars and the upper and lower edges. I hadn't realized that aircraft glass—toughened perspex—could be so tough, nor, when it came to clambering through into the control cabin in my bulky furs, that windscreens could be so narrow.

I landed on top of a dead man. Even in the darkness I knew he was dead. I fumbled under my parka, brought out the torch, switched it on for a couple of seconds, then put it out. It was the co-pilot, the man who had taken the full impact of the crash. He was pinned, crushed between his seat and the twisted, fractured wreckage of what had been control columns, levers and dashboard instruments: not since I had once been called out to the scene of a head-on collision between a racing motor-cyclist and a heavy truck had I seen such dreadful injuries on any man. Whatever any of the survivors, the shocked and injured survivors in the plane, must see, it mustn't be this. It was ghastly beyond description.

I turned and leaned out the windscreen. Jackstraw was directly below, cupped gloved hands shielding his eyes against the flying ice spicules as he stared upwards.

'Bring a blanket,' I shouted. 'Better, bring a full gunny sack. And the morphia kit. Then come up yourself.'

He was back in twenty seconds. I caught both sack and morphia box, placed them on the twisted cabin floor behind me, then reached out to help Jackstraw, but it wasn't necessary. Athleticism wasn't the forte of the short and stocky Greenlanders, but Jackstraw was the fittest and most agile man I had ever met. He sprang, caught the lower sill of the left windscreen in his left hand, the central pillar in the other and swung legs and body through the centre screen as if he had been doing this sort of thing all his life.

I gave him my torch to hold, rummaged in the gunny sack and dragged out a blanket. I spread it over the dead co-pilot, tucking the corners down among twisted and broken ends of metal, so that it shouldn't blow free in the icy wind that swirled and gusted through the wrecked control cabin.

'Waste of a good blanket, I suppose,' I muttered. 'But—well, it isn't pretty.'

'It isn't pretty,' Jawstraw agreed. His voice was quite steady, devoid of all inflection. 'How about this one?'

I looked across at the left-hand side of the cabin. It was almost completely undamaged and the chief pilot, still strapped in his seat and slumped against his sidescreens, seemed quite unmarked. I stripped fur glove, mitten and silk glove off my right hand, reached out and touched the forehead. We had been out of doors now for over fifteen minutes in that ferocious cold, and I would have sworn that my hand was about as cold as the human flesh could get. But I was wrong. I pulled the gloves back on and turned away, without touching him further. I wasn't carrying out any autopsies that night.

A few feet farther back we found the radio operator in his compartment. He was half-sitting, half-lying against the for'ard bulkhead of his shack where he must have been catapulted by the crash. His right hand was still clutched firmly round the handgrip of the front panel of his radio set—it must have been ripped clear off the transmitter, which didn't look as if it would ever transmit anything again.

On the bulkhead, behind his head, blood gleamed dully in the torch-light. I bent over the unconscious man—I could see that he was still breathing—removed my gloves once more and gently slid my fingers behind his head. Just as gently I withdrew them. How the hell, I thought, part hopelessly, part savagely, am I to carry out a head operation on a person with a telescoped occiput: the state he was in, I wouldn't have given a fig for his chance in the finest operating theatre in London. At the very least he would be blind for life, the sight centre must have been completely destroyed. I reached for his pulse: racing, faint, erratic to a degree. The thought came to me, a thought compounded as much of cowardice as of regret, that in all likelihood the possibility of my having to operate on him was remote, very remote. If he were to survive the inevitably rough handling that would be needed to get him out of that aircraft and then the journey back to the cabin through that ice-laden sub-zero gale it would be a miracle indeed.

It seemed unlikely that he would ever wake again. But he might, he just conceivably might, so I broached the morphia kit. Then we eased his head and neck into a more comfortable position, covered him with a blanket and left him.

Immediately behind the radio compartment was a long narrow room which extended across two-thirds of the width of the plane. A quick glance at the two chairs and collapsible bunk was enough to show that this must be the crew's rest room, and someone had been resting there at the moment of the crash. That crumpled shirt-sleeved figure on the floor must have been taken completely unawares before he had the slightest knowledge of what was happening: and he would never know now.

We found the stewardess in the pantry, lying on her left side on the floor, the outspread black hair fallen forward over her face. She was moaning softly to herself, but it wasn't the moan of one in pain. Her pulse was steady enough, but fast. Jackstraw stooped down beside me.

'Shall we lift her, Dr Mason?'

'No.' I shook my head. 'She's coming to, I think, and she can tell us far quicker than we can find out whether there's anything broken. Another blanket, and we'll let her be. Almost certainly someone much more in need of our attention.'

The door leading into the main passenger compartment was locked. At least, it appeared to be, but I was pretty certain it would never be locked under normal circumstances. Perhaps it had been warped by the impact of landing. It was no time for half-measures. Together, we took a step back, then flung all the weight of our shoulders against it. It gave suddenly, three or four inches, and at the same time we heard a sharp exclamation of pain from the other side.

'Careful!' I warned, but Jackstraw had already eased his weight. I raised my voice. 'Get back from that door, will you? We want to come in.'

We heard a meaningless mutter from the other side, followed by a low groan and the slipping shuffle of someone trying to haul himself to his feet. Then the door opened and we passed quickly inside.

The blast of hot air struck me in the face like an almost physical blow. I gasped, fought off a passing moment of weakness when my legs threatened to give under me, then recovered sufficiently to bang the door shut behind me. With the motors dead and the arctic chill striking through the thin steel of the fuselage this warmth, no matter how efficient the cabin insulation, wouldn't last long: but while it did, it might be the saving of all those who still lived. A thought struck me and, ignoring the man who stood swaying before me, one hand clutching a seat grip for support, the other rubbing at a blood-masked forehead, I turned to Jackstraw.

'Carry the stewardess in here. We'll take a chance—and it's not all that much of a chance either. There's a damned sight more hope for her in here with a broken leg than out there with only a bump on the head. Throw her blanket over the wireless operator—but whatever you do don't touch him.'

Jackstraw nodded and went out, closing the door quickly behind him. I turned to the man who still stood shakily in the aisle, still dazedly rubbing his hand, a big brown square hand matted on the back with black hair, across a bleeding forehead. He look at me for a moment, then stared down uncomprehendingly at the blood dripping on to the bright red tie and blue shirt that contrasted so oddly with the light grey gaberdine suit. He closed his eyes tightly, then shook his head to clear it.

'Sorry to ask the inevitable question.' The voice was quiet, deep, well under control. 'But—what happened?'

'You crashed,' I said shortly. 'What do you remember?'

'Nothing. Well, that is, just a bump, then a loud screeching tearing noise——'

'Then you hit the door.' I gestured at the blood stains behind

154

me. 'Sit down for a moment. You'll be all right.' I'd lost interest in him and was staring down the length of the cabin. I'd expected to see most of the seats wrenched off their bases, but instead they were all there exactly as they should have been, three wide to the left of me, two to the right, the seats in the front half facing aft, those to the rear facing forward. More than that, I had expected to see people, injured, broken and moaning people, flung all over the seats and aisles: but the big passenger compartment seemed almost empty, and there wasn't a sound to be heard.

But it wasn't quite empty, not quite. Apart from the man by my side there were, I found, nine others altogether. Two men lay in the front part of the aisle. One, a big broad shouldered man with curly dark hair, was propped up on an elbow, staring around him with a puzzled frown on his face; near him, lying on his side, was a smaller, much older man, but all I could see of him were a few wisps of black hair plastered across a bald head, a Glenurquhart plaid jacket that seemed a couple of sizes too big for him and the loudest check tie it had ever been my misfortune to see. It seemed obvious that they had been sitting together in the left-hand seat adjacent to them and had been flung out when the plane crashed into the ice mound and slewed violently to one side.

In the seat beyond that, also on the left, a man sat by himself. My first reaction was surprise that he, too, hadn't been hurled into the aisle, but then I saw that he was awake and fully conscious. He was sitting rigidly in his seat, pressed in hard against the window, legs braced on the floor, holding on with both hands to the table fixed to the seat in front: tautened tendons ridged the backs of his thin white hands, and his knuckles gleamed in the torch-light. I lifted the beam higher, saw that he was wearing a close-fitting clerical collar.

'Relax, Reverend,' I said soothingly. 'Terra firma, once more, and this is far as you are going.' He said nothing, just stared at me through rimless glasses, so I left him. He seemed unhurt.

Four people sat in the right-hand side of the front part of the plane, each one in a window seat; two women, two men. One of the women was fairly elderly, but so heavily made-up and with her hair so expensively dyed and marcelled that I couldn't have guessed her age within ten years: her face, somehow, seemed vaguely familiar. She was awake, and looking slowly about her, her eyes empty of understanding. So, too, was the woman in the next seat, an even more expensive looking creature with a

155

mink coat flung cape-wise over her shoulders to show a simple green jersey dress that I suspected cost a small fortune: she was about twenty-five I guessed, and with her blonde hair, grey eyes and perfect features would have been one of the most beautiful women I had ever seen, if it weren't for the overfull and rather sulky mouth. Maybe, I thought uncharitably, she remembered to do something about that mouth when she was fully awake. But right then, she wasn't fully awake: none of them was, they all behaved as if they were being dragged up from the depths of an exhausting sleep.

Still more asleep than awake were the other two men in the front, one, a big, burly, high-coloured man of about fifty-five, with the gleaming thick white hair and moustache of the carica-ture of a Dixie colonel: the other was a thin elderly man, his face heavily lined, unmistakably Jewish.

Not bad going so far, I thought with relief. Eight people, and only one cut forehead among the lot of them—the perfect argument, if ever there was one, for having all the seats in a plane face towards the rear. No question but that they all owed, if not their lives, at least their immunity to injury to the fact that their high-backed seats had almost completely cushioned and absorbed the shock of impact.

And the two passengers in the rear end of the cabin were the perfect argument for not having the seats face forward. The first I came to—a brown-haired young girl of about eighteen or nineteen, wearing a belted raincoat—was lying on the floor between two seats. She was stirring, and as I put my hands under her arms to help her up, she screamed in sudden pain. I changed my grip and lifted her gently on to the seat.

'My shoulder.' Her voice was low and husky. 'It is very sore.'

'I'm not surprised.' I'd eased back the blouse at the neck and closed it again. 'Your clavicle—the collar bone—is gone. Just sit there and hold your left arm in your right hand . . . yes, so. I'll strap you up later. You won't feel a thing, I promise you.'

She smiled at me, half-timidly, half-gratefully, and said nothing. I left her, went to the very rear seat in the plane, stooped to examine the man there then straightened in almost the same in-stant: the weirdly unnatural angle of the head on the shoulders made any examination superfluous.

I turned and walked forward. Everybody was awake now, sitting upright or struggling dazedly to their feet, their half-formed questions as dazed as the expressions on their faces. I ignored them for the moment, looked questioningly at Jackstraw as he came through the forward door, closely followed by Joss.

'She won't come.' Jackstraw jerked his thumb over his shoulder. 'She's awake, but she won't leave the wireless operator.'

'She's all right?'

'Her back hurts, I think. She wouldn't say.'

I made no answer and moved across to the main door—the one we'd failed to open from the outside. I supposed it was no business of mine if the stewardess chose to devote her attention to a member of the crew instead of to the passengers who were her charges. But it was damned queer all the same—almost as queer as the fact that though the inevitability of the crash must have been known for at least fifteen minutes before the actual event, not one of the ten passengers in the cabin had been wearing a seat-belt—and the stewardess, wireless operator and the crew member in the rest room appeared to have been caught completely unprepared.

The circular door handle refused to budge. I called Jackstraw, but even the extra weight made not the slightest impression on it. Obviously, it was immovably jammed—there must have been a slight telescoping effect along the entire length of the fuselage as the plane had crashed into the ice-mound. If the door I had noticed behind the control cabin was as badly warped as this one—and, being nearer the point of impact, it almost inevitably would be—then they'd all have to leave via the windscreens of the control cabin. I thought of the wireless operator with his dreadful head wound and wondered bleakly whether even trying to move him out could be more than a futile gesture, anyway.

A figure barred my way as I turned from the door. It was the white-haired, white moustached Dixie Colonel. His face was dark red, his eyes light blue, choleric and protuberant. It only required someone to get this man good and mad and he would be no more than a debit entry in the account book of some life assurance company. And he seemed good and mad now.

'What's happened? What in the devil *is* all this?' He had a voice like a Dixie colonel too, the Mason-Dixon line lay far to the north of wherever he had been born. 'We've landed. Why? What are we doing here? What's the noise outside? And—and who in the name of heaven are you?'

157

A big business tycoon, I thought wryly, with money enough and power enough to indulge an obviously over-generous capacity for righteous indignation: if I was going to meet any trouble, it wasn't hard to guess the direction it was going to come from. But, right then, there was some excuse for his attitude: I wondered how I would have felt if I had gone to sleep in a trans-Atlantic airliner and woken up to find myself landed in the freezing middle of nowhere with three fur-clad people, complete with snow-goggles and snow-masks, waddling about the aisle of the plane.

'You've crash-landed,' I said briefly. 'I don't know why—how the hell should I? The noise outside is an ice-blizzard rattling against the fuselage. As for us, we are scientists manning an International Geophysical Year station half a mile from here. We saw and heard you just before you crashed.'

I made to push past him, but he barred my way.

'Just a minute, if you don't mind.' The voice was more authoritative than ever and there was a surprising amount of muscle in that arm across my chest. 'I think we have a right to know——'

'Later.' I knocked his arm away and Jackstraw completed the job by pushing him down into his seat. 'Don't make a damned nuisance of yourself. There's a critically injured man who has to have attention, and at once. We'll take him to safety and then come back for you. Keep the door shut.' I was addressing all of them now, but the white-haired man's wrathful spluttering attracted my attention again. 'And if you don't shut up and co-operate, you can stay here. If it weren't for us you'd be dead, stiff as a board, in a couple of hours. Maybe you will be yet.'

I moved up the aisle, followed by Jackstraw. The young man who had been lying on the floor pulled himself on to a seat, and he grinned at me as I passed.

'How to win friends and influence people.' He had a slow cultured drawl. 'I fear you have offended our worthy friend.'

'I fear I have.' I smiled, passed by, then turned. These wide shoulders and large, capable hands could be more than useful to us. 'How are you feeling?'

'Recoverin' rapidly.'

'You are indeed. You didn't look so good a minute ago.'

'Just takin' a long count,' he said easily. 'Can I help?'

'That's why I asked,' I nodded.

'Glad to oblige.' He heaved himself to his feet, towering inches above me. The little man in the loud tie and the Glenurquhart jacket gave an anguished sound, like the yelp of an injured puppy.

'Careful, Johnny, careful!' The voice, the rich, nasal and rather grating twang, was pure Bowery. 'We got our responsibilities boy, big commitments. We might strain a ligament——'

'Relax, Solly.' The big man patted him soothingly on his bald head. 'Just takin' a little walk to clear my head.'

'Not till you put this parka and pants on first.' I'd no time to bother about the eccentricities of little men in loud jackets and louder ties. 'You'll need them.'

'Cold doesn't bother me, friend.'

'This cold will. Outside that door it's 110 degrees below the temperature of this cabin.'

I heard a murmur of astonishment from some of the passengers, and the large young man, suddenly thoughtful, took the clothes from Jackstraw. I didn't wait until he had put them on, but went out with Joss.

The stewardess was bent low over the injured wireless operator. I pulled her gently to her feet. She offered no resistance, just looked wordlessly at me, the deep brown eyes huge in a face dead-white and strained with shock. She was shivering violently. Her hands were like ice.

'You want to die of cold, miss?' This was no time for soft and sympathetic words, and I knew these girls were trained how to behave in emergencies. 'Haven't you got a hat, coat, boots, anything like that?'

'Yes.' Her voice was dull, almost devoid of life. She was standing alone by the door now, and I could hear the violent rat-a-tat of her elbow as it shook uncontrollably and knocked against the door. 'I'll go and get them.'

Joss scrambled out through the windscreen to get the collapsible stretcher. While we were waiting I went to the exit door behind the flight deck and tried to open it, swinging at it with the back of my fireaxe. But it was locked solid.

We had the stretcher up and were lashing the wireless operator inside as carefully as we could in these cramped conditions, when the stewardess reappeared. She was wearing her uniform heavy coat now, and high boots. I tossed her a pair of caribou trousers.

'Better, but not enough. Put these on.' She hesitated, and I added roughly, 'We won't look.'

'I—I must go and see the passengers.'

'They're all right. Bit late in thinking about it, aren't you?'

'I know. I'm sorry. I couldn't leave him.' She looked down at the young man at her feet. 'Do you—I mean——' She broke off, then it came out with a rush. 'Is he going to die?'

'Probably,' I said, and she flinched away as if I had struck her across the face. I hadn't meant to be brutal, just clinical. 'We'll do what we can for him. It's not much, I'm afraid.'

Finally we had him securely lashed to the stretcher, his head cushioned against the shock as best we could. When I got to my feet, the stewardess was just pulling her coat down over the caribou pants.

'We're taking him back to our cabin,' I said. 'We have a sledge below. There's room for another. You could protect his head. Want to come?'

'The passengers——' she began uncertainly.

'They'll be all right.'

I went back inside the main cabin, closing the door behind me, and handed my torch to the man with the cut brow. The two feeble night or emergency lights that burned inside were poor enough for illumination, worse still for morale.

'We're taking the wireless operator and stewardess with us,' I explained. 'Back in twenty minutes. And if you want to live, just keep this door tight shut.'

'What an extraordinary brusque young man,' the elderly lady murmured. Her voice was low-pitched, resonant, with an extraordinary carrying power.

'Only from necessity, madam,' I said dryly. 'Would you really prefer long-winded and flowery speeches the while you were freezing to death?'

'Well, do you know, I really don't think I would,' she answered mock-seriously, and I could hear her chuckling—there was no other word for it—as I closed the door behind me.

Working in the cramped confines of that wrecked control cabin, in almost pitch darkness and with that ice-laden bitter gale whistling through the shattered windscreens, we had the devil's own time of it trying to get the injured wireless operator down to that waiting sledge below. Without the help of the big young stranger I don't think we would ever have managed it, but manage it we eventually did: he and I lowered and slid the stretcher down to Jackstraw and Joss, who took and strapped it on the sledge. Then we eased the stewardess down: I thought I heard her cry

160

out as she hung supported only by a hand round either wrist, and remembered that Jackstraw had said something about her back being injured. But there was no time for such things now.

I jumped down and a couple of seconds later the big young man joined me. I hadn't intended that he should come, but there was no harm in it: he had to go sometime, and there was no question of his having to ride on the sledge.

The wind had eased a little, perhaps, but the cold was crueller than ever. Even the dogs cowered miserably in the lee of the plane; now and again one of them stretched out a neck in protest and gave its long, mournful wolf call, a sound eerie beyond description. But their misery was all to the good: as Jackstraw said, they were mad to run.

And, with the wind and ice-drift behind them, run they did. At first I led the way with the torch, but Balto, the big lead dog, brushed me aside and raced on into the darkness: I had sense enough to let him have his head. He followed the twisting route of the plane's snow-furrow, the bamboos, homing spool and antenna line as swiftly and unerringly as if it had been broad daylight, and the polished steel runners of the sledge fairly hissed across the snow. The frozen ground was smooth and flat as river ice; no ambulance could have carried the wireless operator as comfortably as our sledge did that night.

It took us no more than five minutes to reach the cabin, and in three more minutes we were on our way again. They were a busy three minutes. Jackstraw lit the oil stove, oil lamp and Colman pressure lamp, while Joss and I put the injured man on a collapsible cot before the stove, worked him into my sleeping-bag, slid in half a dozen heat pads—waterproof pads containing a chemical which gave off heat when water was added—placed a rolled up blanket under his neck to keep the back of his head off the cot, and zipped the sleeping-bag shut. I had surgical instruments enough to do what had to be done, but it had to wait: not so much because we had others still to rescue, urgent enough though that was, but the man lying at our feet, so still, so ashen-faced, was suffering so severely from shock and exposure that to touch him would have been to kill him: I was astonished that he had managed to survive even this long.

I told the stewardess to make some coffee, gave her the necessary instructions, and then we left her and the big young man together: the girl heating a pan over a pile of meta tablets, the

161

young man staring incredulously into a mirror as he kneaded a frost-bitten cheek and chin with one hand, and with the other held a cold compress to a frozen ear. We took with us the warm clothes we had lent them, some rolls of bandages, and left.

Ten minutes later we were back inside the plane. Despite its insulation, the temperature inside the main cabin had already dropped at least thirty degrees and almost everyone was shivering with the cold, one or two beating their arms to keep themselves warm. Even the Dixie colonel was looking very subdued. The elderly lady, fur coat tightly wrapped around her, looked at her watch and smiled.

'Twenty minutes, exactly. You are very prompt, young man.'

'We try to be of service.' I dumped the pile of clothes I was carrying on a seat, nodded at them and the contents of a gunny sack Joss and Jackstraw were emptying. 'Share these out between you and be as quick as you can. I want you to get out at once—my two friends here will take you back. Perhaps one of you would be kind enough to remain behind.' I looked to where the young girl still sat alone in her back seat, still holding her left forearm in her hand. 'I'll need some help to fix this young lady up.'

'Fix her up?' It was the expensive young woman in the expensive furs speaking for the first time. Her voice was expensive as the rest of her and made me want to reach for a hairbrush. 'Why? What on earth is the matter with her?'

'Her collar-bone is broken,' I said shortly.

'Collar-bone broken?' The elderly lady was on her feet, her face a mixture of concern and indignation. 'And she's been sitting there alone all this time—why didn't you *tell* us, you silly man?'

'I forgot,' I replied mildly. 'Besides, what good would it have done?' I looked down at the girl in the mink coat. Goodness only knew that I didn't particularly want her, but the injured girl had struck me as being almost painfully shy, and I was sure she'd prefer to have one of her own sex around. 'Would you like to give me a hand?'

She stared at me, a cold surprised stare that would have been normal enough had I made some outrageous or improper request, but before she could answer the elderly lady broke in again.

'I'll stay behind. I'd love to help.'

'Well——' I began doubtfully, but she interrupted immediately. 'Well, yourself. What's the matter? Think I'm too old, hey?'

'No, no, of course not,' I protested.

162

'A fluent liar, but a gallant one.' She grinned. 'Come on, we're wasting this valuable time you're always so concerned about.'

We brought the girl into the first of the rear seats, where there was plenty of space between that and the first of the rearward facing front seats, and had just worked her coat off when Joss called me.

'We're off now, sir. Back in twenty minutes.'

As the door closed behind the last of them and I broke open a roll of bandage, the old lady looked quizzically at me.

'Know what you're doing, young man?'

'More or less. I'm a doctor.'

'Doctor, hey?' She looked at me with open suspicion, and what with my bulky, oil-streaked and smelly furs, not to mention the fact that I hadn't shaved for three days, I suppose there was justification enough for it. 'You sure?'

'Sure I'm sure,' I said irritably. 'What do you expect me to do—whip my medical degree out from under this parka or just wear round my neck a brass plate giving my consulting hours?'

'We'll get along, young man,' she chuckled. She patted my arm, then turned to the young girl. 'What's your name, my dear?'

'Helene.' We could hardly catch it, the voice was so low: her embarrassment was positively painful.

'Helene? A lovely name.' And, indeed, the way she said it made it sound so. 'You're not British, are you? Or American?'

'I'm from Germany, madam.'

'Don't call me "madam". You know, you speak English beautifully. Germany, hey? Bavaria, for a guess?'

'Yes.' The rather plain face was transfigured in a smile, and I mentally saluted the old lady for the ease with which she was distracting the young girl's thoughts from the pain. 'Munich. Perhaps you know it?'

'Like the back of my hand,' she said complacently. 'And not just the Hofbrauhaus either. You're still very young, aren't you?'

'I'm seventeen.'

'Seventeen.' A nostalgic sigh. 'Ah, my dear, I remember when I was seventeen. A different world. There was no trans-Atlantic airliner in those days, I can tell you.'

'In fact,' I murmured, 'the Wright brothers were hardly airborne.' The face had been more than familiar to me, and I was annoyed that I should have taken so long in placing it: I suppose

163

it was because her normal setting was so utterly different from this bleak and frozen world.

'Being insulting, young man?' she queried. But there was no offence in her face.

'I can't imagine anyone ever insulting you. The world was at your feet even in the Edwardian days, Miss LeGarde.'

'You know me, then?' She seemed genuinely pleased.

'It would be difficult to find anyone who doesn't know the name of Marie LeGarde.' I nodded at the young girl. 'See, Helene knows it too.' And it was clear from the awe-struck expression on the young German girl's face that the name meant as much to her as to me. Twenty years queen of the music-hall, thirty years queen of the musical comedy stage, beloved wherever she was known less for her genius than for the innate kindliness and goodness which she tried to conceal from the world with a waspish tongue, for the half-dozen orphanages she maintained in Britain and Europe, Marie LeGarde was one of the few truly international names in the world of entertainment.

'Yes, yes, I see you know my name.' Marie LeGarde smiled at me. 'But how did you know *me*?'

'From your photograph, naturally. I saw it in *Life* the other week, Miss LeGarde.'

' "Marie", to my friends.'

'I don't know you,' I protested.

'I paid a small fortune to have that photograph retouched and made barely presentable,' she answered obliquely. 'It was a splendid photograph, inasmuch as it bore precious little resemblance to the face that I carry about with me. Anyone who recognizes me from that is my friend for life. Besides,' she smiled, 'I bear nothing but the most amicable feelings towards people who save my life.'

I said nothing, just concentrated on finishing the job of strapping up Helene's arm and shoulders as quickly as possible: she was blue with cold, and shivering uncontrollably. But she hadn't uttered a murmur throughout, and smiled gratefully at me when I was finished. Marie LeGarde regarded my handiwork approvingly.

'I really do believe you have picked up some smattering of your trade along the way, Doctor—ah——'

'Mason. Peter Mason. Peter, to my friends.'

' "Peter" it shall be. Come on, Helene, into your clothes as fast as you like.'

Fifteen minutes later we were back in the cabin. Jackstraw went to unharness the dogs and secure them to the tethering cable, while Joss and I helped the two women down the ice-coated steps from the trap-door. But I had no sooner reached the foot of the steps than I had forgotten all about Marie LeGarde and Helene and was staring unbelievingly at the tableau before me. I was just vaguely aware of Joss by my shoulder, the anger and dismay on his face slowly giving way to a kind of reluctant horror. For what we saw, though it vitally concerned us all, concerned him most of all.

The injured wireless operator still lay where we had left him. All the others were there too, grouped in a rough semi-circle round him and round a cleared space to the left of the stove. By their feet in the centre of this space, upside down and with one corner completely stove in on the wooden floor, lay the big metal R.C.A. radio transmitter and receiver, our sole source of contact with, our only means of summoning help from the outer world. I knew next to nothing about radios, but it was chillingly obvious to me—as it was, I could see, to the semi-circle of fascinated onlookers—that the R.C.A. was smashed beyond recovery.

CHAPTER THREE

MONDAY 2 A.M.–3 A.M.

Half a minute passed in complete silence, half a minute before I could trust myself to speak, even bring myself to speak. When at last I did, my voice was unnaturally low in the unnatural hush that was broken only by the interminable clacking of the anemometer cups above.

'Splendid. Really splendid. The perfect end to the perfect day.' I looked round them slowly, one by one, then gestured at the smashed transmitter. 'What bloody idiot was responsible for this—this stroke of genius?'

'How dare you, sir!' The white-haired man whom I had mentally labelled as the Dixie colonel took a step forward, face flushed with anger. 'Mind your tongue. We're not children to be——'

'Shut up!' I said, quietly enough, but there must have been something in my voice rather less than reassuring, for he fell silent, though his fists still remained clenched. I looked at them all again. 'Well?'

'I'm afraid—I'm afraid I did it,' the stewardess faltered. Her brown eyes were as unnaturally large, her face as white and strained as when I had first seen her. 'It's all my fault.'

'You! The one person here who should know just how vital radio really is. I don't believe it.'

'You must, I'm afraid.' The quiet controlled voice belonged to the man with the cut brow. 'No one else was anywhere near it at the time.'

'What happened to you?' I could see he was nursing a bruised and bleeding hand.

'I dived for it when I saw it toppling.' He smiled wryly. 'I should have saved myself the trouble. That damned thing's heavy.'

'It's all that. Thanks for trying anyway. I'll fix your hand up later.' I turned to the stewardess again, and not even that pale and exhausted face, the contrition in the eyes, could quieten my anger

166

—and, to be honest, my fear. 'I suppose it just came to pieces in your hand?'

'I've told you I'm sorry. I—I was just kneeling beside Jimmy here——'

'Who?'

'Jimmy Waterman—the Second Officer. I——'

'Second Officer?' I interrupted. 'That's the radio operator, I take it?'

'No, Jimmy is a pilot. We've three pilots—we don't carry a radio operator.'

'You don't——' I broke off my surprised question, asked another instead. 'Who's the man in the crew rest room? Navigator?'

'We don't carry a navigator either. Harry Williamson is—was —the Flight Engineer.'

No wireless operator, no navigator. There had been changes indeed since I'd flown the Atlantic some years previously in a Stratocruiser. I gave it up, returned to my original question and nodded at the smashed R.C.A.

'Well, how *did* it happen?'

'I brushed the table as I rose and—well, it just fell.' Her voice trailed off uncertainly.

'It just fell,' I echoed incredulously. 'One hundred and fifty pounds of transmitter and you flicked it off the table just like that?'

'I didn't knock it off. The legs collapsed.'

'It's got no legs to collapse,' I said shortly. 'Hinges.'

'Well, hinges, then.'

I looked at Joss, who had been responsible for the erection of the table as well as the radio. 'Is it possible?'

'No.' His voice was flat, definite.

Again the silence in the cabin, the hush, the tension that grew from the merely uncomfortable to the all but unbearable. But I was beginning to see that there was nothing to be gained now by further questioning, much to be lost. The radio was wrecked. Finish.

I turned away without a word, hung up my caribou furs on nails on the walls, took off goggles and gloves and turned to the man with the cut brow.

'Let's have a look at your head and your hand—it's a pretty nasty gash on your forehead. Forget the radio for the moment,

167

Joss—let's have coffee first, lots of it.' I turned to Jackstraw, who had just come down the steps from the hatch and was staring at the smashed radio. 'I know, Jackstraw, I know. I'll explain later—not that I know anything about it. Bring some empty cases for seats out of the food tunnel, will you. And a bottle of brandy. We all need it.'

I'd just started to wash the cut forehead—a nasty gash, as I had said, but surprisingly little signs of bruising—when the big amiable young man who had helped us lower the second officer from the wrecked plane came across to us. I looked up at him, and saw that I could be wrong about the amiability: his face wasn't exactly hostile, but his eyes had the cool measuring look of one who knew from experience that he could cope with most of the situations, pleasant and unpleasant, that he was ever likely to come up against.

'Look,' he began without preamble, 'I don't know who you are or what your name is, but I'm sure we are all most grateful to you for what you have done for us. It's more than probable that we owe our lives to you. We acknowledge that. Also, we know you're a field scientist, and we realize that your equipment is of paramount importance to you. Agreed?'

'Agreed.' I dabbed iodine fairly liberally on the injured man's head—he was tough, all right, he didn't even wince—and looked at the speaker. Not at all a man to ignore, I thought. Behind that strong intelligent face lay a hardness, a tenacity of purpose that hadn't been acquired along with the cultured relaxed voice at the Ivy League college I was pretty certain he had attended. 'You'd something else to say?'

'Yes. We think—correction, I think—that you were unnecessarily rough on our air hostess. You can see the state the poor kid's in. O.K., so your radio's bust, so you're hoppin' mad about it—but there's no need for all this song and dance.' His voice was calm, conversational all the time. 'Radios aren't irreplaceable. This one will be replaced, I promise you. You'll have a new one inside a week, ten days at the most.'

'Kind,' I said dryly. I finished tying the head bandage and straightened up. 'The offer is appreciated, but there's one thing you haven't taken into account. You may be dead inside that ten days. You may all be dead in ten days.'

'We may all——' He broke off and stared at me his expression perceptibly hardening. 'What are you talking about?'

'What I'm talking about is that without this radio you dismiss so lightly your chances—our chances—of survival aren't all that good. In fact, they're not good at all. I don't give a tuppenny damn about the radio, as such.' I eyed him curiously, and a preposterous thought struck me: at least, it was preposterous for all of a couple of seconds, before the truth hit me. 'Have you—have *any* of you *any* idea just where you are, right here, at the present moment.'

'Sure we have.' The young man lifted his shoulders fractionally. 'Just can't say how far to the nearest drugstore or pub——'

'I told them,' the stewardess interrupted. 'They were asking me —just before you came in. I thought Captain Johnson had over-shot the landing field at Reykjavik in a snowstorm. This is Langjökull, isn't it?' She saw the expression on my face and went on hastily. 'Or Hofsjökull? I mean, we were flying more or less north-east from Gander, and these are the only two snowfields or glaciers or whatever you call them in Iceland in that direction from——'

'Iceland?' I suppose there is a bit of the ham actor in all of us, and I really couldn't pass it up. 'Did you say Iceland?'

She nodded, dumbly. Everybody was looking at her, and when she didn't answer they all transferred their gazes to me, as at the touch of a switch.

'Iceland,' I repeated. 'My dear girl, at the present moment you're at an altitude of 8,500 feet, right slam bang in the middle of the Greenland ice-cap.'

The effect was all that anybody could ever have wished for. I doubt whether even Marie LeGarde had ever had a better reaction from an audience. 'Stunned' is an inadequate word to describe their mental state immediately after this announcement; paralysis was nearer it, especially where the power of speech was concerned. And when the power of thought and speech did return, it expressed itself, as I might have expected, in the most violent disbelief. Everybody seemed to start talking at once, but it was the steward-ess who took my attention, by coming forward and catching me by the lapels. I noticed the glitter of a diamond ring on her hand, and remember having some vague idea that this was against airline regulations.

'What kind of joke is this? It can't be, it can't be! Greenland—it just can't be.' She saw by the expression on my face that I wasn't joking, and her grip tightened even more. I had just time to be conscious of two conflicting thoughts—that, wide with fear and

169

dismay though they might be, she had the most extraordinarily beautiful brown eyes and, secondly, that the M.Y.T.H. were slipping in their selection of stewardesses whose calmness in emergency was supposed to match the trimness of their appearance—when she rushed on wildly.

'How—how can it be? We were on a Gander—Reykjavik flight. Greenland—we don't go anywhere near it. And there's the automatic pilot, and radio beams and—and radio base checks every half-hour. Oh, it's impossible, it's impossible! Why do you tell us this?' She was shaking now, whether from nervous strain or cold I had no idea: the big young man with the Ivy League accent put an arm awkwardly round her shoulder, and I saw her wince. Something indeed seemed to be hurting her—but again it could wait.

'Joss,' I called. He looked up from the stove, where he was pouring coffee into mugs. 'Tell our friends where we are.'

'Latitude 72.40 north, longitude 40.10 west,' Joss said unemotionally. His voice cut clearly through the hubbub of incredulous conversation. 'Three hundred miles from the nearest human habitation. Four hundred miles north of the Arctic Circle. Near enough 800 miles from Reykjavik, 1,000 from Cape Farewell, the southernmost point of Greenland, and just a little farther distant from the North Pole. And if anyone doesn't believe us, sir, I suggest they just take a walk—in any direction—and they'll find out who's right.'

Joss's calm, matter-of-fact statement was worth half an hour of argument and explanation. In a moment, conviction was complete—and there were more problems than ever to be answered. I held up my hand in mock protest and protection against the waves of questions that surged against me from every side.

'All in good time, please—although I really don't know anything more than yourselves—with the exception, perhaps, of one thing. But first, coffee and brandy all round.'

'Brandy?' The expensive young woman had been the first, I'd noticed, to appropriate one of the empty wooden cases that Jackstraw had brought in in lieu of seats, and now she looked up under the curve of exquisitely modelled eyebrows. 'Are you sure that's wise?' The tone of her voice left little room for doubt as to her opinion.

'Of course.' I forced myself to be civil: bickering could reach intolerable proportions in a rigidly closed, mutually interdependent group such as we were likely to be for some time to come. 'Why ever not?'

'Opens the pores, dear man,' she said sweetly. 'I thought everyone knew that—how dangerous it is when you're exposed to cold afterwards. Or had you forgotten? Our cases, our night things in the plane—somebody has to get these.'

'Don't talk such utter rubbish.' My short-lived attempt at civility perished miserably. 'Nobody's leaving here to-night. You sleep in your clothes—this isn't the Dorchester. If the blizzard dies down, we may try to get your things tomorrow morning.'

'But——'

'If you're all that desperate, you're welcome to get them yourself. Want to try?' It was boorish of me, but that was the effect she had. I turned away to see the minister or priest hold up his hand against the offered brandy.

'Go on, take it,' I said impatiently.

'I don't really think I should.' The voice was high-pitched, but the enunciation clear and precise, and I found it vaguely irritating that it should so perfectly match his appearance, be so exactly what I should have expected. He laughed, a nervous deprecating laugh. 'My parishioners, you know . . .'

I was tired, worried and felt like telling him what he could do with his parishioners. But it wasn't his fault.

'There's precedent in plenty in your Bible, Reverend. You know that better than I. It'll do you good, really.'

'Oh well, if you think so.' He took the glass gingerly, as if Beelzebub himself were on the offering end, but I noticed that there was nothing so hesitant about his method and speed of disposal of the contents: his subsequent expression could properly be described as beatific. I caught Marie LeGarde's eye, and smiled at the twinkle I caught there.

The Reverend wasn't the only one who found the coffee—and brandy—welcome. With the exception of the stewardess, who sipped at her drink in a distraught fashion, the others had also emptied their glasses, and I decided that the broaching of another Martell's was justified. In the respite from the talk, I bent over the injured man on the floor. His pulse was slower, steadier and his breathing not quite so shallow: I slipped in a few more heat pads and zipped up the sleeping-bag.

'Is he—is he any better, do you think?' The stewardess was so

171

close to me that I brushed against her as I straightened. 'He—he seems a bit better, doesn't he?'

'He is a bit, I think. But nothing like over the shock from the wound and the exposure, though.' I looked at her speculatively and suddenly felt almost sorry for her. Almost, but not quite: I didn't at all like the direction my thoughts were leading me. 'You've flown together quite a bit, haven't you?'

'Yes.' She didn't offer anything more. 'His head—do you think——'

'Later. Let me have a quick look at that back of yours.'

'Look at *what*?'

'Your back,' I said patiently. 'Your shoulders. They seem to give you some pain. I'll rig a screen.'

'No, no, I'm all right.' She moved away from me.

'Don't be silly, my dear.' I wondered what trick of voice production made Marie LeGarde's voice so clear and carrying. 'He *is* a doctor, you know.'

'No!'

I shrugged and reached for my brandy glass. Bearers of bad news were ever unpopular: I supposed her reaction was the modern equivalent of the classical despot's unsheathing his dagger. Probably only bruises, anyhow, I told myself, and turned to look at the company.

An odd-looking bunch, to say the least, but then any group of people dressed in lounge suits and dresses, trilby hats and nylon stockings would have looked odd against the strange and uncompromising background of that cabin where every suggestion of anything that even remotely suggested gracious living had been crushed and ruthlessly made subservient to the all-exclusive purpose of survival.

Here there were no arm-chairs—no chairs, even—no carpets, wall-paper, book-shelves, beds, curtains—or even windows for the curtains. It was a bleak utilitarian box of a room, eighteen feet by fourteen. The floor was made of unfurnished yellow pine. The walls were made of spaced sheets of bonded ply, with kapok insulation between: the lower part of the walls was covered with green-painted asbestos, the upper part and entire roof sheeted with glittering aluminium to reflect the maximum possible heat and light. A thin, ever-present film of ice climbed at least half-way up all four walls, reaching almost to the ceiling in the four corners, the parts of the room most remote from the stove and therefore

172

the coldest. On very cold nights, such as this, the ice reached the ceiling and started to creep across it to the layers of opaque ice that permanently framed the undersides of our rimed and opaque skylights.

The two exits from the cabin were let into the fourteen-foot sides: one led to the trap, the other to the snow and ice tunnel where we kept our food, petrol, oil, batteries, radio generators, explosives for seismological and glacial investigations and a hundred and one other items. Half-way along, a secondary tunnel led off at right angles—a tunnel which steadily increased in length as we cut out the blocks of snow which were melted to give us our water supply. At the far end of the main tunnel lay our primitive toilet system.

One eighteen-foot wall and half of the wall that gave access to the trap-door were lined with twin rows of bunks—eight in all. The other eighteen-foot wall was given over entirely to our stove, work-bench, radio table and housings for the meteorological instruments. The remaining wall by the tunnel was piled with tins and cases of food, now mostly empties, that had been brought in from the tunnel to begin the lengthy process of defrosting.

Slowly I surveyed all this, then as slowly surveyed the company. The incongruity of the contrast reached the point where one all but disbelieved the evidence of one's own eyes. But they were there all right, and I was stuck with them. Everyone had stopped talking now and was looking at me, waiting for me to speak: sitting in a tight semi-circle round the stove, they were huddled together and shivering in the freezing cold. The only sounds in the room were the clacking of the anemometer cups, clearly audible down the ventilation pipe, the faint moaning of the wind on the ice-cap and the hissing of our pressure Colman lamp. I sighed to myself, and put down my empty glass.

'Well, it looks as if you are going to be our guests for some little time, so we'd better introduce ourselves. Us first.' I nodded to where Joss and Jackstraw were working on the shattered R.C.A., which they had lifted back on the table. 'On the left, Joseph London, of the city of London, our radio operator.'

'Unemployed,' Joss muttered.

'On the right, Nils Nielsen. Take a good look at him, ladies and gentlemen. At this very moment the guardian angels of your respective insurance companies are probably putting up a prayer for his continued well-being. If you all live to come home again, the chances are that you will owe it to him.' I was to remember my own words later. 'He probably knows more than any man living about survival on the Greenland ice-cap.'

'I thought you called him "Jackstraw",' Marie LeGarde murmured.

'My Eskimo name.' Jackstraw had turned and smiled at her, his parka hood off for the first time; I could see her polite astonishment as she looked at the fair hair, the blue eyes, and it was as if Jackstraw read her thoughts. 'Two of my grandparents were Danish—most of us Greenlanders have as much Danish blood as Eskimo in us nowadays.' I was surprised to hear him talk like this, and it was a tribute to Marie LeGarde's personality: his pride in his Eskimo background was equalled only by his touchiness on the subject.

'Well, well, how interesting.' The expensive young lady was sitting back on her box, hands clasped round an expensively-nyloned knee, her expression reflecting accurately the well-bred condescension of her tone. 'My very first Eskimo.'

'Don't be afraid, lady.' Jackstraw's smile was wider than ever, and I felt more than vaguely uneasy: his almost invariable Eskimo cheerfulness and good nature concealed an explosive temper which he'd probably inherited from some far distant Viking forbear. 'It doesn't rub off.'

The silence that followed could hardly be described as companionable, and I rushed in quickly.

'My own name is Mason, Peter Mason, and I'm in charge of this I.G.Y. station. You all know roughly what we're doing stuck out here on the plateau—meteorology, glaciology, the study of the earth's magnetism, the borealis, airglow, ionosphere, cosmic rays, magnetic storms and a dozen other things which I suppose are equally uninteresting to you.' I waved my arm. 'We don't, as you can see, normally live here alone. Five others are away to the north on a field expedition. They're due back in about three weeks, after which we all pack up and abandon this place before winter sets in and the ice-pack freezes on the coast.'

'Before the winter sets in?' The little man in the Glenurquhart jacket stared at me. 'You mean to tell me it gets colder than this?'

'It certainly does. An explorer called Alfred Wegener wintered not fifty miles from here in 1930–1, and the temperature dropped to 85 degrees below zero—117 degrees of frost. And that may have been a warm winter, for all we know.'

174

I gave some time to allow this cheering item of information to sink in, then continued.

'Well, that's us. Miss LeGarde—Marie LeGarde—needs no introduction from anyone.' A slight murmur of surprise and turning of heads showed that I wasn't altogether right. 'But that's all I know, I'm afraid.'

'Corazzini,' the man with the cut brow offered. The white bandage, just staining with blood, was in striking contrast to the receding dark hair. 'Nick Corazzini. Bound for Bonnie Scotland, as the travel posters put it.'

'Holiday?'

'No luck.' He grinned. 'Taking over the new Global Tractor Company outside Glasgow. Know it?'

'I've heard of it. Tractors, eh? Mr Corazzini, you may be worth your weight in gold to us yet. We have a broken-down elderly tractor outside that can usually only be started by repeated oaths and assaults by a four-pound hammer.'

'Well.' He seemed taken aback. 'Of course, I can try——'

'I don't suppose you've actually laid a finger on a tractor for many years,' Marie LeGarde interrupted shrewdly. 'Isn't that it, Mr Corazzini?'

'Afraid it is,' he admitted ruefully. 'But in a situation like this I'd gladly lay my hands on another one.'

'You'll have your chance,' I promised him. I looked at the man beside him.

'Smallwood,' the minister announced. He rubbed his thin white hands constantly to drive the cold away. 'The Rev. Joseph Smallwood. I'm the Vermont delegate to the International General Assembly of the Unitarian and Free United Churches in London. You may have heard of it—our biggest conference in many years?'

'Sorry.' I shook my head. 'But don't let that disturb you. Our paper boy misses out occasionally. And you, sir?'

'Solly Levin. Of New York City,' the little man in the check jacket added unnecessarily. He reached up and laid a proprietary arm along the broad shoulders of the young man beside him. 'And this is my boy, Johnny.'

'Your boy? Your son?' I fancied I could see a slight resemblance.

'Perish the thought,' the young man drawled. 'My name is Johnny Zagero. Solly is my manager. Sorry to introduce a discordant note into company such as this'—his eyes swept over us, dwelt significantly longer on the expensive young lady by his

175

side—'but I'm in the way of being a common or garden pugilist. That means "boxer", Solly?'

'Would you listen to him?' Solly Levin implored. He stretched his clenched fists heavenwards. 'Would you just listen to him? Apologizin'. Johnny Zagero, future heavyweight champion, apologizin' for being a boxer. The white hope of the world, that's all. Rated number three challenger to the champ. A household name in all——'

'Ask Dr Mason if he's ever heard of me,' Zagero suggested.

'That means nothing,' I smiled. 'You don't look like a boxer to me, Mr Zagero. Or sound like one. I didn't know it was included in the curriculum at Yale. Or was it Harvard?'

'Princeton,' he grinned. 'And what's so funny about that? Look at Tunney and his Shakespeare. Roland La Starza was a college boy when he fought for the world title. Why not me?'

'Exactly.' Solly Levin tried to thunder the word, but he hadn't the voice for it. 'Why not? And when we've carved up this British champ of yours—a doddery old character rated number two challenger by one of the biggest injustices ever perpetrated in the long and glorious history of boxin'—when we've massacred this ancient has-been, I say——'

'All right, Solly,' Zagero interrupted. 'Desist. There's not a press man within a thousand miles. Save the golden words for later.'

'Just keepin' in practice, boy. Words are ten a penny. I've got thousands to spare——'

'T'ousands, Solly, t'ousands. You're slippin'. Now shut up.'

Solly shut up, and I turned to the girl beside Zagero.

'Mrs. Mrs Dansby-Gregg. You may have heard of me?'

'No.' I wrinkled my brow. 'I'm afraid I haven't.' I'd heard of her all right, and I knew now that I'd seen her name and picture a score of times among those of other wealthy unemployed and unemployable built up by the tongue-in-the-cheek gossip columnists of the great national dailies into an ersatz London society whose frenetic, frequently moronic and utterly unimportant activities were a source of endless interest to millions. Mrs Dansby-Gregg, I seemed to recall, had been particularly active in the field of charitable activities, although perhaps less so in the production of the balance sheets.

She smiled sweetly at me.

'Well, perhaps it's not so surprising after all. You *are* a bit

176

distant from the centre of things, aren't you?' She looked across to where the youngster with the broken collar-bone was sitting. 'And this is Fleming.'

'Fleming?' This time the wrinkling of my brow was genuine. 'You mean Helene?'

'Fleming. My personal maid.'

'Your personal maid,' I said slowly. I could feel the incredulous anger stirring inside me. 'Your own maid? And you didn't even bother to volunteer to stay while I fixed her shoulder up?'

'Miss LeGarde did it first,' she said coolly. 'Why should I?'

'Quite right, Mrs Dansby-Gregg, why should you?' Johnny Zagero said approvingly. He looked at her long and consideringly. 'You might have got your hands dirty.'

For the first time the carefully cultivated façade cracked, the smile stiffened mechanically and her colour deepened. Mrs Dansby-Gregg made no reply, maybe she had none to make. People like Johnny Zagero never got close enough even to the fringes of her money-sheltered world for her to know how to deal with them.

'Well, that leaves just the two of you,' I said hastily. The large Dixie colonel with the florid face and white hair was sitting next to the thin wispy-haired little Jew. They made an incongruous pair.

'Theodore Mahler,' the little Jew said quietly. I waited, but he added nothing. A communicative character.

'Brewster,' the other announced. He made a significant pause. 'Senator Hoffman Brewster. Glad to help in any way I can, Dr Mason.'

'Thank you, Senator. At least I know who you are.' Indeed, thanks to his magnificent flair for self-publicity, half the Western world knew who this outspoken, bitterly—but fairly—anti-communist, near isolationist senator from the south-west was. 'On a European tour?'

'You might say that.' He had the politician's gift for investing even the most significant words with a statesmanlike consideration. 'As Chairman of one of our Appropriation committees, I—well, let's call it a fact-finding tour.'

'Wife and secretaries gone ahead by humble passenger steamer, I take it,' Zagero said mildly. He shook his head. 'That was a fearful stink your Congressional investigation boys raised recently about the expenses of U.S. senators abroad.'

177

'That was quite unnecessary, young man,' Brewster said coldly. 'And insulting.'

'I believe it was,' Zagero apologized. 'Not really intended as such. Sorry, Senator.' He meant it.

What a bunch, I thought despairingly, what a crowd to be stuck with in the middle of the Greenland ice-plateau. A business executive, a musical-comedy star, a minister of religion, a boxer with an uninhibited if cultured tongue, his zany manager, a London society playgirl and her young German maid, a Senator, a taciturn Jew and a near-hysterical hostess—or one apparently so. And a gravely injured pilot who might live or die. But willy-nilly I was stuck with them, stuck with the responsibility of doing my damndest to get these people to safety, and the prospect appalled me. How on earth was I even to start to go about it, go about it with people with no arctic clothing to ward off the razor-edged winds and inhuman cold, people lacking in all knowledge and experience of arctic travel, even lacking, with two or three exceptions, the endurance and sheer muscular strength to cope with the savagery of the Greenland ice-cap? I couldn't even begin to guess.

But whatever else they were lacking in at that moment, it wasn't volubility: the life-giving warmth of the brandy had had the unfortunate side effect of loosening their tongues. Unfortunate, that is, from my point of view: they had a hundred and one questions to ask, and they seemed to think that I should have the answer to all of them.

More accurately, they had only half a dozen questions to ask, with a hundred and one variations of these. How was it possible for a pilot to veer so many hundreds of miles off course? Could the compasses have gone wrong? Could the pilot have had a brain-storm? But then surely both the co-pilot and second pilot would have known something was wrong? Could the radio have been damaged? It had been a bitterly cold afternoon even when they had left Gander, was it possible that some of the flaps and controls had iced, forcing them off course? But if this were the case, why hadn't someone come to warn them of the possibility of a crash?

I answered all of their questions as best I could but these answers were all to the same effect, that I didn't really know anything more about it than they did.

'But you said some time ago that you did, perhaps, know one

thing more than we did.' It was Corazzini who put the question, and he was looking at me shrewdly. 'What was that, Dr Mason?'

'What? Ah, yes, I remember now.' I hadn't forgotten, but the way things were shaping up in my mind I'd had second thoughts about mentioning it, and had time to think up a plausible alternative. 'I need hardly tell you that it's nothing that I actually *know*, Mr Corazzini—how could I, *I* wasn't in the plane—just a reasonably informed guess in the absence of all other solutions. It's based on the scientific observations made here and in other I.G.Y. stations in Greenland, some of them over the past eighteen months.

'For over a year now, we have been experiencing a period of intense sun-spot activity—that's one of the main interests of the I.G.Y. year—the most intense of this century. As you may know, sun-spots, or, rather, the emission of solar particles from these sun-spots, are directly responsible for the formation of the aurora borealis and magnetic storms, both of these being related to disturbances in the ionosphere. These disturbances can and, actually, almost invariably do interfere with radio transmission and reception, and when severe enough can completely disrupt all normal radio communications: and they can also produce temporary alterations of the earth's magnetism which knock magnetic compasses completely out of kilter.' All of which was true enough as far as it went. 'It would, of course, require extreme conditions to produce these effects: but we have been experiencing these lately, and I'm pretty sure that that's what happened with your plane. Where astral navigation—by the stars, that is—is impossible, as it was on a night like this, you are dependent on radio and compasses as your two main navigational aids: if these are knocked out, what have you left?'

A fresh hubbub of talk arose at this, and though it was quite obvious that most of them had only a vague idea what I was talking about, I could see that this idea was finding a fair degree of ready acceptance, satisfying them and fitting the facts as they knew them. I saw Joss gazing at me with an expressionless face, looked him in the eye for a couple of seconds, then turned away. As a radio operator, Joss knew even better than I that, though there was still some sun-spot activity, it had reached its maximum in the previous year: and as an ex-aircraft radio operator, he knew that airliners flew on gyrocompasses, which neither sun-spots nor magnetic storms could ever affect in the slightest.

'We'll have something to eat now.' I cut through the buzz of conversation. 'Any volunteers to give Jackstraw a hand?'

'Certainly.' Marie LeGarde, as I might have guessed, was first on her feet. 'I'm by way of being what you might call a mean cook. Lead me to it, Mr Nielsen.'

'Thanks. Joss, you might give me a hand to rig a screen.' I nodded at the injured pilot. 'We'll see what we can do for this boy here.' The stewardess, unbidden, moved forward to help me also. I was on the point of objecting—I knew that this wasn't going to be nice—but I didn't want trouble with her, not yet. I shrugged my shoulders and let her stay.

Half an hour later, I had done all I could. It indeed hadn't been nice, but both the patient and the stewardess had stood it far better than I had expected. I was fixing and binding on a stiff leather helmet to protect the back of his head and Joss was strapping him down, inside the sleeping-bag, to the stretcher, so that he couldn't toss around and hurt himself, when the stewardess touched my arm.

'What—what do you think now, Dr Mason?'

'It's hard to be sure. I'm not a specialist in brain or head injuries, and even a specialist would hesitate to say. The damage may have penetrated deeper than we think. There may be hæmorrhaging—it's often delayed in these cases.'

'But if there's no hæmorrhaging?' she persisted. 'If the damage is no worse than what you think, what you see?'

'Fifty-fifty. I wouldn't have said so a couple of hours ago, but he seems to have quite astonishing powers of resistance and recuperation. Better than an even chance, I would say—if he had the warmth, the food, the skilled nursing he would have in a first-class hospital. As it is—well, let's leave it at that, shall we?'

'Yes,' she murmured. 'Thank you.'

I looked at her, looked at the washed-out face, the faint blue circles forming under her eyes, and almost felt touched with pity. Almost. She was exhausted, and shivering with cold.

'Bed,' I said. 'You're dying for sleep and warmth, Miss—I'm so sorry, I forgot to ask your name.'

'Ross. Margaret Ross.'

'Scots?'

'Irish. Southern Irish.'

'I won't hold it against you,' I smiled. There was no answering

180

smile from her. 'Tell me, Miss Ross, why was the plane so empty?'

'We were an "X" flight—an extra or duplicate charter for an overflow of passengers—out from London yesterday. Day before yesterday it is now, I suppose. We just stayed the night in Idlewild and had to return after we'd slept. The office phoned up people who had booked out on the evening plane, giving the chance of an earlier flight: ten of them accepted.'

'I see. By the way, isn't it a bit unusual to have only one stewardess aboard? On a trans-Atlantic flight, I mean?'

'I know. There's usually two or three—a steward and two stewardesses—or two stewards and a stewardess. But not for ten people.'

'Of course. Hardly worth stewarding, you might say. Still,' I went on smoothly, 'it at least gives you time for the odd forty winks on these long night-flights.'

'That wasn't fair!' I hadn't been as clever as I thought, and her white cheeks were stained with red. 'That's never happened to me before. Never!'

'Sorry, Miss Ross—it wasn't really meant as a dig. It doesn't matter anyhow.'

'It does so matter!' Her extraordinary brown eyes were bright with unshed tears. 'If I hadn't been asleep I would have known what was going to happen. I could have warned the passengers. I could have moved Colonel Harrison to a front seat facing the rear——'

'Colonel Harrison?' I interrupted sharply.

'Yes. The man in the back seat—the dead man.'

'But he hadn't a uniform on when——'

'I don't care. That was his name on the passenger list. . . . If I'd known, he wouldn't be dead now—and Miss Fleming wouldn't have had her collar-bone broken.'

So that's what has been worrying her, I thought. That accounts for her strange distraught behaviour. And then a moment later I realized that it didn't account for it all—she had been behaving like that before ever she had known what had happened to any of the passengers. My slowly forming suspicions came back with renewed force: the lady would bear watching.

'You've nothing to reproach yourself with, Miss Ross. The captain must have been flying blind in the storm—and we're more than 8000 feet up here. Probably he'd no knowledge of what was going to happen until the actual moment of crashing.' In my mind's eye I saw again the doomed airliner, landing lights on, circling our cabin for at least ten minutes, but if Miss Ross had any such thing in *her* mind's eye, it was impossible for me to detect it. She had no idea at all—or she was an extraordinarily good actress.

'Probably,' she murmured dully. 'I don't know.'

We had a hot and satisfying meal of soup, corned meat, potatoes and vegetables—everything out of cans, but passable enough for all that. It was the last satisfying meal that our guests—or ourselves, for that matter—were likely to have for some considerable time to come, but I felt the moment unpropitious for breaking that sort of news. Time enough for that tomorrow—or later in the day, rather, for it was now already after three o'clock in the morning.

I suggested that the four women sleep in the top bunks—not from any delicacy of sentiment but because it was at least twenty-five degrees warmer there than it was at ground level, and the proportional difference would increase as the night wore on after the stove had been put out. There were some half-hearted protests when they learnt that I intended to shut down the fire, but I didn't even bother arguing with them. Like all people who have lived for any length of time in the arctic, I had an almost pathological dread of fire.

Margaret Ross, the stewardess, refused the offer of a bunk, and said she would sleep by the injured pilot, lest he should wake and want anything during the night. I had intended doing that myself, but I saw her mind was set on it, and though I felt unaccountably uneasy about the idea, I raised no objection.

That left five empty bunks among six men—Jackstraw, Joss and I could sleep reasonably enough in our furs. Inevitably, there was some magnanimous argument over the allocation of these bunks, but Corazzini settled the argument by producing a coin and beginning to toss for it. He himself lost in the end, but accepted defeat and the prospect of a cold uncomfortable night on the floor with amiable grace.

When they were all settled down, I picked up a torch and our weather log book, glanced at Joss and made for the trap. Zagero turned on his bunk to look at me.

'What gives, Dr Mason? Especially at this hour of night, what gives?'

182

'Weather reports, Mr Zagero. That's why we're here, remember? And I'm already three hours late with these.'

'Even tonight?'

'Even tonight. Continuity is the most important thing in weather observation.'

'Sooner you than me.' He shivered. 'If it's only half as cold outside as it is in here. . . .'

He turned his back, and Joss rose to his feet. He'd correctly interpreted my look, and I knew he was consumed with curiosity.

'I'll come with you, sir. Better have a last look at the dogs.'

We didn't bother looking at either the dogs or the weather instruments. We went straight towards the tractor and huddled under the tarpaulin for what miserable shelter it could afford. True, the wind had eased, but it was colder than ever: the long winter night was beginning to close down on the ice-cap.

'It stinks,' Joss said flatly. 'The whole set-up stinks.'

'To high heaven,' I agreed. 'But it's finding out where the smell comes from that the trouble lies.'

'This fairy tale of yours about magnetic storms and compasses and radios,' he went on. 'What was the idea?'

'I'd previously said I knew something they didn't. I did. But when it came to the bit I knew I'd better keep it to myself. You know how this damnable cold slows up your mind—I should have realized it sooner.'

'Realized what?'

'That I should keep it to myself.'

'Keep what, for heaven's sake?'

'Sorry, Joss. Not trying to build up suspense. The reason none of them knew anything about the crash until after it had happened is that they were all doped. As far as I could see, all of them, or nearly all, were under the influence of some sleeping drug or narcotic.'

In the darkness I could almost feel him staring at me. After a long time he said softly, 'You wouldn't say this unless you were sure of it.'

'I am sure of it. Their reactions, their dazed fumbling back to reality—and, above all, the pupils of their eyes. Unmistakable. Some kind of sleeping tablet mixtures, of the fast-acting kind. What is known to the trade, I believe, as Mickey Finns.'

'But——' Joss broke off. He was still trying to orientate his mind to this new line of thought. 'But—they would be bound to know of it, to be aware that they had been doped, when they came to.'

'In normal circumstances, yes. But they came to in what was, to say the least, most abnormal circumstances. I'm not saying that they didn't experience any symptoms of weakness, dizziness and lassitude—they must have done—and what more natural than that they should ascribe any such unusual physical or mental symptoms to the effects of the crash. And what more natural, too, than that they should conceal these symptoms as best they could —and refrain from mentioning them? They would be ashamed to admit or discuss weakness—it's a very human trait to show to your neighbours the very best face you can put on in times of emergency or danger.'

Joss didn't reply at once. The implications of all this, as I'd found out for myself, took no little time for digestion, so I let him take his time and waited, listening to the lost and mournful wailing of the wind, the rustling hiss of millions of ice spicules scudding across the frozen snow of the ice-cap, and my own thoughts were in keeping with the bleak misery of the night.

'It's not possible,' Joss muttered at length. I could hear his teeth chattering with the cold. 'You can't have some maniac rushing around an aircraft cabin with a hypo needle or dropping fizz-balls into their gin and tonics. You think they were all doped?'

'Just about.'

'But how could anyone——'

'A moment, Joss,' I interrupted. 'What happened to the R.C.A.?'

'What?' The sudden switch caught him momentarily off-balance. 'What happened—you mean, how did it go for a burton? I've no idea at all, sir. All I know is that these hinges couldn't have been knocked into the wall accidentally—not with radio and equipment weighing about 180 pounds sitting on top of them. Someone shoved them in. Deliberately.'

'And the only person anywhere near it at the time was the stewardess, Margaret Ross. Everyone agreed on that.'

'Yes, but why in the name of heaven should anyone want to do a crazy thing like that?'

'I don't know,' I said wearily. 'There's a hundred things I don't know. But I do know she did it. . . . And who's in the best position to spike the drinks of aircraft passengers?'

'Good God!' I could hear the sharp hissing intake of breath. 'Of course. Drinks—or maybe the sweets they hand out at take off.'

184

'No.' I shook my head definitely in the darkness. 'Barley sugar is too weak a covering-up agent to disguise the taste of a drug. Coffee, more likely.'

'It must have been her,' Joss said slowly. 'It must have been. But—but she acted as dazed and abnormal as any of the others. More so, if anything.'

'Maybe she'd reason to,' I said grimly. 'Come on, let's get back or we'll freeze to death. Tell Jackstraw when you get him by himself.'

Inside the cabin, I propped the hatch open a couple of inches—with fourteen people inside, extra ventilation was essential. Then I glanced at the thermograph: it showed 48° below zero—eighty degrees of frost.

I lay down on the floor, pulled my parka hood tight to keep my ears from freezing, and was asleep in a minute.

CHAPTER FOUR

MONDAY 6 A.M.–6 P.M.

For the first time in four months I had forgotten to set the alarm-clock before I went to sleep, and it was late when I awoke, cold and stiff and sore all over from the uneven hardness of the wooden floor. It was still dark as midnight—two or three weeks had passed since the rim of the sun had shown above the horizon for the last time that year, and all the light we had each day was two or three hours dim twilight round noon—but a glance at the luminous face of my watch showed me that it was nine-thirty.

I pulled the torch out from my parka, located the oil-lamp and lit it. The light was dim, scarcely reaching the far corners of the cabin, but sufficient to show the mummy-like figures lying huddled on the bunks and sprawled grotesquely across the floor, their frozen breath clouding before their faces and above their heads, then condensing on the cabin walls. The walls themselves were sheeted with ice which had extended far out across the roof, in places reaching the skylights, a condition largely brought about by the cold heavy air that had flooded down the opened hatchway during the night: the outside temperature registered on the drum at 54° below zero.

Not everyone was asleep: most of them, I suspected, had slept but little, the numbing cold had seen to that: but they were as warm in their bunks as they would be anywhere else and nobody showed any inclination to move. Things would be better when the cabin heated up a little.

I had trouble starting the stove—even though it was gravity fed from a tank above and to one side of it, the oil fuel had thickened up in the cold—but when it did catch it went with a roar. I turned both burners up to maximum, put on the water bucket that had lain on the floor all night and was now nearly a solid mass of ice, pulled on snow-mask and goggles and clambered up the hatchway to have a look at the weather.

The wind had died away almost completely—I'd known that

from the slow and dispirited clacking of the anemometer cups—and the ice-drift, which at times could reach up several hundred feet into the sky, was no more than gentle puffs of dust stirring lazily and spectrally, through the feeble beam of my torch, across the glittering surface of the ice-cap. The wind, such as it was, still held out of the east. The cold, too, was still intense, but more bearable than it had been on the previous night. In terms of the effect of cold on human beings in the Arctic, absolute temperature is far from being the deciding factor: wind is just as important—every extra mile per hour is equivalent to a one degree drop in temperature—and humidity far more so. Where the relative humidity is high, even a few degrees below zero can become intolerable. But today the wind was light and the air dry. Perhaps it was a good omen. . . . After that morning, I never believed in omens again.

When I got below, Jackstraw was on his feet, presiding over the coffee-pot. He smiled at me, and his face was as fresh and rested as if he'd had nine hours on a feather bed behind him. But then Jackstraw never showed fatigue or distress under any circumstances: his tolerance to sleeplessness and the most exhausting toil was phenomenal.

He was the only one on his feet, but far from the only one awake: of those in the bunks, only Senator Brewster was still asleep. The others were facing into the centre of the room, a few propped up on their elbows: all of them were shivering, and shivering violently, their faces blue and white and pinched with the cold. Some were looking at Jackstraw, wrinkling their noses in anticipation of the coffee, the pungent smell of which already filled the cabin; others were staring in fascination at the sight of the ice on the roof melting as the temperature rose, melting, dripping down to the floor in a dozen different places and there beginning to form tiny stalagmites of ice, building up perceptibly before their eyes: the temperature on the cabin floor must have been almost forty degrees lower than that at the roof.

'Good morning, Dr Mason.' Marie LeGarde tried to smile at me, but it was a pathetic effort, and she looked ten years older than she had on the previous night: she was one of the few with a sleeping-bag, but even so she must have passed a miserable six hours, and there is nothing so exhausting to the human body as uncontrollable night-long shivering, a vicious circle in which the more one shivers the tireder one becomes, and the tireder the

187

less resistance to cold and hence the more shivering. For the first time, I knew that Marie LeGarde was an old woman.

'Good morning,' I smiled. 'How did you enjoy your first night in your new home?'

'First night!' Even in the sleeping-bag her movements of clasping her arms together and huddling her head down between her shoulders were unmistakable. 'I hope to heaven that it's the last night. You run a very chilly establishment here, Dr Mason.'

'I'm sorry. Next time we'll keep watches and have the stove on all night.' I pointed to the water splashing down to the floor. 'The place is heating up already. You'll feel better when you have some hot coffee inside you.'

'I'll never feel better again,' she declared vigorously, but the twinkle was back in her eye. She turned to the young German girl in the next bunk. 'And how do you feel this morning, my dear?'

'Better, thank you, Miss LeGarde.' She seemed absurdly grateful that anyone should even bother to ask. 'I don't feel a thing now.'

'Means nothing,' Miss LeGarde assured her cheerfully. 'Neither do I. It's just that we're both frozen stiff. . . . And how did you survive the night, Mrs Dansby-Gregg?'

'As you say, I survived.' Mrs Dansby-Gregg smiled thinly. 'As Dr Mason observed last night, this is not the Ritz. . . . That coffee smells delicious. Bring me a cup over, Fleming, will you?'

I picked up one of the cups Jackstraw had poured out and took it across to the young German girl who was struggling to unzip her sleeping-bag with her one good arm. Her embarrassment and discomfort were obvious, but I knew I'd no option, the time to stop this nonsense was before ever it had a chance to start.

'You stay where you are, young lady, and drink this.' She took the cup reluctantly, and I turned away. 'You've surely forgotten, Mrs Dansby-Gregg, that Helene has a broken collar-bone?'

The expression on her face made it quite obvious that she hadn't forgotten, but she was no fool. The gossip columnists would murder her for this, if they got hold of it. In her circle, an outward if meaningless conformity to the accepted mores and virtues of the day was *sine qua non*: the knife between the ribs was permitted, but only to the accompaniment of the well-bred smile.

188

'I'm so sorry,' she said sweetly. 'I'd quite forgotten, of course.' Her eyes were cold and hard, and I knew I had an enemy. That didn't worry me, but I found the very triviality of the whole thing irritating beyond measure when there were so many other and vastly more important things to talk about. But less than thirty seconds later we had forgotten all about it, even, I am sure, Mrs Dansby-Gregg herself.

I was just handing Marie LeGarde a cup when someone screamed. It wasn't really loud, I suppose, but in that confined space it had a peculiarly piercing and startling quality. Marie LeGarde's arm jerked violently and the scalding contents of the coffee-cup were emptied over my bare hand.

I hardly noticed the pain. It was Margaret Ross, the young stewardess, who had screamed, and she was now kneeling, half in and half out of her sleeping bag, one rigidly spread-fingered hand stretched out at arm's length before her, the other clasped over her mouth as she stared down at the figure lying near her on the floor. I pushed her to one side and sank on to my own knees.

In that bitter cold it was impossible to be any way sure, but I felt reasonably certain that the young pilot had been dead for several hours. I knelt there for a long time, just looking down at him, and when I finally rose to my feet I did so like an old man, a defeated old man, and I felt as cold, almost, as the dead man lying there. Everyone was wide awake now, everyone staring at me, the eyes of nearly all of them reflecting the superstitious horror which the presence of sudden and unexpected death brings to those who are unaccustomed to it. It was Johnny Zagero who broke the silence.

'He's dead, isn't he, Dr Mason?' His low voice sounded a little husky. 'That head injury——' His voice trailed off.

'Cerebral hæmorrhage,' I said quietly, 'as far as I can tell.'

I lied to him. There was no shadow of doubt in my mind as to the cause of death. Murder. The young boy had been ruthlessly, cold-bloodedly murdered: lying there unconscious, gravely injured and with his hands strapped helplessly to his sides, he had been smothered as easily, as surely, as one might smother a very little child.

We buried him out on the ice-cap, not fifty yards from the place where he had died. Bringing his stiffened body out of the hatch was a grisly job, but we managed it and laid him on the snow while we sawed out a shallow grave for him in the light of one of our torches. It was impossible to dig it out: that frozen ringing surface turned shovel blades as would a bar of iron: even at eighteen inches, the impacted *névé* of snow and ice defied the serrated spearpoints of our special snow saws. But it was deep enough and within a few hours the eternal ice-drift would have smoothed its blanket across the grave, and we would never be able to find it again. The Reverend Joseph Smallwood murmured some sort of burial service over the grave, but his teeth chattered so violently in the cold and his voice was so low and indistinct and hurried that I could hardly catch a word of it. I thought wryly that heavenly forgiveness for this indecent haste was unlikely to be withheld: by all odds it must have been by far the coldest funeral service that Mr Smallwood had ever conducted.

Back in the cabin, breakfast was a sketchy and silent affair. Even in the steadily rising warmth, the melancholy gloom was an almost palpable blanket under the dripping ceiling. Hardly anybody said anything, hardly anybody ate anything. Margaret Ross ate nothing, and when she finally set down her coffee-cup, the contents had scarcely been touched.

You're overdoing it, my dear, I thought viciously, you're carrying the grief-stricken act just a little too far: a little longer, and even the others will start wondering—and they have no suspicions at all, you damned inhuman little murderess.

For I had no suspicions either—only certainty. There was no doubt in my mind at all but that she had smothered the young pilot. She was only slightly built—but then it would have required only slight strength. Lashed to the cot as he had been, he wouldn't even have been able to drum his heels as he had died. I could feel my flesh crawl at the very thought.

She had killed him, just as she had broken the radio and doped the passengers. He had been killed, obviously, to keep him from talking—about what, I couldn't even begin to guess, any more than I could guess the reason for the destruction of the radio, except that she clearly did not want the news of the crash broadcast to the outer world. But why in the world destroy the radio in the first place, surely she must have known how essential it was for survival? But then, after all, how was she even to have guessed that: she might well have thought that we had big fast tractors that could have whipped them down to the coast in a matter of a couple of days. For that matter, she might have thought she was a great deal nearer the coast than we really were—it was impossible, surely, that she had genuinely imagined that we were in Iceland. Or was it?

My thoughts were spinning now in an unbreakable circle. I knew I was getting nowhere, couldn't possibly get anywhere without some fresh information. As it was, I was only confusing myself the more with the passing of every moment. I gave it up then, promising myself that from now on I would watch her every possible minute of the day. I looked at her again, covertly, and she was staring vacantly at one of the glowing embers of the stove. Planning her next move, no doubt, planning it as cleverly as the last: asking me last night about the pilot's chances of survival, doubtless to decide whether he would have to be killed or could safely be left to die, had been clever enough, but insisting on sleeping next to the man she had meant to kill had been nothing short of brilliant. On that account alone no one would ever suspect her, even if the fact that it had been murder became known. And it wouldn't: I intended keeping that to myself. Or did she suspect that I suspected? Heaven only knew. All I knew was that she must be playing for tremendous stakes. Or that she was mad.

It was just after eleven o'clock. Joss and Jackstraw were in a corner by themselves, stripping down the smashed transmitter, while the rest were grouped in a large semi-circle round the stove. They looked wan and sickly and were sitting very still indeed. They looked unwell because the first greyness of the noon twilight was stealing through our rimed skylights and it did unflattering things to any complexion: and they sat so still because I had just explained to them in detail exactly what their situation was, and they didn't like it one little bit. Neither did I.

'Let's get this quite straight, Dr Mason.' Corazzini leant forward, his lean brown face intent and serious. He was worried all right, but he wasn't scared. Corazzini didn't look as if he would scare easily: I had the idea that he would be a pretty good man to have around. 'The others left here three weeks ago in a big modern Sno-Cat, and aren't expected back for another three weeks. You've overstayed your welcome on the ice-cap, you say, and things have been cut a trifle too fine—you had already started rationing yourselves to make your food spin out until they returned. With thirteen of us here, we have food for less than five days. Therefore we may be a fortnight without food before they return.' He smiled, but there was no humour in it. 'My arithmetic is correct, Dr Mason?'

'It is. Unfortunately.'

'How long would the tractor you have take to get to the coast?'

'There's no guarantee that it ever would. I told you, it's falling to pieces. I'll show you later. Maybe a week—given the right conditions. Any bad weather would stop it in its tracks.'

'You doctors are all the same,' Zagero drawled. 'Always spreadin' sweet cheerfulness and light. Why don't we wait for the other machine to get back?'

'Indeed?' Senator Brewster said heavily. 'And how do you propose to live in the meanwhile, Mr Zagero?'

'People can live for longer than fourteen days without food, Senator,' Zagero said cheerfully. 'Think what it would do for that figure of yours. Tush, Senator, you surprise me. Too gloomy by half.'

'Not in this case,' I said flatly. 'The senator is right. Sure you can live a long time without food in normal conditions. You might even do it here—if you had proper day clothes and night coverings. You haven't—and how many of you have stopped shivering since you came here? Cold burns up your energy and depletes your reserves at a fantastic pace. Do you want me to list all the Arctic and Antarctic explorers—and Himalayan climbers—who have died within forty·eight hours of their food running out? And don't kid yourselves about the life-giving warmth of this cabin. The floor temperature is about zero now—and that's as hot as it is ever likely to get.'

'You said there was a radio on your old tractor,' Corazzini said abruptly. 'What range does it have? Couldn't you possibly reach your friends—or your Uplavnik base—with that?'

I nodded in Joss's direction. 'There's the man to ask.'

'I heard,' Joss said without enthusiasm. 'Do you think I'd be trying to salvage this wreckage, Mr Corazzini, if there was any chance. It's an eight-watt transmitter with hand-cranked generator and battery receiver, it came out of the ark and was never meant for anything more than walkie-talkie use.'

'But what is its range?' Corazzini persisted.

'Impossible to say.' Joss shrugged. 'You know how it is with transmission and reception. One day you can hardly pick up the B.B.C. a hundred miles away, another you can pick up a taxi-cab at twice the distance, if you have the right receiver. All depends on conditions. This one? Hundred miles, maybe—hundred fifty in perfect conditions. In the present conditions, you'd be better with a megaphone. I'll have a go with it this afternoon, perhaps. Might as well waste my time that way as any other.' Joss turned away and it was obvious that, as far as he was concerned, the subject was closed.

'Perhaps your friends will move within transmission range?' Corazzini suggested. 'After all, you said they're not much more than a couple of hundred miles away.'

'And I said they'll be staying there. They've set up their equipment and instruments and they won't move until they have to. They're too short of petrol for that.'

'They can refuel here, of course?'

'That's no worry.' I jerked a thumb towards the tunnel. 'There's eight hundred gallons out there.'

'I see.' Corazzini looked thoughtful for a moment, then went on. 'Please don't think I'm being annoyingly persistent. I just want to eliminate possibilities. I believe you have—or have had—a radio schedule with your friends. Won't they worry if they fail to hear from you?'

'Hillcrest—that's the scientist in charge—never worries about anything. And unfortunately, their own radio, a big long-range job, is giving trouble—they said a couple of days ago that the generator brushes were beginning to give out—and the nearest spares are here. If they can't raise us, they'll probably blame themselves. Anyway, they know we're as safe as houses here. Why on earth should they worry?'

'So what do we do?' Solly Levin asked querulously. 'Starve to death or start hikin'?'

'Succinctly and admirably put,' Senator Brewster boomed. 'In a nutshell, one might say. I propose we set up a small committee to investigate the possibilities——'

'This isn't Washington, Senator,' I said mildly. 'Besides, we already have a committee—Mr London, Mr Nielsen and myself.'

'Indeed?' It seemed to be the Senator's favourite word, and long years of practice had matched it perfectly to the lift of his eyebrows. 'You will remember, perhaps, that we have rather a personal stake in this also?'

'I'm unlikely to forget it,' I said dryly. 'Look, Senator, if you

193

were adrift in a hurricane and were picked up by a ship, would you presume to advise the captain and his officers of the course they should adopt to survive the hurricane?'

'That's not the point.' Senator Brewster puffed out his cheeks. 'This is not a ship——'

'Shut up!' It was Corazzini who spoke, his voice quiet and hard, and I could suddenly understand why he had reached the top in his own particularly tough and competitive business. 'Dr Mason is absolutely right. This is their own backyard, and our lives should be left in the hands of experts. I take it you have already reached a decision, Dr Mason?'

'I reached it last night. Joss—Mr London—stays here to contact the others when they return. He will be left enough food for three weeks. We take the remainder, and we leave tomorrow.'

'Why not today?'

'Because the tractor is at present unfit for winter travel, especially travel with ten passengers. It's still got the canvas hood on it that it had when we hauled stuff up from the coast. We have the prefabricated wooden sides and top that we need to arcticize it, plus the bunks and portable stove, but it will take several hours.'

'We start on that now?'

'Soon. But first your luggage. We'll go out to the plane now, and bring that back.'

'Thank goodness for that,' Mrs Dansby-Gregg said stiffly. 'I was beginning to think I'd never see my stuff again.'

'Oh, you will,' I said. 'Briefly.'

'Just what do you mean by that?' she asked suspiciously.

'I mean that you'll all put on as many clothes as you're able to stagger about in,' I said. 'Then you have a small attache-case for your valuables, if you have any. The rest of the stuff we'll have to abandon. This is no Cook's tour. We'll have no room on the tractor.'

'But—but I have clothes worth hundreds of pounds,' she protested angrily. 'Hundreds?—Thousands would be nearer it. I have a Balenciaga alone that cost over five hundred pounds, not to mention——'

'How much do you reckon your own life is worth?' Zagero said shortly. He grinned. 'Or maybe we should abandon you and save the Balenciaga. Better still, wear it on top of everything— you know, how the well-dressed woman leaves the ice-cap.'

'Excruciatingly funny.' She stared at him icily.

194

'Frequently fracture myself,' Zagero agreed. 'Can I give you a hand with the stuff, Doc?'

'You stay here, Johnny Zagero!' Solly Levin jumped up in agitation. 'One little slip on that ice——'

'Calm yourself, calm yourself.' Zagero patted his shoulder. 'Merely goin' in a supervisory capacity, Solly. How about it, Doc?'

'Thanks. You want to come, Mr Corazzini?' I could see he was already shrugging into a parka.

'I'd be glad to. Can't sit here all day.'

'These cuts on your head and hands aren't sealed yet. They'll sting like the devil when you get out into this cold.'

'Got to get used to it, haven't I? Lead the way.'

The airliner, crouching in the snow like some great wounded bird, was faintly visible in the twilight now, seven or eight hundred yards away to the north-east, port wing-tip facing us, lying at exactly right angles to our line of sight. There was no saying how often we might have to go out there, the quasi daylight would be gone in another hour or so, and it seemed pointless to follow in darkness the zigzag route we had been compelled to make the previous night, so with help from Zagero and Corazzini I staked out a route, with bamboo markers about five yards apart, straight out to the plane. Some of the bamboos I fetched from the tunnel, but most of them were transplanted from the positions where they had been stuck the previous night.

Inside the plane itself it was as cold as the tomb and as dark as the tomb. One side of the plane was already thickly sheeted in drift ice, and all the windows were completely blanked off, made opaque, by rime frost. In the light of a couple of torches we ourselves moved around like spectres, our heads enveloped in the clouds of our frozen breath, clouds that remained hanging almost stationary above our heads. In the silence we could faintly hear the crackling of our breath in the super-chilled air, followed by the curious wheezing noise that men make in very low temperatures when they are trying not to breathe too deeply.

'God, this is a ghastly place,' Zagero said. He shivered, whether or not from cold it was impossible to say, and flashed his torch at the dead man sitting in the back seat. 'Are we—are we going to leave them there, Doc?'

'Leave them?' I dumped a couple of attaché-cases on to the

195

pile we were making in the front seat. 'What on earth do you mean?'

'I don't know, I thought—well, we buried the second officer this morning, and——'

'Bury them? The ice-cap will bury them soon enough. In six months time this plane will have drifted over and be vanished for ever. But I agree—let's get out of here. Give anyone the creeps.'

As I made my way to the front I saw Corazzini, a doleful look on his face, shaking an ebonite and metal portable radio and listening to the rattling that came from inside.

'Another casualty?' I inquired.

'Afraid so.' He twiddled some dials, without result. 'Battery and mains model. A goner, Doc. Valves, I expect. Still, I'll tote it along—cost me two hundred dollars two days ago.'

'Two hundred?' I whistled. 'You should have bought two. Maybe Joss can give you some valves. He's got dozens of spares.'

'No good.' Corazzini shook his head. 'Latest transistor model —that's why it was so damn expensive.'

'Take it with you,' I advised. 'It'll only cost you another two hundred to get it repaired in Glasgow. Listen, there's Jackstraw now.'

We could hear the barking of dogs, and we lost no time in lowering the odds and ends down to Jackstraw, who loaded them on the sledge. In the forward hold we found about twenty-five suitcases of various sizes. We had to make two trips to bring all the stuff back, and on the second trip the rising wind was in our faces, already lifting the drift off the ice-cap. The climate on the Greenland plateau is one of the most unstable in the world, and the wind, which had all but stopped for a few hours, had now veered suddenly to the south. I didn't know what it presaged, but I suspected it wasn't anything good.

We were all chilled to the bone by the time the luggage had been lowered down into the cabin, and Corazzini looked at me, his eyes sober and speculative. He was shaking with cold, and his nose and one of his cheeks were white with frostbite, and when he pulled off one of his gloves the hand, too, was limp and white and dead.

'Is this what it's like to be exposed to this stuff for half an hour, Dr Mason?'

'I'm afraid it is.'

'And we're to be out in this for maybe seven days and seven nights! Good God, man, we'll never make it! And the women, old Miss LeGarde, and Brewster and Mahler, they're no chickens either——' He broke off, wincing—and I was beginning to suspect that it would take a great deal to make this man wince—as the circulation returned under the influence of vigorous rubbing. 'It's nothing short of suicide.'

'It's a gamble,' I corrected. 'Staying here and starving to death is suicide.'

'You put the alternative so nicely.' He smiled, a smile that never touched the cold and determined eyes. 'But I guess you're right at that.'

Lunch that day was a bowl of soup and crackers, poor fare at any time, shockingly insufficient to stay and warm men who would have to work for the next few hours in these bitter sub-zero temperatures above. But there was no help for it: if it would take us a week to reach the coast, and in all optimism I couldn't count on less, rationing would have to start now.

In a matter of a couple of hours the thermometer reading had risen with astonishing speed—these dramatic temperature variations were commonplace on the ice-cap—and it was beginning to snow when we emerged from the hatch and moved across to where the tractor lay. The rise in temperature flattered only to deceive: the south wind brought with it not only snow but a rapidly climbing humidity, and the air was almost unbearably chill.

We ripped off the covering tarpaulin—it cracked and tore but I was no longer concerned with preserving it—and our guests saw for the first time the vehicle upon which all their lives were to depend. Slowly I played my torch over it—the dark shroud of the arctic night had already fallen across the ice-cap—and I heard the quick indrawn hiss of breath beside me.

'Drove it out when the museum attendant wasn't looking, I suppose.' Corazzini kept his voice carefully expressionless. 'Or did you just find it here—left over from the last ice-age?'

'It is a bit old,' I admitted. 'Pre-war. But all we can afford. The British Government isn't quite so lavish with its I.G.Y. expenditure as the Russians and your people. Know it? It's the prototype, the ancestor of the modern arctic tractor.'

'Never seen it before. What is it?'

'French. A 10–20 Citroën. Underpowered, narrow-tracked as

197

you can see, and far too short for its weight. Lethal in crevasse country. Plods along fairly well on the frozen ice-cap, but you'd be better with a bicycle when there's any depth at all of new-fallen snow. But it's all we have.'

Corazzini said no more. As the managing director of a factory producing some of the finest tractors in the world, I suppose his heart was too full to say any more. But his disappointment made no difference to his drive, his sheer unflagging determination. For the next few hours he worked like a demon. So, too, did Zagero.

Less than five minutes after we had started work we had to stop again to rig up a canvas screen, lashed to aluminium poles brought up from the tunnel, round three sides of the tractor: work had been impossible in that snow and knife-like wind that lanced through even the bulkiest layers of clothing—and most of them were now wearing so many that they could move only with difficulty—as if they were tissue paper. Behind this screen we placed a portable oil stove—the very illusion of warmth was better than nothing—two storm lanterns and the blow-torches without which we could have made no progress at all. Even with this shelter, practically everyone had to go below from time to time to rub and pound life back into his freezing body: only Jackstraw and I, in our caribou furs, could stay up almost indefinitely. Joss was below all the afternoon: after spending a couple of hours trying to raise our field party on the tractor's emergency radio he gave it up and went doggedly back to work on the R.C.A.

Our first job, the removal of the hooped canvas hood, gave us some measure of the difficulty of the task that lay before us. The hood was secured by only seven bolts and nuts, but these had been in position for over four months now, were frozen solid and took over an hour to remove: each set had to be thawed out separately by blow-torch before the heavy wrenches could get the nuts to turn.

Then came the assembly of the wooden body. This was in fifteen prefabricated pieces, three each for the floor, sides, roof and front—the back was only a canvas screen. Each set of three pieces had to be brought out singly through the narrow hatchway before assembly, and it was the devil's own job, in that numbing cold and flickering semi-darkness, to locate and line up the bolt-holes in the wood with the matching holes in the connecting iron cross-pieces. It took us well over an hour to assemble and fit the floor section alone, and it was beginning to look as if we would be there until midnight when Corazzini had the idea—and a brilliant one it seemed at the time—of assembling the various sections in the comparative warmth and brightness of the cabin, sliding the completed piece out vertically into the food and fuel tunnel, sawing a long narrow slit through the snow roof, which was no more than a foot thick in the middle, and hauling the sections up from below.

After this we made rapid progress. By five o'clock the entire body shell was completed and with the end in sight less than a couple of hours away, everyone worked more furiously than ever. Most of them were unskilled, ham-handed and completely unused to any physical work at all, far less work of this cruel, exacting nature, but my opinion of them was rising all the time. Corazzini and Zagero, especially, were tireless, and Theodore Mahler, the silent little Jew whose entire conversational range so far had been limited to 'Yes', 'No', 'Please' and 'Thank you', was indefatigable, completely selfless and uncomplaining, driving his slight body to lengths of which I would never have believed it capable. Even the senator, the Rev. Smallwood and Solly Levin did what they could, as best they could, trying their best to hide their misery and their pain. By this time everyone, even Jackstraw and myself, were shaking almost uncontrollably with the cold so that our hands and elbows rat-tat-tatted like machine-guns against the wooden sides of the tractor: and our hands themselves, through constant contact with metal, were in a shocking state, puffed and bleeding and blistered, the mittens continuously filled with lumps and slivers of ice that never melted.

We had just installed the four collapsible bunks and were fitting the stove-pipe through its circular hole in the roof when someone called me. I jumped down and all but knocked over Marie LeGarde.

'You shouldn't be out here,' I scolded. 'It's far too cold for you, Miss LeGarde.'

'Don't be silly, Peter.' I could never bring myself to call her 'Marie', though she had asked me to several times. 'I have to get used to it, don't I? Would you come below for a moment or two, please?'

'Why? I'm busy.'

'But not indispensable,' she retorted. 'I want you to have a look at Margaret.'

199

'Margaret—oh, the stewardess. What does she want?'

'Nothing. It's I who want it. Why are you so hostile towards her?' she asked curiously. 'It's not like you—at least, I don't think it is. She's a fine girl.'

'What does the fine girl want?'

'What in the world's got into you? Why—oh, forget it. I'm not going to fight with you. Her back hurts—she's in considerable pain. Come and see it, please.'

'I offered to see it last night. If she wants me now, why doesn't she come and ask me?'

'Because she's scared of you, that's why,' she said angrily. She stamped a foot in the frozen snow. 'Will you go or not?'

I went. Below, I stripped off my gloves, emptied the ice out of them and washed my blistered, bleeding hands in disinfectant. I saw Marie LeGarde's eyes widen at the sight of my hands, but she said nothing: maybe she knew I wasn't in the mood for condolences.

I rigged up a screen in the corner of the room remote from the table where the women had been gathering and dividing out the remaining food supplies, and had a look at Margaret Ross's back. It was a mess, all right, a great ugly blue and purpling bruise from the spine to the left shoulder: in the centre, just below the shoulder blade, was a deep jagged cut, which looked as if it had been caused by a heavy blow from some triangular piece of sharp metal. Whatever had caused it had passed clean through her tunic and blouse.

'Why didn't you show me this yesterday?' I asked coldly

'I—I didn't want to bother you,' she faltered.

Didn't want to bother me, I thought grimly. Didn't want to give yourself away, you mean. In my mind's eye I had a picture of the pantry where we had found her, and I was almost certain now that I could get the proof I needed. Almost, but not quite, I'd have to go to check.

'Is it very bad?' She twisted round, and I could see there were tears in the brown eyes from the pain of the disinfectant I was rubbing on none too gently.

'Bad enough,' I said shortly. 'How did you get this?'

'I've no idea,' she said helplessly. 'I just don't know, Dr Mason.'

'Perhaps we can find out.'

'Find out? Why? What does it matter?' She shook her head wearily. 'I don't understand, I really don't. What *have* I done, Dr Mason?'

It was magnificent, I had to admit. I could have hit her, but it was magnificent.

'Nothing, Miss Ross. Just nothing at all.' By the time I had pulled on my parka, gloves, goggles and mask she was fully dressed, staring at me as I climbed up the steps and out through the hatch.

The snow was falling quite heavily now, gusting in swirling ghostly flurries through the pale beam of my torch: it seemed to vanish as it hit the ground, freezing as it touched, or scudding smoke-like over the frozen surface with a thin rustling sound. But the wind was at my back, the bamboo markers stretched out in a dead straight line ahead, never less than two of them in the beam of my torch, and I had reached the crashed plane in five or six minutes.

I jumped for the windscreen, hooked my fingers over the sill, hauled myself up with some difficulty and wriggled my way into the control cabin. A moment later I was in the stewardess's pantry, flashing my torch around.

On the after bulkhead was a big refrigerator, with a small hinged table in front of it, and at the far end, under the window, a hinged box cover over what might have been a heating unit or sink or both. I didn't bother investigating, I wasn't interested. What I was interested in was the for'ard bulkhead, and I examined it carefully. It was given up entirely to the small closed doors of little metal lockers let in flush to the wall—food containers, probably—and there wasn't a single metal projection in the entire wall, nothing that could possibly account for the wound in the stewardess's back. And if she had been here at the moment of impact, that was the wall she must have been flung against. The inference was inescapable—she must have been elsewhere at the time of the crash. I remembered now, with chagrin, that I hadn't even bothered to see whether or not she was conscious when we'd first found her lying on the floor.

Across the passage in the radio compartment I found what I was looking for almost immediately—I'd a pretty good idea where to look. The thin sheet metal at the top left-hand corner of the radio cabinet was bent almost half an inch out of true: and it

201

didn't require any microscope to locate or forensic expert to guess at the significance of the small dark stain and the fibres of navy blue cloth clinging to the corner of the smashed set. I looked inside the set itself, and now that I had time to spare it more than a fleeting glance it was abundantly clear to me that the wrenching away of the face-plate didn't even begin to account for the damage that had been done to the set: it had been systematically and thoroughly wrecked.

If ever there was a time when my thoughts should have been racing it was then, but the plain truth is that they weren't. It was abominably cold inside the chilled metal of that dead plane, and my mind was sluggish, but even so I knew that this time I couldn't be wrong about what had happened. I could see now why the second officer had sent out no distress messages. I could see now why he had almost certainly been sending out his regular "on route—on time" checks to base. Poor devil, he hadn't had much option—not with the stewardess sitting there with a gun on him. It must have been a gun. It was no consolation at all that the crash had caught her unprepared.

A gun! Gradually, ever so gradually, in infuriating slow-motion process, thoughts were beginning to click into place in my numbed mind. Whoever had landed that plane, landed it so skilfully into the blinding maelstrom of last night's blizzard, it hadn't been a dead man. I straightened, walked forward into the control cabin and shone my torch on the dead captain of the plane. As I'd noticed when I'd first seen him, he appeared to be completely unmarked, and I don't know whether it was some unconscious process of logical reasoning or some strange instinct that made me right away lift up the crackling ice-stiffened tunic jacket far enough to see the black powder-ringed bullet hole in the middle of the spine. I had been expecting it, I had been uncannily certain that I would find such a hole, and find it just there: but my mouth was suddenly dry, dry as if I had drunk nothing for days, and my heart was thudding heavily in my chest.

I lowered the jacket, pulled it down into position, turned away and walked slowly towards the rear of the plane. The man the stewardess had called Colonel Harrison was still sitting as I had left him, propped up stiffly in a corner, as stiffly as he would remain there for heaven only knew how many frozen centuries to come.

202

The jacket was fastened by a central button. I undid it, saw nothing except a curious thin leather strap running across the chest, undid a shirt button, another, and there it was, the same deadly little hole, the same powder-ringed evidence of point-blank firing staining the whiteness of the singlet. But in this case the powder marks were concentrated on the upper part of the ring, showing that the pistol had been directed in a slightly downward angle. On a hunch, but still like a man in a dream, I eased him forward, and there, less like a bullet hole in the jacket than an inconsequential rip one might easily overlook, was the point exit, matched by an equally tiny tear in the padding of the upholstered seat behind. At the time, that carried no special significance for me. Heaven knows that I was in no mental frame of mind at the moment, anyway, to figure anything out. I was like an automaton, the movements of which were controlled by something outside me. I felt nothing at the time, not even horror at the hideous thought that the man's neck might well have been cold-bloodedly broken after death to conceal its true cause.

The leather strap across the man's chest led to a felt-covered holster under the arm. I took out the little dark snub-nosed automatic, pressed the release switch and shook the magazine out from the base of the grip. It was an eight shot clip, full. I replaced it and shoved the gun into the inside pocket of my parka.

There were two inside breast pockets in the jacket. The left-hand one held another clip of ammunition, in a thin leather case. This, too, I pocketed. The right-hand pocket held only passport and wallet. The picture on the passport matched the face, and it was made out in the name of Lieut.-Colonel Robert Harrison. The wallet contained little of interest—a couple of letters with an Oxford postmark, obviously from his wife, British and American currency notes and a long cutting that had been torn from the top half of a page of the New York *Herald Tribune*, with a mid-September date-mark, just over two months previously.

For a brief moment I studied this in the light of my torch. There was a small, indistinct picture of a railway smash of some kind, showing carriages on a bridge that ended abruptly over a stretch of water, with boats beneath, and I realized that it was some kind of follow-up story on the shocking train disaster of about that time when a loaded commuters' train at Elizabeth, New Jersey, had plunged out over an opened span of the bridge into the waters of Newark Bay. I was in no mood for reading it

203

then, but I had the obscure, unreasonable idea that it might be in some way important.

I folded it carefully, lifted up my parka and thrust the paper into my inside pocket, along with the gun and the spare ammo clip. It was just at that moment that I heard the sharp metallic sound coming from the front of the dark and deserted plane.

CHAPTER FIVE

MONDAY 6 P.M.–7 P.M.

For maybe five seconds, maybe ten, I sat there without moving, as rigid and motionless as the dead man by my side, bent right arm frozen in the act of folding the newspaper cutting into my parka pocket. Looking back on it, I can only think that my brain had been half numbed from too long exposure to the cold, that the shock of the discovery of the savagely murdered men had upset me more than I would admit even to myself, and that the morgue-like atmosphere of that chill metal tomb had affected my normally unimaginative mind to a degree quite unprecedented in my experience. Or maybe it was a combination of all three that triggered open the floodgates to the atavistic racial superstitions that lurk deep in the minds of all of us, the nameless dreads that can in a moment destroy the tissue veneer of our civilization as if it had never been, and send the adrenalin pumping crazily into the bloodstream. However it was, I had only one thought in mind at that moment, no thought, rather, but an unreasoning blood-freezing certainty: that one of the dead pilots or the flight engineer had somehow risen from his seat and was walking back towards me. Even yet I can remember the frenzy of my wild, frantic hope that it wasn't the co-pilot, the man who had been sitting in the right-hand pilot's seat when the telescoping nose of the airliner had folded back on him, mangling him out of all human recognition.

Heaven only knows how long I might have sat there, petrified in this superstitious horror, had the sound from the control cabin not repeated itself. But again I heard it, the same metallic scraping sound as someone moved around in the darkness among the tangled wreckage of the flight deck, and as the touch of an electric switch can turn a room from pitch darkness to the brightness of daylight, so this second sound served to recall me, in an instant, from the thrall of superstition and panic to the world of reality and reason, and I dropped swiftly to my knees behind the high padded back of the seat in front of me, for what little shelter it offered. My heart was still pounding, the hairs still stiff on the back of my neck, but I was a going concern again, my mind beginning to race under the impetus invariably provided by the need for self-preservation.

And that self-preservation entered very acutely into it I did not for a moment doubt. A person who had killed three times to achieve her ends—I had no doubt at all as to the identity of the person in the control cabin, only the stewardess had seen me leave for the plane—and protect her secret wouldn't hesitate to kill a fourth. And she knew her secret was no longer a secret, not while I lived, I had stupidly made my suspicions plain to her. And not only was she ready to kill, but she had the means to kill —of the fact that she carried a gun and was murderously ready to use it I'd had grisly evidence in the past few minutes. Nor need she hesitate to use it: apart from the fact that falling snow had a peculiarly blanketing effect on all sound, the south wind would carry the crack of a pistol-shot away from the cabin.

Then something snapped inside my mind and I was all of a sudden fighting mad. Perhaps it was the thought of the four dead men—five, including the co-pilot—perhaps it was the inevitable reaction from my panic-stricken fear of a moment ago, and perhaps, too, it had no little to do with the realization that I, too, had a gun. I brought it out from my pocket, transferred the torch to my left hand, jumped up, pressed the torch button and started running down the aisle.

It was proof enough of my utter inexperience in this murderous game of hide-and-seek that it was not until I was almost at the door at the forward end of the cabin that I remembered how easy it would have been for anyone to crouch down behind the backs of one of the rearward facing front seats and shoot me at point-blank range as I passed. But there was no one there and as I plunged through the door I caught a fleeting glimpse of a dark muffled figure, no more than a featureless silhouette in the none too powerful beam of my torch, wriggling out through the smashed windscreen of the control cabin.

I brought up my automatic—the thought that I could be indicted on a murder charge for killing a fleeing person, no matter how criminal a person, never entered my mind—and squeezed the trigger. Nothing happened. I squeezed the trigger again, and before I remembered the existence of such a thing as a safety-

catch the windscreen was no more than an empty frame for the thickening snow that swirled greyly in the darkness beyond, and I plainly heard the thud of feet hitting the ground.

Cursing my stupidity, and again oblivious of the perfect target I was presenting, I leaned far out of the window. Again I was lucky, again I had another brief sight of the figure, this time scurrying round the tip of the left wing before vanishing into the snow and the dark.

Three seconds later I was on the ground myself. I landed awkwardly but picked myself up at once and skirted round the wing, pounding after the fleeing figure with all the speed I could muster in the hampering bulkiness of my furs.

She was running straight back to the cabin, following the line of the bamboo sticks, and I could both hear the thudding of feet in the frozen snow and see the wildly erratic swinging of a torch, the beam one moment pooling whitely on the ground beside the flying feet, the next reaching ahead to light up the bamboo line. She was moving swiftly, much more so than I would have thought her capable of doing, but nevertheless I was steadily overhauling her when suddenly the torch beam ahead curved away in a new direction, as the runner angled off into the darkness, about forty-five degrees to the left. I turned after her, still following both my sight of the torch and sound of the feet. Thirty yards, forty, fifty—then I stopped and stood very still indeed. The torch ahead had gone out and I could hear nothing at all.

For the second time that night I cursed my unthinking folly. What I should have done, of course, was to carry straight on back to the cabin and await the moment she turned up there, as she inevitably must: no person could hope to survive for any great length of time, without shelter of some kind, in the deadly cold of that arctic night.

But it wasn't too late yet. The wind had been blowing almost directly in my face as I had been running: all I had to do was walk back, keeping it on my left cheek, and I would be bound to hit the line of bamboos at right angles, and the chances of my passing unwittingly between two of them, with the light of my torch to help me, did not exist. I turned, took one step, then two, then halted in my tracks.

Why had I been lured out here away from the bamboo line? Not so that she could thereby escape me—she couldn't do it that way. As long as we both lived, we were both utterly dependent on the cabin and would have to meet there sooner or later.

As long as we both lived! God, what a fool I was, what a veriest amateur at this game. The only way she could escape me, really and permanently escape me, was if I no longer lived. I could be shot down here and no one would ever know. And as she had stopped running before I had and been first to switch out her torch, she must have a much better idea of my position than I of hers. And these two rash, incautious steps I had taken had given her a new and even more accurate bearing on my position. Perhaps she was only feet away now, lining her gun up for the kill.

I switched on my torch and whirled round in a complete circle. Nobody there, nothing to be seen at all. Only the frozen feathers of the snow brushing my cheeks in the blackness of the night, the low moaning lament of the soughing south wind and the faint rustle of ice spicules brushing their blind way across the iron-hard surface of the ice-cap.

Swiftly, softly, I moved half a dozen steps to my left. My torch was out now, I'd been crazy ever to switch it on in the first place. Nothing could have been better calculated to betray my position —the light of a torch, seen head on, can be seen at twenty times the farthest distance that its beam will reach. I prayed that a flurry of snow had hidden it.

Where would the attack come from—downwind, so that I could see nothing in that blinding snow, or upwind, so that I could hear nothing? Downwind, I decided—on the ice-cap one could move as silently as on a tar-macadam road. The better to hear, I pulled the parka hood off my head: the better to see, I slipped up my goggles and stared out unwinkingly under my visored hands.

Five minutes passed, and nothing happened—if, that is, the freezing of my ears and forehead could be called nothing. Still no sound, still no sight of anything: the strain, the nerve-racking expectancy could not be borne for much longer. Slowly, with infinite care, I moved off in a circle of about twenty yards diameter, but I saw nothing, heard nothing, and so well adjusted now were my eyes to the darkness, so well attuned my ears to the ice-cap's mournful symphony of sound, that I would have sworn that had there been anyone there to be seen or heard, I would have seen or heard them. It was as if I were alone on the ice-cap.

And then the appalling truth struck me—I was alone. I was alone, I realized in a belated and chilling flash of understanding, because shooting me would have been a stupid way of disposing of both myself and my dangerous knowledge—the discovery of a bullet-riddled body on the ice-cap during the brief hours of daylight would have provoked a hundred questions and suspicions. Much more desirable, from the killer's point of view, would be my dead body without a trace of violence. Even the most experienced man can get lost in a snow-storm on the ice-cap.

And I was lost. I knew I was lost, I was convinced of it even before I got the wind on my left and walked back to the line of bamboo piles. The bamboos were no longer there. I made a wide circle, but still I found nothing. For at least twenty yards back in the direction of the plane, and probably all the way towards the cabin, the poles had been removed, that slender series of markers which alone meant all the difference between safety and being irrecoverably lost on the ice-cap, were no longer there. I was lost, really and truly lost.

For once, that night, I didn't panic. It wasn't just that I knew that panic would be the end of me. I was consumed by a cold fury that I should have been so ignominiously tricked, so callously left to die. But I wasn't going to die. I couldn't even begin to guess what the tremendously high stakes must be in the murderous game that this incredibly ruthless, wickedly-deceptive gentle-faced stewardess was playing, but I swore to myself that I wasn't going to be one of the pawns that were going to be brushed off the table. I stood still, and took stock.

The snow was increasing now, thickening by the minute, building up into a blizzard with visibility cut down to a few feet: the yearly precipitation on the ice-cap was no more than seven or eight inches, and it was just my evil luck that it should fall so heavily that night. The wind was southerly, or had been, but in that fickle Greenland climate there was no knowing what minute it might back or veer. My torch was failing: continual use plus the cold had left it with a pale yellowish beam that reached not much more than a few yards: but that was the limit of visibility anyway, even downwind. The plane, I calculated, was not much more than a hundred yards away, the cabin six hundred. My chances of stumbling upon the latter, flush as it almost was with the surface of the ice-cap, were no better than one in a hundred. But my chances of finding the plane, or what came to the same thing, the great quarter-mile trench that it had gouged out in the frozen snow when it had crash-landed, were far better than even: it was impossible that it could have already been filled in with drift. I turned until I had the wind over my left shoulder and started walking.

I reached the deep furrow in the snow inside a minute—I'd switched off my torch to conserve the battery but my stumble and heavy fall as I went over the edge was intimation enough—turned right and reached the plane in thirty seconds. I suppose I might possibly have lasted out the night inside the wrecked fuselage, but such was my singleness of purpose at the moment that the thought never even occurred to me. I walked round the wing, picked up the first of the bamboos in the dim beam of my torch and started to follow them.

There were only five altogether. After that, nothing. Every one of the others had been removed. These five, I knew, pointed straight towards the cabin and all I had to do was to keep shifting the last of the five to the front, lining it up straight with the others in the light of my torch, and it would be bound to bring out to the cabin. Or so I thought, for perhaps ten seconds. But it was a task that really required two people to achieve anything like accuracy: what with that, the feebleness of my rapidly dying torch and the hopeless visibility, I couldn't be accurate within two or three degrees at the least. That seemed a trifle, but when I stopped and worked it out I discovered that, over the distance, even one degree out would have put me almost forty feet off course. On a night like that, I could pass by the cabin ten feet away and never see it. There were less laborious means of committing suicide.

I picked up the five sticks, returned to the plane and walked along the furrowed trench till I came to the depression where the plane had touched down. The 250-foot line of the antenna, I knew, was roughly four hundred yards away, just a little bit south of west—slightly to my left, that was, as I stood with my back to the plane. I didn't hesitate. I strode out into the darkness, counting my steps, concentrating on keeping the wind a little more than on my left cheek but not quite full-face. After four hundred long paces I stopped and pulled out my torch.

It was quite dead—the dull red glow from the filament didn't even register on my glove six inches away, and the darkness was as absolute as it can ever become on the ice-cap. I was a blind

man moving in a blind world, and all I had left to me was the sense of touch. For the first time fear came to me and I all but gave way to an almost overpowering instinct to run. But there was no place to run to.

I pulled the drawstring from my hood and with numbed and clumsy hands lashed together two of the bamboos to give me a stick seven feet in length. A third bamboo I thrust into the snow, then lay down flat, the sole of my boot touching it while I described a complete circle, flailing out with my long stick into the darkness. Nothing. At the full stretch of my body and the stick I stuck the last two bamboos into the snow, one upwind, the other downwind from the central bamboo, and described horizontal flailing circles round both of these. Again, nothing.

I gathered up the bamboos, walked ten paces more, and repeated the performance. I had the same luck again—and again and again. Five minutes and seventy paces after I had stopped for the first time I knew I had completely missed the antenna line and was utterly lost. The wind must have backed or veered, and I had wandered far off my course: and then came the chilling realisation that if that were so I had no idea now where the plane lay and could never regain it. Even had I known the direction where it lay, I doubted now whether I could have made my way back anyway, not because I was tired but because my only means of gauging direction was the wind in my face, and my face was now so completely numbed that I could no longer feel anything. I could hear the wind, but I couldn't feel it.

Ten more paces, I told myself, ten more and then I must turn back. Turn back where, a mocking voice seemed to ask me, but I ignored it and stumbled on with leaden-footed steps, doggedly counting. And on the seventh step I walked straight into one of the big antenna poles, staggered with the shock, all but fell, recovered, grabbed the pole and hugged it as if I would never let it go. I knew at that moment what it must be like to be condemned to death and then live again, it was the most wonderful feeling I have ever experienced. And then the relief and the exultation gradually faded and anger returned to take its place, a cold, vicious, all-consuming anger of which I could never have believed myself capable.

With my stick stretched up and running along the rimed antenna cable to guide me, I ran all the way back to the cabin. I was vaguely surprised to see shadows still moving in the lamp-lit screen that surrounded the tractor—it was almost impossible for me to realise that I had been gone no more than thirty minutes —but I passed by, opened the hatch and dropped down into the cabin.

Joss was still in the far corner, working on the big radio, and the four women were huddled close round the stove. The stewardess, I noticed, wore a parka—one she had borrowed from Joss—and was rubbing her hands above the flame.

'Cold, Miss Ross?' I inquired solicitously. At least, I had meant it to sound that way, but even to myself my voice sounded hoarse and strained.

'And why shouldn't she be, Dr Mason?' Marie LeGarde snapped. 'Dr Mason', I noted. 'She's just spent the last fifteen minutes or so with the men on the tractor.'

'Doing what?'

'I was giving them coffee.' For the first time the stewardess showed some spirit. 'What's so wrong with that?'

'Nothing,' I said shortly. Takes you a damned long time to pour a cup of coffee, I thought savagely. 'Most kind, I'm sure.' Massaging my frozen face, I walked away into the food tunnel, nodding to Joss. He joined me immediately.

'Somebody just tried to murder me out there,' I said without preamble.

'Murder you!' Joss stared at me for a long moment, then his eyes narrowed. 'I'll believe anything of this lot.'

'Meaning?'

'I was looking for some of the radio spares a moment ago —a few of them seem to be missing, but that's not the point. The spares, as you know, are next to the explosives. Someone's been tampering with them.'

'The explosives!' I had a momentary vision of some maniac placing a stick of gelignite under the tractor. 'What's missing?'

'Nothing, that's what so damned funny. I checked. All the explosives are there. But they're scattered everywhere, all mixed up with the fuses and detonators.'

'Who's been in here this afternoon?'

He shrugged. 'Who hasn't?'

It was true enough. Everyone had been coming and going there all afternoon and evening, the men for a hundred and one pieces of equipment for the tractor body, the women for food and stores. And, of course, our primitive toilet lay at the farthest end of the tunnel.

'What happened to you, sir?' Joss asked quietly.

I told him, and watched his face tighten till the mouth was a thin white line in the dark face. Joss knew what it meant to be lost on the ice-cap.

'The murderous, cold-blooded she-devil,' he said softly. 'We'll have to nail her, sir, we'll have to, or God only knows who's next on her list. But—but won't we have to have proof or confession or something? We can't just——'

'I'm going to get both,' I said. The bitter anger still dominated my mind to the exclusion of all else. 'Right now.'

I walked out of the tunnel and across the cabin to where the stewardess was sitting.

'We've overlooked something, Miss Ross,' I said abruptly. 'The food in your galley on the plane. It might make all the difference between life and death. How much is there?'

'In the galley? Not very much, I'm afraid. Only odds and ends for snacks, if anyone was hungry. It was a night flight, Dr Mason, and they had already had their evening meal.'

Followed by a very special brand of coffee, I thought grimly. 'Doesn't matter how little it is,' I said. 'It might be invaluable. I'd like you to come and show me where it is.'

'Can't it wait?' The protest came from Marie LeGarde. 'Can't you see that the poor girl is chilled to death?'

'Can't you see that I am too,' I snapped. It was a measure of the mood I was in when I could bring myself to speak like that to Marie LeGarde. 'Coming, Miss Ross?'

She came. I was taking no chances this time, so I carried with me the big searchlight with its portable battery and another torch, and gave the stewardess an armful of bamboos. When we had reached the top of the hatchway steps she waited for me to lead the way, but I told her to walk in front. I wanted to watch her hands.

The snow was easing now, the wind dropping and visibility just a little improved. We walked the length of the antenna line, angled off a little way north of east, setting down an occasional bamboo, and were at the plane within ten minutes of leaving the cabin.

'Right,' I said. 'You first, Miss Ross. Up you go.'

'Up?' She turned towards me, and though the big searchlight

lying on the ground was no help in letting me see the expression on her face, the puzzled tone of her voice was exactly right. 'How?'

'Same way as you did before,' I said harshly. My anger was almost out of control now, I couldn't have restrained myself any longer. 'Jump for it.'

'The same way——' She stopped in mid-sentence and stared at me. 'What do you mean?' Her voice was only a whisper.

'Jump for it,' I said implacably.

She turned away slowly and jumped. Her fingers didn't come within six inches of the sill. She tried again, got no nearer, and on her third attempt I boosted her so that her hands hooked over the sill. She hung there for a moment, pulled herself up a few inches, cried out and fell heavily to the ground. Slowly, dazedly, she picked herself up and looked at me. A splendid perfomance.

'I can't do it,' she said huskily. 'You can see I can't. What are you trying to do to me? What's wrong?' I didn't answer, and she rushed on. 'I—I'm not staying here. I'm going back to the cabin.'

'Later.' I caught her arm roughly as she made to move away 'Stand there where I can watch you.' I jumped up, wriggled inside the control cabin, reached down and pulled her up after me, none too gently, and without a word I led her straight into the galley.

'The Mickey Finn dispensary.' I observed. 'An ideal quiet spot it is, too.' She had her mask off now, and I held up my hand to forestall her as she opened her mouth to speak. 'Dope Miss Ross. But of course you wouldn't know what I'm talking about.'

She stared at me unblinkingly, made no answer.

'You were sitting here when the plane crashed,' I went on. 'Possibly on this little stool here? Right?'

She nodded, again without speaking.

'And, of course, were flung against this front bulkhead here. Tell me, Miss Ross, where's the metal projection that tore this hole in your back?'

She stared at the lockers, then looked slowly back at me.

'Is—is that why you've brought me here——'

'Where is it?' I demanded.

'I don't know'' She shook her head from side to side and took a backward step. 'What does it matter. And—and dope—what *is* the matter? *Please.*'

I took her arm without a word and led her through to the radio cabin. I trained the torch beam on to the top of the radio cabinet.

214

'Blood, Miss Ross. And some navy blue fibres. The blood from the cut on your back, the fibres from your tunic. Here's where you were sitting—or standing—when the plane crashed. Pity it caught you off balance. But at least you managed to retain your hold on your gun.' She was gazing at me now with sick eyes, and her face was a mask carved from white papier-mache. 'Missed your cue, Miss Ross—your next line of dialogue was "What gun?". I'll tell you—the one you had lined up on the second officer. Pity you hadn't killed him then, isn't it? But you made a good job of it later. Smothering makes such a much less messy job, doesn't it?'

'Smothering?' She had to try three times before she got the word out.

'On cue, on time,' I approved. 'Smothering. When you murdered the second officer in the cabin last night.'

'You're mad,' she whispered. Her lips, startlingly red against the ashen face, were parted and the brown eyes enormous with fear and sick despair. 'You're mad,' she repeated unsteadily.

'Crazy as a loon,' I agreed. Again I caught her arm, pulled her out on to the flight deck and trained my flashlight on the captain's back. 'You wouldn't, of course, know anything about this either.' I leaned forward, jerked up the jacket to expose the bullet hole in the back, then stumbled and all but fell as she gave a long sigh and crumpled against me. Instinctively I caught her, lowered her to the floor, cursed myself for having fallen for the fainting routine even for a second, and ruthlessly stabbed a stiff couple of fingers into the solar plexus, just below the breast bone.

There was no reaction, just no reaction at all. The faint had been as genuine as ever a faint can be and she was completely unconscious.

The next few minutes, while I sat beside her on the front seat of the plane waiting for her to recover consciousness, were some of the worst I have ever gone through. Self-reproach is a hopeless word to describe the way I swore at myself for my folly, my utter stupidity and unforgiveable blindness, above all for the brutality, the calculated cruelty with which I'd treated this poor, crumpled young girl by my side. Especially the cruelty in the past few minutes. Perhaps there had been excuse enough for my earlier suspicions, but there was none for my latest actions: if I hadn't been so consumed by anger, so utterly sure of myself so that the possibility of doubt never had a chance to enter my mind, if my mind hadn't been concentrated, to the exclusion of all else, on the exposure of her guilt, I should have known at least that it couldn't have been she who had jumped down from the control cabin half an hour ago when I had rushed up the aisle, for the simple but sufficient reason that she had been incapable of getting up there in the first place. Quite apart from her injury, I should have been doctor enough to know that the arms and shoulders I had seen while attending to her back that evening weren't built for the acrobatic performance necessary to swing one's self up and through that smashed windscreen. That had been no act she had put on when she had fallen back into the snow, I could see that clearly now; but I should have seen it then.

I still hadn't got beyond the stage of calling myself by every name I could think of when she stirred, sighed and straightened in the crook of the arm with which I was supporting her. Her eyes opened slowly, focused themselves on me, and I could feel the pressure on my forearm as she shrank away.

'It's all right, Miss Ross,' I urged her. 'Please don't be afraid. I'm not mad—really I'm not—just the biggest blundering half-witted idiot you're ever likely to meet in all the rest of your days. I'm sorry, I'm most terribly sorry for all I've said, for all I've done. Do you think you can ever forgive me?'

I don't think she heard a word I said. Maybe the tone of my voice gave her some reassurance, but it was impossible to tell. She shuddered, violently, and twisted her head to look in the direction of the flight deck.

'Murder!' The word was so low that I could hardly catch it. Suddenly her voice became high-pitched, unsteady. 'He's been murdered! Who—who killed him?'

'Now take it easy, Miss Ross.' My heavens, I thought, of all the fatuous advice. 'I don't know. All I know is that you had nothing to do with it.'

'No.' She shook her head tiredly. 'I don't believe it. I can't believe it. Captain Johnson. Why should anyone—he hadn't an enemy in the world, Dr Mason!'

'Maybe Colonel Harrison hadn't an enemy either.' I nodded towards the rear of the plane. 'But they got him too.'

She stared down the plane, her eyes wide with horror, her lips moving as if to speak, but no sound came.

'They got him too,' I repeated. 'Just as they got the captain.

Just as they got the second officer—and the flight engineer.'

'They?' she whispered. 'They?'

'Whoever it was. I only know it wasn't you.'

'No,' she whispered. Again she shuddered, even more uncontrollably than before, and I tightened my arm round her. 'I'm frightened, Dr Mason. I'm frightened.'

'There's nothing——' I'd started off to say there was nothing to be frightened of, before I realised the idiocy of the words. With a ruthless and unknown murderer among us, there was everything in the world to be frightened of. I was scared myself: but admitting that to this youngster wasn't likely to help her morale any. So I started talking, telling her of all the things we had found out, of the suspicions we had and of what had happened to me, and when I finished she looked at me and said: 'But why was I taken into the wireless cabin? I must have been, mustn't I?'

'You must have been,' I agreed. 'Why? Probably so that someone could turn a gun on you and threaten to kill you if the second officer—Jimmy Waterman, you called him, wasn't it—didn't play ball. Why else?'

'Why else?' she echoed. She gazed at me, the wide brown eyes never leaving mine, and then I could see the slow fear touching them again and she whispered: 'And who else?'

'How do you mean "Who else"?'

'Can't you see? If someone had a gun on Jimmy Waterman, someone else must have had one on the pilots. You can see yourself that no one could cover both places at the same time. But Captain Johnson must have been doing exactly as he was told, just as Jimmy was.'

It was so glaringly obvious that a child could have seen it: it was so glaringly obvious that I'd missed it altogether. Of course there must have been two of them how else would it have been possible to force the entire crew to do as they were ordered Good heavens, this was twice as bad, ten times as bad as it had been previously. Nine men and women back there in the cabin, and two of them killers, ruthless merciless killers who would surely kill again, at the drop of the hat, as the needs of the moment demanded. And I couldn't even begin to guess the identity of either of them. . . .

'You're right, of course, Miss Ross.' I forced myself to speak calmly, matter-of-factly. 'It was blind of me, I should have known,' I remembered how the bullet had passed clear through the man in the back seat. 'I did know, but I couldn't add one and one.

217

Colonel Harrison and Captain Johnson were killed by different guns—the one by a heavy carrying weapon, like a Colt or a Luger, the other by a less powerful, a lighter weapon, like something a woman might have used.'

I broke off abruptly. A woman's gun! Why not a woman using it? Why not even this girl by my side? It could have been her accomplice that had followed me out to the plane earlier in the evening, and it would fit in beautifully with the facts. . . . No, it wouldn't, faints couldn't be faked. But perhaps——

'A woman's gun?' I might have spoken my thoughts aloud, so perfectly had she understood. 'Perhaps even me—or should I say perhaps still me?' Her voice was unnaturally calm. 'Goodness only knows I can't blame you. If I were you, I'd suspect every-one too.'

She pulled glove and mitten off her left hand, took the gleaming ring off the third finger and passed it across to me. I examined it blankly in the light of my torch, then bent forward as I caught sight of the tiny inscription on the inside of the gold band: 'J. W.-M. R. Sept. 28, 1958'. I looked up at her and she nodded, her face numb and stricken.

'Jimmy and I got engaged two months ago. This was my last flight as a stewardess—we were being married at Christmas.' She snatched the ring from me, thrust it back on her finger with a shaking hand and when she turned to me again the tears were brimming over in her eyes. 'Now do you trust me?' she sobbed. 'Now do you trust me?'

For the first time in almost twenty-four hours I acted sensibly —I closed my mouth tightly and kept it that way. I didn't even bother reviewing her strange behaviour after the crash and in the cabin, I knew instinctively that this accounted for everything: I just sat there silently watching her staring straight ahead, her fists clenched and tears rolling down her cheeks, and when she suddenly crumpled and buried her face in her hands and I reached out and pulled her towards me she made no resistance, just turned, crushed her face into the caribou fur of my parka and cried as if her heart was breaking: and I suppose it was.

I suppose, too, that the moment when a man hears that a girl's fiancé has died only that day is the last moment that that man should ever begin to fall in love with her, but I'm afraid that's just how it was. The emotions are no respecters of the niceties, the proprieties and decencies of this life, and, just then, I was clearly aware that mine were stirred as they hadn't been since that dreadful day, four years ago, when my wife, a bride of only three months, had been killed in a car smash and I had given up medicine, returned to my first great love, geology, completed the B.Sc. course that had been interrupted by the outbreak of World War Two and taken to wandering wherever work, new surroundings and an opportunity to forget the past had presented themselves. Why, when I gazed down at that small dark head pressed so deeply into the fur of my coat, I should have felt my heart turn over I didn't know. For all her wonderful brown eyes she had no pretensions to beauty and I knew nothing whatsoever about her. Perhaps it was just a natural reaction from my earlier antipathy: perhaps it was pity for her loss, for what I had so cruelly done to her, for having so exposed her to danger—whoever knew that I knew too much would soon know that she knew it also: or perhaps it was just because she was so defenceless and vulnerable, so ridiculously small and lost in Joss's big parka. And then I caught myself trying to work out the reasons and I gave it up: I hadn't been married long, but long enough to know that the heart has its own reasons which even the acutest mind couldn't begin to suspect.

By and by the sobbing subsided and she straightened, hiding from me what must have been a very badly tear-stained face.

'I'm sorry,' she murmured. 'And thank you very much.'

'My crying shoulder.' I patted it with my right hand. 'For my friends. The other one's for my patients.'

'For that, too, but I didn't mean that. Just for not saying how sorry you were for me, or patting me or saying "Now, now" or anything like that. I—I couldn't have stood it.' She finished wiping her face with the palm of her mitten, looked up at me with brown eyes still swimming in tears and I felt my heart turn over again. 'Where do we go from here, Dr Mason?'

'Back to the cabin.'

'I didn't mean that.'

'I know. What am I to say? I'm completely at a loss. A hundred questions, and never an answer to one of them.'

'And I don't even know all the questions, yet,' she murmured. 'It's only five minutes since I even knew that it wasn't an accident.' She shook her head incredulously. 'Who ever heard of a civilian airliner being forced down at pistol point?'

'I did. On the radio, just over a month ago. In Cuba—some of

219

Fidel Castro's rebels forced a Viscount to crash land. Only they picked an even worse spot than this—I think there were only one or two survivors. Maybe that's where our friends back in the cabin got the idea from. I shouldn't be surprised.'

She wasn't even listening, her mind was already off on another track.

'Why—why did they kill Colonel Harrison?'

I shrugged. 'Maybe he had a high resistance to Mickey Finns. Maybe he saw too much, or knew too much. Or both.'

'But—but now they know *you've* seen too much and know too much.' I wished she wouldn't look at me when she was talking, these eyes would have made even the Rev. Smallwood forget himself in the middle of his most thundering denunciations—not that I could imagine Mr Smallwood going in for thundering denunciations very much.

'A disquieting thought,' I admitted, 'and one that has occurred to me several times during the past half-hour. About five hundred times, I would say.'

'Oh, stop it! You're probably as scared as I am.' She shivered. 'Let's get out of here please. It's—it's ghastly, it's horrible. What—what was that?' Her voice finished on a sharp high note.

'What was what?' I tried to speak calmly, but that didn't stop me from glancing around nervously. Maybe she was right, maybe I was as scared as she was.

'A noise outside.' Her voice was a whisper and her fingers were digging deep into the fur of my parka. 'Like someone tapping the wing or the fuselage.'

'Nonsense.' My voice was rough, but I was on razor-edge. 'You're beginning to——'

I stopped in mid-sentence. This time I could have sworn I *had* heard something, and it was plain that Margaret Ross had too. She twisted her head over her shoulder, looking in the direction of the noise, then slowly turned back to me, her face tense, her eyes wide and staring.

I pushed her hands away, reached for gun and torch, jumped up and started running. In the control cabin I checked abruptly —God, what a fool I'd been to leave that searchlight burning and lined up on the windscreens, blinding me with its glare, making me a perfect target for anyone crouching outside with a gun in hand— but the hesitation was momentary only. It was then or never—I could be trapped in there all night, or until the searchlight battery died. I dived head first through the windscreen, caught a pillar at the very last moment and was lying flat on the ground below in less time than I would have believed possible.

I waited five seconds, just listening, but all I could hear was the moan of the wind, the hiss of the ice spicules rustling along over the frozen snow—I'd never before heard that hissing so plainly, but then I'd never before lain with my uncovered ear on the ice-cap itself—and the thudding of my heart. And then I was on my feet, the probing torch cutting a bright swathe in the darkness before me as I ran round the plane, slipping and stumbling in my haste. Twice I made the circuit, the second time in the opposite direction, but there was no one there at all.

I stopped before the control cabin and called softly to Margaret Ross. She appeared at the window, and I said: 'It's all right, there's no one here. We've both been imagining things. Come on down.' I reached up my hands, caught her and lowered her to the ground.

'Why did you leave me up there, why did you leave me up there?' The words came rushing out, tumbling frantically one over the other, the anger drowned in the terror. 'It was—it was horrible! The dead men. . . . Why did you leave me?'

'I'm sorry.' There was a time and a place for comment on feminine injustice, unreasonableness and downright illogicality, but this wasn't it. In the way of grief and heart break, shock and ill-treatment, she had already had far more than she could stand. 'I'm sorry.' I repeated. 'I shouldn't have done it. I just didn't stop to think.'

She was trembling violently, so I put my arms round her and held her tightly until she had calmed down, took the searchlight and battery in one hand and her hand in my other and we walked back to the cabin together.

CHAPTER SIX

MONDAY 7 P.M.–TUESDAY 7 A.M.

Jackstraw and the others had just completed the assembly of the tractor body when we arrived back at the cabin, and some of the men were already going below. I didn't bother to check the tractor: when Jackstraw made anything, he made a perfect job of it.

I knew he must have missed me in the past hour, but I knew, too, that he wasn't the man to question me while the others were around. I waited till the last of these had gone below, then took him by the arm and walked out into the darkness, far enough to talk in complete privacy, but not so far as to lose sight of the yellow glow from our skylights—twice lost in the one night was twice too many.

He heard me out in silence, and at the end he said: 'What are we going to do, Dr Mason?'

'Depends. Spoken to Joss recently?'

'Fifteen minutes ago. In the tunnel.'

'How about the radio?'

'I'm afraid not, Dr Mason. He's missing some condensers and spare valves. He's looked for them everywhere—says they've been stolen.'

'Maybe they'll turn up?' I didn't believe it myself.

'Two of the valves already have. Crushed little bits of glass lying in the bottom of the snow tunnel.'

'Our little friends think of everything.' I swore softly. 'That settles it, Jackstraw. We can't wait any longer, we'll leave as soon as possible. But first a night's sleep—that we must have.'

'Uplavnik?' That was our expedition base, near the mouth of the Strömsund glacier. 'Do you think we will ever get there?'

He wasn't thinking, just as I wasn't, about the rigours and dangers of arctic winter travel, daunting enough though these were when they had to be faced with a superannuated tractor like the Citroën, but of the company we would be keeping en route. If any fact was ever so glaringly obvious that it didn't need mention, it was that the killers, whoever they were, could only escape justice, or, at least, the mass arrest and interrogation of all the passengers, by ensuring that they were the only ones to emerge alive from the ice-cap.

'I wouldn't like to bet on it,' I said dryly. 'But I'd bet even less on our chances if we stay here. Death by starvation is kind of final.'

'Yes, indeed.' He paused for a moment, then switched to a fresh line of thought. 'You say they tried to kill you to-night. Is that not surprising? I would have thought that you and I would have been very safe, for a few days at least.'

I knew what he meant. Apart from Jackstraw and myself, there probably wasn't a handful of people in all Greenland who could start that damned Citroën, far less drive it, only Jackstraw could handle the dogs, and it was long odds indeed against any of the passengers knowing anything at all about astral or magnetic compass navigation—the latter very tricky indeed in these high latitudes. These special skills should have been guarantee enough of our immediate survival.

'True enough,' I agreed. 'But I suspect they haven't given any thought to these things simply because they haven't realised the importance of them. We'll make it our business to point out that importance very plainly. Then we're both insured. Meantime, we'll have one last effort to clear this business up before we get started. It's not going to make us very popular, but we can't help that.' I explained what I had in mind, and he nodded thoughtful agreement.

After he had gone below, I waited a couple of minutes and then followed him. All nine of the passengers were sitting in the cabin now—eight, rather, watching Marie LeGarde presiding over a soup pan—and I took a long, long look at all of them. It was the first time I had ever examined a group of my fellow-men with the object of trying to decide which among them were murderers, and I found it a strange and unsettling experience.

In the first place, everyone of them looked to me like a potential or actual murderer—or murderess—but even with that thought came the realisation that this was purely because I associated murder with abnormality, and in these wildly unlikely surroundings, clad in the layered bulkiness of these wildly unlikely clothes, everyone of them seemed far removed from normality. But on a second and closer look, when one ignored the irrelevancies of surroundings and clothes, there remained only a group of shivering, feet-stamping, miserable and very ordinary people indeed.

Or were they so ordinary? Zagero, for instance, was he ordinary? He had the build, the strength and, no doubt, also the speed and temperament for a top-ranking heavyweight, but he was the most unlikely looking boxer I had ever seen. It wasn't just that he was obviously a well-educated and cultured man—there had been such boxers before: it was chiefly because his face was absolutely unmarked, without even that almost invariable thickening of skin above the eyes. Moreover, I had never heard of him, although that, admittedly, didn't go for much: as a doctor, I took a poor view of *homo sapiens* wreaking gratuitous physical and mental injury on *homo sapiens*, and took little interest in the sport.

Or take his manager, Solly Levin, or, for that matter of it, the Rev. Joseph Smallwood. Solly wasn't a New York boxing manager, he was a caricature of all I had ever heard or read about these Runyonesque characters, and he was just too good to be true: so, also, was the Rev. Smallwood, who was so exactly the meek, mild, slightly nervous, slightly anæmic man of God that preachers are so frequently represented to be—and almost invariably never are—that his movements, reactions, comments and opinions were predictable to the nth degree. But, against that, I had to set the fact that the killers were clever calculating men who would have carefully avoided assuming the guise of any character so patently cut from cardboard: on the other hand, they might have been astute enough to do just that.

There was a question mark, too, about Corazzini. America specialised in producing shrewd, intelligent, tough business leaders and executives, and Corazzini was undoubtedly one such. But the toughness of the average business man was purely mental: Corazzini had physical toughness as well, a ruthlessness I felt he wouldn't hesitate to apply to matters lying far outside the immediate sphere of business. And then I realised, wryly, that I was prepared to suspect Corazzini for reasons diametrically opposed to those for which I was prepared to suspect Levin and the Rev. Smallwood: Corazzini didn't fit into any pattern, any prefabricated mental image of the American business man.

Of the two remaining men, Theodore Mahler, the little Jew, and Senator Brewster, I would have taken the former any time as the more likely suspect. But when I asked myself why, I could

224

adduce no more damaging reasons than that he was thin, dark, rather embittered looking and had told us absolutely nothing about himself: and if that weren't prejudice on my part, I couldn't guess what was. As for Senator Brewster, he was surely above suspicion: and then the startling thought struck me that if one wished to be above suspicion surely there were no better means of achieving that than by assuming the identity of someone who *was* above suspicion. How did I know he was Senator Brewster? A couple of forged papers, a white moustache and white hair on top of a naturally florid complexion, and anyone could have been Senator Brewster. True, it would be an impersonation impossible to sustain indefinitely: but the whole point was that any such impersonation didn't have to be sustained indefinitely.

I was getting nowhere, and I knew it: I was more confused, more uncertain, and infinitely more suspicious than ever. I was even suspicious of the women. The young German girl, Helene —Munich was her home town, near enough Central Europe and the skulduggery that went on in the neighbourhood of the iron curtain for anything to be possible: but on the other hand the idea of a seventeen-year-old master criminal—we certainly weren't dealing with apprentices—was ridiculously far-fetched, and the fact that she had fractured her collar-bone, almost sure proof that the crash had been unexpected, was a strong point in her favour. Mrs Dansby-Gregg? She belonged to a world I knew little about, except for what slight information I had gleaned from my psychiatric brethren, who found rich fishing in the troubled waters of what passed for the younger London society: but instability and neuroses—not to mention the more than occasional financial embarrassment—were not criminal in themselves, and, in particular, that world lacked what people like Zagero and Corazzini had in full measure—the physical and mental toughness required for a job like this. But particularising from the general could be every bit as dangerous and misleading as generalising from the particular: of Mrs Dansby-Gregg, as a person, I knew nothing.

That left only Marie LeGarde. She was the touchstone, the one rock I could cling to in this sea of uncertainty, and if I were wrong about her so too had been a million others. There are some things that cannot be because they are unthinkable, and this was one of them. It was as simple as that. Marie LeGarde was above suspicion.

I became gradually aware of the muted clack of the anemometer cups turning sluggishly in the dying wind above and that the hiss of the Colman lamp had become abnormally loud: a total silence had fallen over the cabin and everyone was staring at me with mingled puzzlement and curiosity. So much for my impassive features, my casual negligent ease: so clearly had I betrayed the fact that something was far wrong that not one of the nine had missed it. But to be the centre of attraction at the moment suited me well enough: Jackstraw had just made his entry unobserved, a Winchester repeater cradled under his arm, his finger ready through the trigger guard.

'Sorry,' I apologized. 'Rude to stare, I know. However, now it's your turn.' I nodded in Jackstraw's direction. 'Every expedition carries a gun or two—for coast use against prowling bears and wolves and to get seal-meat for the dogs. I never thought that it would come in so handy right in the middle of the ice-cap—and against far more dangerous game than we ever find on the coast. Mr Nielsen is a remarkably accurate shot. Don't try anything—just clasp your hands above your heads. All of you.'

As if controlled by a master switch, all the eyes had now swivelled back to me. I'd had time and to spare to pull out the automatic —a 9 mm. butt-loading Beretta—that I'd taken off Colonel Harrison: and this time I didn't forget to slide off the safey-catch. The click was abnormally loud in the frozen silence of the room. But the silence didn't last long.

'What damnable outrage is this?' Senator Brewster shouted out the words, his face purpling in rage. He leapt to his feet, started to move forwards towards me then stopped as if he had run into a brick wall. The crash of Jackstraw's Winchester was a deafening, ear-drum shattering thunderclap of sound in that confined space: and when the last reverberations of the rifle-shot had faded and the smoke cleared away, Senator Brewster was staring down whitely at the splintered hole in the floor boards, almost literally underneath his feet: Jackstraw must have miscalculated the Senator's rate of movement, for the bullet had sliced through the edge of the sole of Brewster's boot. However it was, the effect couldn't have been bettered: the Senator reached back blindly for the support of the bunk behind him and lowered himself shakily to his seat, so terrified that he even forgot to clasp his hands above his head. But I didn't care about that: there would be no more trouble from the Senator.

'O.K., so you mean business. Now we're convinced.' It was

Zagero who drawled out the words, but his hands were tightly enough clasped above his head. 'We know you wouldn't do this for nothin', Doc. What gives?'

'This gives,' I said tightly. 'Two of you people are murderers— or a murderer and murderess. Both have guns. I want those guns.'

'Succinctly put, dear boy,' Marie LeGarde said slowly. 'Very concise. Have you gone crazy?'

'Unclasp your hands, Miss LeGarde, you're not included in this little lot. No, I'm not crazy. I'm as sane as you are, and if you want evidence of my sanity you'll find it out on the plane there—or buried out on the ice-cap: the captain of the plane with a bullet through his spine, the passenger in the rear with a bullet through his heart and the second officer smothered to death. Yes, smothered. Not cerebral haemorrhage, as I said: he was murdered in his sleep. Believe me, Miss LeGarde? Or would it take a personal tour of the plane to convince you?'

She didn't speak at once. Nobody spoke. Everyone was too stunned, too busy fighting incredulity and trying to assimilate the meaning of the shocking news I'd given them—everyone, that is, except two. But though I scanned eight faces with an intensity with which I had never before examined people I saw nothing—not the slightest off-beat gesture, the tiniest guilty reaction. As for what I'd secretly hoped—a guilty interchange of glances—well, the idea now seemed hopelessly, laughably improbable. Whoever the killers were, they were in perfect control of themselves. I felt despair touch me, a sure knowledge of defeat.

'I must believe you.' Marie LeGarde spoke as slowly as before, but her voice was unsteady and her face drained of colour. She looked at Margaret Ross. 'You knew of this, my dear?'

'Half an hour ago, Miss LeGarde. Dr Mason thought I had done it.'

'Good God! How—how utterly ghastly! How horrible! Two of us murderers.' From her position by the stove, Marie LeGarde glanced round the eight seated people, then looked quickly away. 'Suppose—suppose you tell us everything, Dr Mason?'

I told them everything. On the way back from the plane with Miss Ross I had debated this with myself—the question of secrecy or not. The no secrecy decision had won hands down: keeping quiet wouldn't fool the killers—they knew I knew: no secrecy would mean each and everyone of the passengers watching the others like hawks, making my task of constant vigilance all that

227

much easier, the killers' chance of making further mischief all that more difficult.

'You will stand up one at a time,' I said when I'd finished. 'Mr London will search you for your guns. And please don't forget—I know I'm dealing with desperate men. I'm prepared to act accordingly. When your turn comes stand very still indeed and make no suspicious move, not the slightest. I'm not very good with a pistol, and I shall have to aim at the middle of your bodies to make certain.'

'I believe you would at that,' Corazzini said thoughtfully.

'It doesn't matter what you believe,' I said coldly. 'Just don't be the one to find out.'

Joss started on Zagero. He searched him thoroughly—I could see the anger in Zagero's face, but his eyes didn't leave my gun—and found nothing. He moved on to Solly Levin.

'Might I ask why I'm being excused?' Marie LeGarde asked suddenly.

'You?' I said shortly. My eyes didn't move from Solly. 'Marie LeGarde? Don't be so damned silly!'

'The choice of words and tone of voice leave a lot to be desired.' Her voice was soft and warm, though still shaky. 'But I've never had a greater compliment. All the same, I insist on being searched: I don't want to be the one under a cloud if the guns don't turn up.'

And the guns didn't turn up. Joss finished searching the men, Margaret Ross the women—Mrs Dansby-Gregg under icy protest—and neither found anything. Joss looked at me, his face empty of all expression.

'Get their luggage,' I said harshly. 'The small cases they're taking with them. We'll try these.'

'You're wasting your time, Dr Mason,' Nick Corazzini said quietly. 'To any characters smart enough to guess that you were going to frisk them, the next move would stick out a mile. A child could guess it. You might find those guns you talk about hidden on the tractor or the sledges or buried under a couple of inches of snow, ready to be picked up whenever required, but you won't find them in our grips. A thousand to one, in dollars, that you don't.'

'Maybe you're right,' I said slowly. 'On the other hand, if I were one of the killers and did have a gun in my case—well, that's exactly the way I'd talk too.'

'As you said to Miss LeGarde just now, don't be so damned

silly!' He jumped to his feet, walked over to a corner of the cabin under the watchful eyes of Jackstraw and myself, picked up a handful of small cases and dumped them on the floor before me, his own nearest me. 'Where are you going to start? There's mine, that's the Reverend's robe case, this'—he picked it up and looked at the initials—'this is the Senator's brief-case. I don't know whose the last is.'

'Mine,' Mrs Dansby-Gregg said coldly.

Corazzini grinned. 'Ah, the Balenciaga. Well, Doc, who——' He broke off, straightened slowly, and gazed up through the skylight. 'What—what the devil is happening up there?'

'Don't try to pull any fast stuff, Corazzini,' I said quickly. 'Jackstraw's gun——'

'The hell with Jackstraw's gun!' he snapped impatiently. 'Have a look for yourself.'

I motioned him out of the way and had a look. Two seconds later I had thrust my automatic into Joss's hand and was on my way up top.

The airliner was a blazing torch in the darkness of the night. Even at that distance of half a mile and against the light wind, I could clearly hear the fierce roaring and crackling of the flames —not flames, rather, but one great solid column of fire that seemed to spring from the wings and centre of the fuselage and reach up clear and smokeless and sparkless two hundred feet into the night sky, brushing its blood-red stain across the snow for hundreds of yards around, transforming the rest of the still ice-sheathed fuselage into a vast effulgent diamond, a million constantly shifting points of refracted white and red and blue and green that glittered and gleamed with an eye-dazzling scintillating brilliance that no jewels on earth could have matched. It was a fantastically beautiful spectacle, but I'd had time to watch it for barely ten seconds when the dazzling coloured irradiation turned to a blaze of white, the central flame leapt up to twice, almost three times its original height and, two or three seconds later, the roar of the exploding petrol tanks came at me across the frozen stillness of the ice-cap.

Almost at once the flames seemed to collapse in upon themselves and the perimeter of the blood-red circle of snow shrank almost to vanishing point, but I waited to see no more. I dropped down into the cabin, pulling the hatch shut behind me, and looked at Jackstraw.

229

'Any chance at all of accounting for the presence of our various friends here during the past half-hour?'

'I'm afraid not, Dr Mason. Everyone was on the move all the time, finishing off the tractor body or bringing up the stores and petrol drums and lashing them on the sledge.' He glanced up through the skylight. 'The plane, wasn't it?'

' "Was" is right.' I glanced at the stewardess. 'My apologies, Miss Ross. You did hear somebody out there.'

'You mean—you mean it wasn't an accident?' Zagero asked.

There's a fair chance that you know damned well that it wasn't, I thought. Aloud, I said: 'It was no accident.'

'So there goes your evidence, eh?' Corazzini asked. 'The pilot and Colonel Harrison, I mean.'

'No. The nose and tail of the plane are still intact. I don't know what the reason could be—but I'm sure there's a damned good one. And you can put these bags away, Mr Corazzini. We're not, as you say, playing with children or amateurs.'

There was silence while Corazzini returned the bags, then Joss looked at me quizzically.

'Well, that explains one thing at least.'

'The messed-up explosives?' I remembered with chagrin how I had listened to the abnormally loud hissing out by the plane, but had ignored it. Someone who had known very clearly what he was doing had led a fuse into petrol lines or tanks or carburettors. 'It certainly does.'

'What's all this about explosives and fuses?' Senator Brewster demanded. It was the first word he had spoken since Jackstraw had scared the wits out of him, and even yet the colour wasn't all back in his face.

'Somebody stole the fuses to set fire to the plane. For all I know it may have been you.' I held up my hand to still his outraged spluttering and went on wearily: 'It may equally well have been one of the other seven of you. I don't know. All I know is that the person or persons responsible for the murders were responsible for the theft of the fuses. And for the smashing of the radio valves. And for the theft of the condensers.'

'And for the theft of the sugar,' Joss put in. 'Though heaven only knows why they should want to steal that.'

'Sugar!' I exclaimed, and then the question died in my throat. I happened to be looking straight at the little Jew, Theodore Mahler, and the nervous start he gave, the quick flicker of his eyes in Joss's direction, was unmistakable. I knew I couldn't have imagined it. But I looked away quickly, before he could see my face.

'Our last bag,' Joss explained. 'Maybe thirty pounds. It's gone. I found what little was left of it—just a handful lying on the floor of the tunnel—mixed up with the smashed valves.'

I shook my head and said nothing. The reason for this last theft I couldn't even begin to imagine.

Supper that night was a sketchy affair—soup, coffee and a couple of biscuits each as the only solids. The soup was thin, the biscuits no more than a bite and the coffee, for me at any rate, all but undrinkable without sugar.

And the meal was as silent as it was miserable, conversation being limited to what was absolutely necessary. Time and again I would see someone turn to his neighbour and make to say something, then his lips would clamp tightly shut, the expression drain out of his face as he turned away without a word: with almost everyone thinking that his or her neighbour might be a murderer, or, what was almost as bad, that his or her neighbour might be thinking that he was a murderer, the meal was by all odds the most awkward and uncomfortable that I'd ever had. Or, that is, the first part of it was: but by and by I came to the conclusion that I'd a great deal more to worry about than the niceties of social intercourse.

After the meal I rose, pulled on parka and gloves, picked up the searchlight, told Jackstraw and Joss to come with me and headed for the trap-door. Zagero's voice stopped me.

'Where you goin', Doc?'

'That's no concern of yours. Well, Mrs Dansby-Gregg?'

'Shouldn't you—shouldn't you take the rifle with you?'

'Don't worry.' I smiled thinly. 'With everyone watching everyone else like hawks, that rifle's as safe as houses.'

'But—but someone could jump for it,' she said nervously. 'They could get you when you're coming down the hatch——'

'Mr Nielsen and I are the last two persons they'd ever shoot. Without us, they couldn't get a mile from here. The most likely candidates for the next bullet are some of yourselves. You're absolutely inessential and, as far as the killers are concerned, represent nothing more than a waste of priceless rations.' With this comforting thought I left them, each person trying to watch all the others at one and the same time, while doing his level best to give the appearance of watching no one.

The wind was so slight now that the anemometer cups had stopped turning. The dying embers of the burnt-out plane were a dull smouldering glow to the north-east. The snow had gone, completely and the first faint stars were beginning to show through the thinning cloud above. It was typically Greenland, this swift change in the weather, and so, too, was the temperature inversion that would surely follow in the morning, or before morning. Twelve hours from now it was going to be very cold indeed.

With searchlight and torches we examined every inch of the tractor and sledges, above and below, and if there had been a pin there I would have sworn that we couldn't have missed it, far less anything so large as a couple of guns. We found nothing.

I straightened, and turned to look at the glow that was lightening the sky to the east, and even as I stood there with Joss and Jackstraw by my side the moon, preternaturally large and rather more than half full, heaved itself above the distant horizon and flooded the ice-cap with its pale and ghostly light, laying down between itself and our feet a bar-straight path of glittering silver grey. We watched in silence for a full minute, than Jackstraw stirred. Even before he spoke, I knew what was in his mind.

'Uplavnik,' he murmured. 'Tomorrow, we set off for Uplavnik. But first, you said, a good night's sleep.'

'I know,' I said. 'A traveller's moon.'

'A traveller's moon,' he echoed.

He was right, of course. Travel in the Arctic, in winter, was regulated not by daylight but by moonlight. And to-night we had that moon—and we had a clear sky, a dying wind and no snow at all. I turned to Joss.

'You'll be all right alone?'

'I have no worries,' he said soberly. 'Look, sir, can't I come too?

'Stay here and stay healthy,' I advised. 'Thanks, Joss, but you know someone must remain behind. I'll call you up on the usual schedules. You might get a kick out of the R.C.A. yet. Miracles still happen.'

'Not this time, they won't.' He turned away abruptly and went below. Jackstraw moved across to the tractor—we didn't say another word to each other, we didn't have to—and I followed Joss down to the cabin. No one had moved an inch, as far as I could see, but they all looked up as I came in.

'All right,' I said abruptly. 'Get your stuff together and pile on every last stitch of clothes you can. We're leaving now.'

We left, in fact, just over an hour later. The Citroën had been lying unused for the better part of a fortnight, and we had the devil's own job getting it to start. But start it eventually did, with a roar and a thunderous clatter that had everybody jumping in startlement then looking at it in dismay. I knew the thoughts in their minds, that they'd have to live with this cacophony, this bedlam of sound assaulting their shrinking eardrums for no one knew how many days to come, but I wasted little sympathy on them: at least they would have the protection of the wooden body while I would be sitting practically on top of the engine.

We said our good-byes to Joss. He shook hands with Jackstraw and myself, with Margaret Ross and Marie LeGarde, and, pointedly, with no one else. We left him standing there by the hatchway, a lonely figure outlined against the pale light of the steadily climbing moon, and headed west by south for Uplavnik, three hundred long and frozen miles away. I wondered, as I knew Joss was wondering, whether we would ever see each other again.

I wondered, too, what right I had in exposing Jackstraw to the dangers which must lie ahead. He was sitting beside me as I drove, but as I looked at him covertly in the moonlight, at that strong lean face that, but for the rather broad cheekbones, might have been that of any Scandinavian sea-rover, I knew I was wasting my time wondering. Although nominally under my command, he had only been lent me, as other Greenlanders had been lent as an act of courtesy by the Danish Government to several I.G.Y. stations, as a scientific officer—he had a geology degree from the University of Copenhagen and had forgotten more about the ice-cap than I would ever know—and in times of emergency, especially where his own pride, and he had plenty of that, was concerned would be extremely liable to do what he thought best, regardless of what I thought or said. I knew he wouldn't have remained behind even if I had ordered him to—and, if I were honest with myself, I was only too damned glad to have him along, as a friend, as an ally, and as insurance policy against the disaster that can so easily overtake the careless or the inexperienced on the ice-cap. But even so, even though I quieted my conscience as best I could, it was difficult to push from

233

my mind the picture of his dark vivacious young school-teacher wife and little daughter, the red and white brick house in which I'd lived for two weeks as a guest in the summer. What Jackstraw thought was impossible to say. He sat immobile as if carved from stone, only his eyes alive, constantly moving, constantly shifting, as he probed for sudden dips in the ice-cap, for differences in the structure of the snow, for anything that might spell trouble. It was purely automatic, purely instinctive: the crevasse country lay, as yet, two hundred and fifty miles away, where the ice-cap started to slope sharply to the sea, and Jackstraw himself maintained that Balto, his big lead dog, had a surer instinct for crevasses than any human alive.

The temperature was dropping down into the minus thirties, but it was a perfect night for arctic travel—a moonlit, windless night under a still and stary sky. Visibility was phenomenal, the ice-cap was smooth and flat, the engine ran sweetly with never a falter: had it not been for the cold, the incessant roar and body-numbing vibration of the big engine, I think I would almost have enjoyed it.

With the wide tractor body blocking off the view behind, it was impossible for me to see what was happening there: but every ten minutes or so Jackstraw would jump off and stand by the side of the trail. Behind the tractor body and its shivering occupants— because of the tractor fuel tank beneath and the spare fuel drums astern the stove was never lit while we were in motion—came the sledge with all our stores: 120 gallons of fuel, provisions, bedding and sleeping-bags, tents, ropes, axes, shovels, trail flags, cooking utensils, seal meat for the dogs, four wooden bridging battens, canvas sheets, blow lamps, lantern, medical equipment, radio-sonde balloons, magnesium flares and a score of minor items. I had hesitated over including the radio-sondes, especially the relatively heavy hydrogen cylinders for these: but they were ready crated with tents, ropes, axes and shovels and—this was the deciding factor—had saved lives on at least one occasion when a trail party, lost on the plateau with defective compasses, had saved themselves by releasing several balloons in the brief daylight hours thereby enabling base to see them and send accurate radio bearings.

Behind the heavy transport sled was towed the empty dogsled, with the dogs on loose traces running astern of it, all except Balto who always ran free, coursing tirelessly backwards and forwards

234

all night long, one moment far ahead of us, the next ranging out to one side, the next dropping astern, like some destroyer circling a straggling convoy by night. When the last of the dogs had passed him by, Jackstraw would run forward to overtake the tractor and jump in alongside me once more. He was as tireless, as immune to fatigue, as Balto himself.

The first twenty miles were easy. On the way up from the coast, over four months previously, we had planted big marker flags at intervals of half a mile. On a night such as this, with the moonlight flooding the ice-cap, these trail flags, a bright luminous orange in colour and mounted on aluminium poles stuck in snow beacons, were visible at a great distance, with never less than two and sometimes three in sight at the same time, the long glistening frost feathers stretching out from the poles sometimes twice the length of the flags themselves. We counted twenty-eight of these flags altogether—about a dozen were missing—then, after a sudden dip in the land, completely lost them: whether they had been blown away or just drifted under it was impossible to say.

'Well, there it is, Jackstraw,' I said resignedly. 'This is where one of us starts getting cold. Really cold.'

'We've been cold before, Dr Mason. Me first.' He slid the magnetic compass off its brackets, started to unreel a cable from a spool under the dashboard, then jumped out, still unwinding the cable, while I followed to help. Despite the fact that the magnetic north pole is nowhere near the north pole—at that time it was almost a thousand miles south of it and lay more to the west than north of us—a magnetic compass, when proper variation allowances are made, is still useful in high latitudes: but because of the counter-acting magnetic effects of a large mass of metal, it was quite useless when mounted on the tractor itself. Our plan, therefore, was that someone should lie with the compass on the dog-sled, fifty feet behind the tractor, and, by means of a switch which operated red and green lights in the tractor dashboard, guide the driver to left or right. It wasn't our original idea, it wasn't even a recent idea: it had been used in the Antarctic a quater century previously but, as far as I knew, had not been improved upon yet.

With Jackstraw established on the sledge, I walked back to the tractor and pushed aside the canvas screen at the back of the wooden body. What with the faces of the passengers, drawn and

235

pinched and weirdly pale in the light of the tiny overhead bulb, the constant shivering, the chattering of teeth and the frozen breath drifting upwards to condense and freeze on the wooden roof, it was a picture of utter and abject misery: but I was in no mood to be moved at that moment.

'Sorry for the delay,' I said. 'Just off again now. But I want one of you for a lookout.'

Both Zagero and Corazzini volunteered almost in the same breath, but I shook my head.

'You two get what sleep or rest you can—I'm liable to need you very much later on. Perhaps you, Mr Mahler?'

He looked pale and ill, but he nodded silently, and Zagero said in a quiet voice: 'Corazzini and myself too high up on the list of suspects, huh?'

'I wouldn't put either of you at the very foot,' I said shortly. I waited till Mahler had climbed down then dropped the canvas and walked round to the driver's seat.

Theodore Mahler, strangely enough, proved only too anxious to talk—and keep on talking. It was so completely out of keeping with the idea I had formed of his character that I was more than surprised. Loneliness, perhaps, I thought, or trying to forget the situation, or trying to divert my thoughts and suspicions: how wrong I was on all three counts I wasn't to find out until later.

'Well, Mr Mahler, it looks as if the itinerary of your European trip is going to be upset a bit.' I had almost to shout to make my words heard above the roar of the tractor.

'Not Europe, Dr Mason.' I could hear the machine-gun-like chatter of his teeth. 'Israel.'

'You live there?'

'Never been there in my life.' There was a pause, and when his voice came again it was all but drowned in the sound of the engine. I thought I caught the words 'My home'.

'You—you're going to start a new life there, Mr Mahler?'

'I'm sixty-nine—to-morrow,' he answered obliquely. 'A new life? Let's say, rather, that I'm going to end an old one.'

'And you're going to live there, make your home there—after sixty-nine years in another country?'

'Millions of us Jews have done just that, in the past ten years. Not that I've lived in America all my lfe. . . .'

And then he told me his story—a story of refugee oppression that I'd heard a hundred times, with a hundred variations. He

236

was a Russian Jew, he said, one of the millions of the largest Jewry in the world that had been 'frozen' for over a century in the notorious Pale of Settlement, and in 1905 had been forced to flee with his father—leaving mother and two brothers behind—to escape the ruthless massacres carried out by the 'Black Hundreds' at the behest of the last of the Romanoff Tzars who was seeking scapegoats for his crushing defeat by the Japanese. His mother, he learned later, had just disappeared, while his two brothers had survived only to die in agony long years afterwards, one in the rising in the Bialystok ghetto, the other in the Treblinka gas chambers. He himself had found work in the clothing industry in New York, studied in night school, worked for an oil company, married and with the death of his wife that spring had set about fulfilling the agelong ambition of his race, the return to their holy land.

It was a touching story, pathetic and deeply moving, and I didn't believe a word of it.

Every twenty minutes I changed position with Jackstraw and so the long hours of the night dragged by as the cold deepened and the stars and the moon wheeled across the black vault of the sky. And then came moonset, the blackness of the arctic night rushed across the ice-cap, I slowed the Citroën gratefully to a stop and the silence, breathless and hushed and infinitely sweet came flooding in to take the place of the night long clamour of the deafening roar of the big engine, the metallic clanking of the treads.

Over our black sugarless coffee and biscuits I told our passengers that this would be only a brief three-hour halt, that they should try to get what sleep they could: most of them, myself included, were already red-eyed and drooping from exhaustion. Three hours, no more: not often did Greenland offer travel weather like this, and the chance was not to be missed.

Beside me, as I drank my coffee, was Theodore Mahler. He was for some reason, restless, ill at ease, jerky and nervous, and his eyes and attention both wandered so much that it was easy enough for me to find out what I wanted.

When my cup was empty, I whispered in Mahler's ear that there was a little matter that I wished to discuss privately with him. He looked at me in surprise, hesitated, then nodded in agreement, rising to follow me as I moved out into the darkness.

A hundred yards away I stopped, switched on my torch so that he blinked in its beam, and slid my Beretta forward until its barrel was clearly visible, sharply outlined in the harsh white glare. I heard the catch of the breath, saw the eyes widening in fear and horror.

'Save the act for the judge, Mahler,' I said bleakly. 'I'm not interested in it. All I want is your gun.'

CHAPTER SEVEN

TUESDAY 7 A.M.–TUESDAY MIDNIGHT

'My gun?' Mahler had slowly lifted his arms until his hands were at shoulder level, and his voice wasn't quite steady. 'I—I don't understand, Dr Mason. I have no gun.'

'Naturally.' I jerked the barrel of the Beretta to lend emphasis to my words. 'Turn round.'

'What are you going to do? You're making a——'

'Turn round!'

He turned. I took a couple of steps forward, ground the muzzle of the automatic none too gently into the small of his back and started to search him with my free hand.

He was wearing two overcoats, a jacket, several sweaters and scarves, two pairs of trousers and layer upon layer of under-clothes: searching him was easier said than done. It took me a full minute to convince myself that he wasn't carrying a weapon of any kind. I stepped back, and he came slowly round to face me.

'I hope you're quite satisfied now, Dr Mason?'

'We'll see what we find in your case. As for the rest, I'm satisfied enough. I have all the proof I want.' I dipped the torch beam to illuminate the handful of sugar I'd taken from the pocket of his inner overcoat—there had been well over a pound in either pocket. 'You might care to explain where you got this from, Mr Mahler?'

'I don't have to tell you that, do I?' His voice was very low. 'I stole it, Dr Mason.'

'You did indeed. A remarkably small-time activity for a person who operates on the scale you do. It was just your bad luck, Mahler, that I happened to be looking directly at you when the theft of the sugar was mentioned back in the cabin. It was just your bad luck that when we had our coffee just now it was dark enough for me to have a swig from your cup without your knowledge: it was so stiff with sugar that I couldn't even drink the damn' stuff. Curious, isn't it, Mahler, that such a tiny thing as giving way to a momentary impulse of greed should ruin everything? But I believe it's always the way: the big slip-up never brings the big criminal to book, because he never makes any. If you'd left that sugar alone when you were smashing up the valves, I'd never have known. Incidentally, what did you do with the rest of the sugar? In your grip? Or just thrown away?'

'You're making a very grave mistake, Dr Mason.' Mahler's voice was steady now, and if it held any trace of worry or guilt I couldn't detect it. But I was now far beyond the naïve stage of expecting to detect anything of the sort. 'I didn't touch these valves. And, apart from the few handfuls I took, the sugar bag was quite intact when I left it.'

'Of course, of course.' I waved the Beretta. 'Back to the tractor, my friend, and let's have a look at this case of yours.'

'No!'

'Don't be crazy,' I snapped. 'I have a gun, Mahler. Believe me, I won't hesitate to use it.'

'I believe you. I think you would be quite ruthless if the need arose. Oh, I don't doubt you're tough, Doctor, as well as being headstrong, impulsive and not very subtle, but because I rather respect your efficient and selfless handling of an awkward and ugly situation for which you were in no way responsible, I don't want to see you make a complete fool of yourself in public.' He lifted his right hand towards the lapel of his coat. 'Let me show you something.'

I jerked the Beretta forward, but the gesture was quite needless. As he pushed his hand under his topcoats, Mahler's gestures were smooth and unhurried, just as smooth and unhurried when he brought his hand out again and passed over to me a leather-covered card. I stepped back a few feet, flipped open the card and glanced down at it.

That one glance was enough—or should have been enough. I'd seen these cards scores of times before, but I stared down at this one as if I'd never seen one in my life. This was a completely new factor, it knocked all my preconceived notions on the head, and I needed time, time for reorientation, for understanding, for quelling the professional fear that came hard on the heels of that understanding. Then, slowly, I folded the card, pulled down my snow-mask, stepped close to Mahler and pulled his down also.

In the harsh glare of the torch, his face was blue and white with the cold, and I could see the jutting of the jaw muscles as he clamped his teeth together to keep them from chattering uncontrollably.

'Breathe out,' I said.

He did as I asked, and there was no mistaking it, none at all: the sweet acetone breath of the advanced and untreated diabetic can't possibly be confused with anything else. Wordlessly, I handed him back the card and thrust the automatic into my parka pocket.

At last I said quietly: 'How long have you had this, Mr Mahler?'

'Thirty years.'

'A pretty advanced condition?' When it came to discussing a man's illness with him, I had little time for the professional reticence of many of my colleagues: besides, the average elderly diabetic had survived to that age simply because he was intelligent about the dietary and medical treatment of his trouble, and usually knew all about it.

'My doctor would agree with you.' I caught the smile on his face as he pushed his mask up, and there wasn't much humour in it. 'So would I.'

'Twice daily injections?'

'Twice,' he nodded. 'Before breakfast and in the evening.'

'But don't you carry a hypo and——'

'Normally,' he interrupted. 'But not this time. The Gander doctor gave me a jab and as I can usually carry on a few hours overdue without ill effects I thought I'd wait until we got to London.' He tapped his breast pocket. 'This card's good anywhere.'

'Except on the Greenland ice-cap,' I said bitterly. 'But then I don't suppose you anticipated a stop-over here. What diet were you on?'

'High protein, high starch.'

'Hence the sugar?' I looked down at the white crystals still clenched in my left mitten.

'No.' He shrugged. 'But I know sugar used to be used for the treatment of coma. I thought maybe if I stuffed enough into myself. . . . Well, anyway, you know now why I turned criminal.'

'Yes, I know now. My apologies for the gun-waving act, Mr Mahler, but you must admit I had every justification. Why

241

in the hell didn't you tell me before now? I *am* supposed to be a doctor, you know.'

'I would have had to tell you sooner or later, I suppose. But right now you'd plenty troubles of your own without worrying about mine also. And I didn't think there would be much chance of your carrying insulin among your medical stores.'

'We don't—we don't have to. Everybody gets a thorough medical before going on an I.G.Y. station, and diabetes hardly develops overnight. . . . You take it all very calmly, I must say Mr Mahler. Come on, let's get back to the tractor.'

We reached there inside a minute. I pulled back the canvas screen and a thick white opaque cloud formed almost immediately as the relatively warm air inside met the far sub-zero arctic air outside. I waved my hand to dispel it, and peered inside. They were all still drinking coffee—it was the one thing we had in plenty. It seemed difficult to realize that we'd been gone only a few minutes.

'Hurry up and finish off,' I said abruptly. 'We're on our way within five minutes. Jackstraw, would you start the engine, please, before she chills right down?'

'On our way!' The protest, almost inevitably, came from Mrs Dansby-Gregg. 'My dear man, we've hardly stopped. And you promised us three hours' sleep only a few minutes ago.'

'That was a few minutes ago. That was before I found out about Mr Mahler here.' Quickly I told them all I thought they needed to know. 'It sounds brutal to say it in Mr Mahler's presence,' I went on, 'but the facts themselves are brutal. Whoever crashed that plane—and, to a lesser extent, stole the sugar—put Mr Mahler's life in the greatest danger. Only two things, normally, could save Mr Mahler—a properly balanced high-calorie diet as a short term measure, insulin as a long term one. We have neither. All we can give Mr Mahler is the chance to get one or other of these things with all speed humanly possible. Between now and the coast that tractor engine is going to stop only if it packs up completely, if we run into an impassable blizzard—or if the last of the drivers collapses over the wheel. Are there any objections?'

It was a stupid, unnecessary, gratuitously truculent question to ask, but that's just the way I felt at that moment. I suppose, really, that I was inviting protest so that I could have some victim for working off the accumulated rage inside me, the anger that could find its proper outlet only against those responsible for this fresh infliction of suffering, the anger at the near certainty that no matter what effort we made to save Mahler it would be completely nullified when the time came, as it inevitably must come, that the killers showed their hand. For one wild moment I considered the idea of tying them all up, lashing them inside the tractor body so that they couldn't move, and had the conditions been right I believe I would have done just that. But the conditions couldn't have been more hopeless: a bound person wouldn't have lasted a couple of hours in that bitter cold.

There were no objections. For the most part, I suppose, they were too cold, too tired, too hungry and too thirsty—for with the rapid evaporation of moisture from the warm, relatively humid body thirst was always a problem in dry, intensely cold air—to raise any objections. To people unaccustomed to the Arctic, it must have seemed that they had reached the nadir of their sufferings, that things could get no worse than they were: I hoped as much time as possible would elapse before they found out how wrong they were.

There were no objections, but there were two suggestions. Both came from Nick Corazzini.

'Look, Doc, about this diet Mr Mahler must have. Maybe we can't balance it, but we can at least make sure that he gets a fair number of calories—not that I know how you count the damn' things. Why don't we double his rations—no, even that wouldn't keep a decent sparrow alive. What say each of the rest of us docks a quarter of his rations and hands them over? That way Mr Mahler would have about four times his normal——'

'No, no!' Mahler protested. 'Thank you, Mr Corazzini, but I cannot permit——'

'An excellent idea,' I interrupted. 'I was thinking along the same lines myself.'

'Good,' Corazzini grinned. 'Carried unanimously. I also suggest we'd get along farther and faster if, say, Mr Zagero and I were to spell you two on the tractor.' He held up a hand as if to forestall protest. 'Either of us may be the man you want, in fact, we might be the two men you want—if it is two men. But if I'm one of the killers, and I know nothing about the Arctic, navigation, the maintenance of this damned Citroën and wouldn't as much as recognize a crevasse if I fell down one, it's as plain as the nose on your face that I'm not going to make a break for it until I'm within shouting distance of the coast. Agreed?'

'Agreed,' I said. Even as I spoke, there came a coughing clattering roar as Jackstraw coaxed the still-warm Citroën back into life, and I looked up at Corazzini. 'All right,' I went on. 'Come on down. You can have your first driving lesson now.'

We left at half-past seven that morning, in driving conditions that were just about perfect. Not the slightest breath of air stirred across the ice-cap and the deep blue-black vault of the sky was unmarred by even the tiniest wisp of cloud. The stars were strangely remote, pale and shimmering and unreal through the gossamer gauze of the glittering ice needles that filled the sky and sifted soundlessly down on to the frozen snow, but even so visibility was all that could have been desired: the powerful headlights of the Citroën, striking a million sparkling diamond points of light off the ice spicules, reached a clear three hundred yards ahead into the darkness, leaving the ground to either side of the twin interlocking beams shrouded in impenetrable darkness. The cold was intense, and deepening by the hour: but the Citroën seemed to thrive on it that morning.

Luck was with us almost right away. Within fifteen minutes of starting off, Balto, ranging free as always, appeared out of the darkness to the south-west and ran alongside the dog-sledge, barking to attract Jackstraw's attention. Jackstraw gave us the signal to stop—a rapid flickering of the red and green lights on the tractor dashboard—and two or three minutes later appeared out of the darkness, grinning, to tell us that Balto had picked up a standing trail flag. That was good news in itself, in that it meant that our navigation the previous night had been all that could have been wished for and that we were almost exactly on course: even more important, however, was the fact that if this flag was the first of a series we could dispense with the navigator on the dog-sledge and that Jackstraw and I could have some sleep—if sleep were possible in that miserably cold and lurching tractor body. And, indeed, that flag proved to be the first of an almost unbroken series that was to guide us all the length of that interminable day, so that from eight o'clock onwards Jackstraw, Zagero, Corazzini and I took it in turns to drive, with the Senator, the Reverend Smallwood or Solly Levin up front as lookout. Theirs was probably the coldest, certainly the most unwelcome job of all: but all three bore up uncomplainingly, even to the extent of thawing out in silent agony at the end of their hour on duty.

Shortly after eight o'clock I left an obviously competent Corazzini to his own devices, dropped back to the shelter of the tractor body and asked the Senator to go up front. I then set about breaking the strictest rule of all, where these old tractors were concerned—that no fire should ever be lit inside when they were in motion. But even the most stringent rules are to be observed only until such time as the need for breaking them is paramount: and now both the need and the time were here. My concern was not for the warmth and comfort of the passengers, or even for the cooking of the food—we had little enough of that, heaven knew, though a constant supply of warm water would come in useful for dealing with the inevitable cases of frostbite—but purely and simply for the life of Theodore Mahler.

Even following Corazzini's suggestion we couldn't give him enough food, and what we could didn't, and wouldn't, even begin to resemble a balanced diet. His best chance of survival, and that was slender enough, lay in conserving his body reserves and his energy as far as lay within our power. To achieve that, work, or exercise of even the lightest kind, was out: he had to remain as immobile as possible, which was why I had him climb into a sleeping-bag and lie down on one of the bunks, wrapped in a pair of heavy blankets, as soon as I entered. But without work or exercise he would have no means to combat that numbing cold except by a constant shivering which would deplete his reserves just as quickly as the most violent exercise would. So he had to have heat: heat from the stove, heat from the warm fluids which I told Margaret Ross that he was to have at least every two hours. Mahler protested strongly against all these arrangements being made on his behalf, but at the same time he was sensible enough to realize that his only chance of survival depended on doing what I said: but I believe that the main factor which finally made him yield was not so much my medical explanations as the pressure of public opinion.

That all the passengers should suddenly, and so vehemently, be concerned with Theodore Mahler's welfare seemed, on the face of it, inexplicable. But only on the face of it. It did not require a great deal of thought or probing beneath the surface to discover that the true motivating factor was not selflessness—though there may have been some of that, too—but selfishness. Mahler represented not so much a sufferer as a most welcome diversion from their own thoughts and suspicions, from the tension, from the never-ending constraint that had laid its chilling hand over the entire company for the past twelve hours.

This constraint, apart from its awkwardness and sheer unpleasantness, had the further effect of splitting up the passengers into tiny groups. Communal speech had ceased entirely, except where necessity and the barest demands of common politeness made it inevitable.

Marie LeGarde and Margaret Ross, each of whom knew that the other was not under suspicion, kept very much to themselves and talked only between themselves. So, too, did Zagero and Solly Levin, and also—though this would have seemed ridiculously improbable only twenty-four hours ago—Mrs Dansby-Gregg and her maid, Helene. Improbable then, but inevitable now: whether guilty or not, both knew exactly where the other stood, and, of all the passengers, each could only fully trust the other. They could, of course, as could all the others, trust Marie LeGarde and Margaret Ross: but the fact that they knew that Marie LeGarde and Margaret Ross couldn't trust them was enough to prohibit any attempts to establish an easier relationship. As for Corazzini, the Rev Smallwood, the senator and Mahler, they kept very much to themselves.

In the circumstances, then, it was inevitable that they should welcome the introduction of an absolutely innocuous subject of interest and conversation, something that would ease, however slightly, the coldness and discomfort of the social atmosphere, something that would divert their unwelcome and suspicious thoughts into some more tolerable channel. Theodore Mahler promised to be the best looked after patient I had ever had.

I had just got the oil stove going to my satisfaction when Zagero called to me from his seat by the rear canvas screen.

'There's somethin' funny goin' on outside, Doc. Come and have a look.'

I had a look. Far off to the right—the north-west, that was—and high above the horizon a great diffuse formless volume of luminosity, spreading over almost a quarter of the dark dome of the sky, was beginning to pulse and fade, pulse and fade, strengthening, deepening, climbing with the passing of every moment. At first it was no more than a lightening in the sky, but already it was beginning to take form, and faint colours beginning to establish themselves in definite patterns.

246

'The aurora, Mr Zagero,' I said. 'The Northern Lights. First time you've seen it?'

He nodded. 'Yeah. Amazin' spectacle, ain't it?'

'This? This is nothing. It's just starting up. It's going to be a curtain—you get all sorts, rays, bands, coronas, arcs and what have you, but this is a curtain. Best of the lot.'

'Get this sort of thing often, Doc?'

'Every day, for days on end, when the weather is like this—you know, cold and clear and still. Believe it or not, you can even get so used to it that you won't bother looking.'

'I don't believe it. It's amazin',' he repeated, 'just amazin'. Tired of it, you say—I hope we see it every day.' He grinned. 'You don't have to look, Doc.'

'For your own sake you'd better hope for something else,' I said grimly.

'Meanin'?'

'Meaning that radio reception is hopeless when the aurora is on.'

'Radio reception?' He crinkled his brows. 'What we gotta lose, with the radio set in the cabin smashed and your friends in the trail party gettin' farther away every minute? You couldn't raise either of them anyway.'

'No, but we can raise our Uplavnik base when we get a bit nearer the coast,' I said, and the next moment I could have bitten my tongue off. I had never thought of the matter until then, but as soon as the words were out I realized that I should have kept this piece of knowledge to myself. The chances of Uplavnik listening in at the right time and on the right frequency were remote enough, but it was always a chance: we could have sent out a warning, summoned help long before the killers would have thought of making a break for it. But, now, if Zagero were one of the killers, he would make good and certain that the set would be smashed long before we got within radio range of the Uplavnik base.

I cursed myself for a blundering idiot, and stole a quick glance at Zagero. In the light streaming out from the gap in the curtain and in the fainter light of the aurora, his every feature was plain, but I could tell nothing from his expression. He was playing it casual, all right, but not too stupidly casual. The slow nod, the pursing of the lips, the thoughtful lifting of the eyebrows could not have been improved upon. Not even the best professional actor could have improved on it, and hard on the heels of that

247

came the second thought that there were a couple of extraordinarily fine actors among us. But, then, if he hadn't reacted at all, or had reacted too violently, I would have been doubly suspicious. Or would I? If Zagero were one of the guilty men, wouldn't he have known that too much or too little reaction would have been the very thing to excite suspicion, and taken due precaution against registering either? I gave it up and turned away. But in my mind there was growing a vague but steadily strengthening suspicion against Johnny Zagero: and on the basis of the success and validity of my previous suspicions, I thought bitterly, that just about guaranteed Zagero's innocence.

I turned and touched Margaret Ross on the shoulder.

'I'd like to have a few words with you, Miss Ross, if you don't mind the cold outside.'

She looked at me in surprise, hesitated for a moment, then nodded. I jumped down, reached up a hand to steady her, then helped her aboard the big sled as it passed by a few seconds later. For a short time we just sat there, side by side on a petrol drum, watching the aurora while I wondered how to begin. I stared almost unseeingly at the tremendous sweep of the developing aurora, the great folded, fluted curtain of yellow-green with red-tipped feet that seemed almost to brush the surface of the ice-cap, a translucent transparent drapery—for even at its brightest the stars still shone faintly through—that waved and shimmered and pulsed and glowed, a pastel poem in insubstantiality, like the ethereal backdrop to some unimaginably beautiful fairyland. Margaret Ross sat there gazing at it like one lost in a trance. But she might have been looking at it with the same uncaring eyes as myself, lost not in wonder but in the memory of the man we had left behind in the ice-cap. And when she turned at the sound of my voice, and I saw the glow of the aurora reflected in the sad depths of the wide brown eyes, I knew I was right.

'Well, Miss Ross, what do you think of the latest developments?'

'Mr Mahler?' She'd slipped up her snow-mask—in her case just a gauze and cotton-wool pad with a central breathing aperture —and I had to lean forward to catch her soft voice against the steady roar of the tractor engine in front. 'What can one say about anything so—so dreadful. What chance does the poor man have, Dr Mason?'

'I've honestly no idea. There are far too many unpredictable factors involved. . . . Did you know that after I'd crossed you off I'd lined him up as number one on my list of suspects?'

'No!'

'But yes, I'm afraid. I fear I'm no sleuth, Miss Ross. I may be long on the empirical, trial and error method—and it at least has had the negative advantage of reducing the number of suspects by two—but I'm pretty short on the deductive.' I told her what had happened between Mahler and myself during the brief stop we had made.

'And now you're as badly off as ever,' she said, when I had finished. 'I suppose all we can do now is to sit and wait to see what happens?'

'Wait for the axe to fall, you mean?' I said grimly. 'Not quite. I haven't much hope from it, but I thought I might try the the deductive reasoning act for a change. But before we can deduce, we have to have some facts we can deduce from. And we're very short on facts. That's why I asked you out here—to see if you could help me.'

'I'll do anything I can, you know that.' She lifted her head as the aurora swelled and flamed to the incandescent climax of its performance, and shivered violently as its unearthly beautiful colourings struck a million sparks of coloured light, red and green and yellow and gold, off the ice spicules in the sky. 'I don't know why, that makes me feel colder than ever. . . . But I think I've already told you everything I know, everything I can remember, Dr Mason.'

'I'm sure you have. But you may have missed some things just because you couldn't see they mattered anyway. Now, as I see it, we have three big questions looking for an answer. How come the crash in the first place? How was the coffee spiked? How was the radio broken? If we can turn up anything that can throw a light on even one of these, we may be a long way towards finding out what we want to know.'

Ten freezing minutes later we were still a long way from finding out anything. I'd taken Margaret Ross step by step from the Customs Hall, where she'd met her passengers, to the plane where she had settled them down, flown with them to Gander, watched them go through the same process again, flown with them out of Gander, watched her as she'd served their evening meal, and still I'd learnt nothing, turned up nothing suspicious, off-beat or abnormal that could even begin to account for the crash.

Then, slowly, just as she was describing the serving of the meal, her voice trailed away into silence, and she turned and stared at me.

'What's the matter, Miss Ross?'

'Of course,' she said softly. 'Of course! What a fool I am! Now I see. . . .'

'What do you see?' I demanded.

'The coffee. How it was tampered with. I'd just served Colonel Harrison—he was in the rear seat, so he was the last to be served—when he wrinkled his nose and asked if I could smell something burning. I couldn't, but I made some sort of joke about something burning on the galley hotplate, and I'd just got back there when I heard the Colonel calling, and when I looked round he had the door of the starboard wash-room open and smoke was coming out. Not much, just a little. I called the captain, and he hurried aft to see what it was, but it was nothing serious, just a few papers burning—somebody had been careless with a cigarette, I suppose.'

'And everybody rose out of their seats and crowded to have a look?' I asked grimly.

'Yes. Captain Johnson ordered them all back to their seats—they were upsetting the trim of the plane.'

'And you didn't think this worth mentioning to me,' I said heavily. 'No importance at all?'

'I'm sorry. It—it *did* seem unimportant, unrelated to anything. That was hours before the crash, so——'

'It doesn't matter. Who could have gone into the galley then—anybody in the front seats, I suppose?'

'Yes. They all seemed to crowd down past the middle——'

'They? Who were "they"?'

'I don't know. What—why do you ask?'

'Because by knowing who *was* there, we might find out who wasn't.'

'I'm sorry,' she repeated helplessly. 'I was a little upset for a moment, then Captain Johnson was in front of me shooing everybody back to their seats and I couldn't see.'

'All right,' I changed my approach. 'This was the men's wash-room, I take it?'

'Yes. The powder-room is on the port side.'

'Can you remember who went in there, say, any time up to an hour beforehand?'

'An hour? But a cigarette end——'

'Do you believe now that the fire was caused deliberately?' I asked.

'Of course.' She stared at me, wide-eyed.

'Right. And we're dealing, obviously, with hardened professional criminals. The whole success of their plan depended on causing this excitement. Do you for a moment believe that they were going to let the whole thing hinge on the mere off-chance of a smouldering butt-end setting some papers alight—especially setting them alight at the correct moment?'

'But how——'

'Easy. You can get a little plastic tube with a central composition shield dividing it into two compartments. In one compartment you have a free acid, in the other a different acid enclosed in a glass tube. All you have to do is to crush the tube, break the glass, drop the tube in your chosen spot, walk away and after a predetermined time the acid that was in the glass eats through the shield, meets the other acid and starts a fire. It's been used hundreds of times, especially in war-time sabotage. If you're an arsonist looking for a cast-iron alibi and want to be five miles away when the fire starts, it's the perfect answer.'

'There *was* a funny smell——' she began slowly.

'You bet there was. Can you remember who went there?'

'It's no good.' She shook her head. 'I was in the galley most of the time, getting the meal ready.'

'Who were in the front two seats—those nearest the galley?'

'Miss LeGarde and Mr Corazzini. And I'm afraid that's not much help. We know Marie LeGarde can't have had anything to do with it. And Mr Corazzini is the one person I'm sure *didn't* leave his seat before dinner. He had a gin soon after take-off, then switched off his reading light, draped a newspaper over his head and went to sleep.'

'Are you sure?'

'Quite sure. I always peek through the cabin door from time to time, and he was always there.'

'That seems to cut him out,' I said thoughtfully. '*And* reduce the number of suspects—though, I suppose, he could still have had an accomplice to plant the acid tube.' Then, suddenly, I had what was, for me, an inspiration. 'Tell me, Miss Ross, did anyone ask you earlier in the evening, when dinner would be?'

She looked at me for a long moment before answering, and

even in the fading light of the aurora I could see the understanding coming into her eyes.

'Mrs Dansby-Gregg did, I'm sure.'

'She would. Anyone else?'

'Yes. I remember now.' Her voice was suddenly very quiet. 'Colonel Harrison—but he doesn't count any more—and Mr Zagero.'

'Zagero?' In my excitement I bent forward until my face was almost touching hers. 'Are you sure?'

'I'm sure. I remember when he asked me, I said, "Are you feeling peckish, sir?" and he grinned and said, "My dear air hostess, I *always* feel peckish".'

'Well, well. This is most interesting.'

'Do you think Mr Zagero——'

'I'm at the stage where I'm afraid to think anything. I've been wrong too often. But it's a straw in the wind all right—a straw about the size of a haystack. . . . Was he anywhere near you when the radio fell? Behind you, for instance, when you rose and brushed against the radio table?'

'No, he was by the hatch, I'm sure of that. Could he——'

'He couldn't. Joss and I worked it out. Somebody had pushed one of the table hinges right home and the other until it was at the critical point of balance. Then as you stood up he pushed the other in. From a distance. There was a long-handled brush lying there—but it had no significance for us at the time. . . . When you heard the crash you whirled round, didn't you?' She nodded without speaking.

'And what did you see?'

'Mr Corazzini——'

'We know he dived for it,' I said impatiently. 'But in the background, against the wall?'

'There *was* someone.' Her voice was barely more than a whisper. 'But no—no, it couldn't have been. He'd been sitting dozing on the floor, and he got the fright of his life when——'

'For heaven's sake!' I cut in harshly. 'Who was it?'

'Solly Levin.'

The brief twilight of noon came and went, the cold steadily deepened and by late in the evening it seemed that we had been on board that lurching, roaring tractor all our lives.

Twice only we stopped in the course of that interminable day, for refuelling at 4 p.m. and 8 p.m. I chose these times because I had arranged with Joss that I would try to contact him every fourth hour. But though we set up the apparatus outside while Jackstraw was refuelling and Corazzini sat astride the bicycle seat and cranked the generator handle while I tapped out our call sign for almost ten unbroken minutes, no shadow of an answer came through. I had expected none. Even if by some miracle Joss had managed to fix the set, the ionosphere turbulence that had caused the aurora would have almost certainly killed any chance of making contact. But I'd promised Joss, and I had to keep faith.

By the time I made the second try, everyone, even Jackstraw and myself, were shaking and shivering in the bitter cold. Normally, we wouldn't have felt it much—in very cold weather, we wore two complete sets of furs, the inner one with the fur inside, the outer with the fur outside. But we'd given our extra pairs away to Corazzini and Zagero—furs were essential in that ice-box of a tractor cabin—and suffered just as much as the others.

Occasionally, someone would jump down from the tractor and run alongside to try to get warm, but so exhausted were most from sleeplessness, hunger, cold and eternally bracing themselves against the lurching of the tractor, that they were staggering from exhaustion within minutes and had to come aboard again. And when they did come aboard, the sweat from their exertions in such heavy clothes turned ice-cold on their bodies, putting them in worse case than ever, until finally I had to stop it.

It grieved me to do what had to be done, what I saw must be done, but there was no help for it. The weariness, the cold and the sleeplessness could be borne no longer. When I finally gave the order to stop it was ten minutes after midnight, and we had been driving continuously, except for brief fuel and radio halts, for twenty-seven hours.

CHAPTER EIGHT

WEDNESDAY 4 A.M.–8 P.M.

Despite our exhaustion, despite our almost overwhelming need for sleep, I don't think anyone slept that night, even for a moment, for to have slept would have been to freeze to death.

I had never known such cold. Even with twelve of us jam-packed inside a tiny wooden box built to hold five sleeping people at the most, even with the oil fire roaring up the chimney all night long and warmed by a couple of cups of piping hot coffee apiece, we all of us suffered agonies during these dark hours. The chattering of teeth, the St Vitus' dance of tremor-ridden limbs knocking against the thin uninsulated wooden walls, the constant rubbing as someone sought to restore life to a frozen face or arm or foot—these were the sounds that never ceased. How the elderly Marie LeGarde or the sick Mahler survived that night was indeed a matter for wonder.

But survive they did, for when I looked at my luminous watch, saw that it was almost four o'clock and decided that enough was enough, both of them were wide awake when I switched on the little overhead light. Weak enough normally, that light was now no more than a feeble yellow glow—an ominous sign, it meant that even the tractor batteries were beginning to freeze up—but enough to see the crowded circle of faces, white and blue and yellowing with frostbite, the smoke-like exhalations that clouded in the air before them with every breath they took, the film of slick ice that already covered the walls and all of the roof except for a few inches round the stove-pipe exit. As a spectacle of suffering, of sheer unrelieved misery, I don't think I have ever seen its equal.

'Insomnia, eh, Doc?' It was Corazzini speaking, his teeth chattering between the words. 'Or just forgotten to plug in your electric blanket?'

'Just an early riser, Mr Corazzini.' I glanced round the haggard and pain-filled faces. 'Anybody here slept at all?'

254

I was answered by mute headshakes from everybody.

'Anybody likely to sleep?'

Again the headshakes.

'That settles it.' I struggled to my feet. 'It's only 4 a.m., but if we're going to freeze to death we might as well freeze on the move. Not only that, but another few hours in this temperature and that tractor engine will never start again. What do you think, Jackstraw?'

'I'll get the blow-torches,' he said by way of answer, and pushed his way out through the canvas screen. Almost at once I heard him begin to cough violently in the deadly cold of the air outside, and, in the intervals between the coughing, we could clearly hear the dry rustling crackling of his breath as the moisture condensed, froze and drifted away in the all but imperceptible breeze.

Corazzini and I followed, choking and gasping in turn as that glacial cold seared through throat and lungs, adjusting masks and goggles until not a millimetre of flesh was left exposed. Abreast the driving cabin I drew out my torch and glanced at the alcohol thermometer—ordinary mercury froze solid at $-38°$—then looked again in disbelief. The red spirit inside the glass had sunk down to within an inch of the bulb and stood on the line of $-68°$—exactly one hundred degrees of frost. Still well below Wegener's $-85°$, further short still of the incredible $-125°$ that the Russians had recorded at the Vostok in Antarctica, but nevertheless the lowest, by almost fifteen degrees, that I had ever experienced. And that it should happen now—now, two hundred miles from the nearest human habitation, with Jackstraw and myself stuck with two murderers, a possibly dying man, seven other passengers rapidly weakening from exposure, exhaustion and lack of food, and a superannuated tractor that was due to pack up at any moment at all.

Over an hour later I had cause to revise the last part of that estimate—it seemed that the tractor had already packed up. I had had my first intimation of trouble to come when I had switched on the ignition and pressed the horn—the faint mournful *beep* could hardly have been heard twenty yards away. The batteries were so gummed up by the cold that they couldn't even have turned over a hot engine, far less one in which the crankcase, transmission and differential were all but locked solid in lubricating oil that had lost all power to lubricate anything and had been turned into a super-viscous liquid with the consistency and intractability of some heavy animal glue. Even with two of us bringing all our weight to bear on the starting handle it was impossible to turn even one cylinder over the top.

We made to light the paraffin blow-torches, but they, too, were frozen solid: paraffin freezes at just over −50°, and even at −40° it still flows like heavy gear-case oil. We had to thaw them out with a petrol blow-torch, then place all five of them on wooden boxes and behind canvas aprons to retain the heat, two to thaw out the crankcase, two for the gear-box and transmission and the last for the differential. After an hour or so, when the engine had begun to turn fairly easily and we had brought out the heavy battery which had been thawing out by the stove, we tried again. But it gave no sign of life at all.

None of us, not even Corazzini whose Global tractors were all diesel-powered, was an expert in engine maintenance, and this was when we came very close to despair. But despair was the one emotion we couldn't afford, and we knew it. We kept the blow-torches burning, returned the battery to the stove, removed and cleaned the plugs, eased the frozen brushes in the generator, stripped and removed the petrol lines, thawed them and sucked out the frozen condensation by mouth, scraped away the ice from the carburettor intake and returned everything in place. We had to remove our gloves for most of this delicate work, the flesh stuck to metal and pulled off like the skin of an orange when we removed our hands, even the backs of our fingers became burnt and blistered from casual knocks on metal, blood oozed out from under our fingernails only to coagulate in the freezing air, and our lips, where they had touched the copper petrol feeds, were swollen and puffed and blistered. It was brutal, killing work, and in addition to the work our arms and legs and faces were almost constantly frozen, despite frequent visits to the stove to thaw ourselves out. It was murderous—but it was worth it. At six-fifteen, two and a quarter hours after we had begun, the big engine coughed and spluttered into life, missed, coughed again, caught and settled down into a steady even roar. I felt my split lips cracking into a painful grin under my mask, thumped Jackstraw and Corazzini—for the moment quite forgetting that the latter might be one of the killers—on the back, turned and went in for breakfast.

Or what passed for breakfast. It was little enough, heaven knew—coffee, crackers and the contents of a couple of corned beef tins shared among the twelve of us, the lion's share going to

Theodore Mahler. That left us with only four more tins of beef, four cans of vegetables, about ten pounds of dried fruit, a little frozen fish, a small tin of biscuits, three packets of cereal and—it was the only thing apart from coffee of which we had an adequate supply—over twenty tins of Nestle's unsweetened milk. We had, of course, seal meat for the dogs—Jackstraw thawed some out for them over the stove while we had breakfast—and the fried meat of young seal is palatable to a degree. But the dogs had first claim on that. It was more important to preserve their strength than our own: should the engine of the Citroën break down completely, our last hope lay with the dogs.

Breakfast over and the dogs fed, we started off just before moonset, Corazzini driving, with the long trailing plume of our exhaust vapour, milk-white but thick as smoke in that bitter air, stretching out far behind us, bar-straight, almost as far as the eye could see in the waning light of the moon. I had arranged that the drivers should change over every fifteen minutes—as long a period as any person could stand in that unheated and largely unprotected cabin. I had heard of a case in the Antarctic where a driver had sat so long in an exposed tractor that his numbed and frozen fingers had locked so immovably that the steering-wheel had had to be unbolted and brought inside still clutched in the driver's grasp before the hands could be thawed sufficiently to release the wheel: I didn't want anything of that kind happening to us.

As soon as we were under way I had a look at Mahler, and his appearance certainly did nothing to inspire any great confidence in his chances. Even although he was fully dressed, lying in an eiderdown sleeping-bag that was zipped all the way to his chin, and covered in blankets, his pinched face was a mottled blue-white and he was shaking continuously with the cold, a handkerchief between his teeth to prevent their chattering. I reached for his wrist. The pulse was very fast, though it seemed strong enough: but I couldn't be sure, so much skin had been sloughed or burnt off in the past two or three hours that I'd lost all sensitivity in my fingertips. I gave him what I hoped was an encouraging smile.

'Well, how do you feel, Mr Mahler?'

'No worse than anyone else, I'm sure, Dr Mason.'

'That could still be bad enough. Hungry?'

'Hungry!' he exclaimed. 'Thanks to the generosity of these good people here, I couldn't eat another crumb.'

It was typical of what I had come to expect of this gentle Jew in the past few hours. Despite the relatively generous amount of food he'd had for his breakfast, he'd wolfed it all down like a famished man. He was hungry, all right: his body, lacking the insulin to break down the mounting sugar in his blood, was crying out for nourishment yet unable to find it no matter what his food intake was.

'Thirsty?'

He nodded. Perhaps he thought he was on safe ground there, but it was another and invariable symptom of the developing acuteness of his trouble. I was pretty certain, too, that he had already begun to weaken, and I knew it wouldn't be long before he began to lose weight rapidly. Indeed, he already looked thinner, the cheekbones were more prominent, than even thirty-six hours ago. But then that was true of all the others also, especially Marie LeGarde: for all her uncomplaining courage, her determined cheerfulness, she now looked more than old: she looked sick, and very tired. But there was nothing I could do for her.

'Your feet?' I asked Mahler. 'How are they?'

'I don't think they're there any longer,' he smiled.

'Let me see them,' I asked abruptly. He protested, but I overruled him. One look at that dead-white ice-cold flesh was enough.

'Miss Ross,' I said. 'From now on you are Mr Mahler's personal Gunga Din. We have a couple of rubber bags in the sled. I want you to keep these alternately filled just as soon as you can get water heated—unfortunately, it takes a long time to melt that damned snow. They're for Mr Mahler's feet.' Again Mahler protested, objecting to what he called 'This babying', but I ignored him. I didn't want to tell him, not yet, that frostbite in the feet of an untreated diabetic could mean only one thing: gangrene and amputation, at the least. Slowly I looked round the occupants of the tractor cabin and I think that had I known for certain who the person responsible for all this was, I would have killed him without compunction.

Just then Corazzini came in. After only fifteen minutes at the wheel of the tractor he had just yielded to Jackstraw he was in a pretty bad way. The bluish-white bloodless face was mottled with yellow frostbite blisters, his lips were cracked, the fingernails were beginning to discolour and his hands were a shocking mess. True, Jackstraw, Zagero and I were little better, but Corazzini was the only one who had so far driven in that

258

intense cold: he was shaking like a man with malarial fever, and from the way he stumbled up the steps I could tell that his legs were gone. I helped him to a vacant seat by the stove.

'Feel anything below the knees?' I asked quickly.

'Not a damned thing.' He tried to smile, but the effort was too painful, the blood started to well again from the open cuts on his lips. 'It's pretty vicious out there, Doc. Better rub the old feet with some snow, huh?' He stooped and fumbled uselessly at laces with his numbed and bleeding fingers, but before I could move Margaret Ross was on her knees, easing off his boots with gentle fingers. Looking down at that slight figure lost beneath the bulky layers of clothing, I wondered for the hundredth time how I could ever have been crazy enough to believe about her all the things I had done.

'In your own idiom, Mr Corazzini,' I said, 'snow is strictly for the birds. Just an old wives' tale as far as these temperatures are concerned. You'd be better rubbing your skin off with emery-paper.' At 70° below, snow had the hard crystalline structure of sandstone, and, when rubbed, granulated into a gritty white powdery sand. I nodded at one of the snow-buckets on the stove. 'When the temperature there reaches 85°, stick your feet in it. Wait till the skin turns red. It won't be pleasant, but it'll work. If there are any blisters I'll puncture and sterilise them to-morrow.'

He stared at me. 'Is this sort of thing going to go on *all* the time, Doc?'

'I'm afraid so.'

And it did go on for all the time—or for the next ten hours, at least, during which time the temperature dropped down to the low seventies, halted and began its slow, ever so slow, upward swing again. Ten hours while the two snow-buckets were never off the stove, ten hours while Mrs Dansby-Gregg, her maid, Helene and, later on, Solly Levin held blow-torches against the sides of the buckets to hurry up the melting and heating process, ten hours while we drivers suffered the regularly recurring pounding agony of circulation returning to our frozen limbs, ten hour during which we began to build up an almost pathological dread of the moment when we must again plunge our feet into hot water, ten hours during which Mahler grew steadily weaker and Marie LeGarde, falling silent for the first time, slipped down and lay huddled in a corner, eyelids closed, like one already dead. Ten hours. Ten interminable, indescribable hours of suffering borrowed from purgatory. But long before these ten hours were up something happened to change the picture completely.

At noon I halted the tractor. While the women were heating up some soup and using a blow-torch to thaw out two cans of fruit, Jackstraw and I rigged up the radio transmitter, strung out an antenna and started triggering out our GFK call-sign. Normally, on these hand-cranked eight-watt jobs, a morse key was used for transmission while reception was by a pair of earphones, but thanks to a skilful improvisation by Joss who knew how hopelessly awkward morse was for everyone in the party except himself; the set had been rigged so that the key was used only for the call-up sign. After the link was made a hand microphone could be used for transmission: and simply by throwing the receiving switch into the antenna lead, the microphone was transformed into a small but sufficiently effective loudspeaker.

Calling up Joss was only a gesture. I'd made a promise and was keeping it, that was all. But by this time, I estimated, we were 120 miles distant from him, near enough the limit of our small set: I didn't know what effect the intense cold would have on radio transmission, but I suspected it wouldn't be anything good: there had been no aurora that morning, but the ionosphere disturbance might still be lingering on: and, of course, Joss himself had declared that his R.C.A. was entirely beyond repair.

Ten minutes passed, ten minutes during which Jackstraw industriously cranked the handle and I sent out the call-sign, GFK three times repeated, a flick of the receiver switch, ten seconds listening, then the switch pushed back and the call-sign made again. At the end of the ten minutes I sent out the last call, pushed over the receiving switch, listened briefly then stood up, resignedly gesturing to Jackstraw to stop cranking. It was just then almost in the very last instant, that the mike in my hand crackled into life.

'GFX calling GFK. GFX calling GFK. We are receiving you, faint but clear. Repeat, we are receiving you. Over.'

I fumbled and nearly dropped the mike in my excitement.

'GFK calling GFX, GFK calling GFX.' I almost shouted the words, saw Jackstraw pointing to the switch which was still in the receiving position, cursed my stupidity, threw it over, called out the signs again and then, quite forgetting the procedure and etiquette of radio communication, rushed on, the words tumbling over one another: 'Dr Mason here, Dr Mason here. Receiving you loud and clear. Is that you, Joss?' I threw the switch

260

'Yes, sir. Glad to hear from you.' Static lent a flat impersonality to the crackling words, robbed them of meaning. 'How are you? What weather, how far out?'

'Going strong,' I replied. 'Cold intense—minus 70°. Approximately 120 miles out. Joss, this is a miracle! How on earth did you fix it?'

'I didn't,' he said unemotionally. There was a pause and then his voice came again. 'Captain Hillcrest is waiting to speak to you, sir.'

'Captain Hillcrest! What on earth is Captain Hillcrest——' I broke off abruptly, not through astonishment, great though that was, that Hillcrest, whom I had believed to be almost 250 miles to the north of our I.G.Y. cabin should have suddenly turned up there, but because the warning glance from Jackstraw had found an echoing answer in the back of my own mind. 'Hold on,' I said quickly. 'Will call you back in two or three minutes.'

We had set up the transmitter just to the rear of the tractor cabin, and I knew that every word said on both sides could be heard by those inside. It was just then that the curtains parted and Corazzini and Zagero peered out, but I ignored them. I never cared less about the hurt I was offering to anybody's feelings, just picked up the radio and generator while Jackstraw unstrung the antenna, and walked away from the tractor. Two hundred yards away I stopped. Those in the tractor could still see us—the brief light of noonday was flooding over the ice-cap—but they could no longer hear us.

We rigged the radio again, and I tried to tap out the call-sign but it was hopeless, we'd been out too long in that dreadful cold and my hand was beating an uncontrollable tattoo on the key. Fortunately, they knew or guessed at the other end what was happening, for Hillcrest's voice, calm, confident, infinitely reassuring, came through as soon as I pressed the receiving switch.

'Surprise, surprise,' the mike crackled mechanically. 'O.K., Dr Mason, from what Joss has said—and the recent delay—I guess you're a good way from the tractor. At seventy below you won't want to stay there too long. Suggest I do all the talking. I'll keep it brief. Receiving me?'

'Loud and clear. What on earth are you—sorry, carry on.'

'Thanks. We heard Monday afternoon, on both British and American broadcasts, of the overdue airliner. Tuesday morning

261

—yesterday, that is—we heard from the Uplavnik base. They say this hasn't been announced officially, but the U.S. and British governments are convinced that the plane has not been lost at sea, but that it has landed somewhere in Greenland or Baffin Island. Don't ask me why they're convinced—I've no idea. Anyway, they've mounted the biggest air-sea rescue search since the war. Merchant vessels of several nationalities have been diverted. American, British, French and Canadian fishing trawlers are moving in to the Greenland coast—the west coast mainly, the east's already blocked with ice. A dozen U.S. air force search bombers are already operating from Thule and Sondre Strömfjord. U.S. coastguard cutters are on the job, a flotilla of Canadian destroyers have been rerouted from mid-Atlantic and are steaming at full speed for the southern entrance of the Davis Strait—although it will take them at least thirty-six more hours to get there—and a British aircraft-carrier, accompanied by a couple of destroyers, has already rounded Cape Farewell: we don't know yet how far north she can get, the ice is solid on the Baffin side, but it's open at least to Disko on the Greenland coast, maybe as far as Svartenhuk. All I.G.Y. stations in Greenland have been ordered to join in the search. That's why we came back non-stop to the cabin—to pick up more petrol.'

I could contain myself no longer, threw over the receiving switch.

'What on earth's all the mad flap about. You'd think the President of the United States and half the Royal Family were aboard that plane. Why no more information from Uplavnik?'

I waited, and then Hillcrest's voice crackled again.

'Radio transmission impossible during preceding twenty-four hours. Will raise them now, tell them we've found the missing plane and that you're on your way to the coast. Any fresh developments with you?'

'None. Correction. One of the passengers—Mahler—turns out to be an advanced diabetic. He's in a bad way. Radio Uplavnik to get insulin. Godthaab will have it.'

'Wilco,' the microphone crackled back. A long pause, during which I could faintly hear the murmur of conversation, then Hillcrest came on again. 'Suggest you return to meet us. We have plenty of petrol, plenty of food. With eight of us on guard instead of two, nothing could happen. We're already forty miles out"—I glanced at Jackstraw, caught the sudden wrinkling of the eyes

262

which I knew to be the tell-tale of a quick grin of astonished delight which so accurately reflected my own feelings—'so not more than eighty miles behind you. We could meet up in five or six hours.'

I felt elation wash through me like a releasing wave. This was wonderful, this was more than anything I had ever dared hope for. All our troubles were at an end. . . . And then the momentary emotion of relief and triumph ebbed, the cold dismaying processes of reason moved in inexorably to take their place, and it didn't require the slow, definite shake of Jackstraw's head to tell me that the end of our troubles was as far away as ever.

'No go.' I radioed back. 'Quite fatal. The minute we turned back the killers would be bound to show their hand. And even if we don't turn they know now that we've been in contact with you and will be more desperate than ever. We must go on. Please follow at your best speed.' I paused for a moment, then continued. 'Emphasize to Uplavnik essential for our lives to know why crashed plane so important. Tell them to find out the passenger list, how genuine it is. This is absolutely imperative, Captain Hillcrest. Refuse to accept "No" for an answer. We *must* know.'

We talked for another minute, but we'd really said all there was to be said. Besides, even during the brief periods that I'd pushed down my snow-mask to speak the cold had struck so cruelly at my cut and bleeding lips that I could now raise scarcely more than a mumble, so after arranging an 8 p.m. rendezvous and making a time-check I signed off.

Back in the tractor cabin curiosity had reached fever pitch, but at least three minutes elapsed—three excruciatingly uncomfortable minutes while Jackstraw and I waited for the blood to come surging back through our frozen veins—before anyone ventured to speak. The inevitable question came from the senator—a now very much chastened senator who had lost much of his choler and all of his colour, with the heavy jowls, hanging more loosely than ever, showing unhealthily pale through the grey grizzle of beard. The very fact that he spoke showed, I suppose, that he didn't regard himself as being heavily under suspicion. He was right enough in that.

'Made contact with your friends, Dr Mason, eh? The field party, I mean.' His voice was hesitant, unsure.

'Yes,' I nodded. 'Joss—Mr London—got the set working after almost thirty hours' non-stop work. He raised Captain

Hillcrest—he's in charge of the field party—and managed to establish a relay contact between us.' I'd never heard of the phrase 'relay contact' in my life, but it sounded scientific enough. 'He's packing up immediately, and coming after us.'

'Is that good?' the senator asked hopefully. 'I mean, how long——?'

'Only a gesture, I'm afraid,' I interrupted. 'He's at least 258 miles away. His tractor's not a great deal faster than ours.' It was in fact, almost three times as fast. 'Five or six days, at the least.'

Brewster nodded heavily and said no more. He looked disappointed, but he looked as if he believed me. I wondered which of them didn't believe me, which of them *knew* I was lying because they knew that they had so thoroughly destroyed all the spare condensers and valves that it would have been quite impossible for Joss to repair the R.C.A.

The long bitter day, a day filled by nothing except that dreadful cold, an endless suffering and the nerve-destroying thunderous roar and vibration of that big engine, crawled by like a dying man. About two-thirty in the afternoon, as the last glow of the noon light faded and the stars began to stand clear in the cold and brittle sky, the temperature reached its nadir—a frightening 73 degrees below zero. Then it was, that strange things happened: flashlights brought from under a parka died out inside a minute: rubber became hard as wood and cracked and fractured like wood: breath was an opaque white cloud that shrouded the heads of every person who ventured outside the tractor-body: the ice-cap froze to such an unprecedented degree of hardness that the tractor treads spun and slipped on flat surfaces, the crimp marks no more than half-seen hairlines on the ground: the dogs, who could with impunity stand up to howling blizzards that would kill any man, whined and wailed in their utter misery in that appaling cold: and, now and again, like some far-off intimation of doom and the end of the world, a dull rumbling sound would come echoing across the ice-cap and the ground shake beneath the treads of the tractor as some great areas of snow and ice contracted still farther under the iron hand of that glacial cold.

It was then, inevitably, that the tractor started to give trouble: it was only a matter for wonder that it hadn't broken down long before that. What I feared above all was the shearing of some moving metal part, made brittle by that intense cold, that would have been the end of us: a valve-stem, a cam-rod, any one part of the delicate timing mechanism, even so small a thing as a crank-shaft pin: it needed just one of these to go, and we would be gone also.

We were spared these lethal mishaps, but what we had was almost as bad. Carburettor ice was a constant problem. The steering box froze up and had to be thawed out by blow-torches. Generator brushes stuck and broke, but fortunately we carried spares enough of these. But the biggest trouble was the radiator. Despite the fact that we had it heavily lagged, the cold penetrated the lagging as if it were tissue paper and the subsequent metal contraction produced distortion. Soon it began to leak, and by three o'clock in the afternoon we were losing water at dismaying speed. I doled out some of our precious reserves of heat pads for Mahler's feet, with the instructions that the water from the snow-buckets on the stove was to be kept solely for the radiator. But even with blow-torches assisting the heat of a stove, the melting of super-chilled snow is a discouragingly slow process: soon we were reduced to pouring half-melted slush down the radiator cap, and finally to cramming snow itself down in order to keep going at all. All this was bad enough: but the frightening thing was that for every pint of radiator liquid lost and every pint of snow-water used to replace it, the anti-freeze became that much more diluted, and though we carried a small reserve drum of ethylene glycol its weight diminished perceptibly with every halt we made.

We had, hours before that, dispensed with a lookout, and the burden of all this work fell on Jackstraw, Zagero, Corazzini and myself. Of the four of us, Jackstraw was the only one who escaped what I knew would be permanent injury or disfigurement in the shape of scars and destroyed tissue. Zagero might never before have borne any of the scars of his trade, but he was going to have what looked peculiarly like one now: we had been too late in getting a cold-water compress to his right ear, and these destroyed tissues would need plastic surgery: two of Corazzini's toes had also been left too long without treatment, and I knew that he, too, would finish up in a surgical ward: and, because I was the one most in contact with the engine, my fingertips were a painful bleeding mess, the nails already blackening and beginning to rot away.

Nor were things a great deal better with those inside the tractor cabin. The first physiological effects of the cold were beginning to assert themselves, and assert themselves strongly—the almost

265

overpowering desire for sleep, the uncaring indifference to all that went on around them. Later would come the sleeplessness, the anaemia, the digestive troubles, the nervousness that could lead to insanity—if the cold continued long enough these conditions would inevitably succeed the picture of huddled, lifeless misery that presented itself to me whenever I sought the shelter of the cabin and the agony of returning circulation after my spell at the wheel. Many times I saw the picture that afternoon, and always the picture was the same.

The senator sat slumped in a corner, a dead man but for the fits of violent shuddering that overtook him at regularly recurring intervals. Mahler appeared to sleep. Mrs Dansby-Gregg and Helene lay huddled in one another's arms—an incredible sight, I thought, but then, next only to death itself, the Arctic was the great leveller, an unparalleled agent in stripping away the pretensions and shoddy veneers of everyday living. I was no great believer in the sudden conversions of human nature, and was pretty certain that, with Mrs Dansby-Gregg, the return to civilisation would coincide with the return to her normal self, and that this moment of common humanity shared by herself and her maid would be no more than a fading and unwelcome memory: but for all my dislike of Mrs Dansby-Gregg, I was beginning to develop more than a sneaking admiration for her. The carefully cherished snobbery, the maddeningly easy and condescending assumption of an inevitable social superiority were irritating enough, heaven knew, but behind that unlovable façade seemed to lie a deep-buried streak of that selflessness which is the hall-mark of the genuine aristocrat: although she complained constantly about the tiny irritations, she was silent on matters that caused her genuine suffering: she was developing a certain brusque helpfulness, as if she were half-ashamed of it, and showed a care for her maid which, though probably no more than that feudal kindness that reaches its best in adversity, nevertheless verged almost on tenderness: and I had seen her take a mirror from her handbag, inspect the ravages frostbite had wreaked on her lovely face, then return the mirror to her bag with a gesture of indifference. Mrs Dansby-Gregg, in short, was becoming for me an object lesson against the dangers of an over-ready classification of people into types.

Marie LeGarde, the lovable, indomitable Marie LeGarde, was a sick old woman, weakening by the hour. Her attempts at cheerful-

266

ness in her fully wakeful moments—she was asleep most of the time—were strained and almost desperate. The effort was too much. There was nothing I could do for her. Like an old watch, her time was running out, the mainspring of her life running down. A day or two more of this would surely kill her.

Solly Levin had taken over the blow-torches which played constantly against the sides of the snow-buckets. Wrapped and huddled in clothes until only one eye was visible, he nevertheless achieved the near impossible of looking a picture of abject misery: but the way my thoughts had been running all day, I had no sympathy to waste on Mr Levin. Margaret Ross dozed by the side of the stove but I turned my eyes away quickly, even to look at that thin white face was a physical hurt.

The marvel of them all was Mr Smallwood, yet another instance, I thought wryly, of how wrong I could get. Instead of being one of the first to go under, he showed every sign of being the last. Three hours ago, when I had been in the cabin, he had brought up his bag from the tractor sled, and as he'd opened it I'd caught a glimpse of a black gown and the red and purple of a divinity hood. He'd brought out a Bible, donned a pair of rimless steel spectacles and, for several hours now, had been reading as best he could in the dim overhead light. He seemed composed, relaxed yet alert, fit to carry on for a long time to come. As a doctor and scientist I didn't go in much for theological speculation, but I could only suppose that Mr Smallwood was in some way sustained by something that was denied the rest of us. I could only envy him.

During the course of the evening two blows fell. The first of these was not in any way figurative. I still have the scar on my forehead to prove it.

We stopped just before eight o'clock that evening, partly in order to keep our radio schedule with Hillcrest, partly—because I wanted to make a long halt, to give Hillcrest all the more opportunity to overtake us—on the pretext that the Citroën's engine was overheating badly in the temperature that had been rising steadily since the early afternoon. But despite the fact that it was now almost twenty-five degrees warmer than in mid-afternoon, it was still bitterly cold—our hunger and physical exhaustion saw to it that we still suffered almost as much as ever—dark and very still. Far away to the south-west we could see the jagged saw-tooth line of the Vindeby Nunataks—that hundred-mile long ridge of

267

hills that we would have to cross the next day—the forbidding peaks a gleaming crystalline white in the light of the moon that had not yet topped our eastern horizon.

I was driving when we stopped. I switched off the motor, walked round to the back of the tractor and told those inside that we were making a halt. I asked Margaret Ross to heat some food on the stove—soup, dried fruit, one of our four remaining tins of corned beef—asked Jackstraw to rig up the antenna for the radio, then went back to the tractor, stooped and turned the radiator drainage cap, catching the liquid in a can. The anti-freeze in the water had been thinned down so much in the course of the day that I was pretty certain that, in those temperatures, it wouldn't take half an hour for the radiator water to freeze up and split open the cylinder jacket.

I suppose it was because of the gurgling of the water into the can that I didn't hear the sound behind me until the last moment, and even so I had no particular reason just then to be suspicious of anything. I half-straightened and turned round to see who was there, but I was too late. The consciousness of a vague blur in the darkness and the blinding white flash of light and pain as something solid smashed into my forehead, just above the goggles on my right eye, came in one and the same instant. I was out, completely unconscious, long before I crumpled down on to the frozen surface of the ice-cap.

Death could easily have supervened then. It would have been easy, ever so easy, for me to drift from unconsciousness into that numbed sleep from which, with almost eighty degrees of frost in the ground, I would never have awaked. But awake I did, slowly, painfully, reluctantly, at the insistence of urgently shaking hands.

'Dr Mason! Dr Mason!' Dimly I realised that it was Jackstraw speaking, that he had my head and shoulders supported in the crook of his arm. His voice was low, but with a peculiarly carrying quality. 'Wake up, Dr Mason. Ah, good, good. Easy does it now, Dr Mason.'

Groggily, Jackstraw's strong arm helping, I levered myself up into an upright sitting position. A brilliant flame of pain lanced like a scalpel through my head, I felt everything blurring once more, consciously, almost violently, shook off the shadows that were creeping in on me again, then looked dazzedly up at Jackstraw. I couldn't see very well, I thought for one frightening moment that the vision centre had been damaged when the back of my head had struck against the iron-hard ice-cap—the ache there was almost as severe as the one in my forehead—but I soon discovered that it was only the blood seeping from the cut on my forehead that had frozen and gummed together the lids of my right eye.

'No idea who did it, Dr Mason?' Jackstraw wasn't the man to ask stupid questions like 'What happened?'

'No idea at all.' I struggled to my feet. 'Have you?'

'Hopeless.' I could sense rather than see the shrug in the darkness. 'As soon as you stopped, three or four of them came out. I don't know where they went— I was out to the south rigging up the antenna.'

'The radio, Jackstraw!' I was beginning to think again. 'Where's the radio?'

'No worry, Dr Mason, I have it with me,' Jackstraw said grimly. 'It's here. . . . Any idea *why*?'

'None. . . . Yes, I have.' I thrust my hand into the inside pocket of my parka, then looked at Jackstraw in disbelief. 'My gun—it's still there!'

'Nothing else missing?'

'No. Spare ammo clip there—wait a moment,' I said slowly. I hunted around in my parka pocket, but with no success. 'A paper —I took a newspaper cutting from Colonel Harrison's pocket— it's gone.'

'A cutting? What was in it, Dr Mason?'

'You're talking to one of the world's prize idiots, Jackstraw.' I shook my head in self-reproach, winced as the pain struck again. 'I've never even read the damn' thing.'

'If you had,' Jackstraw murmured philosophically, 'you'd probably know why it was taken from you.'

'But—but what was the point in it?' I asked blankly. 'For all they know I might have read it a dozen times.'

'I think they know you haven't even read it once,' Jackstraw said slowly. 'If you had, they'd have known it by the fact that you would have said or done something they would have expected you to say or do. But because you haven't—well, they know they're still safe. They must have been desperate to take a chance like this. It is a great pity. I do not think, Dr Mason, that you will ever see that paper again.'

Five minutes later I had washed and bandaged the cut on my forehead—I'd savagely told an inquiring Zagero that I'd walked

269

into a lamp-post and refused to answer all other questions—and set off with Jackstraw in the strengthening light of the newly-risen moon. We were late for our rendezvous, but when I switched the receiver into the antenna I heard Joss's call-up sign come through straight away.

I acknowledged, then asked without preamble: 'What news from Uplavnik?'

'Two things, Dr Mason.' Hillcrest had taken the microphone over from Joss, and, even through the distortion of the speaker, his voice sounded strange, with the flat controlled unemotionalism of one speaking through a suppressed anger. 'Uplavnik has been in touch with H.M.S. *Triton*—the carrier coming up the Davis Strait, *Triton* is in constant communication with the British Admiralty and the Government. Or so I gather.

'The answers to your questions are these. Firstly, the passenger list from M.Y.T.H. in America is not yet through, but it is known from newspaper reports that the following three people were aboard: Marie LeGarde, the musical comedy star, Senator Hoffman Brewster of the United States and a Mrs Phyllis Dansby-Gregg, who appears to be a very prominent London socialite.'

I wasn't greatly excited over this item of news. Marie LeGarde had never been a suspect. Mrs Dansby-Gregg—and, by implication, Helene Fleming—had never had more than a faint question mark against their names, and I had already come to the conclusion that it was long odds against the man who was, or purported to be, Senator Brewster being one of the killers.

'The second thing is this. The Admiralty cannot or will not say why the plane has been forced down, but I gather there must have been a most vital reason. Uplavnik suggests, on what basis I cannot say, perhaps it is officially inspired, that some person aboard the plane must have been in possession of something of the utmost importance, so important that complete secrecy was vital. Don't ask me what it was. A microfilm, a formula, something, perhaps, only committed to memory—it sounds fanciful, but that's all we can guess at. It does seem likely that Colonel Harrison was in possession of it.'

I looked at Jackstraw, and he at me. The man who had so recently knocked me out had been desperate all right. I knew then what I had subconsciously known all along, that I was dealing blindfolded against a man—or men—far cleverer than myself. They knew that Joss couldn't possibly have hoped to repair the R.C.A. They knew, therefore, that I must have been talking direct to Hillcrest. They knew, because I had told them, that the eight-watt radio we had with us had a range of not more than 150 miles under normal conditions, so that the chances were high that Hillcrest was actually speaking from the I.G.Y. cabin—or a point even nearer. I had also told them that Hillcrest and his four companions wouldn't be returning from their field trip for another two or three weeks, so that this premature return could only be accounted for by some unforeseen and extra-ordinary event. It wasn't hard to guess what that event must have been. That I should ask Hillcrest to find out the reason for the crash followed inevitably, but what was not inevitable, what pointed most clearly of all to the shrewdness of the killers, was their guess that whoever knew the reason for the crash would be most reluctant to go into specific detail: and they had robbed me of the only clue that might have helped me discover what that detail was and so also, I felt sure, the identity of the killers. But the time was far past now for crying over spilt milk.

I pressed the switch to 'Transmit'.

'Thank you. But please radio Uplavnik again, emphasize desperate urgency of finding out crash reasons ... How far behind do you estimate you are now? We have made only twenty miles since noon. Cold extreme, bad radiator trouble. Over.'

'We have made only eight miles since noon. It seems——'

I threw the switch over.

'Eight miles?' I demanded harshly. 'Did I hear you say eight miles?'

'You heard.' Hillcrest's voice was savage. 'Remember the missing sugar? Well, it's turned up. Your fine friends dumped the whole bloody lot into the petrol. We're completely immobilized.'

CHAPTER NINE

WEDNESDAY 8 P.M.– THURSDAY 4 P.M.

We were on our way again just after nine o'clock that night. It had been my original intention, by dreaming up a variety of excuses and even, if necessary, by sabotaging the engine, to stay there for several hours or at least what I reckoned to be the longest possible time before the killers became restive, suspected that I was deliberately stalling, and took over. Or tried to take over. For it had been my further intention that, after an hour or two, Jackstraw should produce his rifle—it was strapped to his shoulders night and day—and I my automatic, and hold them all at the point of the gun until Hillcrest came up. If all had gone well, he should have been with us by midnight. Our troubles would have been over.

But all had not gone well, our troubles were as bad as ever, the Sno-Cat was bogged down and with Mahler now seriously ill and Marie LeGarde frighteningly weak and exhausted, I couldn't remain any longer. Had I been made of tougher stuff, or even had I not been a doctor, I might have brought myself to recognize that both Marie LeGarde and Theodore Mahler were expendable pawns in a game where the stakes, I was now certain, were far greater than just the lives of one or two people. I might have held everybody—or the major suspects, at least—at gunpoint until such time, twenty-four hours if need be, as Hillcrest did come up. But I could not bring myself to regard our sick passengers as expendable pawns. A weakness, no doubt, but one that I was almost proud to share with Jackstraw, who felt exactly as I did.

That Hillcrest would come up eventually I felt pretty sure. The dumping of the sugar in the petrol—I bit my lips in chagrin whenever I remembered that it had been I who had told them all that Hillcrest was running short of fuel—had been a brilliant move, but nothing more, now, than I had come to expect of men who thought of everything, made every possible provision against future eventualities. Still, even though furiously angry at the delay, Hillcrest had thought he could cope with the situation. The big cabin of the Sno-Cat was equipped with a regular workshop with tools fit to deal with just about every mechanical breakdown, and already his driver-mechanic—I didn't envy him his murderous task even though he was reportedly working behind heated canvas aprons—had stripped down the engine and was cleaning pistons, cylinder walls and valves of the unburnt carbon deposits that had finally ground the big tractor to a halt. A couple of others had rigged up a makeshift distillation unit—a petrol drum, almost full, with a thin metal tube packed in ice leading from its top to an empty drum. Petrol, Hillcrest had explained, had a lower boiling point than sugar, and when the drum was heated the evaporating gas, which would cool in the ice-packed tube, should emerge as pure petrol.

Such, at least, was the theory, although Hillcrest didn't seem absolutely sure of himself. He had asked if we had any suggestion whether we could help him in any way at all, but I had said we couldn't. I was tragically, unforgivably wrong. I could have helped, for I knew something that no one else did, but, at the moment I completely forgot it. And because I forgot, nothing could now avert the tragedy that was to come, or save the lives of those who were about to die.

My thoughts were black and bitter as the tractor roared and lurched and clattered its way south-west by west under the deepening darkness of a sky that was slowly beginning to fill with cloud. A dark depression filled me, and a cold rage, and there was room in my mind for both. I had a strange fey sense of impending disaster, and though I was doctor enough to know that it was almost certainly a psychologically induced reaction to the cold, exhaustion, sleeplessness and hunger—and a physical reaction to the blow on the head—nevertheless I could not shake it off: and I was angry because I was helpless.

I was helpless to do anything to protect any of the innocent people with me, the people who had entrusted themselves to my care, the sick Mahler and Marie LeGarde, the quiet young German girl, the grave-faced Margaret Ross—above all, I had to admit to myself, Margaret Ross: I was helpless because I knew the murderers might strike at any time, for all I knew they might believe that Hillcrest had already told me all I needed to know and that I was just waiting my chance to catch them completely off guard; on the other hand they, too, were almost certainly just biding their time, not knowing how much I knew, but just taking a calculated gamble, letting things ride as long as the tractor kept moving, kept heading in the right direction, but prepared to strike once and for all when the time came: and, above all, I was helpless because I still had no definite idea as to who the killers were.

For the hundredth time I went over everything I could remember, everything that had happened, everything that had been said, trying to dredge up from the depths of memory one single fact, one isolated word that would point the finger in one unmistakable direction. But I found nothing.

Of the ten passengers Jackstraw and I had with us, six of them, I felt certain, were almost beyond suspicion. Margaret Ross and Marie LeGarde were completely beyond it. The only things that could be said against Mrs Dansby-Gregg and Helene was that I hadn't absolute proof of their innocence, but I was certain that such proof was quite unnecessary. United States Senators, as recent bribery and corruption cases had lamentably shown, had as many human failings—especially cupidity—as the next man: but, even so, the idea of a senator getting mixed up with murder and criminal activities on this massive scale was too preposterous to bear further examination. As for Mahler, I was quite aware that being a diabetic didn't bar a man from criminal pursuits, and he could have been one of the guilty men—just possibly he had thought they would force-land near some easily available insulin supplies. But that was just a little too far-fetched, and even if it weren't, I wasn't seriously interested in Mahler. I was concerned only with killers who might kill again at any moment, and he most certainly wasn't included in that category: Mahler was a dying man.

That left only Zagero, Solly Levin, Corazzini and the Rev Smallwood, and the Rev Smallwood was too good *not* to be true. The Bible was hardly ever out of his hands these days: there were certain lengths to which any impostor might reasonably be expected to go to convince us of his identity, but lengths such as these passed the bounds of the superfluous into the realms of the ridiculous.

I had reason to suspect Corazzini. As a tractor specialist, he knew precious little about tractors—although I had to be fair and admit that Citroën and Global tractors were a quarter of a century different in time and a world different in design. But he had been the only person I had found on his feet when I had opened the door of the passenger cabin in the plane. It was he who, back in the I.G.Y. cabin, had questioned me so closely about Hillcrest's movements. It was he, I had learnt, who had helped Jackstraw and Zagero bring up the petrol from the tunnel and so had the opportunity to spike the stuff left behind. Finally, I believed he could be utterly ruthless. But there was one great point in his favour: that still-bandaged hand, token of his desperate attempt to save the falling radio.

I had far greater reason to suspect Zagero, and, by implication of friendship, Solly Levin. Zagero had inquired of Margaret Ross when dinner was: a damning point. Solly Levin had been nearest the radio, and in the right position for doing the damage when it had been destroyed: another damning point. Zagero had been one of those working with the petrol. And, most damning of all, Zagero bore no more resemblance to a boxer than Levin did to any boxing manager who had ever lived outside the pages of Damon Runyon. And, as a further negative mark against Zagero, I had Margaret Ross's word that Corazzini had never left his seat in the plane. That didn't, of course, necessarily exclude Corazzini, he could well have had an accomplice. But who could that accomplice be?

It was not until then that the chilling, frightening thought struck me that, because two guns had been used in the plane, I had assumed all along that there were only two criminals. There wasn't a shadow of evidence to suggest why there should not be more than two: why not three? Why not Corazzini, Zagero and Levin all in the conspiracy together? I thought over the implications of this for some minutes, and at the end I felt more helpless than ever, more weirdly certain of ultimate tragedy to come. Forcibly, almost, I had to remind myself that all three were not necesssarily working together: but it was a possibility that had to be faced.

About three o'clock in the morning, still following the flag trail that stretched out interminably before us in the long rake of the headlights, we felt the tractor slow down and Jackstraw, who was driving at the time, change gear as we entered on the first gentle slope of the long foothills that led to the winding pass that cut the Vindeby Nunataks almost exactly in half. We could have gone round the Nunataks, but that would have wasted an entire day, perhaps two, and with the ten-mile route through the hills clearly marked, it was pointless to make a detour.

Two hours later, as the incline perceptibly steepened, the tractor treads began to slip and spin on the frozen snow, but by off-loading almost all the petrol and gear we carried on the tractor sled and stowing it inside the tractor cabin, we managed to build up enough weight to gain a purchase on the surface. Even so, progress was slow and difficult. We could only make ground by following a wide zigzag pattern, and it took us well over an hour to cover the last mile before the entrance to the pass. Here we halted, soon after seven o'clock in the morning. The pass was lined on one side by a deep crevasse in the ice that ran its entire length, and although not particularly treacherous the trail was difficult and dangerous enough to make me determined to wait for the two or three brief hours' light at the middle of the day.

While breakfast was being prepared, I looked at Mahler and Marie LeGarde. The steady rise in temperature—it was now less than −30° F.—had done nothing to help either of them. Marie LeGarde looked as if she hadn't eaten in weeks, her face, pockmarked with sores and frostbite blisters, was appallingly thin and wasted, and the once sparkling eyes lack-lustre, pouched and filled and rimmed with blood. She hadn't spoken a word in ten hours, just sat there, in her increasingly rare moments of waking, shivering and staring ahead with sightless eyes. Theodore Mahler looked in better case than she, but I knew when his defences went down they would do so in a matter of hours. Despite all that we— or, rather, Margaret Ross—had done for him, the insidious talons of frostbite had already sunk deep into his feet, he had developed a very heavy cold—rare indeed in the Arctic, the seeds of it must have been sown before he had left New York—and he had neither the energy nor reserves to fight either that or the boils that were beginning to plague him. His breathing was difficult, the sweet ethereal odour of acetone very strong. He seemed wideawake and rational enough, superficially a much better going concern than Marie LeGarde, but I knew that the collapse, the preliminary to the true diabetic coma, might come at any time.

At eight o'clock Jackstraw and I moved out on to the hillside, and again made contact with Hillcrest. My heart sank when I heard the grim news that they'd hardly progressed a couple of miles in the previous twelve hours. In that bitter cold, it seemed—and where

276

they were temperatures were all of thirty degrees lower than they were with us—heating up an eight-gallon drum of petrol, even using stoves, blow-lamps and every means at their disposal, to the point of boiling was a heartbreakingly slow job, and the Sno-Cat gobbled up in a minute all the pure fuel they could distil in thirty times that. Beyond that, there was no news: Uplavnik, which they had contacted less than an hour previously, had still nothing fresh to report. Without a word, Jackstraw and I packed up the equipment and made our way back to the cabin of the tractor. Jackstraw's almost invariable Eskimo cheerfulness was at the lowest ebb I had ever seen, he seldom spoke now and even more rarely smiled. As for me, I felt our last hope was gone.

We started up the tractor again at eleven o'clock and headed straight into the pass, myself at the wheel. I was the only person left in either the driving compartment or the cabin behind: Mahler and Marie LeGarde, vanished under a great mound of clothing, rode on the dog-sled while the others walked. The tractor was wide, the trail narrow and sometimes sloping outwards and downwards, and with a sideslip into the gaping crevasse that bordered our path nobody inside the cabin would have had any chance of escape.

The first part was easy. The trail, sometimes not more than eight or nine feet broad, more often than not opened out into a shelf wide enough, almost, to be called the flat floor of a valley, and we made rapid progress. At noon—I'd warned Hillcrest that we would be traversing the Vindeby Nunataks then and would have to miss our regular radio schedule—we were more than half-way through and had just entered the narrowest and most forbidding defile in the entire crossing when Corazzini came running up alongside the tractor and waved me down to a stop. I suppose he must have been shouting but I'd heard nothing above the steady roar of the engine: and, of course, I'd seen nothing, because they had all been behind me and the width of the tractor cabin made my driving mirror useless.

'Trouble, Doc,' he said swiftly, just as the engine died. 'Someone's gone over the edge. Come on. Quick!'

'Who?' I jumped out of the seat, forgetting all about the gun I habitually carried in the door compartment as an insurance against surprise attack when I was driving. 'How did it happen?'

'The German girl.' We were running side by side round a

277

corner in the track towards the little knot of people forty yards back, clustering round a spot on the edge of the crevasse. 'Slipped, fell, I dunno. Your friend's gone over after her.'

'Gone after her!' I knew that crevasse was virtually bottomless. 'Good God!'

I pushed Brewster and Levin to one side, peered gingerly over the edge into the blue-green depths below, then drew in my breath sharply. To the right, as I looked, the gleaming walls of the crevasse, their top ten feet glittering with a beaded crystalline substance like icing sugar, and here not more than seven or eight feet apart, stretched down into the illimitable darkness, curving away from one another to form an immense cavern the size of which I couldn't even begin to guess at. To the left, more directly below, at a depth of perhaps twenty feet, the two walls were joined by a snow and ice bridge, maybe fifteen feet long, one of the many that dotted the crevasse through its entire length. Jackstraw was standing on this pressed closely into one edge, holding an obviously dazed Helene in the crook of his right arm.

It wasn't hard to work out Jackstraw's presence there. Normally, he was far too careful a man to venture near a crevasse without a rope, and certainly far too experienced to trust himself to the treachery of a snow-bridge. But when Helene had stumbled over the edge, she must have fallen heavily—almost certainly in an effort to protect her broken collar-bone—and when she had risen to her feet had been so dazed that Jackstraw, to prevent her staggering over the edge of the snow-bridge to her death, had taken the near-suicidal gamble of jumping after her to stop her. Even in that moment I wondered if I would have had the courage to do the same myself. I didn't think so.

'Are you all right?' I shouted.

'I think my left arm is broken,' Jackstraw said conversationally. 'Would you please hurry, Dr Mason? This bridge is rotten, and I can feel it going.'

His arm broken and the bridge going—and, indeed, I could see chunks of ice and snow falling off from the underside of the arch on which he was standing! The matter-of-fact lack of emotion of his voice was more compelling than the most urgent cry could possibly have been. But for the moment I was in the grip of a blind panic that inhibited all feeling, all thought except the purely destructive. Ropes—but Jackstraw couldn't tie a rope round himself, not with an arm gone, the girl couldn't help herself

278

either, both of them were helpless, somebody would have to go down to them, and go at once. Even as I stared into the crevasse, held in this strange motionless thrall, a large chunk of *névé* broke off from the side of the bridge and plummeted slowly down into the depths, to vanish from sight, perhaps two hundred feet below, long before we heard it strike the floor of the crevasse.

I jumped up and raced towards the tractor sled. How to belay the man who was lowered? With only eight or nine feet between the edge of the crevasse and the cliff behind, not more than three men could get behind a rope, and, with perhaps two men dangling at the end of it what possible purchase could those three find on that ice-hard snow to support them, far less pull them up? They would be pulled over the edge themselves. Spikes—drive a spike into the ground and anchor a rope to that. But heaven only knew how long it would take to drive a spike into that icy surface with no guarantee at the end that the ice wouldn't crack and refuse to hold, and all the time that snow-bridge crumbling under the feet of the two people who were depending on me to save their lives. The tractor, I thought desperately—perhaps the tractor. That would take any weight: but by the time we'd disconnected the tractor-sled, pushed it over the edge and slowly backed the tractor along that narrow and treacherous path, it would have been far too late.

I literally stumbled upon the answer—the four big wooden bridging battens sticking out from the end of the tractor sled. God, I must have been crazy not to think of them straight away. I grabbed a coil of nylon rope, hauled out one of the battens— Zagero was already beside me pulling at another—and ran back to the spot as fast as I could. That three-inch thick, eleven-foot long batten must have weighed over a hundred pounds, but such is the supernormal strength given us in moments of desperate need that I brought it sweeping over and had it in position astride the crevasse, directly above Jackstraw and Helene, as quickly and surely as if I had been handling a half-inch plank. Seconds later Zagero had laid the second batten alongside mine. I stripped off fur gloves and mittens, tied a double bowline in the end of the nylon rope, slipped my legs through the two loops, made a quick half-hitch round my waist, shouted for another rope to be brought, moved out and tied my own rope to the middle of the planks, allowing for about twenty feet of slack, and lowered myself down hand over hand until I was standing beside Jackstraw and Helene.

279

I could feel the snow-bridge shake under my feet even as I touched it, but I'd no time to think about that, it would have been fatal if I had even begun to think about it. Another rope came snaking down over the edge and in seconds I had it tied round Helene's waist so tightly that I could hear her gasp with the pain of it: but this was no time for taking chances. And whoever held the other end of the rope up above was moving even as quickly as I was, for the rope tightened just as I finished tying the knot.

I learned later that Helene owed her life to Mahler's quick thinking. The dog-sledge carrying Marie LeGarde and himself had stopped directly opposite the spot where Helene had gone over, and he had shouted to Brewster and Margaret Ross to sit on it and thread the rope through the slats on the sledge top. It had been a chance, but one that came off: even on that slippery surface their combined weights were more than enough to hold the slightly built Helene.

It was then that I made my mistake—my second mistake of that afternoon, though I did not realize that at the time. To help those above I stooped to boost her up, and as I straightened abruptly the suddenly increased pressure proved too much for the already crumbling bridge. I heard the ominous rumble, felt the snow begin to give under my feet, released my hold on Helene —she was already well clear anyway—grabbed Jackstraw by the arm and jumped for the other side of the bridge a second before the spot where we had been standing vanished with a *whroom* and went cascading down into the gloomy depths of the crevasse. At the full extent of my rope I hit the ice on the far side of the crevasse, wrapped both arms tightly round Jackstraw—I heard his muffled exclamation of pain and remembered his injury for the first time—and wondered how long I could hold him when that side of the bridge went too, as go it must, its support on the far side no longer existing. But, miraculously, for the moment it held.

Both of us were pressed hard in against the ice, motionless, hardly daring to breathe, when I heard a sudden cry of pain from above. It came from Helene—she must have caught her injured shoulder as she was being pulled over the edge of the crevasse. But what caught my eye was not Helene, but Corazzini. He was standing very close to the edge, and he had my gun in his hand.

I have never known such chagrin, such profound despair, such bitterness of spirit—or, to be utterly frank, such depths of fear. The one thing I had guarded against all the time, the one thing I had dreaded above all other things, that Jackstraw and I should ever both find ourselves, at the same time, completely at the mercy of the killers, had come to pass. But even in my fear there was savagery—savagery towards the man who had engineered this so beautifully, savagery towards myself for having been so easily and utterly fooled.

Even a child could see how it had been done. The series of snow-bridges had given Corazzini the idea. A little nudge to Helene Fleming at the right place—it was as plain as a pikestaff that it had been no accident—and it was a foregone conclusion that either Jackstraw or myself would have to go down to fix a rope round the youngster who, with her broken collarbone, would be unable to do it herself: I suppose the possibility that she might have crashed straight through the snow-bridge must have occurred to Corazzini, but a man with a record of killings like he had wouldn't be worried unduly on that score—annoyance at the failure of his plan would probably have been his only reaction. And when one of us had gone down and the other was supervising the rescue from above—well, another little nudge would have solved all Corazzini's problems. As it was, I had played into his hands more completely than he could ever have hoped.

Mouth dry, sweat breaking out in the palms of my clenched fists and my heart going like a trip-hammer in my chest, I was wondering desperately how he was going to administer the *coup de grâce* when I saw the Rev. Smallwood approaching him arms ourstretched and saying something I couldn't catch. It was a brave gesture of the little minister's, but a forlorn and hopeless one: I could see Corazzini change his gun to his left hand, strike Mr Smallwood a heavy backhanded blow across the face and the sound of a body falling on the ice above was unmistakable. And then Corazzini was waving the others back at the point of the gun and was advancing towards the wooden battens that straddled the crevasse, and I knew with a dull certainty how he intended to dispose of us. Why waste two bullets when all he had to do was to kick the edges of these battens over the side? Whether these battens, weighing two hundred pounds between them, struck us or smashed away the last remaining buttress of the snow-bridge was quite immaterial: the point was that I was inescapably attached to them by the nylon rope round my waist, and when they plummeted down I would go with them, tearing away the bridge and carrying Jackstraw with me to our deaths in the unthinkable depths below.

Despairingly, I considered the idea of snatching at the rifle still strapped to Jackstraw's back, but dismissed it even with the thought. It would take me seconds to get it off. There was only one thing for it, and it wasn't going to do me any good at all. With a jump I could be half-way up the rope in a second, the increased weight would make the battens difficult to kick over, and while Corazzini was either pushing these or pumping bullets into me as I swarmed up the rope, somebody—Zagero, say—could get him from the rear. That way there might, at least, be a faint chance for Jackstraw. I swung my arms behind me, bent my knees then remained frozen in that ridiculous position as a rope came uncoiling down from above and struck me across the shoulder. I glanced up and saw Corazzini smiling down at me.

'You two characters fixin' on stayin' down there all day? Come on up.'

It would be useless to try to describe the mælstrom of thoughts and emotions that whirled through my mind in the ninety seconds that elapsed before Jackstraw and I stood once more in incredulous safety on the trail above. They ranged from hope to bafflement to wild relief to the conviction that Corazzini was playing a cat-and-mouse game with us, and no one thought was in my mind more than seconds at a time. Even when I was safe, I still didn't know what to think, the overwhelming relief and gladness and reaction blotted out everything. I was trembling violently, and although Corazzini must have noticed it he affected not to. He stepped forward and handed me the Beretta, butt first.

'You're a mite careless about where you stow your armoury, Doc. I've known for a long time where you kept this. But I guess it may have been fairly useful these last few minutes.'

'But—but why——?'

'Because I've got a damned good job and a chair behind a vice-president's desk waiting for me in Glasgow,' he snapped. 'I'd appreciate the chance to sit in that chair some day.' Without another word, he turned away.

I knew what he meant, all right. I knew we owed him our lives. Corazzini was as convinced as I that someone had engineered the whole thing. It didn't require any thought at all to guess who that someone was.

My first thought was for Jackstraw. Jackstraw with a broken arm was going to make things very difficult for me: it might well make things quite impossible. But when I'd worked his parka off it required only one glance at the unnatural twist of the left arm to see that though Jackstraw had had every excuse for thinking his arm gone, it was, in fact, an elbow dislocation. He made no murmur and his face remained quite expressionless as I manipulated the bone back into the socket, but the wide white grin that cracked his face immediately afterwards was proof enough of his feelings.

I walked over to where Helene Fleming sat on the sledge, still shaking from the shock, Mrs Dansby-Gregg and Margaret Ross doing their best to soothe her. The uncharitable thought struck me that it was probably the first time that Mrs Dansby-Gregg had ever tried to soothe anyone, but I was almost ashamed of the thought as soon as it had occurred to me.

'That was a close call, young lady,' I said to Helene. 'But all's well. . . . Any more bones broken, eh?' I tried to speak jocularly, but it didn't sound very convincing.

'No, Dr Mason.' She gave a long shuddering sigh. 'I don't know how to thank you and Mr Nielsen——'

'Don't try,' I advised. 'Who pushed you?'

'What?' She stared at me.

'You heard, Helene. Who did it?'

'Yes, I—I was pushed,' she murmured reluctantly. 'But it was an accident, I know it was.'

'Who?' I persisted.

'It was me,' Solly Levin put in. He was twisting his hands nervously. 'Like the lady said, Doc, it was an accident. I guess I kinda stumbled. Someone tapped my heels and——'

'Who tapped your heels?'

'For cryin' out loud!' I'd made no attempt to hide the cold disbelief in my voice. 'What would I want to do a thing like that for?'

'Suppose you tell me,' I said, and turned away, leaving him to stare after me. Zagero stepped in my way, but I brushed roughly past him and went up towards the tractor. On the sled behind I saw the Rev Smallwood sitting, nursing a bleeding mouth. Corazzini was apologizing to him.

'I'm sorry, Reverend, I'm really and truly sorry. I didn't for a moment think you were one of them, but I couldn't afford to

283

take any chances back there. I hope you understand, Mr Smallwood?'

Mr Smallwood did, and was suitably Christian and forgiving. But I didn't wait to hear the end of it. I wanted to get through the Vindeby Nunataks, and get through with as little loss of time as possible, preferably before it became dark. There was something that I knew now that I had to do, and as soon as possible: but I didn't want to do it while we were all teetering on the edge of that damned crevasse.

We were through without further incident and at the head of that long almost imperceptible slope that fell away for thousands of feet towards the ice-bare rocks of the Greenland coast, before the last of the noon twilight had faded from the sky. I halted the tractor, spoke briefly to Jackstraw, told Margaret Ross to start thawing out some corned beef for our belated mid-day meal, and had just seen Mahler, now semi-conscious, and Marie LeGarde once again safely ensconced in the tractor cabin when Margaret Ross came up to me, her brown eyes troubled.

'The tins, Dr Mason—the corned beef. I can't find them.'

'What's that? The bully? They can't be far away, Margaret.' It was the first time I'd called her that, but my thoughts had been fixed exclusively on something else, and it wasn't until I saw the slight smile touching her lips—if she was displeased she was hiding it quite well—that I realized what I had said. I didn't care, it was worth it, it was the first time I had ever seen her smile, and it transformed her rather plain face—but I told my heart that there was a time and a place for somersaults, and this wasn't it. 'Come on, let's have a look.'

We looked, and we found nothing. The tins were gone all right. This was the excuse, the opportunity I had been waiting for. Jackstraw was by my side, looking at me quizzically as we bent over the sled, and I nodded. 'Behind him,' I murmured.

I moved back to where the others were grouped round the rear of the tractor cabin and took up a position where I could watch them all—but especially Zagero and Levin.

'Well,' I said, 'you heard. Our last tins of beef have gone. They didn't just vanish. Somebody stole them. That somebody had better tell me, for I'm going to find out anyway.'

There was an utter silence that was broken only occasionally by the stirring of the dogs on the tethering cable. No one said anything, no one as much as looked at his neighbour. The silence stretched on and on, then, as one man, they all swung round startled at the heavy metallic click from behind them. Jackstraw had just cocked the bolt of his rifle, and I could see the slow stiffening of Zagero's back and arms as he realised that the barrel was lined up on his own head.

'It's no coincidence, Zagero,' I said grimly. I had my own automatic in my hand by the time he turned round. 'That rifle's pointed just where it's meant to. Bring your bag here.'

He stared at me, then called me an unprintable name.

'Bring it here,' I repeated. I pointed the Beretta at his head. 'Believe me, Zagero, I'd as soon kill you as let you live.'

He believed me. He brought the bag, flung it at my feet.

'Open it,' I said curtly.

'It's locked.'

'Unlock it.'

He looked at me without expression, then searched through his pockets. At last he stopped and said, 'I can't find the keys.'

'I'd expected nothing else. Jackstraw——' I changed my mind, one gun was not enough to cover a killer like Zagero. I glanced round the company, made my choice. 'Mr Smallwood, perhaps you——'

'No, thank you,' Mr Smallwood said hastily. He was still holding a handkerchief to his puffed mouth. He smiled wryly. 'I've never realised so clearly before now how essentially a man of peace I am, Dr Mason. Perhaps Mr Corazzini——'

I glanced at Corazzini, and he shrugged indifferently. I understood his lack of eagerness. He must have known that I'd had him high up among my list of suspects until very recently indeed and a certain delicacy of sentiment might well prevent him from being too forthcoming too soon. But this was no time for delicacy. I nodded, and he made for Zagero.

He missed nothing, but he found nothing. After two minutes he stepped back, looked at me and then, thoughtfully, at Solly Levin. Again I nodded, and again he began to search. In ten seconds he brought out a bunch of keys, and held them up.

'It's a frame-up,' Levin yelped. 'It's a plant! Corazzini musta palmed 'em and put 'em there. I never had no keys——'

'Shut up!' I ordered contemptuously. 'Yours, Zagero?'

He nodded tightly, said nothing.

'O.K., Corazzini,' I said. 'Let's see what we can find.'

The second key opened the soft leather case. Corazzini dug

under the clothes on top and brought out the three corned beef tins.

'Thank you,' I said 'Our friend's iron rations for his take-off. Miss Ross, our lunch. . . . Tell me, Zagero, can you think of any reason why I shouldn't kill you now?'

'You've made nothin' but mistakes ever since I met you,' Zagero said slowly, 'but, brother, this is the biggest you ever made. Do you think I would be such a damn' fool as to incriminate myself that way? Do you think I would be so everlastingly obvious——'

'I think that's exactly the way you expected me to think,' I said wearily. 'But I'm learning, I'm learning. One more job, Corazzini, if you would. Tie their feet.'

'What are you going to do,' Zagero asked tightly.

'Don't worry. The executioner will collect his fee. From now on you and Levin ride, with your feet tied, in the front of the tractor sled—and with a gun on you all the time. . . . What is it, Miss LeGarde?'

'Are you sure, Peter?' It was the first time she had spoken for hours, and I could see that even that tiny effort tired her. 'He doesn't *look* like a murderer.' The tone of her voice accurately reflected the expressions of consternation and shocked disbelief on half a dozen faces: Zagero had spared no effort to make himself popular with everyone.

'Does anybody here?' I demanded 'The best murderers never do.' I then explained to her—and the others—all I knew and had suspected about everything. It shook them, especially the facts of the spiking of the petrol and of Hillcrest having been, at one time, only a few hours behind us: and by the time I was finished I could see that there was as little doubt in their minds about Zagero's guilt as there was in mine.

Two hours later, well down the slope from the Vindeby Nunataks, I stopped and set up the radio gear. I reckoned that we were now less than a hundred miles from the coast, and for half an hour tried to raise our base at Uplavnik. We had no success, but I had hardly expected any: the radio shack at the base was manned by one operator, he couldn't be expected be on watch all the time, and obviously his call-up bell wasn't set for the frequency I was using.

At four o'clock exactly I got through to Hillcrest. This time I hadn't bothered to move the radio out of hearing range—I was actually leaning against the tractor cabin as I spoke—and every word said, both by Hillcrest and myself, could be clearly heard. But it didn't matter any more.

The first thing I did, of course, was to tell him that we had got our men. Even as I spoke, my own voice sounded curiously flat and lifeless. I should, I suppose, have been exultant and happy, but the truth was that I had suffered too much, both physically and psychologically, in the past few days, exhaustion lay over me like a smothering blanket, the reaction from the strain of those days was beginning to set in, the awareness was clearly with me that we weren't out of the wood by a long way yet, the lives of Marie LeGarde and Mahler were now the uppermost thoughts in my mind, and, to be perfectly honest, I also felt curiously deflated because I had developed a considerable liking for Zagero and the revelation of his true character had been more of a shock to me than I would have been prepared to admit to anyone.

Hillcrest's reactions, I must admit, were all that could have been wished for, but when I asked him about his progress the enthusiasm vanished from his voice. They were still bogged down, it seemed, and progress had been negligible. There was no word yet of passenger lists or of what the plane had carried that had been so important. The *Triton*, the aircraft-carrier, had insulin aboard and would fly it up to Uplavnik. A landing barge was moving into Uplavnik through an ice lead and was expected to arrive to-morrow and unload the tractor it was carrying, which would move straight out to meet us. Two ski-planes and two search bombers had been looking for us, but failed to locate us—we'd probably been traversing the Vindeby Nunataks at the time . . . His voice went on and on, but I hadn't heard anything he'd said in the past minute or so. I had just remembered something I should have remembered a long time ago.

'Wait a minute,' I called. 'I've just thought of something.'

I climbed inside the tractor cabin and shook Mahler. Fortunately, he was only asleep—from the look of him an hour or two ago I'd have said the collapse was due any minute.

'Mr Mahler,' I said quickly. 'You said you worked for an oil company?'

'That's right. He looked at me in surprise. 'Socony Mobil Oil Co., in New Jersey.'

'As what?' There were a hundred things he could have been that were of no use to me.

'Research chemist. Why?'

I sighed in relief, and explained. When I'd finished telling him of Hillcrest's solution to his troubles—distilling the petrol—I asked him what he thought of it.

'It's as good a way as any of committing suicide,' he said grimly. 'What does he want to do—send himself into orbit? It only requires one weak spot in the can he's trying to heat. . . . Besides, the evaporation range of petrol is so wide—anything from 30 degrees centigrade to twice the temperature of boiling water—that it may take him all day to get enough to fill a cigaraette lighter.'

'That seems to be more or less the trouble,' I agreed. 'Is there nothing he can do?'

'Only one thing he can do—wash it. What size drums does your petrol come in?'

'Ten gallon.'

'Tell him to pour out a couple of gallons and replace with water. Stir well. Let it stand for ten minutes and then syphon off the top seven gallons. It'll be as near pure petrol as makes no difference.'

'As easy as that!' I said incredulously. I thought of Hillcrest's taking half an hour to distil a cupful. 'Are you sure, Mr Mahler?'

'It should work,' he assured me. Even the strain of a minute's speaking had been too much for him, his voice was already no more than a husky whisper. 'Sugar is insoluble in petrol—it just dissolves in the small amounts of water present in petrol, small enough to be held in suspension. But if you've plenty of water it'll sink to the bottom, carrying the sugar with it.'

'If I'd the Nobel Science Prize, I'd give it to you right now, Mr Mahler.' I rose to my feet. 'If you've any more suggestions to make, for heaven's sake let me know.'

'I've one to make now,' he smiled, but he was almost gasping for breath. 'It's going to take your friend a pretty long time to melt the snow to get all the water he needs to wash the petrol.' He nodded towards the tractor sled, visible through the gap in the canvas screen. 'We're obviously carrying far too much fuel. Why don't you drop some off for Captain Hillcrest—why, in fact, didn't you drop some off last night, when you first heard of this?'

I stared at him for a long long moment, then turned heavily for the door.

'I'll tell you why, Mr Mahler,' I said slowly. 'It's because I'm the biggest damned prize idiot in this world, that's why.'

And I went out to tell Hillcrest just how idiotic I was.

CHAPTER TEN

THURSDAY 4 P.M.–
FRIDAY 6 P.M.

Jackstraw, Corazzini and I took turns at driving the Citroën all through that evening and the following night. The engine was beginning to run rough, the exhaust was developing a peculiar note and it was becoming increasingly difficult to engage second gear. But I couldn't stop, I daren't stop. Speed was life now.

Mahler had gone into collapse shortly after nine o'clock that evening, and from the collapse had gradually moved into the true diabetic coma. I had done all I could, all anyone could, but heaven only knew it was little enough. He needed bed, heat, fluids, stimulants, sugar by mouth or injection. Both suitable stimulants and the heat were completely lacking, the lurching, narrow hard wooden bunk was poor substitute for any bed, despite his great thirst he had found it increasingly difficult to keep down the melted snow water, and I had no means of giving an intravenous injection. For the others in the cabin it was distressing to watch him, distressing to listen to the dyspnoea— the harsh laboured breathing of coma. Unless we could get the insulin in time, I knew no power on earth could prevent death from supervening in from one to three days—in these unfavourable conditions, a day would be much more likely.

Marie LeGarde, too, was weakening with dangerous speed. It was with increasing difficulty that she could force down even the smallest mouthfuls of food, and spent most of her time in restless troubled sleep. Having seen her on the stage and marvelled at her magnificent vitality, it now seemed strange to me that she should go under so easily. But her vitality had really been a manifestation of a nervous energy: she had little of the physical resources necessary to cope with a situation like this, and I had frequently to remind myself that she was an elderly woman. Not that any such reminder was needed when one saw her face: it was haggard and lined and old.

But worried though I was about my patients, Jackstraw was even more deeply concerned with the weather. The temperature had been steadily rising for many hours now, the moaning ululation of the ice-cap wind, which had been absent for over two days, was increasing in intensity with every hour that passed, and the skies above were dark and heavy with black drifting clouds of snow. And when, just after midnight, the wind-speed passed fifteen miles an hour, the wind began to pick up the drift off the ice-cap.

I knew what Jackstraw was afraid of, though I myself had never experienced it. I had heard of the katabatic winds of Greenland, the equivalent of the feared Alaskan *williwaws*. When great masses of air in the heart of the plateau were cooled, as they had been in the past forty-eight hours, by extremely low temperatures, they were set in motion by a gradient wind and cascaded—there was no other word for it—downwards from the edge of the plateau through suitable drainage channels. Set in motion through their own sheer weight of cold air, these gravity or drainage winds, slowly warmed by the friction and compression of their descent, could reach a hurricane force of destructive violence in which nothing could live.

And all the signs, all the conditions for a gravity storm were there. The recent extreme cold, the rising wind, the rising temperature, the outward flowing direction of the wind, the dark star-obscuring clouds scudding by overhead—there could be no mistaking it, Jackstraw declared. I had never known him to be wrong about Greenland weather, I didn't believe him to be wrong now, and when Jackstraw became nervous it was time for even the most optimistic to start worrying. And I was worried all right.

We drove the tractor to its limit, and on the slight downward slope—we had changed direction by this time and were heading due south-west for Uplavnik—we were making very good time indeed. But by four o'clock in the morning, when we were, I reckoned, not more than sixty miles from Uplavnik, we ran into the *sastrugi* and were forced to slow down.

The *sastrugi*, regular undulations in the frozen snow, were the devil on tractors, especially elderly machines like the Citroën. Caused by raking winds, symmetrical as the waves in an eighteenth-century sailing print, hard on the crest and soft in the trough, they made progress possible only by slowing down to a disheartening crawl. Even so the Citroën and the sledges behind rolled and pitched like ships in a heavy seaway, the headlights one moment reaching up into the lowering darkness of the sky, the next dipping to illuminate the barred white and shadowed black of the *sastrugi* immediately ahead. Sometimes it gave way to deceptively clear patches—deceptively, for snow had obviously fallen here recently or been carried down from the plateau, and we were reduced to low gear to make any headway at all on it.

Shortly before eight o'clock in the morning Jackstraw brought the Citroën to a halt, and as the roar of the big engine died the deep moaning of the wind, a wind carrying with it a riding wall of ice and snow, swept in to take its place. Jackstraw had drawn up broadside on to the wind and the slope of the hill, and I jumped down to rig up a canvas shelter extending out from the cabin: it was nothing elaborate, just a triangular sheet of proofed canvas attached to the top of the cabin and the cleat of a caterpillar track on its vertical side, with its apex stretched out to a spike hammered into the surface of the ice-cap: there was no room for us all within the cabin at meal-times, I wanted some protection when we kept our 8 a.m. radio schedule with Hillcrest, and, in particular, it was time that Zagero and Levin had some relief from their sufferings. They had ridden all night on the tractor sled, under the guard of either Jackstraw or myself, and though the temperature was now only a few degrees below zero and though they were sheltering under a mound of clothing, nevertheless they must have spent a miserable night.

Breakfast, such as it was, was waiting and ready to be eaten as soon as the tractor had stopped, but I had little appetite for it: it seemed to me I had forgotten what sleep was like, I had had none for almost three days, I was living now in a permanent state of physical and mental exhaustion and it was becoming almost impossible to concentrate, to think of the hundred and one things that had to be thought of all the time. More than once I caught myself nodding and dozing off over my cup of coffee, and it was only with a conscious effort of will that I forced myself to my feet to keep the radio schedule. I was going to call both Hillcrest and our base—Hillcrest had given me the frequency the previous evening. I decided to call Hillcrest first.

We got through without any difficulty, although Hillcrest said they could hear me only very faintly. I suspected some fault on the generator side, for our receiver was powered by a hundred-hour battery and we could hear Hillcrest's voice clearly.

All the men except Mahler were gathered round me during the transmission—they seemed to find a peculiar reassurance in another voice, however distant and disembodied that voice—and even Zagero and Levin were only seven or eight feet away, sitting in front of the tractor sled with their feet still bound. I was on a canvas chair, with my back to the canvas screen, and Corazzini and Brewster were sitting on the tailboard, the canvas curtains drawn behind them to keep the heat in the cabin. The Rev Smallwood was beside me, turning the generator handle, and Jackstraw a few feet away, watchful as ever, the cocked rifle ready in his hand.

'Receiving you loud and clear,' I said to Hillcrest. My hands were cupped round the microphone and I was holding it close to my mouth to cut out as much as possible of the background noise of the wind. 'What progress?' I threw the receiver switch into the antenna, and Hillcrest's voice came again.

'Great!' He sounded enthusiastic, excited. 'My congratulations to your learned friend. Works like a charm and we're going like a bomb. We are approaching the Vindeby Nunataks and expect to be through by this afternoon.'

This was wonderful news. With any luck he would be up with us late in the evening of that day, and we would have the moral support of his company and the even more important technical resources of everything his big modern Sno-Cat could offer. And Jackstraw and I could get some desperately needed sleep. . . . I became aware that Hillcrest was continuing, his voice still charged with the same suppressed excitement.

'The Admiralty or the Government or whoever it is have loosened up at last! Brother, you're sitting on dynamite and you don't know it. You've got it right there with you and you could exchange it to-morrow for a million pounds in the right place. No wonder the Government were so cagy, no wonder they knew something fishy was going on and mounted the biggest search ever. The carrier *Triton*'s going to collect it personally——'

I threw the receiving switch.

'For heaven's sake!' I shouted in exasperation—an exasperation, I was dimly aware, shared by all the others who were leaning forward to hear Hillcrest's voice. 'What are you talking about? What *was* the plane carrying? Over.'

'Sorry. It's a guided-missile mechanism of such advanced design and so top-secret that its details, I gather, are known only to a handful of scientists in all the United States. It's the only one of its kind, and was being sent to Britain for study under the recent agreement to share knowledge on atomic weapons and guided missiles.' Hillcrest's voice was calm now, measured and sober. There was a pause, then he went on, slowly, impressively. 'I understand the governments concerned are prepared to go to any lengths—*any lengths*—to secure the recovery of this mechanism and prevent its falling into wrong hands.'

There was another, longer pause: Hillcrest, clearly, was giving me an opportunity to say something, but I just didn't know what to say. The magnitude of the entire thing took my breath away, temporarily inhibited all thought and speech. . . . Hillcrest's voice was coming through again:

'To help you identify this mechanism, Dr Mason. It's camouflaged, made up to look like an ebonite and metal portable radio of fairly large size, with a braided leather carrying strap. Find that portable, Dr Mason, and you'll——'

I never heard the end of that sentence. I was still sitting there, dazedly wondering why the words 'portable radio' should have triggered off such a clangorous bell in my mind—I can only plead my extreme physical and mental exhaustion—when Zagero catapulted himself off his seat on the sled, knocking Jackstraw staggering, took one tremendous hop with his bound feet just opposite where I was sitting and hurled himself bodily towards Corazzini who, his face twisted into a vicious and unrecognizable mask, had pushed himself off the tractor tailboard with one hand and with the other was fumbling desperately to bring something out from under his coat. He saw he couldn't make it in time, threw himself to one side, but Zagero, bound though he was, was like a cat on his feet and I knew in that instant, that instant that was too late, that Zagero was indeed the world-class boxer that he claimed to be. If the astonishing speed of his reflexes were not proof enough, that blurring right arm of his carried with it lethal conviction. Corazzini was a very big man, six feet two and at least two hundred pounds and he was swathed in many layers of heavy clothing, but when that fist caught him with such frightening power just under the heart he staggered back against the tailboard and slid slowly to the ground, unseeing eyes turned up to the first driving flakes of the newly fallen snow. I had never seen a blow delivered with such power: nor do I ever want to see it again.

For perhaps five seconds no one moved, no one spoke, men were held in thrall. The soughing, wailing moan of the wind on the ice-cap sounded weirdly, unnaturally loud. I was the first to break the silence. I was still sitting on my canvas stool.

'Corazzini!' I said. 'Corazzini!' My voice was barely more than a whisper, but Zagero heard me.

'Sure it's Corazzini,' he said levelly. 'It always was.' He stooped, thrust his hand under the unconscious man's coat and brought out his gun. 'You'd better keep this, Doc. Not only do I not trust our little playmate here with toys like these, but the state prosecutor or district attorney or whatever you call the guy in England will find that the riflin' on this barrel matches the riflin' marks on some very interestin' bullets.'

He tossed the gun across, and automatically I caught it. It was a pistol, not an automatic, and it had a strange looking cylinder screwed on to the front of the barrel. A silencer, I supposed; I had never seen one before. Nor had I ever seen that type of gun before. I didn't like the look of it at all, and I guessed it might be wise to have a gun in my hand when Corazzini came round. Jackstraw, I could see, had already his rifle lined up on the unconscious man. I placed the pistol on the ground beside me and pulled out the Beretta.

'You were ready for him.' I was still trying to put things in order in my own mind. 'You were waiting for the break. How——'

'Do I have to draw a diagram, Doc?' There was no insolence in his voice, only weariness. 'I knew it wasn't me. I knew it wasn't Solly. So it had to be Corazzini.'

'Yes, I see. It had to be Corazzini.' The words were automatic, meaningless. My thoughts were in a state of utter confusion, as confused, no doubt as those of Corazzini who was now pushing himself groggily into a sitting position, but for the past fifteen seconds another bell had been ringing far back in my mind, not so loud as the first but even more desperately insistent, and all at once I had it and began to rise to my feet. 'But there were two of them, two of them! Corazzini had an accomplice——' That was as far as I got when some metal object smashed across my wrist with brutal force, sending my Beretta flying, and something small and hard ground viciously into the back of my neck.

'Don't move, Dr Mason.' The voice, flat, controlled but alive with a vibrant power that I had never heard before, was almost unrecognizable as the Rev Joseph Smallwood's. 'Nobody is to move. Nielsen, drop that rifle—now! Just one suspicious move and Dr Mason gets his head blown off.'

I stood stock-still. The man behind that voice meant every word he said. I didn't need any convincing of that. The cold certainty in his voice only reinforced the knowledge I already had that the sanctity of human life was a factor which could never enter into this man's considerations.

'All right, Corazzini?' Smallwood was speaking again, his voice empty of all concern for and interest in his accomplice: his only anxiety, if one could by any stretch of imagination call it that, lay in his desire for Corazzini's effectively continued cooperation.

'All right,' Corazzini said softly. He was standing now and that both mind and reactions were back to normal was evident from the dexterity with which he caught the gun Smallwood threw back to him. 'Never thought any man could move so fast with his feet tied. But he won't catch me again. Everybody out, eh?'

'Everybody out,' Smallwood nodded. No question, he was the leader of the two, ridiculously improbable though that would have seemed only two minutes ago: but it didn't seem improbable any longer, it seemed inevitable.

'Jump down! All of you,' Corazzini ordered. Gun in one hand, he held back a flap of the canvas screen with the other. 'Hurry it up.'

'Mahler can't jump down,' I protested. 'He can't move—he's in coma. He——'

'Shut up!' Corazzini interrupted. 'All right, Zagero, inside and get him out.'

'You can't move him!' I shouted furiously. 'You'll kill him if——' My last word was choked off in a grunt of pain as Smallwood's gun barrel caught me viciously across the side of the head. I fell to my hands and knees in the snow and remained there for several seconds, head down and shaking it from side to side as I tried to overcome the dizziness and the pain.

'Corazzini said "shut up". You must learn to listen.' Smallwood's voice was chillingly devoid of all emphasis and inflection. He stood waiting quietly until the last of the passengers had descended or been carried from the tractor cabin, then waved us all into a straight line facing towards Corazzini and himself. Both of them had their backs to the canvas screen, while we were placed just far enough clear of the shelter to be blinded by the increasingly heavy snowfall that swirled down into our eyes, but not so far off as not to be clearly seen by them. Whatever these two did, I was beginning to discover, betrayed that economy of movement and unquestioning sureness of the complete professionals who had long ago worked out the answers to and counters against any of a vast range and permutation of situations they were ever likely to encounter.

Smallwood beckoned me.

'You haven't finished your radio call, Dr Mason. Finish it. Your friend Hillcrest must be wondering at the delay.' The gun in his hand came forward a fraction of an inch, just enough for the movement to be perceptible. 'For your own sake, do nothing to arouse his suspicions. Don't be clever. Keep it brief.'

I kept it brief. I excused the interruption of transmission on the grounds that Mahler had taken a sudden turn for the worse—as indeed, I thought bitterly, he had—said that I'd guard the missile mechanism with my life and apologized for cutting the call short, but said it was essential to get Mahler to Uplavnik with all speed.

'Finish it off,' Smallwood said softly in my ear. I nodded.

'That's the lot then, Captain Hillcrest. Will make the noon schedule. This is Mayday signing off. Mayday, Mayday.'

I switched off, and turned indifferently away. I had taken only one step when Smallwood caught my shoulder and whirled me round. For such an apparently slight man, he was phenomenally strong. I gasped as his pistol barrel dug into my stomach.

' "Mayday", Dr Mason?' he asked silkily. 'What is "Mayday"?'

'Our call-sign, of course,' I said irritably.

'Your call-sign is GFK.'

'Our call-up is GFK. Our signing-off is "Mayday".'

'You're lying.' I wondered how I could ever have thought this face meek and nervous and colourless. The mouth was a thin hard line, the upper eyelids bar-straight and hooded above the unwinking eyes. Flat marbled eyes of a faded light-blue. A killer's eyes. 'You're lying,' he repeated.

'I'm not lying,' I said angrily.

'Count five and die.' His eyes never left mine, the pressure of the gun increased. 'One . . . two . . . three——'

'I'll tell you what it is!' The cry came from Margaret Ross. ' "Mayday" is the international air distress signal, the S O S . . .

I had to tell him Dr Mason, I had to!' Her voice was a shaking sob. 'He was going to kill you.'

'I was indeed,' Smallwood agreed. If he felt either anger or apprehension, no trace of either appeared in the calm conversational voice. 'I should do it now—you've lost us four hours' head start. But courage happens to be one of the few virtues I admire. . . . You are an extremely brave man, Dr Mason. Your courage is a fair match for your—ah—lack of perspicacity, shall we say.'

'You'll never get off the ice-cap, Smallwood,' I said steadily. 'Scores of ships and planes are searching for you, thousands of men. They'll get you and they'll hang you for these five dead men.'

'We shall see.' He gave a wintry smile, and now that he had removed his rimless glasses I could see that the man's smile left his eyes untouched, left them flat and empty and lifeless, like the stained glass in a church and no sun behind it. 'All right, Corazzini, the box. Dr Mason, bring one of the maps from the driver's seat.'

'In a moment. Perhaps you would care to explain——'

'Explanations are for children.' The voice was level, curt, devoid of all inflection. 'I'm in a hurry, Dr Mason. Bring the map.'

I brought it and when I returned Corazzini was sitting on the front of the tractor sled with a case before him. But it wasn't the leather-covered portable radio: it was Smallwood's robe case.

Corazzini snapped open the catches, pulled out Bible, robes and divinity hood, tossed them to one side then carefully brought out a metal box which looked exactly like a tape-recorder: indeed, when he shone his torch on it I could clearly see the word 'Grundig'. But it soon became apparent that it was like no tape-recorder that I had ever seen.

The twin spools he ripped off the top of the machine and sent spinning away into the darkness and the snow, the tape unwinding in a long convoluted streamer. By this time I would have taken long odds that anyone suspicious enough to investigate would have found that tape perfectly genuine: probably, I thought bitterly, Bach's organ music, in keeping with Smallwood's late ecclesiastical nature.

Still in silence, we watched Corazzini undo and fling away the false top of the recorder, but not before I had time to notice the padded spring clips on its underside—the perfect hiding place for a couple of automatics: revealed now were controls and calibrated dials that bore no resemblance to those of a tape recorder.

297

Corazzini straightened and erected a hinged telescopic aerial, clamped a set of headphones to his ears, made two switches and started to turn a dial, at the same time watching a green magic eye similar to those found in tape recorders and many modern radios. Faintly, but unmistakably, I could hear a steady whine coming from the earphones, a whine which altered in pitch and intensity as Corazzini turned the dial. When it reached its maximum strength, he turned his attention to a built-in alcohol compass about three inches in diameter. A few moments later he doffed the earphones and turned round, apparently satisfied.

'Very strong, very clear,' he announced to Smallwood. 'But there's too heavy a deviation factor from all the metal in the tractor and sledge. Back in two minutes. Your torch, Dr Mason.'

He walked away for about fifty yards, taking the machine with him: it was with intense chagrin that I realised that it was perfectly in keeping with all that had gone before that Corazzini had probably forgotten more about navigation than I was ever likely to know. He returned soon, consulted a small chart—correcting for variation, no doubt—then grinned at Smallwood.

'It's them, all right. Perfect signal. Bearing 268.'

'Good.' If Smallwood felt relieved or gratified at the news, no shadow of his feeling touched the thin immobile face. Their quiet certainty, their forethought, their foolproof organization was dismaying, frightening. Now that I could see what manner of men they were it was unthinkable that they should have set themselves down in a vast featureless country such as this without some means of orientating themselves: what we had just seen in operation could only be a battery operated radio direction finder, and even to me, inexperienced though I was in such matters, it was obvious that Corazzini must have been taking a bearing on some continuous directional line-up signals transmitted by a vessel, or vessels, off-shore: trawlers, probably, or some other inconspicuous type of fishing vessel. . . . I would have been less than human had I not wanted to shake this absolute confidence.

'You've miscalculated the hornet's nest you've stirred up. The Davis Strait, the coast of Greenland is alive with ships and planes. The scout planes of the carrier *Triton* will pick up every boat that's larger than a skiff. The trawlers will never get away with it: they won't get five miles.'

'They don't have to.' Implicit in Corazzini's words was confirmation of the accuracy of my guess about trawlers. 'There are such things as submarines. In fact there is one, not far from here.'

'You still won't——'

'Be quiet,' Smallwood said coldly. He turned to Corazzini. 'Two hundred and sixty-eight, eh—due west more or less. Distance?'

Corazzini shrugged, said nothing: Smallwood beckoned to me.

'We'll soon find it. That map, Dr Mason—indicate our position, accurately.'

'You can go to hell,' I said briefly.

'I expected nothing else. However, I'm not blind and your clumsy attempts at concealment have done little to hide the growing attachment between yourself and the young lady here.' I glanced quickly at Margaret, saw the faint colour beginning to stain the pale cheek and looked as quickly away. 'I am prepared to shoot Miss Ross.'

I never doubted him. I knew he'd do it in an instant. I gave him our position, he asked for another map, asked Jackstraw to mark our position on the second, and compared the two.

'They coincide,' he nodded. 'Fortunately for you.' He studied the map briefly, then looked at Corazzini. 'The Kangalak fjord, undoubtedly, at the foot of the Kangalak glacier. Approximately——'

'The Kangalak fjord,' I interrupted. My voice was bitter. 'Why the hell didn't you land there in the first place and save us all this?'

'The plane captain deserved to die,' Smallwood said obliquely. His smile was wintry. 'I had instructed him to put down on the coast just north of the fjord where our—ah—friends had reconnoitred a section of the ice-cap, three miles long and absolutely flat, that is the equal of the finest runway in Europe or America, and it wasn't until I saw the altimeter reading just before the crash that I realised he had deceived me.' He made an impatient gesture and turned to Corazzini. 'We waste time. Approximately sixty miles, you would say?'

Corazzini examined the map. 'Yes, about that.'

'So, come then, on our way.'

'Leaving us here to starve and die of cold, I suppose?' I said bitterly.

'What becomes of you no longer concerns me,' Smallwood said indifferently. Already, in a matter of minutes, it had become almost impossible to think of him, to remember him as the meek retiring minister we had known. 'It is possible, however, that you

299

might be foolish enough to take advantage of the cover of snow and darkness to run after us, waylay and try to overcome us. You might even succeed, even though unarmed. We must immobilize you, temporarily.'

'Or permanently,' Zagero said softly.

'Only fools kill wantonly and unnecessarily. Fortunately—for you—it is not necessary for my plans that you die. Corazzini, bring some rope from the sled. There's plenty of cord there. Tie their feet only. With their numbed hands it will take them an hour to undo their bonds: we will be well on our way by then.' He moved his gun gently from side to side. 'Sit in the snow. All of you.'

There was nothing for it but to do as we were told. We sat down and watched Corazzini bring a hank of cord from the sled. He looked at Smallwood, and Smallwood nodded at me.

'Dr Mason first.'

Corazzini gave his gun to Smallwood—they missed nothing, that pair, not even the remote possibility that one of us might try to snatch Corazzini's gun—and advanced on me. He knelt and had taken a couple of turns round my ankles when the truth struck me with the suddenness, the shocking impact of a physical blow. I sent Corazzini staggering with a violent shove and leapt to my feet.

'No!' My voice was hoarse, savage. 'By God, you're not going to tie me up, Smallwood!'

'Sit down, Mason!' His voice was hard, whip-like, and the light from the tractor cabin was enough for me to see the rock-like pistol barrel centred between my eyes. I ignored it completely.

'Jackstraw!' I shouted. 'Zagero, Levin, Brewster! On your feet if you want to live. He's only got one gun. If he starts firing at any of us, the rest go for him and get him—he can't possibly get us all. Margaret, Helene, Mrs. Dansby-Gregg—first shot that's fired, run off into the darkness—and stay there!'

'Have you gone crackers, Doc?' The words came from an astonished Zagero, but for all that something namelessly urgent and compelling in my voice had got him to his feet, and he was bent forward, crouched like a great cat, ready to launch himself at Smallwood. 'Want to get us all killed?'

'That's just what I don't want.' I could feel my spine, the back of my neck cold with a cold that was not of the Arctic, and my legs were trembling. 'Going to tie us up and leave us here? Is he

300

hell! Why do you think he told us of the trawler, its position, the submarine and all the rest of it? I'll tell you why—because he knew it was safe, because he'd made up his mind that none of us would ever live to tell of these things.' I was rattling the words out with machine-gun rapidity, desperate with the need to convince the others of what I was saying before it was too late: and my eyes never left the gun in Smallwood's hand.

'But——'

'No "but",' I interrupted harshly. 'Smallwood knows that Hillcrest will be coming through here this afternoon. If we're still here—and alive—first thing we'd tell him would be Smallwood's course, speed, approximate position and destination. Within an hour the Kangalak glacier would be sealed, within an hour bombers from the *Triton* would have blasted him off the face of the glacier. Tie us up? Sure—and then he and Corazzini would shoot us at their leisure while we flopped around the ice like birds with broken wings.'

Conviction was immediate and complete. I couldn't see the faces of the other, but the fractional lowering of Smallwood's gun was enough to tell me.

'I underestimated you, Dr Mason,' he admitted softly. His voice was devoid of all trace of anger. 'But you almost died there.'

'What's five minutes more or less?' I asked, and Smallwood nodded absently. He was already working out an alternative solution.

'You—you inhuman monster!' Senator Brewster's voice was shaking with fear or anger or both. 'You were going to tie us up and butcher us like—like——' Words failed him for a moment, then he whispered: 'You must be mad, Smallwood, stark raving mad.'

'He's not in the slightest,' Zagero said quietly. 'Not mad. Just bad. But it's kind of hard to tell the difference at times. Figured out your next jolly little scheme, Smallwood?'

'Yes. As Dr Mason says, we can't possibly dispose of all of you inside a couple of seconds, which is all the time it would take for one—probably more—of you to reach the cover of the snow and darkness.' He nodded towards the tractor sled, lifted his collar high against the snow and biting wind. 'I think you had better ride a little way with us.'

And ride with them we did for the thirty longest miles I have ever driven, for nine hours that had no end. A relatively short distance, but this eternity of time to cover it: partly because of the *sastrugi*, partly because of the increasingly long stretches of soft snow, but mainly because of the weather, which was deteriorating rapidly. The wind had now risen to something better than thirty miles an hour, it carried with it a blinding wall of flying ice-filled drift, and, even though it was directly behind us, it made things troublesome for the driver. For all the others except Smallwood it made the conditions intolerable: had the temperature been what it was only twenty-four hours previously, none of us, I am sure, would have survived that trip.

I would have thought that with either Smallwood or Corazzini driving and the other navigating from the dog-sledge we would have had a chance, slender though it might be, to overpower them or at least make good our escape. But Smallwood never offered even a shadow of a chance of either. Corazzini drove all the time, with the radio direction finder headphones clamped to his ears, so that compass navigation became an inaccurate superfluity. Smallwood sat alone in the back of the tractor cabin, his gun unwaveringly trained on the rest of us who were crammed aboard the big tractor sled, ten feet to the rear of him: when the snow eventually became too heavy he stopped the tractor, detached the portable searchlight and mounted it, facing aft, in the rear of the tractor cabin; this had the double advantage of illuminating us so that he could clearly see us even through the drift and making certain that none of us tried to drop off the sled, and of blinding us so that we were quite unable to see what he was doing, even to see whether he was watching us at all. It was frustrating, maddening. And, for good measure and to prevent any desperate attempt at escape in the occasionally blinding flurries of snow, he brought Margaret and Helene up into the cabin and bound their hands: they were the surety for our good conduct.

That left eight of us on the tractor sled, Theodore Mahler and Marie LeGarde stretched out in the middle, three of us sitting on each side. Almost immediately after we had moved off and pulled a pair of tarpaulins over ourselves for what meagre shelter they could afford, Jackstraw leaned across and tapped me on the shoulder with something held in his hand. I reached up and took it from him.

'Corazzini's wallet,' he said softly. For all the chance of his being overheard by either Smallwood or Corazzini above the

302

roar of the engine and the voice of the gale, he could have shouted out the words. 'Fell from his pocket when Zagero knocked him down. He didn't see it go, but I did—sat on top of it when Smallwood told us to squat in the snow.'

I stripped off my gloves, opened the wallet and examined its contents in the light of the torch Jackstraw had also passed across—a torch with the beam carefully hooded and screened to prevent the slightest chink of light escaping from under the tarpaulin: at this time, Smallwood had not yet switched on the searchlight.

The wallet provided us with that last proof of the thoroughness, the meticulous care with which these two men had provided themselves with false but utterly convincing identities: I knew that whatever Corazzini's name was it wasn't the one he had given himself, but, had I not known, the 'N.C.' stamped on the hand-tooled morocco, the visiting cards with the inscribed 'Nicholas Corazzini' above the name and address of the Indiana head office of the Global Tractor Company, and the leather-backed fold of American Express cheques, each one already signed 'N. R. Corazzini' in its top left-hand corner, would have carried complete conviction.

And, too late, the wallet also presented us, obliquely but beyond all doubt, with the reason for many things, ranging from the purpose of the crash-landing of the plane to the explanation of why I had been knocked on the head the night before last: inside the bill-fold compartment was the newspaper cutting which I had first found on the dead body of Colonel Harrison. I read it aloud, slowly, with infinite chagrin.

The account was brief. That it concerned that dreadful disaster in Elizabeth, New Jersey, where a commuters' train had plunged through an open span of the bridge into the waters of Newark Bay, drowning dozens of the passengers aboard, I already knew from the quick glance I had had at the cutting in the plane. But, as I had also gathered in the plane, this was a follow-up story and the reporter wasted little time on the appalling details: his interest lay in another direction entirely. It was 'reliably reported', he said, that the train had been carrying an army courier: that he was one of the forty who had died: and that he had been carrying a 'super-secret guided missile mechanism'.

That was all the cutting said, but it was enough, and more than enough. It didn't say whether the mechanism had been lost or not, it most certainly never even suggested that there was any connection between the presence of the mechanism aboard the train and the reasons for the crash. It didn't have to, the cheek-by-jowl contiguity of the two items made the reader's own horrifying conclusions inevitable. From the silence that stretched out after I had read out the last words, I knew that the others were lost in the same staggering speculations as myself. It was Jackstraw who finally broke this silence, his voice abnormally matter-of-fact.

'Well, we know now why you were knocked on the head.'

'Knocked on the head?' Zagero took him up. 'What do you——?'

'Night before last,' I interrupted. 'When I told you I'd walked into a lamp-post.' I told them all about the finding of the cutting and its subsequent loss.

'Would it have made all that difference even if you *had* read it?' Zagero asked. 'I mean——'

'Of course it would!' My voice was harsh, savage almost, but the savagery was directed against myself, my own stupidity. 'The fact of finding a cutting about a fatal crash which occurred in strange unexplained circumstances on the person of a man who had just died in a fatal crash in equally strange and unexplained circumstances would have made even me suspicious. When I heard from Hillcrest that something highly secret was being carried aboard the plane, the parallel would have been even more glaringly obvious, especially as the cutting was found on the man— an army officer—who was almost certainly the courier, the carrier of this secret. Anything larger than a match-box in the luggage the passengers were carrying I'd have ripped open and examined, radio and tape-recorder included. Smallwood knew it. He didn't know *what* was in the cutting, but he—or Corazzini— knew it *was* a cutting and they were taking no chances at all.'

'You weren't to know this,' Levin said soothingly. 'It's not your fault——'

'Of course it's my fault,' I said wearily. 'All my fault. I don't even know how to start apologizing. You first, Zagero, I suppose, you and Solly Levin, for tying you——'

'Forget it.' Zagero was curt but friendly. 'We're just as bad— all of us. All the facts that mattered were as available to us as they were to you—and we made no better use of them: less, if anything.' In the tiny glow from the torch I could see him shaking his head. 'Lordy, lordy, but ain't it easy to understand everything

304

when it's too late. Easy enough to understand now why we crashed in the middle of nowhere—the plane captain must have been in on it, he must have known that the mechanism was aboard and thought it important enough to put the passengers' lives second and crash-land in the middle of the ice-plateau, where Smallwood could never reach the coast.'

'Not knowing that I was there waiting to oblige Smallwood,' I said bitterly. I shook my head in turn. 'It's obvious now, all too obvious. How Corazzini damaged his hand in the shack—not by saving or trying to save the radio but by accelerating its fall after he'd pushed the hinges in. How and why he lost the toss and had to sleep on the floor—to give him a chance to smother the second officer.'

'What you might call a good loser,' Zagero said grimly. Then he gave a short laugh. 'Remember when we buried the second officer? I wonder what Smallwood's burial service would have sounded like if we'd really been close enough to hear?'

'I missed that,' I nodded. 'I missed the suggestion you made inside the plane that we should bury the murdered men—if you had been guilty you'd never have dared make that suggestion for then the way these men died would almost certainly have been discovered.'

'*You* missed it,' Zagero said feelingly. 'How about me— *I* said it, and I never even thought of it till now.' He snorted. 'Boy, am I disgusted with myself. As far as I can see the only thing I knew that you didn't was that Corazzini clouted our friend Smallwood back in the pass there simply in order to throw suspicion on me: but, then, I knew that even trying to tell you that would have been crazy.'

There was a long moment's silence, while we listened to the rise and fall of the Citroën's exhaust note in the gusting, strengthening wind, then Solly Levin spoke.

'The plane,' he said. 'The fire—how come?'

'There was enough high-octane fuel in its tanks to take Hillcrest's Sno-Cat a couple of thousand miles,' I explained. 'If Hillcrest's tanks had been empty when he arrived back at base and if he'd found out right away that the spare fuel in the tunnel had been doctored—well, it wouldn't have taken him long to siphon out the stuff in the plane. So, no plane.'

The silence this time was even longer, then Zagero cleared his throat, as if uncertain how to begin.

'Seeing explanations are in the air—well, I guess it's time we made one too.' Zagero to my astonishment, sounded almost embarrassed. 'It's about the phony conduct of that phony character to your left, Doc, one Solly Levin. We'd plenty of time to talk about it when we were lashed to this damned sledge all of last night and——'

'Come to the point,' I interrupted impatiently.

'Sorry.' He leaned across to Solly Levin. 'Want I should make a formal introduction, Pop?'

I stared at him in the darkness.

'Did I hear——'

'Sure you did, Doc.' He laughed softly. 'Pop. The old man. The paternal parent. Says so on my birth certificate and everything.' He was enjoying himself vastly. 'Confirmation on the right here.'

'It's perfectly true, Dr Mason,' Solly Levin smiled. The dreadful Bowery accent was quite gone, yielding place to a crisper, more decisive version of Zagero's cultured drawl. 'I'll put it briefly. I'm the owner and managing director—or was till I retired a year ago—of a plastics factory in Trenton, New Jersey, near Princeton, where Johnny managed to acquire a splendid accent and very little else. It was not, I might add, Princeton's fault; Johnny spent most of his time in the gymnasium, nursing his—ah—pugilistic ambitions, much to my annoyance as I wanted him to take over from me.'

'Alas,' Zagero put in, 'I was almost as stubborn as he is himself.'

'A great deal more so,' his father said. 'So I made him a proposition. I'd give him two years—it seemed enough, he was already amateur heavyweight champion—to prove himself, and at the end of that time if he hadn't made it he was to take his place in the factory. His first manager was as corrupt as they come and Johnny literally kicked him out at the end of a year. So I took over. I'd newly retired, I'd time on my hands, I'd a very strong vested interest in his well-being apart from the fact that he was my son—and quite frankly, I'd begun to see that he really was going to get to the very top.' He broke off there— so I took the opportunity to interrupt.

'Zagero or Levin. Which is it?'

'Zagero,' the elder man answered.

'Why the Levin?'

'Some state and national boxing commissions refuse to permit a close relative to be either manager or second. Especially second. So I used an alias. A practice by no means uncommon, and officially winked at. A harmless deception.'

'Not so harmless,' I said grimly. 'It was one of the worst acting performances I've ever seen, and that was one of the primary reasons for my suspecting your son and, in turn, for Corazzini and Smallwood getting away with what they did. Had you come clean earlier on, I would have known that they were bound, even in the absence of all positive evidence, to be the guilty men. But with Solly Levin—I'll find it very difficult to think of you as Mr Zagero, I'm afraid—with Solly Levin sticking out as a sore thumb as an obvious phony—well, I just couldn't leave you two out of the list of suspects.'

'I obviously modelled myself on the wrong person—or type of person,' Levin said wryly. 'Johnny ribbed me about it all the time. I'm deeply sorry for any trouble we may have caused, Dr Mason. I honestly never looked at it from your point of view, never realized the dangers involved in maintaining the impersonation—if you could call it that. Please forgive me.'

'Nothing to forgive,' I said bitterly. 'A hundred to one I'd have found some other way of messing things up.'

Shortly after five o'clock in the evening Corazzini stopped the tractor—but he didn't stop the engine. He came down from the driver's seat and walked round to the cabin, pushing the searchlight to one side. He had to shout to make himself heard above the roar of the tractor and the high ululating whine of the still strengthenging blizzard.

'Half-way, boss. Thirty-two miles on the clock.'

'Thank you.' We couldn't see Smallwood, but we could see the tip of his gun barrel protruding menacingly into the searchlight's beam. 'The end of the line, Dr Mason. You and your friends will please get down.'

There was nothing else for it. Stiffly, numbly, I climbed down, took a couple of steps towards Smallwood, stopped as the pistol steadied unwaveringly on my chest.

'You'll be with your friends in a few hours,' I told Smallwood. 'You could leave us a little food, a portable stove and tent. Is that too much to ask?'

'It is.'

'Nothing? Nothing at all?'

'You're wasting your time, Dr Mason. And it grieves me to see you reduced to begging.'

'The dog sledge, then. We don't even want the dogs. But neither Mahler nor Miss LeGarde can walk.'

'You're wasting your time.' He turned his attention to the sledge. 'Everybody off, I said. Did you hear me, Levin? Get down!'

'It's my legs.' In the harsh glare of the searchlight we could see the lines of pain deep-etched round Levin's eyes and mouth, and I wondered how long he had been sitting there suffering, saying nothing. 'I think they're frozen or sleeping or something.'

'Get down!' Smallwood repeated sharply.

'In a moment.' Levin swung one of his legs over the edge of the sledge, his teeth bared with the effort. 'I don't seem to be able——'

'Maybe a bullet in one of your legs will help,' Smallwood said unemotionally. 'To get the feeling back.'

I didn't know whether he meant it or not. I didn't think so— gratuitous violence wasn't in character for this man, I couldn't see him killing or wounding without sound reason. But Zagero thought differently. He advanced within six feet of Smallwood.

'Don't touch him, Smallwood,' he said warningly.

'No?' The rising inflection was a challenge accepted, and Smallwood went on flatly: 'I'd snuff you and him like a candle.'

'No!' Zagero said, softly and savagely, the words carrying clearly in a sudden lull in the wind. 'Lay a finger on my old man, Smallwood, and I'll get to you and break your neck like a rotten carrot if you empty the entire magazine into me.' I looked at him as he crouched there like a great cat, toes digging into the frozen snow, fists clenched and slightly in advance of him, ready for the explosive leap that would take him across that tiny space in a split second of time and I believed he could do exactly what he said. So, too, I suspected, did Smallwood.

'Your old man?' he enquired. 'Your father?'

Zagero nodded.

'Good.' Smallwood showed no surprise. 'Into the tractor cabin with him, Zagero. We'll exchange him for the German girl. Nobody cares about her.'

His point was clear. I couldn't see how we could offer any danger to Smallwood and Corazzini now, but Smallwood was a man who guarded even against impossibilities: Levin would be a far better surety for Zagero's conduct than Helene.

Levin half-walked, was half-carried into the tractor cabin. With Corazzini and Smallwood both armed, resistance was hopeless: Smallwood had us summed up to a nicety. He knew we were desperate men, that we would fling ourselves on him and his gun in a moment of desperate emergency: but he also knew that we weren't so desperate as to commit suicide when no lives were in immediate danger.

When Levin was inside, Smallwood turned to the young German girl seated opposite him in the cabin. 'Out!'

It was then that it happened, with the stunning speed and inevitability that violent tragedy, viewed in retrospect, always seems to possess. I thought perhaps that it was some calculated plan, a last-minute desperate effort to save us that made Helene Fleming act as she did, but I found out later that she had merely been driven and goaded into a pain-filled unreasoning anger and resentment and despair by the agony she had suffered in her shoulder from having had her arms bound for so many long hours in the cruel jolting discomfort of the tractor cabin.

As she passed by Smallwood she stumbled, he put up an arm either to help her or ward her off, and before he had realized what was happening—it must have been the last quarter from which he expected any show of violence or resistance—she kicked out blindly and knocked the gun spinning out of his hand to land in the snow beneath. Smallwood sprang after it like a cat—the speed was unnecessary, the low growl of warning from an armed Corazzini put paid to any idea we might have had of taking advantage of the situation—picked up the gun and whirled round, the gun lining up on Helene, his eyes narrowed to slits against the beam of the searchlight, his face twisted into an unrecognizable snarl, the lips drawn far back over the teeth. I'd been wrong once more about Smallwood—he could kill without reason.

'Helene!' Mrs Dansby-Gregg, was the nearest to her, and her voice was high-pitched, almost a scream. 'Look out, Helene!' She plunged forward to push her maid to one side, but I don't think Smallwood even saw her: he was mad with fury, I knew he was, and nothing on earth was going to stop him from pressing that trigger. The bullet caught Mrs Dansby-Gregg squarely in the back and pitched her headlong to fall face down in the frozen snow.

Already Smallwood's moment of uncontrollable rage was spent as if it had never been. He said not another word, just nodded to Corazzini and jumped up on the tail of the tractor cabin to keep us covered with searchlight and gun as Corazzini gunned the motor, engaged gear and lumbered off into the darkness to the west. We stood in a forlorn huddled little group and watched the train pass us by, the tractor, the tractor sled, the dog sledge and finally the huskies themselves, running on the loose traces astern.

I heard Helene murmur something to herself, and when I bent to listen she was saying in a strange, wondering voice: 'Helene. She called me "Helene".' I stared at her as if she were mad, glanced down at the dead woman at my feet then gazed unseeingly after the receding lights of the Citroën until both the lights and the sound had faded and vanished into the snow-filled darkness of the night.

CHAPTER ELEVEN

FRIDAY 6 P.M.–
SATURDAY 12.15 P.M.

The white hell of that night, the agony of the bitter dreadful hours that followed—and God only knows how many hours these were—is a memory that will never die.

How many hours did we stagger and lurch after that tractor like drunk or dying men—six hours, eight, ten? We didn't know, we shall never know. Time as an independent system of measurement ceased to exist: each second was an interminable unit of suffering, of freezing, of exhausted marching, each minute an æon where the fire in our aching leg muscles fought with the ice-cold misery of hands and feet and faces for domination in our minds, each hour an eternity which we knew could never end. Not one of us, I am sure, expected to live through that night.

The thoughts, the emotions of these hours I could never afterwards recall. Chagrin there was, the most bitter I have ever known, an overwhelming mortification and self-condemnation that I had all along been deceived with such childish ease, that I had been powerless to offer any hindrance or resistance to the endless resourcefulness of that brilliant little man. And then I would think of Mrs Dansby-Gregg, and of Margaret bound and hostage and afraid and looking at Smallwood in the dim light of that lurching tractor cabin, looking at Smallwood and the gun in Smallwood's hand, and with that thought anger would flood in to supplant the chagrin, a consuming hatred and a fury that flamed throughout my entire being, but even that anger wasn't all exclusive: it couldn't be, not so long as fear, a fear such as I had never before known, was the dominating factor in my mind. And it was.

It was, too, I should think, in Zagero's mind. He hadn't spoken a word since Mrs Dansby-Gregg had died, had just flung himself uncaringly, ruthlessly, into what had to be done. Head bowed, he plodded on like an automaton. I wondered how many times he must have regretted that impetuous slip of the tongue when he had betrayed to Smallwood the fact that Solly Levin was his father.

And Jackstraw was as silent as we were, non-committal, speaking only when he had to, keeping his thoughts strictly to himself. I wondered if he was blaming me for what had happened but I didn't think so, Jackstraw's mind just didn't work that way. I could guess what he was thinking, I knew the explosive temper that slumbered under that placid exterior. Had we met an unarmed Smallwood and Corazzini then, I do not think we would have stopped short of killing them with our hands.

I suppose, too, that we were all three of us exhausted as we had never been before, frost-bitten, bleeding, thirsty and steadily weakening from lack of food. I say 'suppose', because logic and reason tell me that these things must have been so. But if they were I do not think they touched the minds of any of us that night. We were no longer ourselves, we were outside ourselves. Our bodies were but machines to serve the demands of our minds, and our minds so consumed with anxiety and anger that there was no place left for any further thought.

We were following the tractor. We could, I suppose, have turned back in the hope of stumbling across Hillcrest and his men. I knew Hillcrest well enough to know that *he* would know that those who had taken over our tractor—he had no means of knowing who they were, for all he knew Zagero might have suddenly overpowered us—would never dare make for Uplavnik but would almost certainly head for the coast. The likelihood was that Hillcrest, too, would head for the Kangalak fjord— together with a small bay beside it, the Kangalak fjord was the only break, the only likely rendezvous in a hundred miles of cliff-bound coast—and he could go there arrow-straight: on board his Sno-Cat he had a test prototype of a new, compact and as yet unmarketed Arma gyroscope specially designed for land use which had proved to have such astonishing accuracy that navigation on the ice-cap, as a problem, had ceased to exist for him.

But, even should he be heading towards the coast, our chances of meeting him in that blizzard did not exist, and if we once passed them by we would have been lost for ever. Better by far to head for the coast, where some patrolling ship or plane might just possibly pick us up—if we ever got there. Besides,

I knew that both Jackstraw and Zagero felt exactly as I did—under a pointless but overpowering compulsion to follow Smallwood and Corazzini until we dropped in our tracks.

And the truth was that we couldn't have gone any other way even had we wished to. When Smallwood had dropped us off we had been fairly into the steadily deepening depression in the ice-cap that wound down to the Kangalak glacier and it was a perfect drainage channel for the katabatic wind that was pouring down off the plateau. Although powerful enough already when we had been abandoned, that wind was now blowing with the force of a full gale, and for the first time on the Greenland ice-plateau—although we were now, admittedly, down to a level of 1500 feet—I heard a wind where the deep ululating moaning was completely absent. It howled, instead, howled and shrieked like a hurricane in the upper works and rigging of a ship, and it carried with it a numbing bruising flying wall of snow and ice-particles against which progress would have been utterly impossible. So we went the only way we could, with the lash of the storm ever on our bent and aching backs.

And ache our backs did. Only three people—Zagero, Jackstraw and myself—were able to carry anything more than their own weight: and we had among us three people completely unable to walk. Mahler was still unconscious, still in coma, but I didn't think we would have him with us very much longer: Zagero carried him for hour after endless hour through that white nightmare and for his self-sacrifice he paid the cruellest price of all for when, some hours later, I examined the frozen, useless appendages that had once been his hands, I knew that Johnny Zagero would never step into a boxing ring again. Marie LeGarde had lost consciousness too, and as I staggered along with her in my arms I felt it to be no more than a wasted token gesture: without shelter, and shelter soon, she would never see this night out. Helene, too, had collapsed within an hour of the tractor's disappearance, her slender strength had just given out, and Jackstraw had her over his shoulder. How all three of us, exhausted, starved, numbed almost to death as we were, managed to carry them for so long, even though with so many halts, is beyond my understanding: but Zagero had his strength, Jackstraw his superb fitness and I still the sense of responsibility that carried me on long hours after my legs and arms had given out.

Behind us Senator Brewster blundered along in a blind world

all of his own, stumbling often, falling occasionally but always pushing himself up and staggering gamely on. And in those few hours Hoffman Brewster, for me, ceased to be a senator and became again my earliest conception of the old Dixie Colonel, not the proud, rather overbearing aristocrat but the embodiment of a bygone southern chivalry, when courtesy and a splendid gallantry in the greatest perils and hardships were so routine as to excite no comment. Time and time again during that bitter night he insisted, forcibly insisted, on relieving one of the three of us of our burdens and would stagger along under the load until he reached the point of collapse. Despite his age, he was a powerful man: but he had no longer the heart and the lungs and the circulation to match his muscles, and his distress, as the night wore on, became pitiful to see. The blood-shot eyes were almost closed in exhaustion, his face deep-etched in grey suffering and his breath coming in painful whooping gasps that reached me clearly even above the thin high shriek of the wind.

No doubt but that Smallwood and Corazzini had left us to die, but they had made one mistake: they had forgotten Balto. Balto, as always, had been running loose when they had left us, and they had either failed to see him or forgotten all about him. But Balto hadn't forgotten us, he must have known something was far wrong, for all the hours we had been prisoners on the tractor-sled he had never come within a quarter-mile of us. But as soon as the tractor had dumped and left us, he had come loping in out of the driving snow and settled to the task of leading us down towards the glacier. At least, we hoped he was doing that. Jackstraw declared that he was following the crimp marks of the Citroën's caterpillars, now deep buried under the flying drift and new-fallen snow. Zagero wasn't so sure. Once, twice, a dozen times that night, I heard him muttering the same words: 'I hope to hell that hound knows where it's goin'.'

But Balto knew where he was going. Sometime during the night—it might have been any time between midnight and three o'clock in the morning—he stopped suddenly, stretched out his neck and gave his long eerie wolf call. He seemed to listen for an answer, and if he heard anything it was beyond our range: but he seemed satisfied, for he suddenly changed direction and angled off to the left into the blizzard. At Jackstraw's nod, we followed.

Three minutes later we came upon the dog-sledge, with two

of the dogs curled up beside it, their backs to the wind, their muzzles to their bellies and long brushes of tails over their faces, the drift walling high around them. They were comfortable enough—so splendid an insulation does a husky's thick coat provide that snow at forty degrees below zero can lie on its back indefinitely without being melted by body heat—but they preferred freedom to comfort, for they were on their feet and vanished into the swirling whiteness beyond before we could lay hands on them. That left only the sledge.

I suppose that after Smallwood had gone far enough to consider that we would never be able to reach that point, he had cut loose dogs and dog-sledge as a needless encumbrance—but not before he had severed all the traces attaching the dogs to the sledge and, I noticed grimly, removed all the wraps and the magnetic compass that had been there. He thought of everything. For a moment, admiration for the man's undoubtedly remarkable qualities came in to supplant what had become the motivating reason for my existence, a reason that, as the hours crawled by, were crowding out even the feelings I had for Margaret Ross: my hatred for Smallwood burned like a cold steady flame, an obsession with the idea of sinking my fingers into that scrawny throat and never letting go.

Within three minutes of finding the sledge we had tied together the severed remnants of the traces, changed them to the front and were on our way again, Marie LeGarde, Mahler and Helene propped up on the thin wooden slats. We had, of course, to pull the sledge ourselves, but that was nothing: for Jackstraw, Zagero and myself, the relief was beyond measure. But it was only momentary

We were running on to the smooth, slick ice of the Kangalak glacier, but our progress was no faster than it had been before we found the sledge. The wind was climbing up to its maximum now, the blizzard shrieking along horizontally to the ground and coming in great smoking flurries that cut visibility to zero and made us stop and grab one another lest one of us be knocked flying and for ever lost to sight: several times Theodore Mahler, restless in unconsciousness, rolled off the sledge until I at last made Brewster sit at the back and watch. He protested violently, but he was glad to do as I said.

I don't remember much after that, I think I must have been unconscious, eyes shut, but still plodding along in my sleep on leaden, frozen feet. My first conscious memory after installing Brewster on the back of the sledge was of someone shaking me urgently by the shoulder. It was Jackstraw.

'No more!' he shouted in my ear. 'We must stop, Dr Mason, wait till it's blown itself out. We can't live through this.'

I said something that was unintelligible even to myself, but Jackstraw took it for agreement and began pulling the sledge into the sloping side of the glacier valley and to the leeward side of one of the snowdrifts piled up against some of the ridges on the side of the valley. It wasn't all that much of an improvement, but the wind and the effect of the blizzard were perceptibly less. We unloaded the three sick people on the sledge into what pitiful shelter the ridge offered: I was just about to let my knees buckle and collapse beside them when I realized that someone was missing: it was a fair indication of the toll taken by wind and cold and exhaustion that almost twenty seconds passed before I realized it was Brewster.

'Good God!' I cried in Jackstraw's ear. 'The senator—we've lost him! I'll go back and look. I won't be a minute.'

'Stay here.' The grip on my arm was promise enough that Jackstraw meant to detain me by force, if necessary. 'You'd never come back. Balto! Balto!' He shouted a few Eskimo words which meant nothing to me, but the big Siberian seemed to understand, for he was gone in a moment, following the direction of Jackstraw's pointing hand. He was back again inside two minutes.

'He's found him?' I asked Jackstraw.

Jackstraw nodded silently.

'Let's bring him in.'

Balto led us there, but we didn't bring him in. Instead we left him lying where we found him, face down in the snow, dead. The blizzard was already drawing its concealing shroud over him, in an hour he would be no more than a featureless white mound in a featureless white valley. My hands were too numb to examine him, but I wouldn't have bothered anyway: the half-century of self-indulgence in food and drink and temper, all of which had been so clearly reflected in the heavy florid face when first I'd seen him, had had their inevitable way. The heart, cerebral thrombosis, it didn't matter now. But he had been a man.

How long we lay there, the six of us and Balto huddled close together for warmth, unconscious or dozing while that hurricane of a blizzard reached then passed its howling crescendo, I never knew. Probably only half an hour, perhaps not even that. When I awoke, stiff and numbed, I reached for Jackstraw's torch. It was exactly four o'clock in the morning.

I looked at the others. Jackstraw was wide awake—I was pretty sure he'd never shut an eye lest one of us slip away from sleep into that easy frozen sleep from which there would have been no wakening—and Zagero was stirring. That they—and I—would survive, I didn't doubt. Helene was a question mark. A seventeen-year-old, though short on endurance, was usually high on resilience and recuperative powers, but Helene's seemed to have deserted her. After the death of her mistress and up to the time she had collapsed she had become strangely withdrawn and unresponsive, and I guessed that the death of Mrs Dansby-Gregg had hit her far more than any of us would have guessed. The previous forty-eight hours apart, it seemed to me that she had had little enough to thank Mrs Dansby-Gregg for in the way of affection and warmth: but, then, she was young, Mrs Dansby-Gregg had been the person she had known best and, as a foreigner, she must have regarded Mrs Dansby-Gregg as her sole anchor in an alien sea. . . . I asked Jackstraw if he would massage her hands, then turned to have a look at Mahler and Marie LeGarde.

'They don't look so hot to me.' Zagero, too, was studying them. 'What's their chances, Doc?'

'I just don't know,' I said wearily. 'I don't know at all.'

'Don't take it to heart, Doc. It's no fault of yours.' Zagero waved a hand towards the snow-filled emptiness and desolation of the glacier. 'Your dispensary ain't all that well stocked.'

'No.' I smiled faintly, then nodded at Mahler. 'Bend down and listen to his breathing. The end's coming pretty close. Ordinarily I'd say a couple of hours. With Mahler I don't know—he's got the will to live, sheer guts, his beliefs—the lot. . . . But in twelve hours he'll be dead.'

'And how long do you give *me*, Dr Mason?'

I twisted round and gazed down at Marie LeGarde. Her voice was no more than a weak, husky whisper: she was trying to smile, but the smile was a pitiful grimace and there was no humour in either the eyes or the voice.

'Good lord, you've come to!' I reached out, pulled off her gloves and started to massage the frozen wasted hands. 'This is wonderful. How do you feel, Miss LeGarde?'

317

'How do you think I feel?' she said with a flash of her old spirit. 'Don't try to put me off, Peter. How long?'

'About another thousand curtain calls at the old Adelphi.' The light came from the torch that had been thrust, butt down, into the snow, and I bent forward so that my face was shadowed, my expression unreadable. 'Seriously, the fact that you've recovered consciousness is a good sign.'

'I once played a queen who recovered consciousness only to speak a few dramatic words before she died. Only, I can't think of any dramatic words.' I had to strain to catch the feeble whispered words. 'You're a shocking liar, Peter. Is there any hope for us at all?'

'Certainly,' I lied. Anything to get away from that topic. 'We'll be on the coast, with a good chance of being picked up by ship or plane, tomorrow afternoon—this afternoon, rather. It can't be more than twenty miles from here.'

'Twenty miles!' Zagero interjected. 'In this little lot?' He raised a cupped hand significantly to his ear, a gesture superbly superfluous in the ululating shriek of the blizzard.

'It won't last, Mr Zagero,' Jackstraw put in. 'These *williwaws* always blow themselves out in a short time. This already has gone on longer than most and it's easing a lot. Tomorrow will be clear and calm and cold.'

'The cold will be a change,' Zagero said feelingly. He looked past me. 'The old lady's off again, Doc.'

'Yes.' I stopped massaging her hands and slid the gloves on. 'Let's have a look at these paws of yours, Mr Zagero, will you?'

' "Johnny" to you, Doc. I've been dismissed without a stain on my character, remember?' He thrust his big hands out for inspection. 'Pretty, aren't they?'

They weren't pretty. they were the worst case of frostbite I had ever seen, and I had seen all too many, in Korea and later. They were white and yellow and dead. The original skin had vanished under a mass of blisters, and from the few warm spots I could detect on either hand I knew that much of the tissue had been permanently destroyed.

' 'Fraid I was a mite careless with my gloves,' Zagero said apologetically. 'In fact, I lost the damn' things about five miles back. Didn't notice it at the time—hands were too cold, I reckon.'

'Feel anything in them now?'

'Here and there.' He nodded as I touched some spots where the

318

blood still flowered, and went on conversationally: 'Am I goin' to lose my hands, Doc? Amputation, I mean?'

'No.' I shook my head definitely. I saw no point in mentioning that some of his fingers were beyond hope.

'Will I ever fight again?' Still the same casual, careless tone.

'It's difficult to say. You never know——'

'Will I ever fight again?'

'You'll never fight again.'

There was a long pause, then he said quietly: 'You're sure, Doc? You're absolutely sure?'

'I'm absolutely sure, Johnny. No boxing commission doctor in the world would ever let you climb into a ring. It would cost him his listing in the Medical Register.'

'Okay, so that's how it is. Consolidated Plastics of Trenton, New Jersey, have just got themselves a new factory hand: this boxin' racket was too damn' strenuous anyway.' There was no regret in his voice, no resignation even, but that meant nothing: like me, he had more important things to worry about. He looked away into the darkness, then twisted round: 'What's the matter with that hound of yours, Jackstraw?'

'I don't know. I think I'd better find out.' Twice while we had been talking Balto had left us, vanished into the snow, and returned after a few minutes: he seemed restless, uneasy. 'I won't be long.'

He rose, followed Balto into the darkness, returned in a short time: 'Come and see this, Dr Mason.'

'This' was a spot less than a hundred yards away, close into the side of the glacier valley. Jackstraw flashed his torch on to the snow-dusted ice. I stooped, made out a black circular patch on the ground and, a few feet away, a smaller discoloured area where the surface snow had frozen solid.

'Oil from the gearcase or sump, water from the radiator,' Jackstraw said briefly. He altered the torch-beam. 'And you can still see the crimp marks of the caterpillars.'

'And very recent?' I suggested. The drifting snow, the scouring effect of the flying ice-particles had scarcely begun to obliterate the traces left by the treads.

'I think so. And they were stopped here a long time, Dr Mason —look at the size of that oil patch.'

'Mechanical trouble?' I hazarded. I didn't really believe it myself.

319

'Riding out the storm—Corazzini must have been blind,' Jackstraw said definitely. 'If the engine had stopped on that pair, they'd never had got it started again.'

I knew he was right. Neither Smallwood nor Corazzini had shown any mechanical ability at all, and I was convinced that it had been no act.

'Perhaps they were still here when we arrived back there? My God, if we'd only carried on another hundred yards!'

'Spilt milk, as you say, Dr Mason. Yes, I'm sure they were here then.'

'We wouldn't have heard their engine?'

'Not in this wind.'

'Jackstraw!' A sudden thought, a flash of hope. 'Jackstraw, did you sleep back there?'

'No.'

'How long were we stopped?'

'Half an hour, maybe less.'

'And you think they were still here—Good God, man they can't be more than a mile away! The wind's dropping right away, it's getting colder and we'll only freeze to death if we stay here, maybe there'll be crevasses in the glacier to hold them up——'

I was already on my way, running, slipping, stumbling, Jackstraw by my side, Balto leading the way. Zagero was standing up, waiting—and the young German girl by his side.

'Helene!' I caught her hands. 'You all right? How are you feeling?'

'Better, much better.' She didn't sound all that much better. 'I'm sorry I was so silly, Dr Mason. I don't know——'

'It doesn't matter,' I cut in, rather brusquely. 'You can walk? Fine, fine.' I could feel new hope surging through me as I rapped out a brief explanation to Zagero, within a minute we had Mahler and Marie LeGarde bundled aboard the sledge and were on our way.

But the hope was short-lived. We made the best speed we could, at times breaking into a kind of staggering run, but the sledge slowed us up terribly on that uneven surface of the glacier. Once it overturned, throwing both Mahler and Marie LeGarde heavily on to the snow, and after that we were forced to slow down. Another such violent capsizing, or even too severe a jolting, and that sledge would become a bier. From time to time Jackstraw flashed his failing torch on the crimp marks we were following, and even to my inexperienced eye it was obvious that the tracks in the snow were becoming progressively fainter every time we looked at them until the time came at last when I knew we must call a halt to this pursuit, admit defeat: we had fallen so far behind now, three or four miles I was certain, that the hope and chance of overtaking them no longer existed: we were only chasing a hopeless dream, and killing ourselves doing it.

Jackstraw and Zagero agreed. We put Helene aboard the sledge to steady the two sick people, took a trace apiece over our shoulders and plodded on slowly down the glacier, backs bent, heads bowed, each one of us lost in his own hopeless thoughts.

As Jackstraw had prophesied, the storm had blown itself out. Completely. The wind had gone so that not a breath stirred across the glacier. The snow had vanished, with the dark and heavy clouds that had carried it: the white stars stood high in a dark and frozen sky. It was cold, with a temperature well below zero, but cold was an old friend now. By eight o'clock that morning, some three hours and six miles after we had left our resting-place, the conditions for travel were perfect.

The weather conditions, that was—underfoot, they varied from the indifferent to the abominable. We were now fairly into the Kangalak glacier and the going was often difficult indeed. A glacier is seldom a smooth river of ice that flows evenly down-hill, but much more frequently an irregularly surfaced, fissured and crevassed mass descending as often as not in a series of rounded steps and ledges like a sea of petrified lava. The Kangalak was no exception. Here and there we found some straight stretches, but, for the most part, progress was possible only at the sides where the rate of flow was less and the ice smoother. It was the left-hand side that we were following, but even so it was heavy work, for our path was frequently blocked by the debris of ground moraines that had been forced out on the sides, and when these were absent we were as often as not floundering through the thick drifts that the great wind of the night just gone had piled up high against the sides. The one consolation I found was that if it were difficult for us, it was proving doubly so for the tractor whose irregularly weaving twisting crimp marks we were so doggedly following.

I wondered how far away Hillcrest and the Sno-Cat were. I was as certain as I could be of anything that he would have headed due west as soon as he would have emerged from the Vindeby Nunataks, and he'd had time and to spare to make the coast by this time—not even the blizzard of last night could have stopped the Sno-Cat, the engine was a completely enclosed unit, its great caterpillars would take it over the loosest, the most newly fallen snow. But even had he backed his hunches and headed for the coast, as I hoped, he might still be anything up to twenty miles to the north or south of us, or he might be not only north or south but fifteen miles ahead of us—we had no maps left but I was fairly certain we were about that distance from the coast. Or was it possible that Hillcrest, a shrewd and thoughtful man, might have thought the gambit of a break for the coast too obvious a move? Could it not be that he might have indeed pressed on for Uplavnik, or even turned due north after he had come through the hills? Or, if he were coming west, would he not perhaps be driving in a search pattern, quartering the ground between the Vindeby Nunataks and the coast in a series of wide advancing zigzags? If that were so, he might still be anything up to thirty miles behind. It was infuriating beyond measure to know that he was almost certainly within two or three hours' driving time from where we were, but without a wireless or any means of contacting him he might as well have been a thousand miles away for any hope there was of two tiny moving objects encountering each other by chance in that vast and featureless land.

Soon after eight o'clock in the morning I stopped to have a look at the two sick people on the sledge, professional instinct, I suppose, but an empty token gesture: there was nothing we could do for them, except give massage at frequent intervals. The sound of Mahler's dyspnoea, his whooping gasping breathing, was the tolling of a death-bell in our ears, and this effort to breathe was extinguishing the last embers of life in his emaciated and frozen body. In three hours' time, by noon at the latest, Mahler would be dead. Nothing could ever save him now, it was madness, an utterly wasted effort to continue to drag him along on a sledge: he was past caring or knowing or feeling now, he could die just as peacefully if we left him lying on the glacier. Or so I have thought since then. But Mahler was more than a man to us that day, he was a symbol: we would leave Mahler when he had drawn his last gasping breath, but never before.

Marie LeGarde was dying too, but quietly, softly, peacefully, like a little candle flame flickering to extinction. Maybe she would go first, maybe Mahler. But both of them would die this day.

The going was becoming increasingly difficult now, not so much because of the gradually steepening slope of the glacier which made the sledge overrun us more and more frequently, but because of the fact that Jackstraw's torch had all but completely given out, and the fissures and crevasses that, earlier, had merely been nuisances to be negotiated, now became menaces to be avoided at the cost of our lives. It was now that Balto proved of his greatest value yet: as Jackstraw had said on our first day out from the I.G.Y. cabin, the big Siberian had an uncanny nose for crevasses, both open and hidden, in daytime or dark, and he made never a mistake that morning, constantly running ahead and then back towards us to guide us in the safest direction. Even so, progress was heartbreakingly slow.

Shortly after half-past eight in the morning we came across the tractor sled lying at an angle against a moraine. Even in the near darkness it was plain to see what had happened. The steepness of the glacier, not to mention sudden unaccountable dips to left and right across its width, must have made the heavy sled a dangerous libility, for, from its tracks, we had several times seen where it had slewed wildly at an angle, pivoting round on its iron tow-bar as, brakeless, it had sought to overrun the tractor. Obviously, Smallwood and Corazzini must have feared—and with reason—that on one of these occasions it would pull round the tail of the tractor after it and topple the tractor on its side, or, worse, drag it into a crevasse: so they had unhooked the tow-bar and left the sled.

It was surprising that they hadn't done this earlier: apart from carrying their fuel and food, which reserves could easily have gone into the tractor cabin itself, it had been a useless encumbrance to them. As far as I could judge they had abandoned it with all its contents—apart, of course, from the portable radio—including the wraps we had given Zagero and Levin when they had ridden on it at the point of a gun. We took these, tucked them round Mahler and Marie LeGarde and passed on.

Three hundred yards later I stopped so abuptly that the sledge, bumping into me, made me lose my footing on the slippery ice. I stood up, laughing softly, laughing for the first time for days, and Zagero came up close and peered into my face.

'What gives, Doc?'

323

I laughed again and was just on the point of speaking when his hand struck me sharply across the face.

'Cut it out, Doc.' His voice was harsh. 'That ain't goin' to help us any.'

'On the contrary, it's going to help us a very great deal.' I rubbed a hand across my cheek, I couldn't blame him for what he had done. 'My God, and I almost missed it!'

'Missed what?' He still wasn't sure that I wasn't hysterical.

'Come on back to the tractor-sled and see. Smallwood claims he thinks of everything, but he's missed out at last. He's made his first big mistake, but oh, brother, what a mistake! And the weather's just perfect for it!' I turned on my heel and actually ran up the glacier towards the sled.

Many items were carried as standard equipment in I.G.Y. parties, both in the field and at base camps, and none more standard than the magnesium flares which first came into common use in the Antarctic over a quarter of a century ago—they are indispensable as location beacons in the long polar nights—and radio-sondes. We carried more radio-sondes than any other item of equipment, for our primary purpose on the ice-cap—the garnering of information about density, pressure, temperature, humidity and wind direction of the upper atmosphere—was impossible without them. These sondes, still crated with the tents, ropes, axes and shovels which we had found no occasion to use on this trip, were radio-carrying balloons which wirelessed back information from heights of between 100,000 and 150,000 feet. We also carried rockoons, radio rockets fired from balloons which took them clear of the denser parts of the atmosphere before releasing them. But right then rockoons were useless to me. So too, were balloons at their normal operating height: 5000 feet should serve our purpose admirably.

The dim glow from the torch was more than sufficient, Jackstraw and I had worked with these things a hundred times. To couple the balloon to the hydrogen cylinder, disconnect the radio and substitute a group of three magnesium flares fused with R.D.X. took only minutes. We lit the fuse, cut the holding cord and had a second balloon coupled on to the cylinder before the first was 500 feet up. Then, just as we had the third on the cylinder and were disconnecting its radio, the first flare, now at about a height of 4000 feet, burst into scintillating brilliant life.

It was all I could have wished for, indeed it was more than I'd

324

ever hoped for, and Zagero's heavy thump on my back showed how joyfully he shared my feelings.

'Dr Mason,' he said solemnly, 'I take it all back, all I ever said about you. This, Dr Mason, is genius.'

'It's not bad,' I admitted, and indeed if anyone, in those perfect conditions of visibility, couldn't see the coruscating dazzlement of those flares at any distance up to thirty miles, he would have to be blind. If they were looking in the right direction, that was, but I was sure that with Hillcrest carrying five men and everybody almost certainly on the lookout for us, the chances of missing it were remote.

The second flare, considerably higher, burst into life just as the first went sputtering into extinction and the further thought struck me that if there were any ships patrolling out in the sea beyond, it would give them a bearing the significance of which none of them could surely overlook. And then I saw Jackstraw and Zagero looking at me and though I couldn't read their expressions in the darkness I knew from their stillness what they were both thinking and suddenly I didn't feel so happy any more. The odds were high that Corazzini and Smallwood—they could be no more than a few miles distant—had seen the flares also. They would know what it signified, they would know it was the first tug on the drawstring of the net that might even then be starting to close round them. In addition to being dangerous, ruthless killers they would become frightened killers; and they had Margaret and Johnny Zagero's father with them. But I knew I'd had no option, tried to thrust all thought of the hostages from my mind, turned to look at the third balloon that we had just released, then winced and closed my eyes involuntarily as the third flare, through some flaw or misjudgment in the length of the fuse, ignited not more than five hundred feet above us, the blue-white intensity mingling almost immediately with a bright orange flame as the balloon also caught fire and both started drifting slowly earthwards.

And so intently was I watching this through narrowed eyes that I all but missed something vastly more important, but Jackstraw didn't. He never missed anything. I felt his hand on my arm, turned to see the strong white teeth gleaming in the widest grin I had seen for weeks, then half-turned again to follow the direction of his pointing arm just in time to see low on the horizon in the south-east and not more than five miles away the earthward curving red and white flare of a signal rocket.

Our feelings were impossible to describe—I know, at least, that mine were. I had never seen anything half so wonderful in all my life, not even the sight, twenty minutes later, of the powerful wavering headlight beams of the Sno-Cat as it appeared over a rise in the plateau and headed towards the spot—we had scrambled up from the glacier to the flat land above—where we had just ignited the last of our flares and were waving it round and round our heads on the end of a long metal pole, like men demented. It seemed an age, although I don't suppose it was much more than ten minutes, before the great red and yellow Sno-Cat ground to a halt beside us and willing arms reached down to help us into the incredible warmth and comfort of that superbly equipped and insulated cabin.

Hillcrest was a great bull of a man, red-faced, black-bearded, jovial, confident, with a tremendous zest for living, a deceptive external appearance that concealed a first-class brain and a competence of a very high order indeed. It did me good just to sit there, glass of brandy in hand, relaxed—if only for a moment —for the first time in five days and just to look at him. I could tell that it hadn't done him the same good to look at us—in the bright overhead light I could clearly see our yellowed, blistered, emaciated faces, the bleeding, black-nailed, suppurating all but useless hands, and I was shocked myself—but he concealed it well, and busied himself with handing out restoratives, tucking away Mahler and Marie LeGarde in two deep, heat-pad-filled bunks, and supervizing the efforts of the cook who had a steaming hot meal ready prepared. All this he had done before he had as much as asked us a question.

'Right,' he said briskly. 'First things first. Where's the Citroën? I presume the missile mechanism is still aboard it. Brother, you just don't begin to have any idea how many heart attacks this thing is causing.'

'That's not the first thing,' I said quietly. I nodded to Theodore Mahler, whose hoarse gasping breathing filled the room. 'This man is dying.'

'All under control,' he boomed. He jerked a thumb at Joss who, after the first delighted greeting, had returned to his radio set in the corner. 'The boy here hasn't left his set for over twenty-four hours—ever since we got your "Mayday" call.' He looked at me

326

speculatively. 'You took a chance there. I wonder you didn't stop a bullet for your pains.'

'I just about did. . . . We were talking about Mahler.'

'Yes. We've been in constant contact, same wave-length, with two ships in that time—the destroyer *Wykenham* and the carrier *Triton*. I had a fair idea your friends must be heading in this direction, so the *Wykenham* has been moving up overnight and is lying off the coast. But the leads and patches in the ice aren't big enough for the *Triton* to manoeuvre to fly off planes. She's about eighty miles south, in clear water.'

'Eighty miles!' I didn't bother to conceal my shock and my disappointment, I'd begun to have a faint irrational hope that we might yet save the dying man. 'Eighty miles!'

'I have news for you, Doctor,' Hillcrest announced jovially. 'We have moved into the air age.' He turned towards Joss and raised an inquiring eyebrow.

'A Scimitar jet fighter is just taking off.' Joss tried to speak unemotionally, but failed. 'It's airborne—now. Time-check 0933. We're to fire our first rocket at 0946—thirteen minutes from now. Then two more at intervals of thirty seconds. At 0948 we're to set off a slow-burning magnesium flare where we want the stuff dropped, at least two hundred yards from the tractor.' Joss listened for another few moments and grinned. 'He says we're to get the hell out of it after we've lit the flare or we're liable to collect a headache or worse.'

I didn't know what to say, where to look, moments like this came all too seldom. Not until that moment did I realize how much of a symbol Theodore Mahler had become, how much his survival had meant for me. Hillcrest must have had some intuitive understanding of how I felt, for he spoke at once, his voice normal, matter of fact.

'Service, old boy. Sorry we couldn't have laid it on earlier, but the *Triton* refused to risk an expensive plane and an even more expensive pilot flying low over virtually uncharted territory unless they definitely knew that Mahler was alive.'

'They've done all anyone could ask.' A sudden thought struck me. 'These planes don't usually carry ammunition in peace-time, do they?'

'Don't worry,' Hillcrest said grimly. He ladled some steaming stew on to our plates. 'Nobody's playing any more. There's been a flight of Scimitars standing by since midnight, and every cannon's loaded. . . . Right, Doctor. Give with the story.'

I gave, as briefly and concisely as possible. At the end, he clapped his hands together.

'Maybe five miles ahead, eh? Then it's tallyho down the old glacier and after 'em.' He rubbed his hands in anticipation. 'We're three times as fast and we've three times as many rifles. This is the way any decent I.G.Y. expedition should be run!'

I smiled faintly, a token response to his bubbling enthusiasm. I never felt less like smiling: now that the worry of Mahler—and in that warmth and with hot food, almost certainly also the worry of Marie LeGarde—was off my hands, my anxiety about Margaret had returned with redoubled force.

'We're not tally-ho-ing down any old glacier, Captain Hillcrest. Apart from the fact that it's a rotten surface, which would bring your speed down to about the same as the Citroën's, open pursuit is a pretty sure way of guaranteeing that Margaret Ross and Mr Levin get a bullet through their heads. Incidentally, Mr Levin is the father of Mr Zagero.'

'What?' Both Hillcrest and Joss had spoken at the same time.

'Yes. But later. Have you a map of the area?'

'Sure.' Hillcrest handed it over. Like most Greenland maps it showed topographical detail for no more than the first twenty miles inland, but it was sufficient for my purpose. It showed the twisting Kangalak glacier debouching into the Kangalak Fjord, the wide deep bay beyond the southern headland of the fjord, the northern headland continuing in a wide shallow smooth curve for many miles to the north.

'Where did you say the destroyer was?' I asked.

'The *Wykenham*? I'm not sure.'

'Blocking the Kangalak Fjord here, perhaps?' I indicated the spot on the map.

'No, that I'm certain of.' He shook his head regretfully. 'Captain said the pack-ice was too heavy, he couldn't risk his destroyer in any of the leads in case they closed.' Hillcrest snorted in disgust. 'I gather its hull is made of paper.'

'It's not much thicker—I've served in destroyers. I don't blame him. But I'll bet his trawler, probably a specially strengthened job, is well inside the fjord—and a submarine no great distance away. Look, this is all we can do.' I traced my finger on the map. 'We must parallel the glacier, maybe a mile away. With the slope of the valley sides Smallwood won't see us, and with his own

328

engine running he can't hear us. Down here——'

'What's to stop him from cutting his engine now and again to listen?' Hillcrest demanded.

'Because what Smallwood and Corazzini don't know about engines would fill an encyclopedia. They'd be dead scared to stop it in case they couldn't start it again. . . . Down here, at the base of the headland separating the fjord from the bay to the south— about a mile from the end of the glacier, I would say—the sides of the glacier valley fall away and level off into the plateau on either side. But there's bound to be some kind of moraine or shelter there. That's where we'll ambush them.'

'Ambush?' He frowned at me. 'What's the difference between that and pursuing them? It'll still come to a fight—and they can still hold pistols to the heads of Levin and the stewardess, and bargain from there.'

'There'll be no fight,' I said quietly. 'They've been following the left-hand side of the glacier all the way down, I see no reason why they should change. They should come into sight maybe fifty yards from where we're hiding—farther out on the glacier the going is impossible for tractors.' I nodded at the telescopic-sighted .303 in the corner. 'With that Jackstraw can hit a three-inch target at a hundred yards. A man's head at fifty yards is six times that size. First he get Corazzini, who's probably driving, and when Smallwood sticks his head out the back, as he certainly will—well, that's it.'

'But, good God, man, you can't do that!" Hillcrest was horrified. 'Without a chance, without warning? It's murder, simple murder!'

'Want me to go over the number of people *they've* murdered?' I shook my head. 'You just don't begin to know those two, Hillcrest.'

'But——' He broke off, turned to Jackstraw. 'It's you he's asking to do it. What do you say?'

'It will be a pleasure,' Jackstraw said very softly.

Hillcrest stared at us both, baffled incomprehension in his eyes. I suppose he thought he knew both of us well. And he did. But he didn't know what we had been through, words couldn't even begin to make him understand. The atmosphere was uncomfortable, tense even, and I was grateful for Joss's sudden calm words.

'0943, Captain Hillcrest. Three minutes to go.'

'Good.' He was, I could see, as glad of the interruption as I

329

was. 'Barclay'—this to the cook, the only other of Hillcrest's men there, the other three were in the big driving cabin to make room for us—'three Wessex rockets. Line them up on the stand, wait for the word. I'll go myself with the flare, two for safety. Give a beep on the horn, Joss, when it's time to set 'em off.'

I went with him to watch and the whole thing went off without a hitch. Dead on time, just seconds after the third rocket had been fired to curve upwards and explode into incandescent light in the star-dusted darkness above, we heard the high-pitched whine approaching out of the south-west, and in an incredibly short space of time a vague dark blur, carrying no navigation lights, screamed by five hundred feet overhead, banked in the distance, came in at us again at much reduced speed, banked a second time and then, with a crescendoing banshee shriek of the jet engine, had vanished again into the vaguely lightening darkness to the south-east before we had realized that the pilot had made his drop. It was a measure of his complete self-confidence that he didn't even trouble to check the accuracy of his drop: but for a man skilled in landing on the handkerchief-sized flight deck of a carrier in the middle of the night, this must have been a childishly simple exercise.

There were two packages, not one, attached not to parachutes but to insignificant little drogues that seemed to let them fall much too fast for safety: they landed almost together not forty yards from the magnesium flares and with such force that I was sure that their contents muct be smashed. But I had under-estimated the Fleet Air Arm's skill and experience in these matters, the contents were so beautifully packed and cushioned that everything was completely intact. The packages were duplicated: two ampoules of insulin and three hypodermic syringes in each package: whoever had packed these had been taking no chances. But gratitude was the last thought in my mind at that moment: I just tucked the boxes under my arm and made for the tractor at a dead run.

For close on two hours Hillcrest's driver pushed the big Sno-Cat along at irs maximum speed, and despite the inherent stability afforded by its four wide caterpillars, the tractor swayed and lurched in terrifying fashion. This was bad country, this was crevasse country, and we had been forced to make a wide detour that had carried us more than three miles away from the Kangalak

330

glacier. And once again Jackstraw's big Siberian wolf proved how invaluable he was: running tirelessly ahead, he repeatedly guided the Sno-Cat away from dangerous territory, but even so our route was a necessarily devious and twisted one, though the picking out of a path became considerably easier after the pale grey light of the arctic noon spread across the ice-cap.

For all of us it was a time of tension, of an ever-mounting anxiety that reached intolerable proportions. For the first half-hour or so I was busy enough in broaching the tractor's first-aid kit and doing what doctoring I could to Mahler—a Mahler whose dyspnoea was already dramatically easing—Marie LeGarde, Helene, Jackstraw and, above all, to Zagero's shattered hands. Then I myself submitted to Hillcrest's rough and ready ministrations, but after that there was nothing for me to do, nothing for any of us to do except try to avoid the bitterness of thinking what must happen if the Citroën reached the tongue of the glacier before us.

Suddenly, exactly on noon, the tractor stopped abruptly. We jumped out to see what the matter was, and it became apparent soon enough the driver was awaiting instructions. We had abruptly rounded the humpback of the last ice ridge that had lain between us and the glacier itself.

Even in the half-light of the arctic day the panorama suddenly unfolded before us was a breathtaking one. To the north, the ice-sheet extended all the way down to the coast, forming vertical and in some places overhanging cliffs, the well-known phenomenon of the Chinese Wall fronts: nobody, nothing, could hope to land there.

To the south and separated from the fjord by the mile-long ridgeback of the seaward-projecting southern wall of the fjord, was a wide bay, fringed by a low, ice-bare rocky coast, quilted here and there with drifts of snow blown off the ice-cap. There, if anywhere, was where we would have to leave.

In the centre, between the low walls of the fjord, the Kangalak glacier itself, here, at its tongue, about 300 yards wide, ran down to the waters of the fjord in a great dog-leg curving sharply thirty degrees right about half-way down its length, ending abruptly with its upper surface a hundred, perhaps a hundred and fifty feet above the pack-ice-strewn water beneath. For the first half of its length the tongue of the glacier sloped fairly sharply from right to left down to the *nunataks*, crescent-fringed by the debris of

331

moraines, that thrust up through the ice at the far corner of the dog-leg: the surface of the glacier was a nightmare of transverse and longitudinal fissures, some of them anything up to two hundred feet deep, great gaping chasms fanged with *seracs*—the irregular, often needle-pointed ice pinnacles that reached up between the walls of the larger crevasses. Surely Smallwood could never be so desperate, so insane as to drive the Citroën out on that: apart from the fissures, the very steepness of the slope downwards and to the left would be enough to send him into an uncontrollable slide.

And beyond everything lay the sea, the island-studded, ice-filled waters of Baffin Bay. Off-shore there was a mile-wide belt of loose pressure ice—the season was not yet far enough advanced for the fantastic shapes it would assume in the early spring—streaked with open, ever-changing leads and dotted at rare intervals with small icebergs—probably ones that had broken off from the east coast, drifted south round Cape Farewell and then moved north again, the whole half-lost, unearthly, and impossibly, weirdly, continuously altered in configuration by the white drifting fog that hung miasma-like over the sea.

But two things there were that were not lost: two ships. The one to the south-west, wraith-like and blurred though its lines were through the swirling mist, was quite unmistakable, that raked and slender silhouette would have been unmistakable anywhere: it was a destroyer, it could only be the *Wykenham*, moving slowly, cautiously shorewards through the ice-filled waters of the bay to our left. A heart-warming, immensely reassuring spectacle —or it should have been: but after the first cursory identifying glance I lost interest, my attention was taken and completely held by the second ship.

I couldn't see all of it, most of its hull was hidden by the precipitous end of the glacier, but its small squat bridge, two masts and broad, bluff seaward-pointing bows were clearly etched against the mirror-calm waters of the head of the fjord and the sloping ice-bare rock that brushed its portside fenders. I could see no flag. It was a trawler, unmistakably so, and I thought grimly that it must have been a very special trawler indeed to have battered that still-visible path through the ice choked mouth of the fjord.

My gaze moved back to the trawler again and a second later I was grabbing Hillcrest's binoculars without so much as by your leave. One glance was enough, even in that shadowed gloom of the depth of the fjord I could see all I wanted to see by the grey noon-light. I could see a great deal more than I wanted to. For a few seconds I stood stock-still listening desperately for the sound of the Citroën's engines: moments later I was in the tractor cabin by the radio table.

'Still in contact with the *Triton*, Joss?' He nodded, and I rushed on: 'Tell them there's a group of men coming ashore from a trawler in the Kangalak Fjord. Ten, twelve, I'm not sure. And I'm not sure whether they're armed. I'll be damned surprised if they aren't. Tell them I'm certain they're going to move up on the glacier.'

'Now?'

'Of course!' I snapped. 'Send the message immediately. And——'

'No, I meant are they moving on to the glacier now?'

'Take them ten, fifteen minutes—the fjord walls are pretty steep and it's a tricky climb. . . . After that ask the *Wkyenham* if they will send a landing party ashore. An armed party. And for God's sake tell them it's urgent.'

'Will they get here in time, Doc?' Zagero was behind me. 'By the time they lower a boat, row ashore, cross this headland—it's half a mile if it's an inch—it'll take *them* fifteen minutes, maybe more.'

'I know,' I said irritably—irritably, but softly, for Joss was already talking into the table microphone, in the swift, staccato yet strangely unhurried voice of the trained radioman. 'If you have any better suggestions——'

'It's coming!' Hillcrest's excited face had just appeared at the door of the cabin. 'Come on! We can hear it coming down the glacier.'

And indeed they could. The deep throaty roar of that heavy engine was recognizable anywhere. Hurriedly we moved about a hundred yards away from the moraine-ringed depression where we had parked the tractor, Jackstraw, Hillcrest and I each with a rifle in our hands, and crouched down behind the concealing protection of some ice-covered debris at the edge of the glacier. From where we lay we could command a view of the glacier across its entire width and up to a point several hundred yards away where it curved sharply out of sight.

We needn't have hurried. The Citroën was still some good way off, the sound of its engine being funnelled down through the

333

glacier valley well ahead of it, and I had time to look around me. What I saw seemed good. I was banking everything on the hope that the Citroën would still be on the same side of the glacier as when we had last seen it, and, from what I could see, the chances were high that it still would be. The entire centre of the glacier was a devil's playground of crevasses ranging from hairlines to chasms twenty and more feet in width, transverse, longitudinal and diagonal, and as far as I could see they extended clear to the other side. But here, on the left side, close in to the lining wall of moraine, was a relatively clear path, fissured only at long intervals, and not more than thirty yards broad. Thirty yards! Jackstraw could never miss at this point-blank rifle range, even with a moving target

I stole a glance at him, but his face might have been carved from the glacier itself, it was immobile and utterly devoid of expression. Hillcrest, on the other hand, was restless, forever shifting his cramped position: he was unhappy, I knew; he didn't like this one little bit. He didn't like murder. Neither did I. But this wasn't murder, it was a long overdue execution: it wasn't life-taking, it was life-saving, the lives of Margaret and Solly Levin. . . .

There came the sudden click, abnormally loud even above the closing roar of the tractor, and Jackstraw, stretched his length on the snow, had the rifle raised to his shoulder. And then, suddenly, the Citroën had come clearly into sight and Jackstraw was gently lowering his rifle to the ground. I had gambled, and I had lost. The tractor was on the far side of the glacier, hugging the right bank as closely as possible: even at its nearest point of approach it would still be three hundred yards away.

CHAPTER TWELVE

SATURDAY 12.15 P.M.–12.30 P.M.

The Citroën was travelling in a most erratic fashion—one moment slowing down almost to a stop, the next jerking forward and covering perhaps twenty to thirty yards at a rush. Although we couldn't see the glacier surface at that distance, it was obvious that the driver was picking his way round ice-mounds and threading along between fissures at the best speed he could manage. But his average speed was very low: it would probably take him almost five minutes to reach that point opposite us where the glacier fell away sharply to the left towards the outer angle of the dog-leg half-way down towards the fjord.

All these things I noted mechanically, without in any way consciously thinking of them. All I could think of was that Smallwood and Corazzini had outwitted us right up to the last —almost certainly, I could understand now, they had seen and been warned by the rockets Hillcrest had fired to give the Scimitar our position, and decided to give that side of the glacier the widest possible berth.

But the reasons no longer mattered a damn. All that mattered was the accomplished fact, and the fact was that Corazzini and Smallwood could no longer be stopped, not in the way we had intended. Even yet, of course, they *could* be stopped—but I had no illusions but that that would be at the cost of the lives of the two hostages in the tractor.

Frantically I tried to work out what to do for the best. There was no chance in the world that we might approach them openly over the glacier—we would be spotted before we had covered ten yards, and a pistol at the heads of Margaret and Levin would halt us before we got half-way. If we did nothing, let them get away, I knew the hostages' chances of survival were still pretty slim— that trawler would almost certainly have a name or number or both and I couldn't see Smallwood letting them make an identification of the trawler and then come back to report to us—and to all the waiting ships and planes in the Davis Strait—Baffin Sea area. Why should he take the slightest risk when it would be so easy to shoot them, so much easier still to throw them down a crevasse or shove them over the edge of the glacier into the freezing waters of the fjord a hundred and fifty feet below. . . . Already the Citroën was not more than three minutes away from the nearest point of approach they would make to us.

'Looks like they're going to get away with it,' Hillcrest whispered. It seemed as if he feared he might be overhead, though Smallwood and Corazzini couldn't have heard him had he shouted at the top of his voice.

'Well, that was what you wanted, wasn't it? I asked bitterly.

'What I wanted! My God, man, that missile mechanism——'

'I don't give a single solitary damn about the missile mechanism.' I ground the words out between clenched teeth. 'Six months from now other scientists will have invented something twice as good and ten times as secret. They're welcome to it, and with pleasure.'

Hillcrest was shocked, but said nothing. But someone was in agreement with me.

'Hear, hear!' Zagero had just come up, his hands swathed to the size of boxing gloves in white bandages. The words were light enough, but his face was grim and his eyes bleak as he stared out across the glacier. 'My sentiments exactly, Doc. To hell with their murderous little toys. My old man's in that buggy out there. And your girl.'

'His girl?' Hillcrest turned, looked sharply at me under creased brows for a long moment, then murmured: 'Sorry, boy, I didn't understand.'

I made no response, but twisted my head as I heard footsteps behind me. It was Joss, hatless and gloveless in his excitement.

'*Wykenham*'s anchored, sir,' he panted out. 'Her——'

'Get down, man! They'll see you.'

'Sorry.' He dropped to his hands and knees. 'Her power-boat's already moving inshore. And there was a flight of four Scimitars already airborne: they should be half-way here already. In two minutes' time four or five bombers are taking off, with H.E. and incendiaries. They're slower, but——'

'Bombers?' I snapped irritably. 'Bombers? What do they think this is—the Second Front?'

'No, sir. They're going to clobber the trawler if Smallwood

336

gets away with that missile mechanism. They won't get a hundred yards.'

'The hell with their missile mechanism. Do human lives mean nothing to them? What is it, Jackstraw?'

'Lights, Dr Mason.' He pointed to the spot on the fjord wall where the men from the trawler had already covered two thirds of the horizontal and vertical distance to the end of the glacier. 'Signalling, I think.'

I saw it right away, a small light, but powerful, winking irregularly. I watched it for a few moments, then heard Joss's voice.

'It's morse, but it's not our morse, sir.'

'They're hardly likely to signal in English just for our benefit,' I said dryly. I tried to speak calmly, to hide the fear, the near despair in my mind, and when I spoke again my voice, I knew, was abnormally matter-of-fact. 'It's the tip-off to our friends Smallwood and Corazzini. If we can see the men from the trawler, it's a cinch the men from the trawler can see us. The point is, do Smallwood and Corazzini understand them?'

Five seconds later I had my answer in the form of a suddenly deepening roar coming to us across the glacier from the engine of the Citroën. Corazzini—Hillcrest's binoculars had shown him to be the driver—had understood the danger all right, he was casting caution to the winds and gunning the engine to its maximum. He must have been desperate, desperate to the point of madness, for no sane man would have taken the fearful risks of driving that tractor through sloping crevasse ice with the friction coefficient between treads and surface reduced almost to zero. Or could it be that he just didn't know the suicidal dangers involved?

After a few seconds I was convinced he didn't. In the first place, I couldn't see either Corazzini or Smallwood as men who would panic under pressure, no matter how severe that pressure, and in the second place suidcidal risks weren't absolutely necessary, they would have stood a more than even chance of getting away with their lives and the missile mechanism if they had stopped the tractor, got out and picked their cautious way down the glacier on foot, with their pistol barrels stuck in the backs of their hostages. Or would they—rather, did they think they would?

I tried fleetingly, frantically, to get inside their cold and criminal minds, to try to understand their conception of us. Did they think that we thought, like them, that the mechanism was all

337

important, that human lives were cheap and readily expendable. If they did, and guessing the quality of Jackstraw's markmanship with a rifle, would they not be convinced that they would be shot down as soon as they had stepped out on to the ice, regardless of the fate of their hostages? Or did they have a better understanding than that of minds more normal than their own?

Even as these thoughts flashed through my mind I knew I must act now. The time for thought, had there ever been such a time, was past. If they were left to continue in the tractor, they would either kill themselves on the glacier or if, by a miracle, they reached the bottom safely, they would then kill their hostages. If they were stopped now, there was a faint chance that Margaret and Levin might survive, at least for the moment: they were Smallwood's and Corazzini's only two trump cards, and would be kept intact as long as lay within their power, for they were their only guarantee of escape. I just had to gamble on the hope that they would be desperately reluctant to kill them where they were now, still a mile from the end of the glacier. And the last time I had gambled I had lost.

'Can you stop the tractor?' I asked Jackstraw, my voice a flat lifeless monotone in my own ear.

He nodded, his eyes on me: I nodded silently in return.

'You can't do that!' Zagero shouted in urgent protest. The drawl had gone for the first time ever. 'They'll kill them, they'll kill them! My God, Mason, if you're really stuck on that kid you'd never——'

'Shut up!' I said savagely. I grabbed a coil of rope, picked up my rifle and went on brutally: 'If you think they'd ever let your father come out of this alive you must be crazy.'

A second later I was on my way, plunging out into the open across the narrow thirty-yard stretch of ice that led into the first of the fissures, wincing and ducking involuntarily as the first .303 shell from Jackstraw's rifle screamed past me, only feet to my right, and smashed through the hood of the Citroën and into the engine with all the metallic clamour, the vicious power of a sledge-hammer wielded by some giant hand. But still the Citroën came on.

I leapt across a narrow crevasse, steadied myself, glanced back for a moment, saw that Hillcrest, Joss, Zagero and a couple of Hillcrest's men were following, then rushed on again, weaving and twisting my way through the cracks and mounds in the ice.

What was Zagero doing there, I asked myself angrily? Unarmed, with two useless hands that could hold no firearm, he was nothing but a liability, what could any man do with ruined hands like those? I was to find out just what a man with ruined hands could do. . . .

We were running straight across the narrowest neck of the glacier making straight for the spot where the tractor would arrive if it survived Jackstraw's attempts to halt it: Jackstraw was firing in a line well above us now, but we could still hear the thin high whine of every bullet, the metallic crash as it struck the Citroën. Every bullet went home. But that engine was incredibly tough.

We were about half-way across when we heard the engine change gear, the high unmistakable whine of the tractor beginning to overrun its engine. Corazzini—I could clearly see him now, even without the aid of binoculars—must have found himself losing control on the steepening slope and was using the engine to brake the Citroën. And then, when we were less than a hundred yards away and after a longer than usual lull in the firing—Jackstraw must have stopped to change magazines—the sixth shell smashed through the riddled hood and the engine stopped as abruptly as if the ignition had been switched off.

The tractor stopped too. On that steep slope this was surprising, the last thing I would have expected, but there was no doubt that not only had it stopped but that it had been stopped deliberately: there was no mistaking the high-pitched screech of those worn brakes.

And then I could see the reason why. There was some violent activity taking place in the driving cabin of the tractor, and as we neared—a maddeningly slow process, there were dozens of crevasses to be jumped, as many more to be skirted—we could see what it was, Corazzini and Solly Levin were struggling furiously, and, from thirty or forty yards, it seemed, incredibly enough, that Solly Levin was getting the better of it. He had flung himself on top of Corazzini where the latter sat behind the wheel, and was butting him savagely in the face with the top of his bald head, and Corazzini, trapped in the narrow space, could find no room to make use of his much greater strength.

Then, abruptly, the door on the driver's side burst open—we could see it clearly, having been lower down than the tractor when it had stopped we were approaching it now almost head on

—and the two men fell out fighting and struggling furiously. We could see now why Levin had been using his head—both hands were bound behind his back. It had been an act of desperate courage to attack Corazzini in the first place, but the old man wasn't to get the reward he deserved for his selflessness: even as we came up to them Corazzini got his automatic clear and fired down point-blank at Solly Levin who was lying helplessly on his back but still gamely trying to get a leg lock on the bigger man. I was a split second too late in getting there, even as I crashed into Corazzini and sent his automatic flying away to slide down the glacier, I knew I was too late, Solly Levin was a crumpled little blood-stained figure lying on the ice even before Corazzini's gun went slithering over the edge of a crevasse. And then I felt myself being pushed to one side, and Johnny Zagero was staring down at the outspread stillness of the man huddled at his feet. For what seemed an eternity, but was probably no more than three seconds he stood there without moving, then when he turned to Corazzini his face was empty of all expression.

It might have been a flash of fear, of realization that he had come to the end of his road that I saw in Corazzini's eyes, but I could never swear to it, the turn of his head, the sudden headlong dash for the shelter of the ice-covered moraine rocks by the side of the glacier, ten yards away, were so swift that I could be certain of nothing. But swift as he was, Zagero was even swifter: he caught Corazzini before he had covered four yards and they crashed to the glacier together, clawing, punching and kicking in the grim desperate silence of men who know that the winner's prize is his life.

'Drop that gun!' I whirled round at the sound of the voice behind me, but all I could see at first was the white strained face of Margaret Ross, the brown eyes dulled with sickness and fear. Involuntarily I brought up the rifle in my hands.

'Drop it!' Smallwood's voice was curt, deadly, his face barely visible behind Margaret's shoulder as he peered out through the canvas screen at the rear of the tractor cabin. He was completely shielded by her body—it was typical of the man's cunning, his ice-cold calculation that he should have waited until our attention was completely distracted before making his move. 'And your friend. Quickly now!'

I hesitated, glanced at Hillcrest—the only other man with a weapon—to see how he was placed, then jerked my head back

340

again as there came a sudden *plop* from the silenced automatic and a sharp cry of pain from Margaret. She was clutching her left arm just above the elbow.

'Quickly, I said! The next one goes through her shoulder.' His voice was soft with menace, his face implacable. Not for a moment did I doubt that he would do exactly as he said: the clatter of Hillcrest's rifle and mine falling on the ice came in the same instant

'Now kick them over the edge of that crevasse.'

We did as he said and stood there powerless to do anything except watch the savage, mauling fight on the glacier. Neither man had regained his feet since the struggle had begun, the ice was too slippery for that, and still they rolled over and over, first one on top, now the other. Both were powerful men, but Zagero was severely handicapped by the exhaustion of the terrible night's march that lay behind him, by his crippled useless hands, by thickly-swathed bandages over his hands that not only prevented him from catching or holding Corazzini but softened the impact of every blow he struck. For all that, there was no question how the battle was going: those broken hands I'd said would never fight again were clubbing and hammering the life out of Corazzini. I thought of the tremendous force with which I'd seen Zagero strike a blow only the previous morning and felt a momentary flash of pity for Corazzini: then I remembered he was just as Smallwood was, that Smallwood was prepared to kill Margaret with as little compunction as he would snuff out the life of a fly, I looked at the crumpled figure at my feet and every shadow of pity vanished as if it had never been.

Smallwood, his eyes unblinking, his face expressionless as ever, had his gun on them all the time, waiting for that second when the two men would break far enough apart to give him a clear sight of Zagero. But, now, Zagero was underneath nearly all the time, one arm crooked round Corazzini's neck while the other delivered a murderous series of short-arm jabs, each one drawing a grunting gasp of agony from a white-faced Corazzini: finally, goaded into supreme effort by panic and fear, Corazzini managed to break loose and hurled himself not towards Smallwood, where safety lay, but for the shelter of the moraine rocks, where he would never know safety again. Zagero, cat-like as ever, was only feet behind him, moving so fast, so unexpectedly that Smallwood's swift snapshot missed him altogether.

'Call your friend Nielsen.' Smallwood must have realized how things were going behind the concealing shelter of the rocks for his voice was suddenly savage, urgent. He spared a swift glance in Jackstraw's direction—Jackstraw, followed at some distance by two more of Hillcrest's crew, was crossing the glacier at a dead run and now less than fifty yards away. 'His rifle. In a crevasse. Quickly!'

'Jackstraw!' My voice was hoarse, cracked. 'Throw your rifle away! He's got a gun on Miss Ross, and he's going to kill her.' Jackstraw braked, slipped on the ice, halted and stood there for a moment irresolute, and then at my repeated desperate cry carefully, deliberately dropped his rifle into a nearby fissure and came slowly on to join us. It was at that moment that Hillcrest grabbed me by the arm

'He's moving, Mason! He's alive!' He was pointing down to Levin, who had indeed stirred slightly. I had never thought to examine Levin, it had seemed a ludicrous idea that a professional like Corazzini could have missed at such point blank range, but now, regardless of Smallwood's reaction, I dropped to my knees on the glacier and put my face close to Levin's. Hillcrest was right. The breathing was shallow, but breathing there undoubtedly was, and now I could see the thin red line that extended from the temple almost to the back of the head. I rose to my feet.

'Creased, consussed probably, that's all.' Involuntarily I glanced over my shoulder towards the rocks. 'But too late now for Corazzini.'

And I needed no eyes to know that this was so. The unseen battle behind the rocks had been fought out with a dumb feral ferocity, with a silent savagery that had been far more frightening than all the most maddened oaths and shouting could ever have been, but even now, as Smallwood jumped down from the tail board of the tractor cabin, Margaret Ross still held in front of him, and started hustling her towards the rocks, a hoarse, high-pitched scream that raised the hackles on the back of my neck froze us all, even Smallwood, to immobility: and then came a long quavering moan of agony, cut off as abruptly as it had begun. And now there was no more screaming or moaning, no more slipping of feet on ice, no more gasping or frenzied flurries bespeaking the interchange of desperate blows: there was only silence, a silence chillingly broken by regular rhythmic pounding blows like the stamping feet of a pile-driver.

342

Smallwood had recovered, had just reached the rocks when Zagero came out to meet him face to face. Smallwood moved to one side, his gun covering him, as Zagero came slowly towards us, his face cut and bruised, his blood-saturated bandaged hands hanging by his sides, with two long ribbons of red-stained bandage trailing on the ice behind him.

'Finished?' I asked.

'Finished.'

'Good,' I said, and meant it. 'Your father's still alive, Johnny. Scalp wound, that's all.'

His battered face transformed, first by disbelief then by sheer joy, Zagero dropped on his knees beside Solly Levin. I saw Smallwood line his pistol up on Zagero's back.

'Don't do it, Smallwood!' I shouted. 'You'll only have four shells left.'

His eyes swivelled to my face, the cold flat eyes of a killer, then the meaning of my words struck home, his expression subtly altered and he nodded as if I had made some reasonable suggestion. He turned to Jackstraw, the nearest man to him, and said, 'Bring out my radio.'

Jackstraw moved to obey, and while he was inside the cabin Zagero rose slowly to his feet.

'Does look like though I was a mite premature,' he murmured. He glanced towards the rocks and there was no regret in his face, only indifference. 'Half a dozen witnesses, and you all saw him beatin' himself to death. . . . You're next, Smallwood.'

'Corazzini was a fool,' Smallwood said contemptuously. The man's cold-blooded callousness was staggering. 'I can easily replace him. Just leave that radio here, Nielsen, and join your friends—while I join mine.' He nodded down the glacier. 'Or perhaps you hadn't noticed?'

And we hadn't. But we noticed it now all right, the first of the party from the trawler climbing on to the ice at the precipitous tip of the glacier. Within seconds half a dozen of them were on the ice, running, stumbling, falling, picking themselves up again as they clawed their way up the slippery ice with all the speed they could muster.

'My—ah—reception committee.' Smallwood permitted himself the shadow of a smile. 'You will remain here while Miss Ross and I make our way down to meet them. You will not move. I have the girl.' Victory, complete and absolute victory was in his

343

grasp, but his voice, his face were again devoid as ever of all shadow of expression or feeling. He stooped to pick up the portable radio, then swung round and stared up into the sky.

I had heard it too, and I knew what it was before Smallwood did because it was a factor that had never entered into his calculations. But there was no need for me to explain, within seconds of hearing the first high screaming whine from the south a flight of four lean sleek deadly Scimitar jet fighters whistled by less than four hundred feet overhead, banked almost immediately, broke formation and came back again, speed reduced, flying a tight circle over the tongue of the fjord. I don't like planes, and I hate the sound of jets: but I had never seen so welcome a sight, heard so wonderful a sound in all my life.

'Jet fighters, Smallwood,' I cried exultantly. 'Jet fighters from a naval carrier. We called them up by radio.' He was staring at the circling planes with his thin lips drawn back wolfishly over his teeth, and I went on more softly: 'They've had orders to shoot and destroy any person seen going down that glacier—any person, especially, with a case or radio in his hand.' It was a lie, but Smallwood wasn't to know that, the very presence of the jets above must have seemed confirmation of the truth of my words.

'They wouldn't dare,' he said slowly. 'They'd kill the girl too.

'You fool!' I said contemptuously. 'Not only doesn't human life matter a damn to either side compared to the recovery of this mechanism—*you* should know that better than anyone, Smallwood —but these planes have been told to watch out for and kill *two* people going down the glacier. Wrapped in these clothes, Miss Ross is indistinguishable from a man—especially from the air. They'll think it's you and Corazzini and they'll blast you both off the face of the glacier.'

I knew Smallwood believed me, believed me absolutely, this was so exactly the way his own killer's mind would have worked in its utterly callous indifference to human life that conviction could not be stayed. But he had courage, I'll grant him that, and that first-class brain of his never stopped working.

'There's no hurry,' he said comfortably. He was back on balance again. 'They can circle there as long as they like, they can send out relief planes to take over, it doesn't matter. As long as I'm with you here, they won't touch me. And in just over an hour or so it will be dark again, after which I can leave. Meantime, stay close to me, gentlemen: I don't think *you* would so willingly sacrifice Miss Ross's life.'

'Don't listen to him,' Margaret said desperately. Her voice was almost a sob, her face twisted with pain. 'Go away, *please*, all of you, go away. I know he's going to kill me in the end anyway. It may as well be now.' She buried her face in her hands. 'I don't care any more, I don't, I don't!'

'But I care,' I said angrily. Soft words, sympathetic words were useless here. 'We all care. Don't be such a little fool. Everything will be all right, you'll see.'

'Spoken like a man,' said Smallwood approvingly. 'Only, my dear, I wouldn't pay much attention to the last part of his speech.'

'Why don't you give up, Smallwood?' I asked him quietly. I had neither hope nor intention of persuading this fanatic, I was only talking for time, for I had seen something that had made my heart leap: moving quietly out over the right-hand side of the glacier, from the self-same spot where we had lain in ambush, was a file of about a dozen men. 'Bombers have already taken off from the carrier, and, believe me, they're carrying bombs. Bombs and incendiaries. And do you know why, Smallwood?'

They were dressed in khaki, this landing party from the *Wykenham*, not navy blue. Marines, almost certainly, unless they had been carrying soldiers on some combined manœuvres. They were heavily armed, and had that indefinable but unmistakable look of men who knew exactly what they were about. Their leader. I noticed, wasn't fooling around with the usual pistol a naval officer in charge of a landing party traditionally carried: he had a sub-machine-gun under his arm, the barrel gripped in his left hand. Three others had similar weapons, the rest rifles.

'Because they're going to make good and sure you're never going to get off this glacier alive, Smallwood,' I went on. 'At least, not out of the fjord alive. Neither you nor any of your friends coming to meet you—nor any of the men waiting aboard that trawler down there.'

God, how slowly they were coming! Why didn't one of their marksmen with a rifle shoot Smallwood there and then—at that moment, the thought that a rifle bullet would have gone clear through Smallwood and killed the girl held so tightly in front of him never occurred to me. But if I could hold his attention another thirty seconds, if none of the others standing by my side betrayed by the slightest flicker of expression——

'They're going to destroy that trawler, Smallwood,' I rushed on quickly. The men advancing up from the foot of the glacier were waving their arms furiously now, shouting wildly in warning, and even at over three-quarters of a mile their voices were carrying clearly. I had to try to drown their voices, to make sure that Smallwood kept his eyes fixed only on me. 'They're going to blow it out of the water, it and you and that damned missile mechanism. What's the use of——'

But it was too late. Smallwood had heard the shouts even as I had begun to speak, twisted his head to look down the valley, saw the direction of the pointing arms, glanced briefly over his shoulder, then turned to face me again, his face twisted in a bestial snarl, that monolithic calm shattered at last:

'Who are they?' he demanded viciously. 'What are they doing? Quick—or the girl gets it!'

'It's a landing party from the destroyer in the next bay,' I said steadily. 'This is the end, Smallwood. Maybe you'll stand trial yet.'

'I'll kill the girl!' he whispered savagely.

'They'll kill you. They've been ordered to recover that mechanism at all costs. Nobody's playing any more, Smallwood. Give up your gun.'

He swore, vilely, blasphemously, the first time I had ever heard such words from him, and leapt for the driving cabin of the tractor, pushing the girl in front of him while his pistol swung in a wide arc covering all of us. I understood what he was going to do, what this last desperate suicidal gamble was going to be, and hurled myself at the door of the driving cabin.

'You madman!' My voice was a scream. 'You'll kill yourself, you'll kill the girl——'

The gun coughed softly, I felt the white-hot burning pain in my upper arm and crashed backward on to the ice just as Smallwood released the brakes of the Citroën. At once the big tractor started to move, those murderous treads passing by inches from me as Jackstraw leapt forward and dragged me to safety a second before they would have run over my face. The next moment I was on my feet, running after the tractor, Jackstraw at my heels: I suppose that wound just below my shoulder must have been hurting like hell, but the truth is that I felt nothing at all.

The tractor, with next to no adhesion left on the steepest slope

346

of ice, accelerated with dismaying speed, soon out-distancing us. At first it seemed as if Smallwood was making some attempt to steer it, but it was obvious almost immediately that any such attempts were utterly useless: five tons of steel run amok, it was completely out of control, skidding violently first to one side and then the other, finally making a complete half-circle and sliding backward down the glacier at terrifying speed, following the slope of the ice which led from the right-hand side where we had been standing to the big *nunataks* thrusting up through the ice on the far left-hand corner of the dog-leg half-way down.

How it missed all the crevasses—it went straight across some narrow ones, thanks to its treads—and all the ice-mounds on the way down and across the glacier I shall never know, but miss them it did, increasing speed with every second that passed, its treads screeching out a shrilly metallic cacophony of sound as they scored their serrated way across and through the uneven ice of the glacier. But then, I shall never know either how Jackstraw and I survived all the crazy chances we took on our mad headlong run down that glacier, unable to stop, leaping across crevasses we would never have dared attempt in our normal minds, pounding our sliding way alongside others where the slip of either foot would have been our death.

We were still two hundred yards behind the tractor when, less than fifty yards from the corner, it struck an ice-mound, spun round crazily several times and then smashed, tail first, with horrifying force into the biggest of the *nunataks*—a fifty-foot pinacle of rock at the very corner. We were still over a hundred yards away when we saw Smallwood, obviously dazed, half-fall out of the still upright driving cabin, radio in hand, followed by the girl. Whether she flung herself at him or just stumbled against him it was impossible to say, but both of them slipped and fell together and next moment had disappeared from sight against the face of the *nunatak*.

Still fifty yards away, already trying all we could to brake ourselves, we heard the staccato roar of cannon shells seemingly directly above us and as I flung myself flat on the ice, not to avoid the fire but to stop myself before I, too, plunged into the crevasse by the *nunatak* where I knew Margaret and Smallwood must have disappeared, I caught a glimpse of two Scimitars hurtling low across the glacier, red fire streaking from their guns. For a moment rolling over and over, I saw no more, then I had another glimpse of the lower part of the glacier, of exploding cannon-shells raking a lethal barrier of fragmenting steel across the glacier's entire width, and, about sixty or seventy yards lower down, the men from the trawler lying flat on their faces to escape the whistling flying shrapnel. Even in that brief moment I had time to see a third Scimitar screaming down out of the north, exactly following the path of the other two. They were making no attempt to kill the trawler men, obviously they were under the strictest instructions to avoid any but the most necessary bloodshed. And it wasn't necessary, if ever anything was crystal clear it was the fact that we weren't going to have any trouble at all from those trawler men. Both men and trawler could depart now, unmolested: with the missile mechanism beyond their reach, they no longer mattered.

Ten yards ahead of Jackstraw, sick to the heart and almost mad with fear, I reached the crevasse by the *nunatak*—no more than a three-foot wide gap between ice and rock—peered down over the side, and as I peered I felt faint from the wave of relief that swept over me: the crevasse, narrowing as it went down to not much more than two feet, ended about fifteen feet down in a solid shelf of rock, a ledge sculpted by thousands of years of moving, grinding ice.

Margaret and Smallwood were still on their feet, shaky, I could see, but seemingly unharmed—it had been a short drop and they could have slowed their descent by pressing against both sides of the crevasse as they fell. Smallwood, flattened lips drawn back over his teeth, was staring up at me, his pistol barrel pressed savagely against Margaret's temple.

'A rope, Mason!' he said softly. 'Get me a rope. This crevasse is closing—the ice is moving!'

And it was, I knew it was. All glaciers moved, some of them, on this West Greenland coast, with astonishing speed—the great Upernivik glacier, farther north, covered over four feet every hour. As if in confirmation of his words, the ice beneath my feet groaned and shuddered and slid forward a couple of inches.

'Hurry up!' Smallwood's incomparable nerve held to the last, his voice was urgent but completely under control, his face tight-lipped but calm. 'Hurry up or I'll kill her!'

I knew he meant it absolutely.

'Very well,' I said calmly. My mind felt preternaturally clear, I knew Margaret's life hung on a fraying thread but I had never

348

felt so cool, so self-possessed in my life. I unwound the rope round my shoulders. 'Here it comes.'

He reached up both hands to catch the falling rope, I took a short step forward and then stiff-legged and with my hands pressed close to my sides, fell on top of him like a plummeting stone. He saw me coming, but with the tangle of the rope and the narrowness of the crevasse he had no chance to get clear. My feet caught him on the shoulder and outstretched arm, and we crashed on to the ledge together.

He was, as I have said, phenomenally strong for his size, but he had no chance then. True, he was partially numbed by the shock of my fall, but that was more than cancelled out by my weakness, by the loss of blood from my wounded shoulder. But he still had no chance, I locked my hands round that scrawny throat, ignored his kickings, his eye-gougings, the fusillade of blows rained on my unprotected head, and squeezed and knocked his head against the blue-banded striations of the side of the crevasse until I felt him go limp in my hands. And then it was time to go, the ice-wall was now no more than eighteen inches distant from the polished rock of the *nunatak*.

Smallwood apart, I now found myself alone on that narrowing ledge. Jackstraw had already been lowered by Hillcrest and his men, fastened a rope round Margaret and been pulled up himself after her: I could have sworn that I had fought with Smallwood for no more than ten seconds, but was told later that we had struggled like madmen for three or four minutes. It may well have been so, I have no memory of that time, my coolness, my detachment was something altogether outside me.

My first clear recollection was hearing Jackstraw's voice, quick and urgent, as a rope snaked down over my shoulders.

'Quickly, Dr Mason! It'll close any second now.'

'I'm coming. But another rope first, please.' I pointed to the radio lying at my feet. 'We've come too long a way with this, we've suffered too much for this to leave it now.'

Twenty seconds later, just as I scrambled over the edge of the crevasse, the grinding ice-wall lurched another inch or two towards the rock of the *nunatak*, and, at the same moment, Smallwood's voice came to us again. He had propped himself up on his hands and knees and was staring up numbly, almost disbelievingly, at the narrowing walls above him.

'Throw me a rope.' He could see death's hand reaching out to

349

touch him, but the urgency in his voice was still under that iron control, his face an expressionless mask. 'For God's sake, throw me a rope.'

I thought of the trail of death Smallwood had left behind him, of the plane's dead captain, the three dead crew members, Colonel Harrison, Brewster and Mrs Dansby-Gregg, of how close to the brink of death he had brought Marie LeGarde and Mahler, of how often he had threatened death to the girl now trembling violently in the crook of my arm. I thought of these things, then I looked at Jackstraw, who carried a rope over his arm, and I saw reflected in his face the same implacability, the same bleak mercilessness that informed my own mind. And then Jackstraw moved towards the brink of the crevasse, lifted the tightly coiled rope high above his head, hurled it down on the top of the man below and stepped back without a word.

We turned, Jackstraw and I, with Margaret Ross supported between us, and walked slowly up the glacier to meet the officer in charge of the landing party, and as we walked we could feel the glacier shiver beneath our feet as a million tons of ice lurched down towards the head of the Kangalak Fjord.